William Shillinglaw Crocket

Minstrelsy of the Merse

The Poets and Poetry of Berwickshire - A Country Anthology

William Shillinglaw Crocket

Minstrelsy of the Merse
The Poets and Poetry of Berwickshire - A Country Anthology

ISBN/EAN: 9783743496637

Manufactured in Europe, USA, Canada, Australia, Japa

Cover: Foto ©Andreas Hilbeck / pixelio.de

Manufactured and distributed by brebook publishing software (www.brebook.com)

William Shillinglaw Crocket

Minstrelsy of the Merse

Ashiestiel, Scott's First Border Home.

MINSTRELSY OF THE MERSE

THE
Poets and Poetry of Berwickshire.

A County Anthology.

BY

REV. W. S. CROCKETT, F.S.A.Scot.

Rhymer' Tower, Earlston.

PREFACE BY
PROFESSOR JOHN STUART BLACKIE.

J. AND R. PARLANE, PAISLEY,
JOHN MENZIES AND CO., EDINBURGH AND GLASGOW,
HOULSTON AND SONS, LONDON.
1893.

Rev. W. S. Crockett,
Author of "The Scott
Country."

19 May 1909.

Dear Mr Reid,

I think you will be interested in the enclosed, and perhaps you can help us in several ways. I have heard of your Churchyard Excursions, for one thing, and doubtless you will come across very old tombstones of ministers, which were probably unknown to Hew Scott, and that contain the correct dates, and names of family, which he was not able to give in every case. Are your Excursions being printed?

if and have ya visited? Scott's Forte
is a very valuable work, but since it
was at least 5·000 names are waiting
to be added so that with the revision of the
old matter & the continuing, there is considerable ground to be attacked. Nty
the 84 Presbyters in the church. 75 are
in operation. has Kirriemuir shone to y
assistance to us too, & I think ya
have some smaller parish histories y our
northern Fife towns. These I have not seen.
I shall be glad to hear what ya think of
the Churchyard.
    Kind Regards
            Yours Faithfully
            W. S. Crockett

TO

THE MEN AND WOMEN OF THE MERSE,

NOT ONLY IN SCOTLAND

BUT IN EVERY PART OF THE WORLD,

WHO HAVE NEVER FORGOT THEIR NATIVE COUNTY,

I Dedicate

FOR DEAR MEMORY'S SAKE

THESE SKETCHES

OF ITS SONGS AND SINGERS.

IT may be glorious to write
  Thoughts that shall glad the two or three
High souls, like those far stars that come in sight
    Once in a century ;—

  But better far it is to speak
  One simple word, which now and then
Shall waken their free nature in the weak
    And friendless sons of men ;

  To write some earnest verse or line,
  Which, seeking not the praise of art,
Shall make a clearer faith and manhood shine
    In the untutored heart.

  He who doth this, in verse or prose,
  May be forgotten in his day,
But surely shall be crowned at last with those
    Who live and speak for aye.

—JAMES RUSSELL LOWELL.

DEAR native Merse! a glorious plain,
  Streak'd wi' the sunbeams, mild and sweet
I gaze far o'er thy fair domain,
  Where true hearts in their gladness beat ;

I come to tread thy fields again,
  Where long my fathers till'd thy soil,
And with thee and thy sons remain
  Till there I end life's ceaseless toil.

All that I love on earth is there,
  Land of my fathers ! happy land ;
Be virtuous all thy daughters fair,
  And all thy sons in honour stand !

May tyrants and their minions flee
  Far from the Merse's bounds away !
May truth and genius dwell in thee !
  Thy toiling sons be glad for aye !

The land of Boston and M'Crie,
  Where Erskine preached and Baillie sung,
Where, by the Leader's haughs and lea,
  The Rhymer's wizard harp was strung !

There, o'er thy waters, woods, and rills,
  My heart will pour its warmest lay ;
While morn and eve athwart thy hills,
  Shall all their varied charms display.

No land e'er blessed by sun or shower,
  Beneath the wide skies' azure dome,
Will e'er to me look half so fair
  As that which holds my native home !

Though bleak and bare thy hills may be,
  Though winter tempests scathe thy plain,
O Merse ! I could not part with thee,
  For all the gold beyond the main.

—DR. GEORGE HENDERSON.

CONTENTS.

		PAGE
Preface,		xiii
Note by the Editor,		1
Introduction,		3
Thomas of Ercildoune,		9
Sir Tristrem,		18
Sir Richard Maitland,		22
The Blind Baron's Comfort,		26
Na Kyndnes at Court without Siller,		27
Gude Counsels,		28
Baron Maitland of Thirlstane,		29
Aganis Sklanderous Toungis,		31
Thomas Maitland,		34
Mary Maitland,		35
Earl of Lauderdale,		36
Sir Patrick Hume,		37
Alexander Hume,		38
The Day Estivall,		42
David Hume of Godscroft,		48
James Hume, M.D.,		50
Anna Hume,		51
Lady Grisell Baillie,		53
Werena My Heart Licht,		61
The Ewe Buchtin's Bonnie,		62
Patrick Hume,		63
Earl of Haddington,		64
Lord Binning,		66
Ungrateful Nannie,		67
In Praise of Emilius,		69
Robert Crawford,		70
Leader Haughs and Yarrow,		71
Cowdenknowes,		72

	PAGE
JAMES GRAINGER, M.D.,	74
Ode to Solitude	76
Bryan and Pereene,	79
RALPH ERSKINE,	82
SIR JOHN SWINTON,	83
LORD SWINTON,	84
MRS. JOHN HUNTER,	85
Queen Mary's Lamentation,	87
The Farewell,	88
My Mother bids me Bind my Hair,	88
The Death-Song of the Cherokee Indian,	89
The Lot of Thousands,	89
The Spirit's Song,	90
The Flowers of the Forest,	90
DAVID STUART ERSKINE, Earl of Buchan,	91
SIR DAVID ERSKINE,	95
JAMES BARRIE,	97
WILLIAM DUDGEON,	99
The Maid that tends the Goats,	101
REV. JAMES GRAY,	102
A Sabbath among the Mountains,	104
Love,	105
Youth,	106
WILLIAM CRAW,	107
ALEXANDER BROWN ("Berwickshire Sandie"),	110
My Native Vale,	111
The Eagle Troop,	112
ALEXANDER HEWIT,	114
William and Madeline,	115
JOHN ROBERTSON,	117
The Lassie by the Water Side,	117
THOMAS DICKSON,	119
"Lovest Thou Me?"	119
JAMES SANDERSON,	121
My Youthful Haunts on Leaderside,	124
The Bower by Leaderside,	126
The Banks o' Tweed,	127
CAPTAIN JOHN MARJORIBANKS,	128
Liberty,	129

		PAGE
JOHN WHITEHEAD,		131
Sonnet,		131
The Miser's Heart is set on Gold,		132
ROBERT MENNON,		133
Chirnside,		134
The Lily o' the Valley,		135
Juke an' let the Jaw gae by,		136
WILLIAM SUTHERLAND,		137
The Enthusiast Lover,		137
DR. GEORGE HENDERSON,		139
Crunkly's Braes,		140
A Fancy Flight to Leader Water,		142
The Return Home,		145
WILLIAM AIR FOSTER,		149
O ! List the Mavis' Mellow Note,		150
Gude Coldstream Toon,		151
The Trystin' Tree,		152
On the Ettrick Shepherd bearing off the Prize at the Competition of the Border Bowmen in 1832,		153
JOHN WILSON, D.D.,		155
ALEXANDER HOME,		156
A Week in the Country,		156
ANDREW STEELE,		158
My Native Border Home,		159
The Hirsel yet for Me,		160
Hey for a Wife wi' a Hunner or Twa,		162
WILLIAM BROCKIE,		163
Lawther East Mains,		167
Ye'll never gang back to yer Mither nae mair,		171
LADY HUME CAMPBELL,		172
When Thou art near Me,		172
THOMAS KNOX,		173
Undying Work,		176
Earth an Eden-Bower,		177
The Tree and the Storm,		178
REV. ANDREW CUNNINGHAM,		179
Knox,		180
Luther,		180

	PAGE
JOHN GIBSON,	181
Take Life as we find it,	181
WILLIAM FORSYTH,	183
A Lay of Loch Leven,	184
The Cottage by the Quarry,	186
PETER M'CRAKET,	187
The Lammermoor Hills,	188
THOMAS WATTS,	190
The Friend of Bygone Days,	191
Winter Evenings,	193
Oor Wee Wean,	194
WALTER CHISHOLM,	198
Scotia's Border Land,	200
Oor Only Bairnie,	201
" It Micht be Muckle Waur,"	202
The Missed Tryst,	204
MARGARET HAY HOME TOUGH,	205
MARY ANNE LORIMER,	205
The Family Gathering,	205
My Longings	206
JOHN USHER,	208
Lammermoor.	208
GEORGE GILMOUR,	209
The Sabbath,	209
LADY JOHN SCOTT,	211
Annie Laurie,	213
Lammermoor,	214
Duris-Deer,	215
Katherine Logie,	215
The Foul Fords,	216
Ettrick,	216
GEORGE PAULIN,	218
The Tweed Revisited,	221
Baby Song,	222
It's No Worth the Warstle For't,	223
Soun' Sleepin' Noo,	223
Aunty's Sangs,	224
Retrospect,	225

PAGE

REV. JAMES BALLANTYNE, . . 226
   The Dying Infidel, . . 226
ANDREW WANLESS, ... 228
   Our Mither Tongue, ... 230
   The Scott Centenary, ... 232
   A Scotch Bangster's Comin', ... 234
   The Men o' the Merse, ... 235
   Lammermoor, ... 236
JESSIE WANLESS BRACK, ... 237
   Among the Leaves so Green, ... 238
CHRISTOPHER DAWSON, ... 239
   To the Tweed at Coldstream, ... 242
   The Rose, ... 244
WILLIAM TELFORD, ... 245
   Scotia's Heather, ... 247
THOMAS MILLER, ... 248
   My Heart aye Warms to the Tartan, . . . 248
THOMAS HAPPER, ... 250
   The Parting, ... 251
   Christian Charity, ... 252
ROBERT M'LEAN CALDER, ... 254
   When the Days are Creepin' in, ... 256
   Polart Burn, ... 257
   The Auld Schule Hoose on the Green, . . . 258
ROBERT PRINGLE, ... 261
   The Virtue Well, ... 261
JEANNIE DODDS, ... 263
   A Mother's Test, ... 263
   Friendship, ... 264
GEORGE DEANS, ... 265
   Hume Castle, ... 266
   Darlingfield, ... 267
   Birgham Bowers, ... 268
AGNES MACK DENHOLM, ... 270
   A Legend of Lammermoor, ... 270
   After Many Years, ... 272
REV. CHARLES MILLER, ... 275
   Duns Law, ... 276

	PAGE
CHARLES PHILIP GIBSON.	279
Cheerfulness,	280
REV. ROBERT NAISMITH,	282
The Martyr's Grave,	283
E. V. O. E.,	285
The Herring Drave,	285
Low Summer Wind,	286
REV. PETER MEARNS,	287
Scripture Study,	287
JOHN REID,	288
The Lass o' Kidshiel Glen,	288
ANNIE BURTON EASTON,	290
" Dinna Forget Me,"	290
MISCELLANEOUS,	292
THE BALLADS OF BERWICKSHIRE—	
The Broom o' the Cowdenknowes,	295
Tea-Table Miscellany Version,	299
Gilfillan's Version,	301
Bell's Version,	302
Auld Maitland,	303
Leader Haughs and Yarrow,	313
The Grey Peel Glen,	317
The Ballad of the Twinlaw Cairns,	320
Polwarth on the Green,	324
Grieve's Version,	325
Tibby Fowler,	326
Thomas the Rhymer,	327
Additional Note to Thomas of Ercildoune,	331
" Delta's " " Tower of Ercildoune,"	332
Note on Berwickshire Ballads	334

ADDENDA.

	PAGE
PETER COLDWELL,	335
Cuddy Peggy,	337
MARY INGLIS,	339
The Auld Manse,	339
Yon Burnside,	341
Last Longings,	342
Let the Bairnies Play,	343
INDEX OF NAMES,	344

PREFACE.

THE name of Burns occupies such a prominent position in Scottish song that persons are apt to speak of him as the creator of the lyrical art of his country, which owes all its merit to the stamp placed upon it by his powerful genius. Nothing could be a greater mistake. Burns was not the creator of the lyrical genius of his country, but only its highest representative. He was the biggest tree in the forest, but not the only big tree; he was not the forest, and did not make the forest; the forest rather made him, as growing out of the same soil, breathing the same atmosphere, and reared in the same environment. The most common Scottish song-book is studded over with songs of first-rate excellence which derive no inspiration from Burns, and which Burns, with the loftiest flight of his genius, could not have surpassed. Equally unfair would it be to say that the lyric poetry of Scotland belonged specially, as her religious struggles did, to the West Country. No doubt Hew Ainslie and Tannahill stand before the public as closely associated with Lugar Water

and the Banks of Doon as Robert Burns himself;
but there were famous Scottish song-writers from the
earliest times who were as far removed from the land
of Burns as the east is from the west, and to whom
the sharp air from the German Ocean was no less
provocative of sweet song than the soft breezes from
the Western Channel. With one of the most popular
branches of Scottish song, the Jacobite ballads, the
genius of Burns had nothing to do; and on the
eastern side of the country sloping down towards the
sea, the names of Lady Nairne, Sir Walter Scott,
and James Hogg are a prolonged echo of a native
school of Scottish song, flowing from its own source
as distinctly as the Tweed flows diverse from the
Clyde. In the poetry of this eastern side of the
country nothing is more notable than a certain
aristocratic character which belonged to it, as con-
trasted with the strongly-marked peasant features of
the poetry of the west. Not a few of the leading
nobility of Scotland, in the times immediately
following the Reformation, are honourably named
among the popular singers of an eminently singing
age; pity only that, like George Buchanan, living at
a time when the Latin tongue was the only organ of
polite culture, they gave their Scottish sentiments
voice in a language which is now dead. Of their

honourable place, however, and of that of their untitled compeers on the banks of the Leader and the Tweed, an instructive memorial lies now before me in the work of the Rev. W. S. Crockett—a work which worthily fills a felt blank in the history of Scottish song, and which will be perused with no less pleasure than profit by all who know that in the general eye of Europe Scotland holds a proud place, no less by her wealth of popular song than by her thoughtful seriousness, her practical good sense, and her power of persistent work. This is a national characteristic, the growth of centuries, of which we have great reason to be thankful and to be proud; and when Scotsmen forget to cherish this thankfulness and this pride, History will not be slow to forget them.

JOHN STUART BLACKIE.

THE Editor begs to acknowledge, with heartiest thanks, the help he has received from Professor Blackie in kindly writing the PREFACE to this volume; and from his friend Mr. J. Cuthbert Hadden, who has most generously read the proofs of the work while going through the press.

To many others who have given much valuable information thanks is also justly due, and more particularly to the Keepers of the various libraries in Edinburgh and Glasgow, through whose never-failing courtesy he has been largely aided in his work of research.

To himself it has been a labour of love, and his hope is that it may prove a useful and instructive record of Berwickshire song and ballad to all who are interested in such literature.

W. S. C.

Earlston, August, 1893.

INTRODUCTION.

SCOTTISH song is the world's admiration. Perhaps no other country has been more prolific in song and ballad. Every county has its band of singers who are helping to swell the great chorus of national sentiment, and to keep alive with ever-increasing enthusiasm the grand old traditions and hallowed memories that cluster round the fair name of Scotia.

Every district in the land has contributed to this rich heritage of song. The Highlands with the weird, wild music of the clansmen, the songs of Ossian—great Minstrel of the North—the stirring strains of the Rebellion, and the pathetic plaints of Hope become forlorn, are all full of strong Celtic fire in preserving unimpaired the scenes and incidents of most notable times in our national annals. The Lowlands inspire us with their matchless minstrelsy in song and ballad, collected and pieced together by skilful and loving hands, from among the hills and glens of the romantic Borderland. They tell a thousand tales of old-world life, of battle-blade and warrior wight, of death and glory, dool and pain. Central Scotland, too, is pleasingly rich in pastoral poetry. From its fair straths and glorious woodlands have come, full of sweetest symphony, the glad, joyous notes of love and youth, of friendship and freedom, of delight in homely country ways, and pleasure in quiet country scenes.

The whole land has thus been helping to create and mould the nation's song. We are essentially a singing people, proud of our nationality, proud of our country, and no less proud of our achievements in the divine art of poesy. If to the West of Scotland —to Ayrshire—we turn to find the great *master* of Scottish song, it is in Berwickshire, to the East, we find the *father* of our national poetry. The first notes of national song mingled with the music of the Leader. Its true birthplace is among the hills and glens of Lauderdale. Thomas of Ercildoune is the "day-starre of Scottish poetry." He is our earliest minstrel, the first of that bright band who have carried into all the world the sweet cadence of Scottish song.

Situated so near the Scottish Border, in a land laden with legendary lore—the very home of romance —where are castled crag and ruined tower, river and streamlet, forest, field, and moor, each with its own peculiar association and special beauty, it is no wonder that the Merse has so many singing children.

Three things combine to make Berwickshire a nursery of song Nature has formed it one of the loveliest of Scottish counties. To wander by the sloping wood-clad banks of the Tweed and Leader, or by the fertile haughs of the Blackadder and Whitadder, is the very essence of life. To climb the Lammermoors, purpled with autumnal heather, and to drink in from every side the fresh breezes as they blow all around you is the finest of health-invigorators. "Let me see the heather once a year," said Scott, and see it, I pray you, good reader, in the charming uplands of the Merse. May its fields fascinate you with their rich verdure, its broomy braes, its ferny dells, and its wimpling burns—all it has so lavishly received from Nature—delight your heart and mind and soul!

History, too, has left its mark upon the Merse. There are memories on every hand of past days and deeds. The struggle for independence and the conquests of Wallace are not confined to the West. The Stuarts were fond of the county. The " Sair Sanct" founded several of its churches and its finest abbey. There are hallowed associations around Duns Law, and sweet memories of Covenanting

heroism by the winding Whitadder. Its frowning
"keeps," moss-grown now and grey with the
gathering years, speak of stern defiance and of many
a doughty deed of arms in the rough days of yore.
We can almost see them yet—these stout-souled
warriors of an age long gone—fearless and true, as
they strike for sweet liberty in every blow.

There is also the influence of the supernatural.
The mystery of the seer of Ercildoune has bound the
land in awe. The realm of Faëry is strangely near.
Each hill and glen has some story of association
with this interesting locality and its still more
interesting inhabitants.

A further influence is the bright, genial disposition
of Merse men and women. They are ideal Scots.
They love their fatherland with a great love. They
are most loyal to its highest interests, and never fail
to seek its supremest good. Beautiful in character,
they are no less beautiful in body—strong in *physique*,
comely in countenance, true sons and daughters of
the old Border blood. All combined, the effect of
Nature, History, and the Unseen has been to set
some minds thinking and some voices singing with
the rapture these evoked. For our Merse lads and
lassies are in no way dull to such influences. Ever a
religious people, they rise from Nature to Nature's

God, and recognise the Hand Divine weaving each thread into the great warp of history, until all Life's varied movements become clearly understood in the light of that all-perfect plan which the truer Unseen shall at length reveal.

Sing on, then, ye singers of the Merse! Remember those who have sung before you, whose voice is hushed, but whose song still lingers in the vale; catch up their spirit, emulate their example, nay, if you may, rise to even higher achievements, like him whose boyhood years were passed on the very threshold of your land, whose eyes feasted on its scenery, whose mind was stored with its old traditions, and whose dust is handed over to your keeping by the "fair river" in your own beloved Dryburgh.

MINSTRELSY OF THE MERSE.

THOMAS OF ERCILDOUNE.

1216 (?)—1294 (?).

THE story of Thomas of Ercildoune, popularly known as Thomas the Rhymer, is shrouded in much obscurity. The history of this remarkable man borders so closely on the mythical and traditional, that there is great difficulty in determining what in it is really authentic. He has now become little more than a dim, almost unrecognisable figure of the past. The enlightenment and learning of modern days have stripped him of that superstitious veneration and almost religious reverence which our too credulous forefathers were ever eager to accord to their gifted contemporaries. The ignorance of the period in which he lived, the easy, unquestioning credence of succeeding generations, and a readiness to regard as fulfilled predictions the many recurring changes in national life, have been the chief agents in preserving to this day with such freshness and vigour the reputation of Thomas of Ercildoune.

For in the popular mind he is more the prophet than
the poet, and is better remembered for his alleged
powers of vaticination and mystic intercourse with
the Faëry realms, than for any of the metrical
romances that have been attributed to his genius.
Thousands who have never heard of *Sir Tristrem*,[1]
or of the Auchinleck MS.,[1] are perfectly familiar with,
and cling with strongest attachment to those rhyming
couplets of prophetic import which generation after
generation has ascribed to the weird sage of Ercildoune.

Thomas of Ercildoune derived his territorial designation from the ancient village of that name in the
south-west of Berwickshire. This place appears to
have been of considerable importance during the
earlier years of Scottish history. It was frequently
a royal residence. During a visit in June, 1136,
David I. subscribed there the foundation charter of
Melrose Abbey, and in 1143 his son, Prince Henry,
subscribed, also "at Ercheldu," the confirmatory
charter of the same abbey. Among the local barons

---

[1] This now famous romance was discovered in the Advocates'
Library, Edinburgh, by Ritson, the well-known antiquary, and is
part of a vellum MS. volume presented to the library in 1744 by a
judge of the Court of Session, Alexander Boswell of Auchinleck,
father of Dr. Johnson's biographer, and thence called the Auchinleck
MS. It contains in 334 leaves upwards of forty poems and fragments,
a full account of which is given by Scott as an appendix to the introduction to his *Sir Tristrem*. The volume has been much mutilated
from the cutting out of the illuminated initials, and the concluding
stanzas of *Sir Tristrem* are lost, but have been supplied in the published
copy by Scott, after a French romance of the same name, with which
it in certain measure corresponds.

the family of Lindsay held at first the chief position. "William de Lindsei de Ercildun" granted to the monks of Coldingham the church at Ercildoune with one ploughgate of land. The ecclesiastical documents of this period are nearly all associated with this family. Then the Earls of March and Dunbar come upon the scene, and remain for some time the real owners and lords of Ercildoune. But they in turn pass away, and so now, of the very extensive territory in Lauderdale and the Merse formerly belonging to this old Border house, not a single acre is held by an immediate representative of the family. In the village of Ercildoune, at the east end, they had a stronghold, for long known as the Earl's Tower, but now demolished, and a group of buildings close at hand, probably remnants of feudal residences, was called the Earl's Toun. From this circumstance the original name of Ercildoune or Ercheldun [1] gradually blended into the growing Earl's Toun, which modern usage has transformed into one word—Earlston. The residence of Thomas the Rhymer stood at the west end, close by the Leader, and distant about half a mile from the Earl's Tower. While the latter has long since given place to the plough, only a green knoll now marking the site of

[1] In old records, etc., the name has the following forms : — Erceldun, Ercildoune, Ercheldoun, Ercildon, Ersylton, Hersilton, Hersildoune, Erslington, Arseldon, Earthelton, Ersyldowne. The modern form is also rendered Earlstown and Earlstoun, and the latter is more correct than Earlston. Ercildoune is derived from the Cambro-British *Arciol-dun*, that is, the "look-out" or "prospect" hill — the hill to the south which gives an extensive view of the Leader and Tweed valleys.

the great retainer's "keep," the visitor may still stand by the ivy-clad ruins of the Rhymer's dwelling, feeling that here indeed is one of Scotland's sacred places, the habitation of her earliest poet, the nursery of her world-admired song. "While I was yet ignorant," writes David Macbeth Moir ("Delta"), the poet, "that any part of the ruins were in existence, they were pointed out to me, and, I need not add, awakened a thousand stirring associations connected with the legends, the superstitions, and the history of mediæval ages, when nature brought forth 'Gorgons and hydras and chimeras dire,' and social life seemed entirely devoted to 'Ladye love and war, renown and knightly worth.'"

The period at which Thomas of Ercildoune flourished is generally given as the greater part of the thirteenth century—from about 1216 to at least 1285. Henry the Minstrel introduces him into an incident in the career of Wallace in 1296; Pinkerton supposes him to have been alive in 1300; while Patrick Gordon, in his heroic poem *The Bruce*, places his death in the year 1307. In 1294—not 1299 as usually stated—we find his son conveying to the Trinity House of Soltré the lands which he possessed "by inheritance" at Ercildoune. The actual words of the accompanying charter are: "Thomas of Ercildoune, son and heir of Thomas Rimour of Ercildoune," from which it is evident that the elder Thomas must either have been dead by this time, or have retired from the more active duties of life in favour of his son, at whose disposal he had placed

the family property. The former is the more
plausible conjecture, since Thomas of Ercildoune,
the Rhymer, according to Scott's calculations, must
have then been a man considerably advanced in
years. His death may have occurred in the religious
house near Ayr to which he frequently resorted.[1]
One tradition has it that he met his death through
treachery when negotiating with a neighbouring
baron, and the popular story of his translation to
fairyland is too well known to be repeated here,
whilst also, of course, too absurd to be believed.

With reference to his alleged surname of Learmont
there is no satisfactory evidence. Persons of the name
of Learmont living in Earlston *did* claim kinship
with the Rhymer, and down to a late period the right
also of burial immediately in front of the parish
church, in the wall of which is a very ancient stone
with the inscription :

> " Auld Rymr race
> Lyees in this place."

The late Mr. Campbell Swinton supposes that
Thomas's territorial appellation as proprietor of a
mount or hill at Ercildoune may have grown into
Laird of Ercilmount, and have thence been corrupted
into Lairsilmount or Lairmont, but how far this somewhat ingenious theory is tenable cannot be said.

---

[1] The Faile or Feale, a priory of the Cluniacenses which was still
flourishing in the sixteenth century. Henry the Minstrel says :—

> " Thomas Rimour into the Faile was then,
> With the mynystir, quhilk was a worthi man,
> He usyt offt to that religiouss place."

One thing is worthy of note. The biographers of
Russia's great poet, Michael Lermontof (1811-1841),
refer to his ancestral connection with and descent
from Thomas of Ercildoune. In many of his
poems Lermontof himself proudly alludes to his
Scottish lineage :

> " Beneath the curtain of mist,
>   Beneath a heaven of storms,
>   Among the hills of my Scotland
>   Lies the grave of Ossian ;
>   Thither flies my weary soul,
>   To breathe its native gale,
>   And from that forgotten grave
>   A second time to draw its life."

And in another poem called *The Wish* he longs to
have the wings of the bird that he might fly "to the
west, to the west, where shine the fields of my
ancestors, and where, in the deserted tower among
the misty hills, rests their forgotten dust." Above
the sword and shield hanging on the ancient walls
he would fly, and with his wing flick off the gathered
dust of ages.

Into the question of Thomas the Rhymer's poetical
powers I shall not meantime go far. The chief poem
of which he is the reputed author is the romance of
Sir Tristrem. The tale is not original by any
means, but, as the Welsh authorities state, is founded
on very ancient though quite authentic history. It
had appeared on the Continent before it reached the
form in which it now stands. Throughout it is
written in a very difficult and complicated stanza,
and in language which, although English, is almost

unintelligible to an ordinary reader of to-day. The construction is jerky and concise, so much so as to be in some places obscure, and the poem occasionally sinks into a wearying minuteness of unnecessary detail, though it rises again into vigorous and animated verse. There is evidence both for and against its being written by Thomas. Sir Walter Scott, in his elaborate introduction to the poem, confidently attributes the authorship to the Rhymer. Robert of Brunne regrets that "in recited tales of Ercildoune and Kendale no one repeats them as *they* made them." He ranks *Sir Tristrem* in the foremost place, if men would only repeat it "as *Thomas* made it." But in the poem itself there is much mystification. The opening stanza, for example, runs thus :

> " I was at Ertheldoune ;
> With tomas spak I there,
> There herd I rede in roun [1]
> Who tristem gat and bare ;
> Who was king with croun ;
> And who him forsterd yare ;
> And who was bold baroun,
> As their elders were ;
>   By 'yere ;
> Tomas tells in toun
> This aventours [2] as thai ware."

Other passages contain similar reference to a Thomas, "as tomas us hath taught," etc., and so far as this goes the evidence from the poem itself is against the Rhymer's authorship. It has been suggested that he might have woven his name into the verses for

---

[1] Told in tale.   [2] Adventures.

the purpose of perpetuating his fame, but we can
hardly imagine him speaking of himself in such a
way. Most critics are adverse to the Rhymer's first-
hand connection with the romance, and Warton,
Wright, Halliwell, Paris, Murray, and Kölbing agree
in thinking that when the unknown translator from
the French original found a Thomas mentioned he
at once gave the place of honour to Thomas of
Ercildoune, whose reputation as a seer would be
somewhat extensive at the time. It may be, however, that this Scottish version of *Sir Tristrem* was
written by some one who received it immediately
from Thomas, who we might expect had no small
acquaintance with continental and ancient British
traditionary literature. Other poems are said to
have been written by him, but in nearly every case
the evidence is quite as puzzling and contradictory
as that in regard to *Sir Tristrem.*

And what as to his prophetic fame? There is no
evidence to show that he himself assumed the character of a prophet, but it is certain that in a very
few years after his death he had come to be looked
upon as one possessing in no slight degree a spirit
of divination. Barbour, who wrote about 1375,
refers to a reputed prophecy of Thomas concerning
the exploits and succession of Robert I. After
Bruce had slain Comyn at Dumfries in 1306, Bishop
Lamberton is introduced as saying :

> " I hop Thomas's prophecy
> Of Hersildoune sall verified be
> In him."

Bower, who wrote in 1449, has given a circumstantial account of the celebrated prediction of the Rhymer relative to the death of Alexander III.; and Henry the Minstrel makes him utter an avenging word over the apparently lifeless body of Wallace. He is affirmed to have foretold the Union of Scotland and England by one removed in the ninth degree from the Bruce's blood, and there are not wanting many instances, still in popular belief, in which his prophetic genius has cast a weirdsome spell over many of the places and families of the Scottish Border-land.[1]

Beyond mere traditional reputation, however, there is not the remotest evidence to justify the ascription of any prophetic power to the Rhymer of Ercildoune, and as to the rational probability of the thing no argument is necessary. "The reverence of the people for a man, extraordinary for his learning and venerable for his years, seems to have been the sole foundation of Thomas's claims to rank among the prophets. The allegories of the poet were converted, as events chanced to suit, into prophecies of which he never dreamed; and the attributes of a seer being thus once fixed upon him, it is not surprising that in an age when all history was of a poetic structure, his name and authority should often have been fictitiously

---

[1] In addition to the above the following old Scottish and English writers refer to Thomas as a prophet-bard:—Robert Mannyng of Brunne, contemporary with Thomas (1303); Sir Thomas Gray, Constable of Norham, 1355; Andro of Wyntoun, 1424; Hector Boece, 1465; John Mair or Major, 1430; John Bellenden, 1490; John Leland, 1543; Archbishop Spottiswood, 1565; Nisbet the Heraldist, and many others. See additional note at end of book.

employed to throw into the commencement of historic narratives those shadows of coming events, of which poetry has made such frequent and happy use, to heighten the curiosity with which we pursue their development."

From *Sir Tristrem.*

THE COMBAT OF TRISTREM WITH URGAN, A FORMIDABLE GIANT.

[Sir Tristrem, banished from Cornwall, enters the service of Triamour, King of Wales. This monarch is unjustly attacked by Urgan, a neighbouring prince, who besieges him in his capital and lays waste his country. Triamour promises Tristrem a part of his Welsh dominions if he can recover them from the enemy. Tristrem and Urgan join battle, and at length meet in single combat. Urgan, a knight of gigantic stature, upbraids Tristrem with the death of his brother Morgan, slain by him "at the west." They fight desperately. Tristrem cuts off Urgan's right hand; but the giant continues the encounter with his left. Urgan, being hard pressed, flies to his castle. Sir Tristrem seizes and rides off with the bloody hand. Urgan, returning with potent salves to re-unite his hand to the stump, finds that Tristrem has carried it away. The giant pursues Tristrem and overtakes him upon a bridge, where the battle is renewed in presence of a multitude of spectators. Urgan presses Tristrem hard and cleaves his shield, but Tristrem, avoiding his next blow, thrusts him through the body, and in the agony of death he springs over the bridge.]

I.

In Wales tho was a king,
  That hight [1] Triamour ;
He hadde a doughter ying,
  Was hoten [1] Blaunche Flour ;
Urgan with gret wering,
  Biseged him in his tour.
To winne that swete thing,
  And bring hir to his bour,
    With fight ;
  Tristrem with gret honour,
Bicom the Kinges knight.

---

[1] Named.

II.

Urgan gan Wales held,
　With wrong, for sothe to say ;
Oft and unselde,[1]
　Of Triamour tok he prey :
Triamour to Triamour told,
　Opon a somers day,
Wales he wald him yeld,
　Yif he it winne may,
　　　　Right than :
　Tristrem with outen nay,
With were, Wales wan.

III.

Tristrem mett Urgan,
　In that feld to fight ;
To him seyd he than,
　As a douhti knight,
—" Thou slough mi brother Morgan,
　At the mete ful right ;
As Y am douhti man,
　His deth thou bist to-night,
　　　　Mi fo ; "—
　Tristrem seyd aplight,
" So hope Y the to slo."

IV.

Tuelue fete was the wand,
　That Urgan wald with play :
His strok may no man stand,
　Ferly yif Tristrem may :
Tristrem vantage fand,
　His clobbe fel oway ;
And of the geauntes[2] hand,
　Tristrem smot, that day,
　　　　In lede :
　Tristrem, for sothe to say,
The geaunt gert he blede.

---

[1] Not seldom.　　　[2] Giant's

V.

Urgan al in tene,[1]
　Faught with his left hand ;
Oghain Tristrem kene,
　A stern stroke he fand,
Opon his helme so schene,
　That to the grounde he wand,
Bot up he stirt bidene,[2]
　And he cried Godes sand,
　　　　Almight ;
　Tristrem with his brand,
Fast gan to fight.

VI.

The geaunt aroume[3] he stode,
　His hond he tint Y wis ;
He fleighe[4] as he wer wode,
　Ther that the castel is ;
Tristrem trad in the blod,
　And fond the hond that was his ;
Oway Sir Tristrem yode ;
　The geaunt com with this,
　　　　And sought,
　To hele his honde that was his,
Salves hadde he brought.

VII.

Urgan the geaunt unride
　After Sir Tristrem wan ;
The cuntre fer and wide,
　Y-gadred was bi than ;
Tristrem thought that tide,
　—" Y take that me Gode an ; "—
On a brigge he gan abide :
　Biheld ther mani a man :
　　　　Thai mett :
　Urgan to Tristrem ran,
And grimli there thai gret.

---

[1] Anger.　　　[2] Immediately.　　　[3] At a distance.　　　[4] Flew

VIII.

Strokes of michel might,
　Thai delten hem bituene :
That thurch her brinies¹ bright,
　Her bother blode² was sene :
Tristrem faught as a knight,
　And Urgan al in tene,
Yaf him a stroke unlight :
　His scheld he clef bituene,
　　　A-two
　Tristrem with outen wene,
Nas neuer³ are so wo.

IX.

Eft Urgan smot with main,
　And of that stroke he miste :
Tristrem smot ogayn,
　And thurch his body he threste :
Urgan lepe unfain,
　Ouer the bregge he deste :
Tristrem hath Urgan slain,
　That alle the cuntre wist,
　　　With wille :
The King tho Tristrem kist,
And Wales tho yeld him tille.

---

¹ Helmets.　　　² The blood of both.　　　³ Was not.

SIR RICHARD MAITLAND.

1496-1586.

IT was a fortunate day for Scottish literature when
Sir Richard Maitland, the blind baron of Thirlstane, prompted by his patriotism, began to collect
and transcribe into two portly volumes the writings
of many of the old Scottish "makars." For such an
undertaking he is most worthily entitled to the
remembrance of posterity. It was, in truth, a patriot's
legacy to his country, and as such has largely
enriched the treasury of Scottish song. But Sir
Richard was himself a poet of no mean repute. In
spite of adverse circumstances he had all the poet's
enthusiasm, and wrote with grace and dignity, though
his memory is cherished rather for the kindly act of
seeking to preserve the musings of his predecessors
and contemporaries. There is a mixture of pathos
and romance in the picture of this old man, with
his daughter for amanuensis, plodding patiently and
perseveringly at the self-imposed task of gathering
together for the benefit of future ages the scattered
gems of Scotland's song.

Sir Richard Maitland was the twelfth baron of
Thirlstane, but is more frequently known by his
territorial designation of "Lethington."[1] He was

---

[1] Lethington, an estate near Haddington, and now called Lennox-
love, in token of its having been purchased by an ancestor of the
Lauderdale family with a legacy bequeathed to him by a beautiful
Countess of Lennox.

the son of William Maitland of Lethington, who was
killed at Flodden in 1513, and Martha, daughter of
George, second Lord Seaton. On the 13th October,
1513, we find him served heir to his father. He
received his education at St. Andrews and in France,
where he completed his studies for the Bar. On his
return home he was frequently employed by James V.
in various public commissions. In May, 1551, he
was created an Extraordinary Lord of Session, and
received the honour of knighthood. He was sent
occasionally to settle affairs on the Borders, and in
1559 concluded the treaty of Upsettlington. In
October, 1560, he lost his eyesight, a misfortune
which, however, did not incapacitate him for professional work. In November, 1561, he was raised
to the rank of an Ordinary Lord of Session as Lord
Lethington. In December, 1562, he was made Lord
Privy Seal, which office he held till 1567, when he
resigned it in favour of his second son. In 1584 he
gave up his seat on the Bench, and was the recipient
of a congratulatory letter from the king—James VI.—
which bore testimony to the faithful discharge of
important public duties in the service of his "grandsire, good-sire, good-dame, mother, and himself."[1]
Sir Richard died 30th March, 1586, at the age of
ninety. In 1530 he had married Mary, daughter of
Sir Thomas Cranstoun of Corsbie, who died on the
day of her husband's interment. By her he had a
large family, of whom three sons and four daughters

---

[1] James V.; Earl of Lennox; Mary of Guise; Queen Mary;
James VI.

survived their parents. His daughters were all wedded to Border gentlemen: Helen, to John Cockburn of Clerkington; Margaret, to William Douglas of Whittinghame; Mary, to Alexander Lawder of Hatton; and Isabel, to James Heriot of Trabroun. His eldest son, William, was the celebrated Secretary Maitland[1] of Queen Mary's reign, a man "who possessed more than his father's talents, but less than his father's virtues."

It was exactly two centuries after the death of Sir Richard Maitland when Pinkerton drew from obscurity and gave to the public a selection from the now famous manuscript,[2] and fifty-three years later the Maitland Club printed separately Sir Richard's own contributions.[3] The collection consists of two MS. volumes, one of which is in the handwriting of his daughter Mary. These are now in the Pepysian Library of Magdalen College, Cambridge, having been presented along with other MSS. by the only Duke of Lauderdale to Samuel Pepys the diarist. A third volume, containing most of Maitland's own poems, was presented to the Edinburgh University Library by William Drummond of Hawthornden. Sir Richard Maitland's poetry can scarcely be termed striking. He was nearly sixty

---

[1] See Dr. Skelton's "Maitland of Lethington." Edin., 1890.

[2] "Ancient Scottish Poems, never before in print, but now published from the MS. Collections of Sir Richard Maitland of Lethington, Knt." 2 vols. 8vo, London, 1786. In the appendix to Vol. II. he gives a full account of the Maitland MSS.

[3] Poems of Sir Richard Maitland of Lethington. Edited by Joseph Bain for the Maitland Club. 4to. Edin., 1839.

when he began to cultivate the writing of verse.
There is consequently a lack of that intensity
of feeling common to younger men, but withal
he writes with wonderful energy and spirit. He
can be humorous or pathetic, strongly satirical or
commendatory. There is manliness in his verse,
straightforwardness, charity, and good taste. "His
compositions breathe the genuine spirit of piety and
benevolence. The cheerfulness of his natural disposition and his affiance in Divine aid seem to have
supported him with singular equanimity under the
pressure of blindness and old age"—(*Irving*). He
has been lauded by his contemporary poets as a man
adorned by every virtue. Thomas Hudson, for
example, wrote the following sonnet on his death:—

> " The sliding time so slyly slips away,
>   It reaves from us remembrance of our state,
> And while we do the care of time delay
>   We tyne the tide, and so lament too late.
> Then to eschew much dangerous debait,
>   Propose for pattern manly Maitland knight :
> Learn by his life to live in simple rait,
>   With love to God, religion, law, and right.
> For as he was of virtue lucent light,
>   Of ancient blood, of noble spirit and name,
> Beloved of God and every gracious wight,
>   So died he auld, deserving worthy fame,
> A rare example set for us to see
> What we have been, now are, and ought to be."

Sir Richard's prose works are a "Chronicle and
History of the House of Seytoun,"[1] and "Decisions

---

[1] Edited for the Maitland Club by John Fullerton. 4to. Edin.,
1829. With the continuation of the History by Alexander, Viscount
Kingston, to the year 1687.

of the Court of Session between 1550 and 1565," a
work still in MS.—a folio of 120 pages—and preserved in the Advocates' Library at Edinburgh.

THE BLIND BARON'S COMFORT.

[Written after the despoiling, in 1570, of Sir Richard's House and Lands of
Blythe, in Lauderdale.]

Blind man be blyth, althoch that thow be wrangit ;
  Thoch Blythe be herreit, tak no melancholie.
Thow shall be blyth, when that they shall be hangit
  That Blythe has spulyeit [1] sa maliciouslie.
Be blyth and glad ; that nane perceive in thee
  That thy blythness consists in ryches ;
Bot that thow art blyth that eternalie
  Shall reign with God in eternal blythness.

Thoch thai have spulyeit Blythe of guidis and gear,
  Yet have thai thieves left lyand still the land :
Quhilk to transport was nocht in thair poweir,
  Nor yet will be, thoch na men thame ganstand.
Thairfor be blyth : the tym may be at hand,
  Quhen that Blythe shall be yit, with Godis grace,
As weel plenneist as ever thai it fand,
  Quhil sum shall rew the rinning of that race.

Ay to be blyth ay utwardlie appeir ;
  That be na man it may perceivit be.
That thow pantis for tynsal of thy geir.
  Lest thy unfriendis, that are proud and hie,
Be blyth and glad of thy adversitie.
  Thairfor be stout, and gar them understand
For loss of geir thow takest na suffrie :
  For yit be glad thow hast eneuch of land.

Be blyth and glad, then ay in thy intent :
  For lesum [2] blythness is ane happie thing.
Be thow nocht blyth, what vaileth land or rent ?
  And thow be blyth is cause of lang leiving.

[1] Despoiled.   [2] Lawful.

Be thow nocht blyth, thoch that thow war an king,
　Thy lyf is nocht but cair without blythness.
Thairfor be blyth : and pray to God us bring
　Till his blythness ; and joy that is endless.

AA KYNDNES AT COURT WITHOUT SILLER.

[Kyndnes = acquaintance.]

Sumtyme to court I did repair,
　Therein sum errands for to dres :
Thinking I had sum friendis thair
　To help fordwart my beseynes.
　　Bot, not the less,
I fand nathing bot doubilnes.
Auld kyndnes helpis not ane hair.

To ane grit court-man I did speir :
　That I trowit my friend had bene,
Because we were of kyn sa neir,
　To him my mater I did mene.[1]
　　Bot, with disdene,
He fled as I had done him tene :[2]
And wald not byd my tale to heir.

I wend that he, in word and deid,
　For me, his kynsman, sould have wrocht.
But to my speich he tuk na heid :
　Neirnes of blude he set at nocht.
　　Than weel I thocht,
When I for sibness[3] to him socht,
It was the wrang way that I geid.

My hand I put into my sleif,
　And furthe of it ane purs I drew ;
And said I brocht it him to geif,
　Bayth gold and silver I him schew.
　　Then he did rew
That he unkindlie me mis-knew ;—
And hint[4] the purs fest in his neif.

[1] Mention.　　[2] Sorrow.　　[3] Kindred.　　[4] Caught.

Fra tyme he gat the purs in hand
  He kyndlie cousin callit me.
And bade me gar him understand
  My beseynes all haillalie.[1]
      And swair that he
My trew and faythfull friend suld be
In court as I ples him command.

For which better it is, I trow,
  Into the courte to get supplé,
To have ane purs of fyne gold fow
  Nor to the hiast of degre
      Of kyn to be.
Sa alters our nobilitie,
Grit kynrent helpis lytil now.

Thairfor, my friends. gif you will mak
  All courte men youris as ye wald,
Gude gold and silver with yow tak ;
  Than to tak help ye may be bald
      For it is tauld,
Kyndnes of courte is coft and sald,
Neirness of kyn na thing thai rak.[2]

GUDE COUNSELS.

Luif vertew ever and all vycis flee,
  Wickitness hait alway, gudeness embrace,
Remuve rancour and aye keip charitie,
  Proudness detest, envy frae ye far chace ;
Greediness never let in thee tak place ;
  Be honourable and weil credence keip ;
Beseynes to give ever tyme and space,
  Trewlie serve God, and as for synnis weip.

[Thir aucht lynes ye may begin at ony nuke ye will ; and reid backward or foreward, and ye sall find the lyk sentence and meter.]

1 Completely.   2 Stretch.

BARON MAITLAND OF THIRLSTANE.

1545-1595

JOHN MAITLAND, second son of Sir Richard Maitland, was born in 1545. He received part of his education in Scotland, and was afterwards sent to France to study law. Upon his return to his native country he practised as an advocate, in which profession he soon made himself famous. From 1566 to 1573 he was Commendator of Coldingham, and on 26th August, 1567, he received the office of Lord Privy Seal in succession to his father, both of which offices he held till 1570, when, for his loyalty to the queen, he lost the latter, which was conferred on George Buchanan. He was made a Lord of Session in April, 1581, Secretary of State to James VI. in 1584, and Lord High Chancellor in June, 1586. In 1589 he attended the king on his voyage to Norway for his bride, the Princess Anne of Denmark. In 1590 he was raised to the peerage under the title of Baron Maitland of Thirlstane. About this time he married Jean, only daughter of James, Lord Fleming. Towards the end of 1592 he incurred the queen's displeasure for refusing to relinquish his lordship of Musselburgh, which she claimed as being part of that of Dunfermline. He absented himself for some time from court, but was eventually restored to royal favour. He died of a lingering illness on the 3rd of October, 1595. His only son was created Earl of

Lauderdale by James VI. in 1624, and this earl's son became the first and only Duke of Lauderdale (1616-1682).

Spottiswood thus sums up the character of Baron Maitland: " He was a man of rare parts, and of deep wit, learned, full of courage, and most faithful to his king and master. No man did ever carry himself in his place more wisely, nor sustain it more courageously against his enemies." [1]

He was a great favourite with James VI., who wrote four " Visions " in his praise, and mourned his death in the following poetical epitaph :

> " Thou passenger ! that spies with gazing eyes
>   This trophy sad of Death's triumphant dart,
> Consider when this outward tomb thou sees,
>   How rare a man leaves here his earthly part ;
> His wisdom and his uprightness of heart,
>   His piety, his practice of our state,
> His quick engine so versed in every art
>   As equally not all were in debate.
> Thus justly hath his death brought forth of late
>   An heavy grief in prince and subjects all
> That virtue love, and vice do bear a hate.
>   Though vicious man rejoices at his fall.
> So for himself most happy doth he die,
>   Though for his prince it most unhappy be."

Lord Thirlstane wrote a large number of Latin poems, epigrams, etc.,[2] most of which are to be found in the "Delitiæ Poetarum Scotorum," Vol. II. Several of these have been inserted in the collection of his

---

[1] " History of the Church of Scotland," p. 412.

[2] Joannes Metellani Thirlstonii domini Scotiae quondam Cancellarii Epigrami, in D.P,S., Vol. II., p. 160.

father's poems printed by the Maitland Club in 1830.
He is the author also of the well-known satirical
ballad, "Against Slanderous Tongues," and of "An
Admonition to the Earl of Mar," described by
Pinkerton as the best State poem he had ever read.[1]

AGANIS SKLANDEROUS TOUNGIS.

Gif[2] bissie-branit bodis you bakbyte ;
   And of some wickit wittis ye are invyit,
Quha wald deprave your doings for dispite ;
   Despise thair devilliche deming, and defy it.
For fra that tyme and treuthe thair talis have tryit,
   The suythe sall shew itself out to their shame,
And be thair speche thair spyte sall be espyit,
   And have na fayth, nor foute aganes your fame.

Misknow thair craft ; and kythe[3] not as ye kend it :
   Thair doings will thair deling sone detect,
For gif ye greit, find falt, or be offendit,
   Thair sawis to be suythe sum will suspect.
Bot gif thair leyis ye lichtlie, and neglect,
   And let them lie, and tax you as they list ;
Fra tyme thai find thair fabils faill effect,
   Thai will deny thair deling and desist.

As furious fluds with gritter force ay flowis,
   And starker stevin[4] quhere stoppit are the stremis ;
And gorgit waters ever gritter growis ;
   And forcit fyres with gritter gleids out glemis :
And ay more bricht and burning is the beymis
   Of Phebus' face, that fastest are reflexit ;
So gude renoun, quhilk railer's rage repremis
   Advancis more, the more invyars vex it.

---

[1] See Pinkerton's "Ancient Scottish Poems," Vol. I., p. 160.

[2] If.   [3] Appear.   [4] Broaden

The more thai speik, the sonar are thai spyit,
    The more thai lie, your luk will be the less.
The more thai talk, the treuth is sooner tryit.
    The more planelie thair poysone thai express
The less thai cause thair credit to increase.
    The more thai wirk, the less thair wark avances,
The more thai preis [1] your praysis to oppres,
    The gritter of your gloir is the glancis.

Do quhat ye dow, detrattours ay will deme yow,
    Quhais crafte is to calumpniat but caus :
Bakbytars ay be brutis will blaspheme you ;
    Althoch the contrair all the cuntrie knaws.
And, wald ye ward you upe betwene twa wais,
    Yit so ye sall not frome thair sayings save you
Bot, gif thai see sussie [2] of thair fais,
    Blasone thai will, however ye behave yow.

Gif ye be secreit, sad, and solitair ;
    Peirtlie thai speik that privalie ye play ;
And gif in publick places ye repair
    Ye seke to see and to be sene, thai say.
War ye a sanct, thai suld suspect you ay.
    Be ye humane, our humill thai will hold you.
Gif ye bear strange, thai you esteme ower stay : [3]
    And trows it is ye, or els sum has it tald you.

Gif ye be blyth, your lychtness thai will lak.
    Gif ye be grave, your gravitee is elekit.
Gif ye lyk mask and mirthe, or mirrie mak :
    Thai sweir ye feill ane string : and bowns [4] to brek it.
Gif ye be seik, sum flychtis are suspectit ;
    And all your sairris callet secreit sunyeis.
Claiths thai dispyte, and be ye daylie deckit,
    " Persave," thai say, " the papings that pruinyeis." [5]

---

[1] Excite.   [2] Careful.   [3] Lofty.   [4] Ready.
[5] Parrot that prunes its feathers.

Gif ye be wyis, and well in vertew versit,
   Cunning, thai call, uncumlie for your kynd.
And say it is bot slychtis ye have feirsit
   To clok the crafte, quhairto ye ar inclynd.
Gif ye be meik, yit thai mistak your mind :
   And sweir ye ar far shrewdar nor ye seme.
Sua do your best, thus sall ye be defynd :
   And all your deidis sall detractours deme.

Yit thai will leif thair leeing at the last.
   Fra thay advert invy will not availl :
Bakbytar's brutis bydis bot ane blast :
   Thai flureis sone, but forder fructe thai faill.
Rek not thairfore how raschlie ravars raill :
   For never was vertew yit without invy.
So promptlie sall your patience prevaill,
   Quhere thai perhaps sic deming sall deir by.

THOMAS MAITLAND.

1550-1572.

THOMAS MAITLAND was the third son of the blind Knight of Thirlstane, and was born in 1550. He was a young man of brilliant intellect, wide scholarship, and large sympathies. Had he lived he would undoubtedly have done much to extend the fame of his illustrious house. He composed a number of correct Latin poems which, if they do not display a vigorous imagination, at least evince great command of the Latin tongue, and are written with ease and spirit. They are printed in the "Delitiæ Poetarum Scotorum," Vol. II. pp. 162-171. Besides his poetical works he appears to have written a treatise on undertaking a war against the Turks, and a discourse or oration addressed to Queen Elizabeth, urging the propriety of setting Mary at liberty, and of restoring her to sovereign power. This latter production, in MS., supposed to have been written about 1570, is now in Edinburgh University Library. He is better known as one of the interlocutors with George Buchanan in the dialogue "De jure regni apud Scotos." Thomas Maitland died in Italy in 1572, at the early age of twenty-two.

MARY MAITLAND.

Fl. 1580.

MARY MAITLAND, third daughter of Sir Richard Maitland, was born about the year 1550. In consequence of her father's blindness she became his amanuensis, and, amongst other works, transcribed a considerable portion of the MSS. now in the Pepysian Library. The volumes contain several compositions of her own, but the difficulty of obtaining these hinders a selection being made for this work. She married Alexander Lawder of Hatton, and had a numerous family. One of her sons, George Lawder, holds a respectable place among the poets of the seventeenth century. Several pieces which he wrote between 1629 and 1660 have been printed in a volume entitled " Fugitive Scottish Poetry of the Seventeenth Century," Edin., 1825, edited by Dr. David Laing. His "Tears on the Death of Evander"[1] —a monody on the death by drowning of Sir John Swinton of Swinton is probably the best known of these pieces.

[1] Bannatyne Club Garland, No. XI. 8vo, Edin., 1848.

EARL OF LAUDERDALE.

1653-1695.

RICHARD, fourth Earl of Lauderdale, was born on 20th June, 1653. While quite a young man he held several important public positions, and for three years (1681-1684) the office of Lord Justice-General of Scotland. He married Lady Anne Campbell, second daughter of the ninth Earl of Argyll. In consequence of political troubles through his strong attachment to the House of Stuart, he fled to Paris, where he wrote a translation of Virgil's "Æneid," which was published in two volumes in 1737. It was considered a very fair rendering of the immortal epic, and Dryden, who saw the manuscript, is reported to have stripped it without acknowledgment of not a few of its beauties for the embellishment of his own translation. Dr. Trapp says of Lauderdale's version that "it is pretty near the original, though not so close as its brevity would make one imagine." The Earl occasionally employed his pen in writing English verse, but none of his compositions seem to survive.

SIR PATRICK HUME.

1556-1609.

PATRICK, eldest son of Sir Patrick Hume, fifth laird of Polwarth, by Agnes Home of Manderston, born in 1556, was educated for the Bar, and resided chiefly at the royal court, where he was in great favour with James VI. Among the names of the twenty-five gentlemen appointed to attend on the king "at all times of his riding and passing to the field," we find one of them styled the "young laird of Polwarth." He was made Master of the Household in 1591, one of the Gentlemen of the King's Bedchamber, and Warden of the Marches.[1] He married Juliana, daughter of Sir Thomas Ker of Fernihirst. He died 15th June, 1609.

Hume is best known for his *Flyting*, after the manner of that between Dunbar and Kennedy, addressed to Alexander Montgomery under the name of "Polwart." This *Flyting* is full of rough scurrility and boisterous sarcasm, and the contending parties do not scruple to hurl at each other the most opprobrious epithets. He is, however, the author of a more sensible poem, *The Promine*, addressed to the king, which has been reprinted from the original edition of 1580 in Dr. Laing's "Select Remains of the Ancient Popular and Romance Poetry of Scotland," 1823.[2]

---

[1] Crawford's Peerage, p. 313.

[2] Re-edited with Memorial, Introduction, and Additions, by Dr. John Small, Edin., 1885.

ALEXANDER HUME.

1560-1609.

ALEXANDER HUME, a gifted poet-preacher of
the sixteenth century, was a scion of the noble
house of Polwarth, being the second son of Patrick,
the fifth laird. He was born about 1560, and received
part of his education at St. Andrews, where, in 1574,
he took his degree of B.A. According to the custom
of the time, and as befitted a gentleman's son, he
completed his studies in law—for which profession he
was destined—in France, most probably at the
University of Paris. Upon his return home he
practised for three years, but became disgusted with
his calling on account of the corrupt and venal
practices then prevalent in Scottish courts of justice.
In a poetical epistle to his friend Gilbert Moncreiff,
the king's physician, he gives his own reasons for
quitting the Bar :

> "Three years, or near that space,
> I haunted maist our highest pleading place
> And senate, where great causes reasoned were :
> My breast was bruised with leaning on the bar,
> My buttons brist, I partly spitted blood,
> My gown was trailed and trampled where I stood,
> Mine ears were deaved with macer's cries and din,
> Which procutors and parties callèd in :
> I daily learned but could not pleasèd be :
> I saw sic things as pity was to see."

From the courts of law he turned to the court of
royalty, but with a like result. There also were

many things wholly at variance with the integrity
of his nature. He was a pious man this quondam
barrister and courtier, and had a soul above the
rampant worldliness of his day; it was fitting therefore that the Church should claim his attention, and,
accordingly, we find him, after the usual period of
training, ordained to the pastorate of the lovely
parish of Logie, near Stirling, 30th August, 1597.
Here he lived and laboured, writing poetry and
preaching eloquently, fulfilling the duties of his office
with a large measure of success until his death on
the 4th December, 1609, at the age of forty-nine.
He was survived by one son, Caleb, and two daughters,
and by his wife Marion, daughter of John Duncanson,
Dean of the Chapel Royal.

In 1599 Hume published his "Hymnes and Sacred
Songs,"[1] dedicated to the "faithful and virtuous
Elizabeth Melville, Lady Culross," the authoress of
Ane Godly Dream, a poem long popular among
Scottish Presbyterians. The Bannatyne Club reprinted these "Hymnes" in 1832. The principal
poem in the collection is *The Day Estivall*, an exceedingly fine piece of descriptive scenery, and ranking
very high amongst sixteenth-century productions.
In it he describes with genuine simplicity and pathos
the glories of a long summer day. Leyden delighted
in the poem,[2] and Campbell, in his "Specimens of the
British Poets,"[3] refers to it as a "train of images that

---

[1] Published by Robert Waldegrave, Edin. This edition is now
extremely rare, only *three* copies being known to exist.

[2] "Scottish Descriptive Poems," Edin., 1803, pp. 193-214.

[3] Vol. II., pp. 238-247.

seem singularly pleasing and unborrowed, the picture
of a poetical mind, humble, but genuine in its cast."
The poem presents, says Chambers, "a description of
the progress and effects of a summer's day in Scotland, accompanied by the reflections of a mind full of
natural piety, and a delicate perception of the beauties
of the physical world. The easy flow of the numbers,
distinguishing it from the harsher productions of the
same age, and the arrangement of the terms and
ideas, prove an acquaintance with English poetry,
but the subject and the poetical thought are entirely
the author's own. They speak strongly of the
elegant and fastidious mind, tired of the Bar and
disgusted with the court, finding a balm to the
wounded spirit in being alone with Nature and
watching her progress. The style has an unrestrained
freedom which may please the present age, and the
contemplative feeling thrown over the whole, mingled
with the artless vividness of the descriptions, bringing
the objects immediately before the eye, belong to a
species of poetry at which some of the brightest
minds have lately made it their study to aim."[1]

In his quiet rural parish at the foot of the Ochils,
Hume would find abundant material for that choice
imagery which sparkles in his song. The scenery
around the old kirk and manse of Logie was just
of the kind to fire his poetic soul. Nature in her
many moods lent inspiration, and sermon and song
alike combined in devout thanksgiving. The singer
could rise from Nature to Nature's God, and while he

---

[1] Chambers's "Dictionary of Eminent Scotsmen," Vol. III., p. 95.

praised the glories of the earth that should vanish from his sight, he was drawn towards that grander Glory which is eternal and unchanging—a new heaven and a new earth wherein dwelleth righteousness. He is a poet-preacher of the true stamp, thoroughly conscious of his duty and responsibility, and striving always to inculcate a lofty standard of morality and spiritual life amongst his fellowmen.

His other poems are thus entitled: *The Author's Recantation; God's Benefits on Man; Consolation to his Sorrowing Soul; Thanks for the Deliverance of the Sick; God's Triumph* (a poem on the defeat of the Spanish Armada, greatly praised by Leyden); *Of God's Omnipotence; Epistle to Gilbert Moncreiff* —which latter is the only account we have of Hume's early life.

His prose works are: "Ane Treatise of Conscience," 12mo, Edin., 1594; "On the Felicity of the World to Come," 1594; "Four Discourses of Praises to God," 1594; "Rejoinder to Dr. Adam Hill concerning the Descent of Christ into Hell;" "Ane afold Admonition to the Ministerie of Scotland, be ane Deeing Brother," 1607 — a tractate discovered among the Wodrow MSS. in the Advocates' Library, and printed by the Bannatyne Club. It embraces a strong defence of Church government by Presbytery, and a very telling invective against those ministers who, to gratify the whims of James VI., were appointed to the office of bishops in the Church. It is possibly on account of this tractate that Row has commended Hume in his "History" as one of the faithful presbyters who witnessed "against the hierarchy of prelacy in this kirk."[1]

THE DAY ESTIVALL.

(*A Summer's Day.*)

O perfect light that shed away
  The darkness from the light,
And set a ruler o'er the day,
  Another o'er the night.

Thy glory, when the day forth flies,
  More brightly doth appear
Than at mid-day unto our eyes
  The shining sun is clear!

The shadow of the earth anon
  Removes and drawis by,
Syne in the east, when it is gone,
  Appears a clearer sky,

Which soon perceives the little larks,
  The lapwing and the snipe,
And tune their song, like Nature's clerks,
  O'er meadow, muir, and stripe.

But every bold nocturnal beast
  No longer may abide,
They hie away, both maist and least,
  Themselves in house to hide.

The golden globe incontinent
  Sets up his shining head,
And on the earth and firmament
  Displays his beams abroad.

---

[1] "History of the Church of Scotland," pp. 94, 95.

For joy the birds with bolden [1] throats
  Against his visage sheen.
Take up their kindly music notes,
  In woods and gardens green.

Starts up the careful husbandman
  His corn and vines to see,
And every timeous artisan
  In booths works busily.

The pastor quits the slothful sheep
  And passes forth with speed,
His little camow-nosèd [2] sheep
  And rowting [3] kye to feed.

The passenger from perils sure,
  Goes glady forth the way :
Brief, every living creature near,
  Takes comfort of the day.

The misty reek, the clouds of rain,
  From tops of mountains skails, [4]
Clear are the highest hills and plain
  The vapours take the vales.

Begaired [5] is the sapphire pend [6]
  With spraings [7] of scarlet hue :
And preciously from end to end
  Damasked white and blue.

The ample heaven, of fabric sure,
  In clearness does surpass
The crystal and the silver pure,
  As clearest polished glass.

The time so tranquil is and clear,
  That nowhere shall ye find,
Save on a high and barren hill,
  The air of passing wind.

---

[1] Inflated. [2] Flat-nosed. [3] Lowing. [4] Scatters. [5] Variegated.
[6] Arch. [7] Streaks.

All trees and simples, great and small,
  Which balmy leaf do bare,
Than they were painted on a wall,
  Nor move they more or stir.

The rivers fresh, the caller streams,
  O'er rocks that swiftly rin
The water clear like crystal beams,
  And makes a pleasant din.

Calm is the deep and purple sea,
  Yea, smoother than the sand ;
The waves that woltering wont to be,
  Are stable like the land.

So silent is the cessile air
  That every cry and call
The hills and dales, and forest fair,
  Again repeat them all.

The clogget, busy, humming bees,
  That never think to drone,
On flowers and flourishes of trees
  Collect their liquor brown.

The sun, most like a speedy post,
  With ardent course ascends ;
The beauty of the heavenly host
  Up to the zenith tends.

The breathless flocks draw to the shade
  And freshness of their fauld ;
The startling nolt, as they were mad,
  Run to the rivers cauld.

The herds beneath some leafy trees
  Amidst the flowers lie ;
The stable ships upon the seas
  Hang up their sails to dry.

The hart, the hind, the fallow deer,
    Are tapished[1] at their rest :
The fowls and birds that made the beare,[2]
    Prepare their pretty nest.

The rayons dure[3] descending down
    All kindle in a gleid :[4]
In city or in borough town
    May none set forth their head.

Back from the blue pavemented whun,[5]
    And from ilk plaster wall,
The hot reflection of the sun
    Inflames the air and all.

The labourers that timely rose,
    All weary, faint, and weak,
For heat down to their houses goes,
    Noon-meat and sleep to take.

The caller wine in cave is sought,
    Men's brothing[6] hearts to cool :
The water cold and clear is brought,
    And salads steeped in ale.

With gilded eyes and open wings,
    The cock his courage shows :
With claps of joy his breast he dings,
    And twenty times he crows.

The dove with whistling wings so blue
    The winds can fast collect,
Her purple opens many a hue
    Against the sun direct.

Now noon is gone—gone is mid-day,
    The heat does slake at last :
The sun descends down west away,
    For three o'clock is past.

.   .   .   .   .

[1] Couching.   [2] Noise.   [3] Keen.   [4] Blaze.   [5] Whinstone pavement.   [6] Heated.

The rayons of the sun we see
  Diminish in their strength,
The shade of every tower and tree
  Extended is at length.

Great is the calm, for everywhere
  The wind is settling down,
The reek throws up right in the air
  From every tower and town.

   .   .   .   .   .

The mavis and the philomeen,
  The starling whistles loud,
The cushats on the branches green
  Full quietly they crood.

The gloamin' comes, the day is spent,
  The sun goes out of sight,
And painted is the occident
  With purple, sanguine bright.

The scarlet or the golden thread,
  Who would their beauty try?
Are nothing like the colour red,
  And beauty of the sky.

What pleasure then to walk and see
  Endlong [1] a river clear,
The perfect form of every tree
  Within the deep appear!

The salmon out of cruives [2] and creels [3]
  Uphailed into scouts, [4]
The bells and circles on the weils [5]
  Through leaping of the trouts.

Oh, sure it were a seemly thing,
  While all is still and calm,
The praise of God to play and sing,
  With trumpet and with psalm!

---

[1] Along   [2] Salmon-traps.   [3] Baskets.   [4] Small boats or cobles.   [5] Eddies.

Through all the land great is the guild [1]
  Of rustic folks that cry,
Of bleating sheep, for they be filled,
  Of calves and rowting kye.

All labourers draw hame at even,
  And can to others say,
Thanks to the gracious God of Heaven,
  Who sent this summer day.

[1] Clamour.

DAVID HUME OF GODSCROFT.[1]

1560-1630.

DAVID HUME was the second son of Sir David Hume, seventh Baron of Wedderburn, by his wife Mariota, daughter of Johnstone of Elphinstone, and grandson of that Baron of Wedderburn by whom was planned the slaughter of the French knight De La Bastie. He was born about 1560, and received his education at Dunbar and St. Andrews, and on the Continent. A Latin poem, *Daphn-Amaryllis*, written at the age of fourteen, gained him the commendation of no less an authority than George Buchanan. From 1583 to 1588 he acted as secretary to his relative, Archibald, the "good Earl of Angus." On account of his complicity in the Raid of Ruthven, he fled to London and resided there for some time. In 1605 we find him writing a tractate on the Union of England and Scotland,[2] in favour of which he descanted, as Bishop Nicolson says, in a clear Latin style. In this same year he published a selection of Latin poems under the title of "Lusus Poetici," which were afterwards incorporated with the "Delitiæ

---

[1] His territorial appellation is supposed to have been assumed as more euphonious than the real name of his property—Gowkscroft. It bears, especially in its Latin form, *Theagrius*, a strong analogy to the word so touchingly employed in German to designate a burial ground, as "God's Acre."

[2] "Tractatus De Unione Insulæ Britanniæ," 4to, Lond., 1605.

Poetarum Scotorum.[1] In 1611 he wrote a " History
of the House of Wedderburn," which was first
printed in 1839 from a copy in MS. that had been
preserved at Wedderburn.[2] In 1612 appeared a
poem on the death of Prince Henry, *Henrici Principis
Justa*, and in 1617 a long congratulatory poem on
the king's visit to Scotland, *Regi Suo Gratulatio*.
From 1625 to 1629 he was engaged on his chief
work, a " History of the House and Race of Douglas
and Angus," which was published in 1646 by Evan
Tyler, with a second edition by Ruddiman in 1743,
2 vols., 12mo. Hume died in 1630. A small volume
containing most of his poems was printed at Paris
in 1639.[3]

NOTE.--Hume of Godscroft is not to be confounded, as he has
frequently been, with another David Hume, minister of one of the
Protestant churches on the Continent, and the author of several works
in Latin and French.

---

[1] Two vols., 16mo, printed at Amsterdam in 1637, edited by Arthur
Johnston, M.D. It is now a rare and valuable work. Hume's poems
will be found in Vol. I., pp. 378-438. Johnston (1587-1641) was one
of the foremost Scottish Latin poets, and is said to equal George
Buchanan.

[2] " Davidis Humii de Familia Humia Wedderburnensi Liber,"
edited for the Abbotsford Club by John Miller, M.D., 4to, Edin.,
1839.

[3] " Poemata Omnia," etc., 8vo, Paris, 1639.

JAMES HUME, M.D.

Fl. 1640.

JAMES HUME, son of David Hume of Godscroft,
and therefore sometimes described as "Scotus-
Theagrius," flourished during the seventeenth
century, and resided chiefly in France. On the title-
page of his earliest publication, "Pantaleonis Vati-
cinia Satyra," printed at Rouen in 1633, he is styled
"Med. Doctor." The "Satyra" is a very crude
Latin romance, dedicated to Sir Robert Ker, first
Earl of Ancram, and has an historical appendix on
contemporary affairs, mostly German. In 1634
Hume printed in Latin, "Proelium ad Lipsiam;"
"Gustavus Magnus;" and "De Reditu Ducis Ameli-
ensis ex Flandria," as an appendix to his father's
"De Unione Insulæ Britanniæ," while between 1636
and 1640 he published at Paris a series of mathematical treatises, nine in number, all in Latin and
French. He appears to have edited the 1639 (Paris)
edition of his father's poems, and to have added to
the work several pieces of his own composition.

ANNA HUME.

Fl. 1640.

ANNA HUME, daughter of David Hume of Godscroft, superintended the publication of her father's "History of the House and Race of Douglas and Angus." William Douglas, eleventh Earl of Angus, who was dissatisfied with Hume's work, consulted Drummond of Hawthornden on the subject. Drummond admitted various defects and extravagant views in Hume's work, adding, however, that the suppression of the book would ruin "the gentlewoman who hath ventured, she says, her whole fortune" on its publication. For nearly two years the dispute delayed the publication of the work, which had been printed in 1644 by Evan Tyler, the king's printer. In that same year Tyler published "The Triumphs of Love, Chastity, Death, translated out of the French of Petrarch into English verse by Mrs. Anna Hume." A copy of this very rare work is in the British Museum, and there is a reprint in Bohn's "Translation of Petrarch by various Hands" (1859). Her translation is considered to be faithful and spirited. The second half of "The Triumph of Love," Part III., descriptive of the disappointed lover, and the bright account of the fair maids in the "Triumph of Chastity" is admirably rendered. Anna Hume is said to have also translated her father's

Latin poems, and Drummond of Hawthornden,
acknowledging certain commendatory verses at her
hand, writes to her as "the learned and worthy
gentlewoman, Mrs. Anna Hume," declaring himself unworthy of "the blazon of so pregnant and
rare a wit."

LADY GRISELL BAILLIE.

1665 1746

"THE Merse," says Sarah Tytler in her "Song-
stresses of Scotland," "is famous in old
Scotch tradition for the beauty of its women and
the gallantry of its men." The "Men o' the Merse"
is a proverbial expression for strong physical
endurance on the part of the male population of
the county. Fidelity to duty and loyalty to home
and country have ever been leading characteristics
of the Scottish Borderer, but, as will shortly be seen,
the sterner sex are not alone in exemplifying
these estimable virtues. For the Merse has brave
women also on the scroll of her famous ones, and
Grisell Hume, the sweet-faced girl-heroine, is conspicuous above all others. I write here of her song,
but we can never forget the touching poetry of her
life, exemplified in that deed of filial devotedness
which must ever unite her with the noble women
of all time.

Grisell Hume was born in old Redbraes Castle[1]
on Christmas morning, 1665, and was the eldest of
Sir Patrick Hume's family of eighteen. On her
devolved to a considerable extent the care of this
large household, and opportunities for study and

---

[1] Marchmont House stands on the site of Redbraes Castle. It was
also called Polwarth House. Godscroft refers to "the castle of
Polwarth which is known as Redbraes."

self-improvement were few and far between. Besides
that, the times were troublous. The Covenanting
struggle had drained Scotland of some of its best
blood. Sir Patrick Hume had been a zealous upholder
of Reformation principles. He had fought manfully
for his country's religious freedom, but a fresh
persecution brought again the evil days. Darkness
settled on the home at Redbraes, a warrant was
issued for the speedy arrest of Hume, and to escape
the bitter consequences which his capture entailed,
he had to flee for safety to the family vault beneath
Polwarth Kirk. The story of this trying period and
of his daughter's heroism has been told again and
again. No fact of history is better known in the
county. But such gallant achievements are always
worthy of repetition :

> " Though years come and go,
>   That glorious act of filial love
>   Shall shine in cloudless lustre."

Troopers were quartered in the castle and in the
vicinity, and every possible means taken to break
off the retreat of the illustrious offender. But all to
no purpose. His hiding-place remained a profound
secret, only Grisell, her mother, and an old carpenter
on the estate, Jamie Winter by name, knowing his
whereabouts. On the latter, who was a much
attached servant of the family, they thought they
could depend, and were not deceived. With his
assistance a bed and bedclothes were secretly conveyed to the vault, and here, amongst the ashes of
his ancestors, Sir Patrick Hume lay concealed for

nearly a month. Of this terrible crisis many incidents
have been faithfully recorded. Grisell, of course, is
the chief figure. Her courage and coolness were
the agents most essential to her father's safety.
There was needed great skill in dealing with the
keen questionings of his pursuers. And yet she
held frequent and prolonged intercourse with him.
In the dead of night she set out alone, walking a
distance of over a mile, till she reached the grave-
yard and the old vault, and after supplying his body
with the nourishment it required, and his soul with
true daughterly cheer, this faithful maiden trudged
her lonely road homewards before the day had begun
to break. Of these midnight excursions the following
two authentic incidents are related. The minister's
house was near the church, and on Grisell's going
past upon one occasion his dogs began to bark and
kept up such a noise as put her in the utmost fear
of discovery. On mentioning this circumstance to
her mother, the latter sent the next day for the
minister, and on pretence of a mad dog, got him to
hang all his dogs. The other anecdote has reference
to the difficulty in secreting food for her father's
wants without the servants or any of the family
observing. Sir Patrick appears to have been somewhat fond of boiled sheep's head—for in those days
the aristocracy were content with plain, homely fare
—and one day at dinner, while the children where
supping their broth, Grisell managed to stow away
into her lap the greater part of a sheep's head, when
her brother Sandy looked up in astonishment and

said, " Mother, will ye look at Grisell ? While we have been supping our broth she has eaten the whole sheep's head."

At last the soldiers were withdrawn, and Sir Patrick Hume returned to Redbraes, but the unsettled state of the country made flight imperative, and accordingly he and his family betook themselves from Scotland and took refuge at Utrecht, in Holland, where there was already a considerable number of Scottish exiles. But the years there were hard and heavy. The Berwickshire laird's family began to feel the pinch of poverty. Death came and snatched away Christian, the flower of the flock, the singing favourite. Yet, amid all the vicissitudes of exile, they were a brave and cheerful band. Grisell's unflinching devotion to household duties, her dauntless courage, and gentle, winning ways were strong factors in clearing away the heavy clouds that had settled on this pious home. She and her father made their Dutch abode a characteristically Scottish one. It was the centre of the Scotch community at Utrecht, and the exiled gentlemen gathered there to talk of the land they so much loved, of its past trials, its present troubles, and its future hopes. This was the all-engrossing theme, and right patriotically was it discussed over such plain fare as porridge and milk, with small beer instead of wine. Amid her numerous interests and heavy responsibilities, Grisell found time to fill a manuscript book with poems of her own composition. Unfortunately, however, these are not always in the most finished and perfect condition. Calls of domestic duty would come in the midst of composition, and, often before leisure could be gained to complete the verses, the inspiring thought had fled. But there is one sweetly pathetic ballad which has escaped the ceaseless activity of her Dutch life, and by this quaint, old-fashioned, and touching rhyme, is our Berwickshire heroine remembered as a poetess.

It was at Utrecht that she made the acquaintance of her future husband, young George Baillie of Jerviswood. He was the eldest son of that Robert Baillie who suffered death in the Grassmarket of Edinburgh in 1684 for his faithful adherence to Presbyterian principles and his alleged complicity in the Rye-House Plot. Friendship deepened into love, and it was perfectly understood between both families that, so soon as the darkness overshadowing the fair land of Scotland had disappeared, the marriage would take place. Grisell was a beautiful girl. "She was middle-sized, well-made, clean in her person, very handsome, with a life and sweetness in her eyes very uncommon, and great delicacy in all her features." Her hair was chestnut-coloured, long and wavy, her speech pleasant and musical, always of a bright, joyous disposition, filling old worn-out hearts with renewed energy and gladness, and the fresh and young with sparkling innocent glee.

But better days dawned at length. James II. was deposed, and William of Orange, Stadtholder of Holland, was offered the throne of Britain. He arrived on the 5th of November, 1688, at Torbay, with a numerous retinue, amongst whom was the brave

knight of Polwarth and his equally brave daughter.
Sir Patrick Hume's devotion was now rewarded with
the titles of Earl of Marchmont, Lord of Polwarth,
Redbraes, and Greenlaw ; his estates were restored,
and peace once more reigned. After this he held
the Chancellorship, the highest office in the kingdom.
On the 17th September, 1692, a grand Scottish
wedding took place at Redbraes ; the waiting years
were now over, the old exile life had passed away,
a new and brighter existence was about to begin.
Of Lady Grisell Baillie's married life, her daughter,
Lady Murray of Stanhope, has given a charming
picture.[1]   Not a cloud obscured the sunshine of
forty-eight years' wedded bliss, "in all which time I
have heard my mother declare that they never had a
single quarrel or misunderstanding or dryness betwixt
them, not for a moment." "He never went abroad
but what she went to the window to look after him,
never taking her eyes from him so long as he was in
sight."   It was truly a lovely and pleasant life.
They had both experienced bitterness and sweetness
in their sojourn, and knew how to value the triumph
of faithful love. But the best joys must end. The
husband was taken first ; he died at Oxford, 6th
August, 1738, and was buried in a place of sepulture
at Mellerstain, which three years previously he had
ordered to be built. "There was scarce one that
paid their last duty to him that had not tears in their

---

[1] "Memoirs of the Lives and Characters of the Right Hon. George
Baillie of Jerviswood, and of Lady Grisell Baillie." Edited by Thomas
Thomson, advocate.   Privately printed, 8vo, Edin., 1822.

eyes and heavy hearts; never man being more beloved
nor regretted, nor carried a more unspotted character
to the grave." Lady Grisell died in London eight
years afterwards, 6th December, 1746, and was laid
to rest beside him whom her soul loved on the 25th
day of the same month, being the anniversary of her
birth. Well might Justice Sir Thomas Burnet
inscribe upon their tomb these lines:

> "The pious parents rear'd this hallowed place,
> A monument for them and for their race.
> Descendants, be it your successive cares
> That no degenerate dust ere mix with theirs!"

Two daughters were left behind—Grisell and Rachel.
The former became the wife of Sir Alexander
Murray of Stanhope, Bart.; the latter of Charles,
Lord Binning, from whom are descended the present
families of Haddington and of Baillie of Jerviswood.

The following inscription, which is engraved in
marble on the left side of the monument to Lady
Grisell Baillie at Mellerstain, was written by Sir
Thomas Burnet, youngest son of Bishop Burnet, and
one of the Judges of the Court of Common Pleas:—

Here lieth
The Right Honourable Lady Grisell Baillie,
wife of George Baillie of Jerviswood, Esq.,
eldest daughter
of the Right Honourable Patrick, Earl of Marchmont :
a pattern to her sex, an honour to her country.
She excelled in the characters of a daughter, a wife, a mother.
While an infant,
at the hazard of her own, she preserved her father's life :
who, under the rigorous persecution of arbitrary power,
sought refuge in the close confinement of a tomb,
where he was nightly supplied with necessaries, conveyed by her,
with a caution far above her years,
a courage almost above her sex ;
a real instance of the so much celebrated Roman charity.
She was a shining example of conjugal affection
that knew no dissension, felt no decline
during almost a fifty years' union,
the dissolution of which she survived from duty, not choice.
Her conduct as a parent
was amiable, exemplary, successful,
to a degree not well to be expressed
without mixing the praises of the dead with those of the living :
who desire that all praise, but of her, should be silent.
At different times she managed the affairs
of her father, her husband, her family, her relations,
with unwearied application, with happy economy,
as distant from avarice as from prodigality.
Christian piety, love of her country,
zeal for her friends, compassion for her enemies,
cheerfulness of spirit, pleasantness of conversation.
dignity of mind,
good breeding, good humour, good sense,
were the daily ornaments of an useful life,
protracted by Providence to an uncommon length
for the benefit of all who fell within the sphere of her benevolence.
Full of years, and of good works,
she died on the 6th day of December, 1746,
near the end of her 81st year,
and was buried on her birthday, the 25th of that month.

WERENA MY HEART LICHT.

There once was a may [1] and she lo'ed nae men,
She biggit her bonnie bower doun in yon glen,
But now she cries dule! and a well-a-day,
Come doun the green gate, and come here away.

When bonnie young Johnnie came owre the sea,
He said he saw nothing so lovely as me;
He hecht [2] me baith rings and mony braw things,
And werena my heart licht I wad dee.

He had a wee tittie [3] that lo'ed na me,
Because I was twice as bonnie as she;
She raised sic a pother 'twixt him and his mother,
That werena my heart licht I wad dee.

The day it was set for the bridal to be,
The wife took a dwam [4] and lay doun to dee,
She moaned and she groaned wi' fause dolour and pain,
Till he vowed he never would see me again.

His kin were for ane o' a higher degree,
Said, what had he to do wi' the like o' me?
Albeit I was bonnie I wasna for Johnnie,
And werena my heart licht I wad dee.

They said I had neither cow nor calf,
Nor dribbles o' drink rins through the draff,
Nor pickles o' meal rins through the mill e'e,
And werena my heart licht I wad dee.

His tittie she was baith wylie and slee,
She spied me as I came ower the lea;
And then she ran in and made sic a din,
Believe your ain een if ye trow na me.

His bonnet stood aye fu' round on his broo,
His auld ane looked aye as well as some's new:
But now he lets't wear ony gait it will hing,
And casts himself dowie upon the corn-bing.

---

[1] Fair maid.   [2] Promised.   [3] Sister.   [4] Fainting-fit.

And now he gaes droopin' about the dykes,
And a' he dare do is to hound the tykes ;
The livelang nicht he ne'er steeks an e'e,
And werena my heart licht I wad dee.

Were I young for thee as I hae been,
We should hae been gallopin' doun on yon green,
Or linking it ower the lily-white lea,
And wow 'gin I were but young for thee.

THE EWE BUCHTIN'S BONNIE.

[The following two verses belong to an unfinished song of Lady Grisell Baillie's.
The late Charles Kirkpatrick Sharpe published them in a sheet, along with an
air which his father had composed at an early period of his life. A copy of this,
recovered by Robert Chambers, is entitled *Absence.* Thomas Pringle, the Border
poet, added several stanzas to the original.]

O, the ewe-buchtin's bonnie, baith e'ening and morn,
When our blithe shepherds play on the bog-reed and horn ;
While we're milking, they're lilting, baith pleasant and clear—
But my heart's like to break when I think on my dear.

O, the shepherds take pleasure to blow on the horn,
To raise up their flocks o' sheep soon i' the morn ;
On the bonnie green banks they feed pleasant and free,
But, alas, my dear heart, all my sighing's for thee !

PATRICK HUME.

Fl. 1695.

PATRICK HUME, of the house of Polwarth, a learned commentator on Milton, flourished as a London schoolmaster about the close of the seventeenth century. In 1695 he edited for Jacob Tonson the sixth edition of *Paradise Lost*, in folio, with elaborate notes, and is said to have been the first to attempt a system of exhaustive annotation on the work of an English poet. On the title-page he styles himself P. H Φιλοποιητής. Dr. Newton, in his preface to the edition of *Paradise Lost*, published in 1749, says: "Patrick Hume, as he was the first, so is the most copious annotator. He laid the foundation, but he laid it among infinite heaps of rubbish." Warton, in his "History of English Poetry," refers to Hume's book as "a large and very valuable commentary." Callander, who edited the first book of *Paradise Lost* in 1750, plagiarised Hume's notes. "These notes," says an anonymous writer, "are always curious; his observations on some of the finer passages of the poem show a mind deeply smitten with an admiration for the sublime genius of their author, and there is often a masterly nervousness in his style, which is very remarkable for this age." Hume is said to have also written a number of Latin and English poems, but none of these appear to be extant.

[For a spirited and interesting discussion on Hume's edition of Milton, see *Blackwood's Magazine* for March, 1819, p. 658.]

EARL OF HADDINGTON.

1680-1735.

THOMAS HAMILTON, the sixth Earl of Haddington, was the second son of Charles, the fifth earl, by his wife, Margaret Leslie, Countess of Rothes, and was born 29th August, 1680. According to "Douglas's Peerage" he was a staunch adherent of the Hanoverian family, a great promoter of the Union between England and Scotland, and one of the sixteen Scottish noblemen in three British Parliaments. He married his cousin Helen, only daughter of John Hope of Hopetoun, and sister of the first Earl of Hopetoun. He died at Newhailes, 28th November, 1735. To his lordship have been ascribed—probably erroneously—a large number of ballads and songs on topics mostly of a licentious description.[1] To those to whom they are unknown, it may be sufficient to mention that Pinkerton has described their character as "immodest." But there is a more praiseworthy memorial of the Earl's talents. He took a deep interest in the cultivation of forest trees, and was an active and successful improver of his patrimonial estates of Tyninghame and Mellerstain. His "Treatise" on the subject, published many

---

[1] "Forty Select Poems, on several occasions, by the Right Hon. the Earl of H——n." "Tales in Verse, for the amusement of leisure hours, written by the ingenious Earl of H———n." "Monstrous Good Things," 12mo, 1785 (privately printed), etc.

years after his death, remained for long a standard work.[1] It is a production that may be read with advantage by all improvers of land, and it establishes one fact of great importance, that the oak, while it is one of the most valuable, is at the same time one of the most easily raised of all trees.

Lord Haddington is also the author of a political poem on the Union, entitled *The Vision*, printed in Edinburgh in 1706, irregular in measure, and inferior in merit.[2]

[1] "Treatise on the manner of raising Forest-trees, Acquaticks, Ever-greens, etc.," 12mo, Edin., 1756 (and since reprinted).

[2] *The Vision*: a poem by the Earl of Haddington, 4to, Edin., 1706.

LORD BINNING.

1696-1732.

CHARLES HAMILTON, Lord Binning, eldest son of Thomas, sixth Earl of Haddington, was born in 1696. Very little is known of his early life. He served with his father as a volunteer at the battle of Sheriffmuir, 13th November, 1715 ; married Rachel, youngest daughter, and in process of time sole heiress, of George Baillie of Jerviswood, and Lady Grisell Baillie ; was elected in 1722 M.P. for St. Germains in Cornwall, and appointed Knight Marischal of Scotland ; died of consumption at Naples, 27th December, 1732 [O.S.].

While still a youth he composed a song entitled *In Praise of Emilius*, full of self-commendation, and containing some jocular allusions to his father's terror during the Rebellion, at which time, as a matter of fact, his father's valour was particularly conspicuous. He is allowed to have had fine genius for lyric poetry, and this will be amply justified by a perusal of his best known song, *Ungrateful Nannie*, which appeared originally in the *Gentleman's Magazine* for 1741. A ballad — *The Duke of Argyll's Levee*—of inferior merit, has been erroneously ascribed to Lord Binning, it being the production of Joseph Mitchell the dramatist. His lordship was much beloved for his gentle and amiable disposition, and a quiet courtliness of character and bearing, which drew from Hamilton of Bangour[1] the following epitaph on his departed friend :

> " Beneath this sacred marble ever sleeps,
> For whom a father, mother, consort weeps,
> Whom brothers', sisters' pious grief pursue,
> And children's tears with virtuous drops bedew ;
> The Loves and Graces grieving round appear,
> Ev'n Mirth herself becomes a mourner here,
> The stranger who directs his steps this way
> Shall witness to thy worth, and wondering say—
> 'Thy life, though short, can we unhappy call ?
> Sure thine was blest, for it was social all.
> O may no hostile hand this place invade,
> For ever sacred to thy gentle shade ;
> Who knew in all life's offices to please,
> Sound taste to virtue, and to virtue, ease ;
> With riches blest, did not the poor disdain ;
> Was knowing, humble, friendly, great, humane ;
> By good men honoured, by the bad approv'd,
> And loved the Muses, by the Muses loved.
> Hail and farewell, who bore the gentlest mind,
> For thou indeed hast been of human-kind ! ' "

UNGRATEFUL NANNIE.

> Did ever swain a nymph adore
>   As I ungrateful Nannie do ?
> Was ever shepherd's heart so sore ?
>   Was ever broken heart so true ?
> My cheeks are swell'd with tears ; but she
> Has never shed a tear for me.

---

[1] William Hamilton of Bangour (1704-1754) was one of the "ingenious young gentlemen" who assisted Allan Ramsay with contributions to the *Tea-Table Miscellany*. He wrote the famous Yarrow ballad beginning " Busk ye, busk ye, my bonnie, bonnie bride," which Wordsworth has praised so highly.

If Nannie call'd, did Robin stay,
  Or linger when she bade me run?
She only had a word to say,
  And all she ask'd was quickly done.
I always thought on her; but she
Would ne'er bestow a thought on me.

To let her cows my clover taste,
  Have I not rose by break of day?
When did her heifers ever fast,
  If Robin in his yard had hay?
Though to my fields they welcome were,
I never welcome was to her.

If Nannie ever lost a sheep,
  I cheerfully did give her two;
Did not her lambs in safety sleep
  Within my folds in frost and snow?
Have they not there from cold been free?—
But Nannie still is cold to me.

Whene'er I climb'd our orchard trees
  The ripest fruit was kept for Nan;
Oh, how those hands that drown'd her bees
  Were stung! I'll ne'er forget the pain:
Sweet were the combs as sweet could be;
But Nannie ne'er looked sweet on me.

If Nannie to the well did come,
  'Twas I that did her pitchers fill;
Full as they were, I brought them home;
  Her corn I carried to the mill:
My back did bear her sacks; but she
Could never bear the sight o' me.

To Nannie's poultry, oats I gave;
  I'm sure they always had the best;
Within this week her pigeons have
  Eat up a peck of peas at least.
Her little pigeons kiss; but she
Would never take a kiss from me.

Must Robin always Nannie woo?
 And Nannie still on Robin frown?
Alas, poor wretch! what shall I do
 If Nannie does not love me soon?
If no relief to me she'll bring,
 I'll hang me in her apron strings.

IN PRAISE OF EMILIUS.

Some cry up little Hyndy[1] for this thing and for that,
And others James Dalrymple, though he be somewhat fat:
But of all the pretty gentlemen of whom the town do tell,
Emilius, Emilius, he bears away the bell.

Some cry up Rantin' Rothes, whose face is like the moon,
Nor Highlander nor minister can put him out of tune.
 But of all, etc.

Some cry up Binning's father for fechting at Dunblane,
But Binning says it only was for fear of being ta'en.
 But of all, etc.

Some cry up Earl Lauderdale, though he be grim and black,
For at the battle of Sheriffmuir he never turned his back.
 But of all, etc.

Some cry up pretty Polwarth for his appearance great,
For wi' his Orange regiment the rebels he defeat.
 But of all, etc.

Some cry up the Laird o' Grant, 'cause he came foremost in:
And others wee Balgony for nothing but his chin.
 But of all, etc.

Some cry up our great general[2] for managing the war,
Though at the battle o' Dunblane he pushed the foe too far.
 But of all, etc.

I have no skill in politics, therefore I haud my tongue:
But ye'll think I hae gab enough, though I be somewhat young.
But I'll tell you a secret, my fairy Binning elf,
Emilius, Emilius. I swear it is yourself!

[1] Earl of Hyndford, British Ambassador at St. Petersburg.
[2] John, Duke of Argyll.

ROBERT CRAWFORD.

1700-1733.

ROBERT CRAWFORD was the second son of Patrick Crawford, a merchant in Edinburgh, who was the third son of David Crawford, sixth laird of Drumsoy. Patrick Crawford purchased the estate of Auchinames in 1715, as well as that of Drumsoy about 1731, which explains the statement of Burns that the son Robert was of the house of Auchinames. Of Robert Crawford's career very little is known. He passed a number of years in France, and was drowned when returning from that country in 1733. He assisted Allan Ramsay in his *Tea-Table Miscellany*, contributing a number of charming lyrics, of which several have attained a wide popularity. "The true muse of native pastoral," says Allan Cunningham, "seeks not to adorn herself with unnatural ornaments: her spirit is in homely love and fireside joy; tender and simple, like the religion of the land, she utters nothing out of keeping with the character of her people and the aspect of the soil; and of this spirit, and of this feeling, Crawford is a large partaker." The following are the best known of Robert Crawford's productions :—*The Broom o' the Cowdenknowes; Tweedside.* (It is stated that when the first Lady Grisell Baillie sang this song she generally drew tears from her audience.)

*The Bush aboon Traquair ; My Dearie, if Thou Dee ;
The Rose in Yarrow; and Leader Haughs and Yarrow.*

LEADER HAUGHS AND YARROW.

The morn was fair, saft was the air,
  All Nature's sweets were springing ;
Then buds did bow with silver dew,
  Ten thousand birds were singing ;
When on the bent [1] with blythe content,
  Young Jamie sang his marrow ; [2]
No bonnier lass e'er trod the grass
  On Leader Haughs and Yarrow.

How sweet her face, where every grace
  In heavenly beauty's planted !
Her smiling een and comely mein,
  That no perfection wanted.
I'll never fret nor bann my fate,
  But bless my bonnie marrow ;
If her dear smile my doubts beguile,
  My mind shall ken no sorrow.

Yet though she's fair, and has full share
  Of every charm enchanting,
Each good turns ill, and soon will kill
  Poor me, if love be wanting.
O, bonnie lass ! have but the grace
  To think e'er ye gae further,
Your joys maun flit if ye commit
  The crying sin of murder.

My wand'ring ghaist will ne'er get rest,
  And day and night affright ye ;
But if ye're kind, with joyful mind,
  I'll study to delight ye.
Our years around, with love thus crowned,
  From all things joy shall borrow ;
Thus none shall be more blest than we,
  On Leader Haughs and Yarrow.

[1] Pasture-land.   [2] Mate.

O, sweetest Sue ! 'tis only you
    Can make life worth my wishes,
If equal love your mind can move,
    To grant this best of blisses.
Thou art my sun, and thy least frown
    Would blast me in the blossom ;
But if thou shine and make me thine,
    I'll flourish in thy bosom.

COWDENKNOWES.

When summer comes, the swains on Tweed
    Sing their successful loves :
Around the yowes the lambkins feed,
    And music fills the groves.

But my loved song is then the broom,
    So fair on Cowdenknowes ;
For sure so sweet, so soft a bloom
    Elsewhere there never growes !

There Colin tuned his aiten reed,
    And won my yielding heart ;
No shepherd e'er that dwelt on Tweed
    Could play with half such art.

He sung of Tay, of Forth, of Clyde,
    The hills and dales around,
Of Leader-haughs and Leader-side :
    Oh, how I blessed the sound !

Yet more delightful is the broom,
    So fair on Cowdenknowes ;
For sure so fresh, so fair a bloom,
    Elsewhere there never growes.

Not Teviot braes, so green and gay,
    May with this broom compare ;
Not Yarrow's banks in flow'ry May,
    Nor the Bush aboon Traquair.

More pleasing far are Cowdenknowes.
  My peaceful, happy home,
Where I was wont to milk my yowes
  At even, among the broom.

Ye powers that haunt the woods and plains
  Where Tweed with Teviot flows ;
Convey me to the best of swains,
  And my loved Cowdenknowes !

JAMES GRAINGER, M.D.

1723-1766.

THE town of Duns has been the birth-place of a number of distinguished Scotchmen, and among them we desire to include here the name of James Grainger. He was the son, by a second marriage, of James Grainger, Esq., formerly of Houghton Hall, Cumberland, but who from some unfortunate mining speculations, and his attachment to the House of Stuart in 1715, had been obliged to sell his estate and accept of an appointment in the Excise. Born in 1723, young Grainger grew up into a gentle and lovable boy, attended for a time the parish school, but on the death of his father was sent to an academy at North Berwick. He then studied for three years in the medical classes at Edinburgh, and was apprenticed to Mr. George Lauder, a surgeon in that city. Naturally clever, he rose quickly in his profession, and during the "'45" acted as surgeon to General Pulteney's Regiment of Foot, serving in the same capacity under the Earl of Stair in Germany during the European wars. At the peace of Aix-la-Chapelle in 1748 he quitted the army, made a tour of Europe, and returned to Scotland. On 13th March, 1753, he graduated M.D. at his old college, and journeying south, settled in London as a physician. In the metropolis he met and associated with the leading literary men of the day, and was on intimate terms with Shenstone, Dr. Johnson, Bishop Percy, Glover, Armstrong, Smollett, Dodsley, Goldsmith, and Sir Joshua Reynolds. His medical practice was not a success, and he had to support himself mainly through writing. In 1755 he published in "Dodsley's Collection," Vol. IV., his well-known *Ode to Solitude*, which at once brought him into repute. In the first part are many passages in which the author manifests great power in depicting the sublime and beautiful in Nature. From May, 1756, to May, 1758, he wrote articles on poetry, the drama, and physic in the *Monthly Review* and other journals. In 1759 he published in two volumes a "Poetical Translation of the Elegies of Tibullus, and of the Poems of Sulpicia." In the same year he began a four years' tour with a former pupil, John Bourryau, who was heir to some property in the West Indies. On the voyage thither Grainger prescribed successfully for a lady who had been attacked with small-pox. She was the widow of a Nevis planter, and on arrival at his destination he married her daughter, Miss Daniel Mathews Burt. Her brother was Governor of the island of St. Christopher, and through this lucky alliance Dr. Grainger soon succeeded in establishing a large and lucrative practice. In 1764 he published a lengthy didactic poem in four books, entitled *The Culture of the Sugar-Cane*, a successful imitation of Milton's *L'Allegro* and *Il Penseroso*, which was honoured with the highest praise. The "Notes" to this poem he in the same year expanded into an "Essay on the more Common West India Diseases." He died at Bassetterre of fever 16th December, 1766.

The personal, as well as the literary, character of Dr. Grainger appears to have stood high in the estimation of his intimate friends. "He was not only," says Dr. Percy, "a man of genius and learning, but had many excellent virtues, being one of the most generous, friendly, and benevolent men I ever knew;" and Dr. Johnson with more brevity but perhaps with equal comprehensiveness, says that "he was an agreeable man who would do any good that was in his power." Grainger bequeathed his MSS. to his friend Percy, and, in accordance with his wish, a complete edition of his poetical works was in 1798 suggested to Dr. Robert Anderson, who published the same, with a life of the author, in 1836.[1] Most of the copies were destroyed, and the work is now extremely scarce. It contains, among other miscellaneous pieces, the fragment of a blank verse tragedy entitled *The Fate of Capua.*

FROM ODE TO SOLITUDE.

O Solitude, romantic maid !
Whether by nodding towers you tread,
Or haunt the desert's trackless gloom,
Or hover o'er the yawning tomb,
Or climb the Andes' clifted side,
Or by the Nile's coy source abide.
Or, starting from your half-year's sleep,
From Hecla view the thawing deep,

---

[1] "Poetical Works of James Grainger, M.D., with Memoirs of his Life and Writings," by Robert Anderson, M.D. 2 vols., 8vo. Edin., 1836.

Or, at the purple dawn of day,
Tadmor's marble wastes survey,
You, recluse, again I woo,
And again your steps pursue.

Plumed Conceit himself surveying,
Folly with her shadow playing,
Purse-proud, elbowing Insolence,
Bloated empirie, puffed Pretence,
Noise that through a trumpet speaks,
Laughter in loud peals that breaks,
Intrusion with a fopling's face,
Ignorant of time and place,
Sparks of fire Dissension blowing,
Ductile, court-bred Flattery bowing,
Restraint's stiff neck, Grimace's leer,
Squint-eyed Censure's artful sneer,
Ambition's buskins, steeped in blood,
Fly thy presence, Solitude.

Sage Reflection, bent with years,
Conscious Virtue, void of fears,
Muffled Silence, wood-nymph shy,
Meditation's piercing eye,
Halcyon Peace on moss reclined,
Retrospect that scans the mind,
Wrapt earth-gazing Reverie,
Blushing, artless Modesty,
Health that snuffs the morning air,
Full-eyed Truth with bosom bare,
Inspiration, Nature's child,
Seek the solitary wild.

Darkness clapped her sable wing,
While you touched the mournful string;
Anguish left the pathless wild,
Grim-faced Melancholy smiled,
Drowsy Midnight ceased to yawn,
The starry host put back the dawn;

Aside their harps even seraphs flung,
To hear thy sweet complaint, O Young![1]
When all Nature's hushed asleep,
Nor Love nor Guilt their vigils keep,
Soft you leave your caverned den,
And wander o'er the works of men ;
But when Phosphor brings the dawn,
By her dappled coursers drawn,
Again you to the wild retreat,
And the early huntsman meet,
Where, as you pensive pace along,
You catch the distant shepherd's song,
Or brush from herbs the pearly dew,
Or the rising primrose view.
Devotion lends her heaven-plumed wings,
You mount, and Nature with you sings.
But when mid-day fervours glow,
To upland airy shades you go,
Where never sunburnt woodman came,
Nor sportsman chased the timid game :
And there beneath an oak reclined,
With drowsy waterfalls behind,
  You sink to rest.
Till the tuneful bird of night
From the neighbouring poplar's height,
Wake you with her solemn strain,
And teach pleased Echo to complain.

With you roses brighter bloom,
Sweeter every sweet perfume :
Purer every fountain flows,
Stronger every wildling grows.
Let those toil for gold who please,
Or for fame renounce their ease.
What is fame?—an empty bubble.
Gold?—a transient shining trouble.
Let them for their country bleed,
What was Sydney's—Raleigh's—meed?

[1] *Young's Night Thoughts.*

Man's not worth a moment's pain,
Base, ungrateful, fickle, vain.
Then let me, sequestered fair,
To your sibyl grot repair ;
On yon hanging cliff it stands,
Scooped by Nature's salvage hands,
Bosomed in the gloomy shade
Of cypress not with age decayed.
Where the owl still hooting sits,
Where the bat incessant flits,
There in loftier strains I'll sing,
Whence the changing seasons spring ;
Tell how storms deform the skies,
Whence the waves subside and rise,
Trace the comet's blazing tail,
Weigh the planets in a scale ;
Bend, great God, before Thy shrine,
The bournless microcosm's Thine.

BRYAN AND PEREENE.

[A West Indian ballad, founded on an incident which occurred in the island of
St. Christopher, contributed to the first volume of Percy's " Reliques."]

The north-east wind did briskly blow,
  The ship was safely moor'd,
Young Bryan thought the boat's crew slow,
  And so leap'd overboard.

Pereene, the pride of Indian dames,
  His heart did long enthral ;
And whoso his impatience blames,
  I wot ne'er loved at all.

A long, long year, one month and day,
  He dwelt on English land,
Nor once in thought would ever stray.
  Though ladies sought his hand

For Bryan he was tall and strong,
  Right blithesome roll'd his een ;
Sweet was his voice when'er he sung,
  He scant had twenty seen.

But who the countless charms can draw,
  That grac'd his mistress true ?
Such charms the old world never saw,
  Nor oft, I ween, the new.

Her raven hair plays round her neck,
  Like tendrils of the vine ;
Her cheeks red dewy rosebuds deck,
  Her eyes like diamonds shine.

Soon as his well-known ship she spied,
  She cast her weeds away,
And to the palmy shore she hied,
  All in her best array.

In sea-green silk so neatly clad,
  She there impatient stood ;
The crew with wonder saw the lad,
  Repel the foaming flood.

Her hands a handkerchief display'd,
  Which he at parting gave :
Well pleas'd, the token he survey'd,
  And manlier beat the wave.

Her fair companions one and all,
  Rejoicing crowd the strand ;
For now her lover swam in call,
  And almost touch'd the land.

Then through the white surf did she haste,
  To clasp her lovely swain ;
When, ah ! a shark bit through his waist ;
  His heart's blood dy'd the main !

He shriek'd, his half sprung from the wave,
  Streaming with purple gore :
And soon it found a living grave,
  And, ah ! was seen no more.

Now haste, now haste, ye maids, I pray,
  Fetch water from the spring :
She falls, she swoons, she dies away,
  And soon her knell they ring.

Now each May morning round her tomb,
  Ye Fair, fresh flow'rets strew,
So may your lovers 'scape his doom,
  Her hapless fate 'scape you.

RALPH ERSKINE.

1685-1752.

THE leaders of the first secession movement from the Church of Scotland—Ebenezer and Ralph Erskine—were intimately connected with the county of Berwick. Their father was the Rev. Henry Erskine, for many years minister of Chirnside, and himself a Merse man, sprung from the old families of Shielfield and Dryburgh. Ralph Erskine was born at Monilaws, near Cornhill, on the 15th March, 1685. He studied at Edinburgh University, was licensed to preach the Gospel in 1709, and ordained to the second charge of the parish of Dunfermline in 1711, being translated to the first charge in 1716. He took an active part in the Marrow controversy, and in the controversy regarding Patronage. In 1737 he seceded from the Church of Scotland and joined the Associate Presbytery. He died 6th November, 1752.

He was the author of a large number of sermons, many of which were published during his lifetime, but it is by his "Gospel Sonnets" and "Scripture Songs" that he is now best remembered. The whole of his works were published in two large folio volumes at Glasgow in 1764-1766, and have since been frequently re-printed.

> " His silver tongue did living truth impart,
> With raiséd hand fit emblem of his heart ;
> He saw, he felt, he sung redeeming love,
> Death called him home, he tunes his harp above."

SIR JOHN SWINTON.[1]

1624 (?)-1679.

SIR JOHN SWINTON, son of Sir Alexander Swinton of Swinton, was a man of great ability and varied fortunes. He warmly espoused the cause of the Society of Friends, and wrote in vindication of their views several learned and elaborate treatises both in prose and verse. Here is a specimen: "England's Warning, or a friendly admonition to the rulers thereof to beware of persecuting the Righteous for yielding obedience to the law of God," etc., 4to, London, 1664. Beginning thus:

> " O foolish nation, void of grace
>   And understanding true,
> The cruel acts that thou hast made,
>   Thou maist have time to rue !
> Dost think thy peace doth stand in this—
>   To persecute the poor,
> And eke the meek that fear the Lord,
>   And do His Name implore ? "

it continues in a similar strain throughout one hundred and five stanzas. The following are also in defence of the Quaker movement:—"A Testimony for the Lord, by John Swinton, to all the world to whom these shall come, greeting," 6 pp., no date ; "The Spirit of Alexander the Coppersmith. lately revived, now justly rebuked," 1673 ; "One Warning more to the Hypocrites of this generation." Several MSS. of Swinton's are preserved in the library of the Society of Friends at London.

[1] See " The Swintons of that Ilk," p. 73.

LORD SWINTON.[1]

1722-1799.

JOHN SWINTON of Swinton, eldest son of John Swinton and Mary Semple, was destined to have a distinguished judicial career. He was called to the Bar in 1743; appointed Sheriff of Perthshire in 1754; raised to the Bench as Lord Swinton in 1782; and died in 1799. To his pen is generally attributed *An Elegy inscribed to the Duke of Cumberland*, in avowed imitation of Milton's *Lycidas*, 4to, Edin., 1746. The subject is the rumoured death at the battle of Falkirk of the author's friend, Colonel Thornton. The piece, it must be confessed, loses much of its pathos when, in the course of it, the "awful genius of the British Isles" reveals to the poet that the hero whom he was lamenting, instead of having fallen in the battle, had escaped unhurt from the field. After this revelation the principal motive of the elegy seems to be the loyal effusion with which it concludes:

> " Behold a hero of a warlike line,
> His fame already floats along the Rhine,
> His youthful valour Gaul hath seen with fear,
> And, seeking respite, stirs sedition here ;
> He soon rebellion's children will dismay,
> And scatter all their glory far away ;
> Confound their councils, turn their joy to shame,
> And every tongue shall echo William's name."

[1] See " The Swintons of that Ilk," p. 96.

MRS. JOHN HUNTER.

1742-1821.

ANNE HOME, born in 1742, was the eldest daughter of Robert Boyne Home, surgeon, Greenlaw. She was a sister of the celebrated Sir Everad Home [1753-1832], and also of Robert Home, the painter [d. 1836], descended from the Homes of Greenlaw Castle. In July, 1771, she became the wife of John Hunter, the anatomist, and during the lifetime of her distinguished husband, received at her house in London the most eminent literary and scientific personages of the day. Dr. Hunter died in 1793, and after this event his widow sought a life of retirement, giving herself over to literary pursuits, especially the writing of verse, which she composed with wonderful facility and grace. She died of a lingering illness on the 7th June, 1821, leaving a son and daughter—the former a major in the army, and the latter the wife of General Campbell, son of Sir James Campbell of Inverneil.

In 1802 Mrs. Hunter published a collection of her poems dedicated to her son, John Banks Hunter.[1] In a modest note to the reader she says: "The very favourable reception which has for some years been given to lyric poetry, whether ancient or modern, induces me to offer this small volume to the public,

---

[1] "Poems by Mrs. Hunter," Lond., 12mo, 1802. T. Payne. 2nd edition, 1803. [Now a scarce volume.]

consisting chiefly of odes, ballads, and songs, and I
have been further encouraged to take this step by
the success which has attended some of the latter
description of composition, already well known to the
musical world.[1] My little book will, I hope, escape
the censure of being tedious ; what other merit it
may have besides its brevity, and whether its contents
will bear to be *read* as well as to be *sung*, my readers
must now be left to judge for themselves." The
book contains a number of poems addressed to her
son when at school, at college, and in the army ;
Carisbrooke Castle, a historical poem in twenty-two
stanzas ; several old English ballads, and many
beautiful songs. Several of Mrs. Hunter's compositions have had a deserved popularity, and have been
wedded to inspiring music by the illustrious Haydn,
with whom she was on terms of much intimacy.
When in London in 1791-93 the great composer was
a frequent and honoured guest at her house.

There is a certain irresistible charm in the poetry
of this fair singer—a sweetness and homeliness of
expression which at once will rivet the attention, and
touch a chord of sympathy in the heart of every reader.
One who knew her well thus writes : " She possessed
personal attractions of the highest order. Into whatever assembly she entered, the delicacy of her face,
with the commanding grace of her person, gave her
a peculiar air of distinction, and seldom failed to

---

[1] She refers here to those compositions which were set to music by
Haydn :—*The Indian Death-Song : The Spirit's Song : Queen Mary's
Lament*, etc.

attract attention. But she never ascribed to her own merit the notice she received in society. Feeling herself the wife of a celebrated man, she was fond of imputing the attention she received to the influence of his character, doing injustice to herself from a generous pride of owing everything to him, and she never appeared so much gratified by attention as when she supposed it was shown to her for his sake."

THE LAMENTATION OF MARY STUART, QUEEN OF SCOTS.

I sigh and lament me in vain,
   These walls can but echo my moan;
Alas! it increases my pain,
   To think of the days that are gone.

Through the grate of my prison I see
   The birds as they wanton in air;
My heart, how it pants to be free,
   My looks they are wild with despair.

Ye roofs, where cold damps and dismay
   With silence and solitude dwell;
How comfortless passes the day,
   How sad tolls the evening bell!

The owls from the battlements cry,
   Hollow winds seem to murmur around,
"O Mary, prepare thee to die!"
   My blood it runs cold at the sound.

Unchang'd by the rigours of fate,
   I burn with contempt for my foes;
Though fortune has clouded my state,
   This hope shall enlighten its close.

False woman! in ages to come
   Thy malice detested shall be:
And when we are cold in the tomb
   The heart still shall sorrow for me.

THE FAREWELL.

Far from hope, and lost to pleasure,
  Haste away to war's alarms !
Sad I leave my soul's dear treasure,
  For the dismal din of arms.

But, ah ! for thee I follow glory,
  To gain thy love I dare to die ;
And when my comrades tell my story,
  Thou shalt lament me with a sigh.

All my griefs will then be over,
  Sunk in death's eternal rest ;
You may regret a faithful lover,
  Though you refuse to make him bless'd.

Bestow a tear of kind compassion,
  To grace a hapless soldier's tomb ;
And, ah ! forgive a fatal passion,
  Which reason could not overcome.

MY MOTHER BIDS ME BIND MY HAIR.

My mother bids me bind my hair
  With bands of rosy hue,
Tie up my sleeves with ribbons rare,
  And lace my boddice blue.

For why, she cries, sit still and weep,
  While others dance and play ?
Alas ! I scarce can go or creep
  While Lubin is away.

'Tis sad to think the days are gone
  When those we love were near ;
I sit upon this mossy stone
  And sigh when none can hear.

And while I spin my flaxen thread
  And sing my simple lay,
The village seems asleep, or dead,
  Now Lubin is away.

THE DEATH-SONG OF THE CHEROKEE INDIAN.

The sun sets in night, and the stars shun the day,
But glory remains when their lights fade away,
Begin, ye tormentors, your threats are in vain,
For the son of Alknomook will never complain.

Remember the arrows he shot from his bow;
Remember your chiefs by his hatchet laid low.
Why so slow? Do you wait till I shrink from the pain?
No! the son of Alknomook shall never complain.

Remember the wood where in ambush we lay,
And the scalps which we bore from your nation away.
Now the flame rises fast; ye exult in my pain;
But the son of Alknomook can never complain.

I go to the land where my father is gone;
His ghost shall rejoice in the fame of his son.
Death comes like a friend, to relieve me from pain;
And thy son, O Alknomook, has scorn'd to complain!

———

THE LOT OF THOUSANDS.

When hope lies dead within the heart,
 By secret sorrow close concealed,
We shrink, lest looks or words impart
 What must not be revealed.

'Tis hard to smile when one would weep;
 To speak when one would silent be;
To wake when one would wish to sleep,
 And wake to agony.

Yet such the lot of thousands cast,
 Who wander in this world of care,
And bend beneath the bitter blast,
 To save them from despair.

But Nature waits her guests to greet,
 Where disappointment cannot come;
And time guides with unerring feet
 The weary wanderers home.

THE SPIRIT'S SONG.

Hark what I tell to thee,
  Nor sorrow o'er the tomb,
My spirit wanders free,
  And waits till thine shall come.

All pensive and alone,
  I see thee sit and weep,
Thy head upon the stone
  Where my cold ashes sleep.

I watch thy speaking eyes,
  And mark each precious tear ;
I catch thy parting sighs,
  Ere they are lost in air.

THE FLOWERS OF THE FOREST.

Adieu ! ye streams that smoothly glide
  Through mazy windings o'er the plain :
I'll in some lonely cave reside,
  And ever mourn my faithful swain.

Flower of the forest was my love,
  Soft as the sighing summer's gale ;
Gentle and constant as the dove,
  Blooming as roses in the vale.

Alas ! by Tweed my love did stray,
  For me he searched the banks around :
But, ah ! the sad and fatal day,
  My love, the pride of swains, was drown'd.

Now droops the willow o'er the stream ;
  Pale stalks his ghost in yonder grove ;
Dire fancy paints him in my dream ;
  Awake, I mourn my hopeless love.

DAVID STUART ERSKINE, EARL OF BUCHAN.

1742-1829.

DAVID STUART ERSKINE, eleventh Earl of Buchan, was born 12th June, 1742, and died 19th April, 1829. His immediate connection with the county of Berwick dates from his purchase, in 1786, of the estate of Dryburgh, which had previously belonged to his ancestors. A man of strong antiquarian tendencies, and a zealous patriot, with a keen sense for the beautiful and romantic in Nature, he began at Dryburgh that labour of love which consisted in restoring the more ruined portions of the venerable pile, and gradually changing its surroundings—always pleasant—into a scene of almost ideal sylvan loveliness. It is to the artistic and historic, though, it must be confessed, somewhat eccentric, conceptions of this worthy laird that Dryburgh to a large extent owes the attractiveness which it has for the modern tourist. For the old Earl has tried to enshrine in the woods and hills of his beautiful home, and by the banks of "Tweed's fair river," many of his country's sweetest memories and most cherished traditions. On the wooded eminence in front is a colossal statue of Sir William Wallace,[1]

---

[1] The monument was erected on 22nd September, 1814, the anniversary of the victory of Stirling Bridge in 1297. It is formed of red sandstone, from the same quarry which furnished the materials for the

> " The peerless knight of Ellerslie,
> Who waved on Ayr's romantic shore
> The beamy torch of liberty ; "

while close by the river's brink is the deserted Temple of the Muses, dedicated by this Scottish Maecenas to the sons of Border song. Dryburgh has ever been a classical region—the centre of much of Scotland's history and the inspiration of much of her literature—and because of this the Earl of Buchan desired to perpetuate here the memory of such associations.

He was himself a dabbler both in prose and verse, and made many contributions to the periodical literature of his day. He wrote a large number of

Abbey building. The statue is 22½ feet high, and was designed by Mr. John Smith of Darnick, from a supposed authentic portrait of the great hero. He is represented in the ancient Scottish (partially Roman) dress, and armour, with a shield hanging from his left hand, and grasping with his right a huge spear in vertical position. On the pedestal is the following inscription :—

> " ERECTED BY DAVID STUART ERSKINE,
> EARL OF BUCHAN.
> WALLACE,
> GREAT PATRIOT HERO!
> ILL REQUITED CHIEF!
> A.D. MDCCCXIV."

In front of the monument, and standing on a cluster of rocky boulders, is a large urn on which are inscribed the following lines : —

> " Erected to the memory of Wallace,
>
> ' The peerless knight of Ellerslie,
> Who waved on Ayr's romantic shore
> The beamy torch of liberty,
> And roamed around from sea to sea.
> From glade obscure or gloomy rock
> His bold compatriots called to free
> The realm from Edward's iron yoke.' "

essays and treatises on various subjects, chiefly antiquarian, and these are nearly all preserved in the Proceedings of the Society of Antiquaries of Scotland, of which he was the founder. In conjunction with Dr. Walter Minto he compiled an "Account of the Life, Writings, and Inventions of Napier of Merchiston" (4to, Perth, 1787); and an essay from his pen on "The Lives and Writings of Fletcher of Saltoun and James Thomson" (1792), received a fair recognition. "The Anonymous and Fugitive Essays of the Earl of Buchan, collected from various periodical works," were reprinted at Edinburgh in 1812, but never got beyond the first volume.

Lord Buchan had a large correspondence with literary and scientific men throughout the world, and it may be interesting to recall the fact that it was mainly at Robert Burns's suggestion that the Wallace statue was erected. To him also Burns sent his *Address to the Shade of Thomson* in September, 1791, when he could not be present at the annual gathering which his lordship had instituted at Ednam, the poet's birthplace. *Scots Wha Hae*, again, received its inspiration from the loyal-hearted Earl, and Burns wrote in the following terms—"If my little ode has your lordship's approbation, it will gratify my highest ambition."

Of the Earl of Buchan a large number of anecdotes are still related. Let one suffice us. It is with reference, not to the eccentricities of his life, but to an incident which occurred at his burial. He was

interred in that part of Dryburgh Abbey called St.
Modan's Chapel.   The apartment lies lengthways
from east to west, and is very narrow.   In accordance
with the Christian method of sepulture the feet end
of the coffin should have been carried into the vault
first.   Sir David Brewster and Sir Walter Scott were
both present at the funeral.   Brewster was the first to
notice the error of bringing in the head of the coffin
first, and he said, " We have brought the Earl's head
in the wrong way."   Scott replied by saying, " Never
mind, his lordship's head was turned before he died,
and it's not worth our while to shift it now." [1]

[1] For a full account of the Earl of Buchan see Kay's " Edinburgh
Portraits ;" Erskine's "Annals and Antiquities of Dryburgh ;"
Anderson's " Scottish Nation," etc., etc.

SIR DAVID ERSKINE.

1772-1837.

DAVID ERSKINE, a natural son of the eleventh Earl of Buchan, was born in 1772. In early life he bore a captain's commission in the 31st Foot, and belonged also to the York Rangers. On the reduction of the 31st Regiment he was appointed to a professorship in the Royal Military College at Sandhurst. The Earl of Munster was there placed under his tuition, as well as several members of William IV.'s family, and at their request Erskine received the honour of knighthood, 11th September, 1830. His father, dying in 1829, bequeathed to him for life the whole of his unentailed estates, and he settled down at Dryburgh. On 17th November, 1798, he had married his cousin, Elizabeth, second daughter of Thomas, Lord Erskine, and after her death, on 2nd August, 1800, he married a Miss Ellis. Sir David Erskine was one of the earliest Fellows of the Scottish Society of Antiquaries; a director of the Royal Academy at Edinburgh; and one of the founders of the Scottish Military and Naval Academy. He died 22nd October, 1837, aged sixty-five.

His reputation as a poet lies chiefly in his dramatic productions, of which he wrote a large number during his residence on Tweedside. They are characterised by splendid descriptive power, and give indication of decided genius. The following is a list of those which have been published :

" King James I. of Scotland, a Tragedy in Five Acts." Kelso, 1827.
" King James II. of Scotland, an Historical Drama in Five Acts."
    Kelso, 1828.
" Mary Queen of Scots : or, Melrose in Ancient Times During the
    Last of the Abbots." Edin., 1829.
" James V.; or, the Warlike Days of Hab o' Hawick." Edin., 1830.
" James III.; or, the Feudal Times of Konrade of Roxburghshire."
    Edin., 1831.
" Dryburgh Abbey Three Hundred Years Ago ; or, the Nun o' Nen-
    thorn." Edin., 1831.
" Airy-form ; or, Ghosts from Nature." Kelso, 1825.
" Dr. Love among the Roses." Kelso, 1827.

Besides these Sir David Erskine compiled the "Annals and Antiquities of Dryburgh and other Places on the Tweed" (Kelso, 1828 ; 2nd edition, 1836), and wrote a number of lyrical compositions.

JAMES BARRIE.

1753-1829.

BECAUSE James Barrie, "the Earl of Buchan's own poet-laureate," as Sir Walter Scott dubbed him, was so well known in the south-west of Berwickshire he is given a place in this collection. A native of the parish of Spott, in East Lothian, he early removed, along with his widowed mother, to Dronshiel, in the parish of Longformacus, and thenceforward his life was entirely spent in the county. He became a wright in Langton, and in a few years started on his own account in Hume, from which he removed to Gordon, and finally to Bemersyde, at that time a considerable village. In 1786 he married Janet Johnston of Hume, and by her had a family of thirteen children, all of whom died during the lifetime of their parents. In later years Barrie suffered much from a rheumatic affection, and, chiefly through the kindness of Lord Buchan, the Haigs of Bemersyde, and the Scotts of Mertoun, a small "fog-house" was erected near the statue of Wallace, and the local "laureate" appointed custodian. Here he sold souvenirs of the district, spruce beer, and copies of his poems, till his death on 26th June, 1829.

Barrie's poems do not rise above mediocrity. They are the quaint and simple effusions of an unlettered rustic, more careful, perhaps, of the rhyme than the reason, but the spirit of the rhymster is honest and manly, pious and patriotic. The following were issued by Barrie during his stay at Bemersyde:

" Poems for the Use of Children," 74 pp., 1808.
" Poems on Various Subjects," 18mo, Kelso, 1815,[1] and enlarged
    edition, 1824.
" New Collection of Poems," 12mo, Kelso, 1819.
" Riverside Poems," 12mo, Kelso, 1821.

----

[1] It is only fair to state that the Kelso edition of 1815 contains several poems which it is more than likely are not the work of Barrie, *e.g.*, " Lines Addressed to the Earl of Buchan on his Erecting a Colossal Statue of Wallace ;" " On the Earl of Buchan's Birthday, 1815 ;" and that the whole of Andrew Scott's inimitable ballad " Symon and Janet" has been incorporated with corrections and additions that too plainly disclose their origin.

WILLIAM DUDGEON.

1753-1813.

ALTHOUGH born in the neighbouring county of East Lothian, William Dudgeon spent the greater part of his life in Berwickshire, and may fittingly rank among its song-writers. He received a liberal education at his native village of Tynninghame, and this, combined with strong natural talent, soon brought him much local repute. He became proficient in many branches of learning, and especially excelled in mathematics. One of his school-fellows was Sir John Rennie, the celebrated engineer, and Gibson, their teacher at a more advanced school in Dunbar, considered these two the best pupils of his scholastic career. Dudgeon was placed by his father in a farm near Duns, upon a lease of thirty years. The farm was extensive, and a large proportion of it in a state of nature. It received the sweet-sounding name of Primrose Hill, and Dudgeon lived to improve it to a very high degree. He died 28th October, 1813, and was buried in the churchyard of Prestonkirk.

Burns, during his Border tour in May, 1787, met Dudgeon at Berrywell, the residence of the father of his friend Robert Ainslie,[1] who was factor to the

---

[1] Robert Ainslie, W.S., the friend and correspondent of Burns, was born 13th January, 1766, at Berrywell, near Duns. In 1787 he formed the acquaintance of Burns in Edinburgh, and in May of the same year he made an excursion with the poet in Teviotdale and

Earl of Douglas. The ploughman-poet has thus recorded his impressions of this farmer-poet of the Merse:—" A Mr. Dudgeon, a poet at times, a worthy, remarkable character, natural penetration, a great deal of information, some genius, and extreme modesty." A relative supplies the additional information that he was "a man of weakly frame of body, but of liberal and enlarged capacity, a poet, a writer of sermons, a first-rate performer on the violin, and could use tolerably well the graving tool, and last and greatest of all, a temperate and well-conducted person."

As a poet Dudgeon is remembered mainly through one song. He wrote a number of lyrics, many of which remain unpublished, but *The Maid that tends the Goats* is the only one which appears to have secured a wide publicity. It is a sweet pastoral, full of the charm of country life and the trustful tenderness of maiden love. The air is Gaelic, *Nian doun nan gobhar.*[2]

Berwickshire. Burns stayed some days at Berrywell. A sister of Ainslie whom Burns met on this occasion was the subject of the impromptu in Duns Kirk, " Fair maid, you need not take the hint," etc. Robert Ainslie wrote two books on religious themes, " A Father's Gift to his Children," and " Reasons for the Hope that is in Us," a Christian evidence treatise ; and he contributed frequently to the *Edinburgh Magazine* and other periodicals. He was on intimate terms with the Ettrick Shepherd and Christopher North. Fourteen letters of Burns to Ainslie are included in the poet's correspondence. According to Mr. W. Scott Douglas (" Works of Burns," II., 188), the fragmentary ballad, " Robin shure in Hairst," refers to a juvenile amour of Ainslie. He died 11th April, 1838.

[2] See Fraser's " Highland Melodies."

The Maid that tends the Goats.

Up amang yon cliffy rocks
Sweetly rings the rising echo
To the maid that tends the goats,
Lilting o'er her native notes.
Hark, she sings, young Sandy's kind
And has promised aye to lo'e me ;
Here's a brooch I ne'er shall tine
Till he's fairly married to me ;
Drive awa, ye drone, time,
And bring about our bridal day.

Sandy herds a flock o' sheep ;
Aften does he blaw the whistle
In a strain so saftly sweet,
Lammies list'ning darena bleat ;
He's as fleet's the mountain roe,
Hardy as the Highland heather,
Wading through the winter snow,
Keeping aye his flocks thegether ;
But a plaid, wi' bare houghs,
He braves the bleakest norlan' blast.

Brawly can he dance and sing
Cantie glee or Highland cronach ;
Nane can ever match his fling
At a reel, or round a ring.
Wightly can he wield a rung ;
In a brawl he's aye the bangster,
A' his praise can ne'er be sung
By the langest-winded sangster.
Sangs that sing o' Sandy
Seem short, though they were e'er so lang.

NOTE.—See "National Choir." Vol. I., p. 247, for music.

REV. JAMES GRAY.

1770-1830.

JAMES GRAY, a very remarkable Berwickshire man, was born in Duns about the year 1770, in which town his father was a shoemaker. He received the usual village school education, and was thereafter sent to Edinburgh to study "the classics," a phrase used in those days with no little pride. The young student must have applied himself with the utmost diligence to this task, for we soon find him appointed to the mastership of the High School at Dumfries, at that time a notable institution. In 1801 he became classical master in the High School at Edinburgh, but resigned in 1822, aggrieved that he did not receive the rectorship on the promotion to the Greek chair of Mr. Dunbar, also a Berwickshire man. He then became rector in Belfast Academy, and distinguished himself by a series of essays on the Greek drama. This was his favourite subject, and he had few rivals. While in Ireland a new development sprung up in his life. He suddenly became animated with the missionary spirit, and, taking holy orders in the Episcopal communion, embarked in 1826 for India as a chaplain in the East India Company's service. He was stationed at Bhuj, in Cutch, and was appointed tutor to a young native prince, being the first Christian so honoured.

He died there 25th September, 1830, deeply deplored by a large circle of friends, both English and Indian.

While in Dumfries Gray was the companion of Robert Burns, the poet's boys being also his pupils, and in after life he was the friend of Thomas Campbell, Professor Wilson, and James Hogg, whose sister-in-law, Mary Philips, he married. The Ettrick Shepherd, who had a high opinion of Gray's genius, his kindliness and large-heartedness, introduced him in *The Queen's Wake* as the fifteenth bard, who sang the ballad of *King Edward's Dream*. Hogg thus writes of him : " He was a man of genius, but his genius was that of a meteor, it wanted steadying. A kinder or more disinterested heart than his never beat in a human bosom."

Gray published anonymously " Cona ; or, the Vale of Clwyd, and other poems,"[1] in 1814, and a second edition, with the author's name, in 1816. He was the author also of a very pleasing rhapsody entitled, " A Sabbath among the Mountains,"[2] full of beautiful pictures in the choicest language, and fit to stand alongside other well-known compositions of a like nature. He edited the poems of his once boon companion, Robert Fergusson, with a life of the poet and remarks on his genius and writings.[3] He employed much of his Indian life in translating the New

---

[1] The volume contains in addition to *Cona*, which is a long historical poem in four books, a second epic in three parts entitled *Minouscamina*, dealing mainly with religious and social themes. 12mo, London.

[2] 8vo, Edin., 1823, 1825.

[3] 12mo, Edin., 1821.

Testament, and a large portion of his work was printed at Bombay in 1834. He left in MS. an epic on *India*, which is said to have been published in America.

FROM "A SABBATH AMONG THE MOUNTAINS."

[Transcribed from the copy which belonged to the poet Southey, presented to him by the author.]

In simple garb the children are in view,
In Sabbath brightness, fresh as morning dew,
And fondly circle round the father's knee
Like clustering roses, beautiful to see,
And musically murmur at the task
That Scottish parents of their children ask.
'Tis from the sacred volume that they read
Words that to heaven their tender spirits lead,
That book of which the knowledge is the pride,
Their youth's companion and their manhood's guide :
The book they read in childhood's sunny hour,
That they shall read when age's clouds shall lower—
When knees are feeble, and when locks are grey,
Eyes dim, and life is fading fast away ;
The book that did their youthful hearts inspire
Shall lend life's dying lamp a kindly fire.

   .   .   .   .

Dear to my spirit, Scotland, hast thou been
Since infant years in all thy glens of green :
Land of my love, where every sound and sight
Comes in soft melody, or melts in light.
Land of the greenwood by the silver rill,
The heather and the daisy on the hill,
The guardian thistle to thy foemen stern.
The wild-rose, hawthorn, and the lady-fern.
Land of the lark, that like a seraph sings
Beyond the rainbow upon quivering wings.
Land of wild beauty and romantic shapes
Of sheltered valleys, and of stormy capes :

Of the bright garden and the tangled brake,
Of the dark mountain and the sun-lit lake ;
Land of my birth and of my father's grave :
The eagle's home, the eyrie of the brave ;
Land of affection and of native worth ;
Land where my bones shall mingle with the earth :
The foot of slave thy heather never stain'd,
Nor rocks that battlement thy sons profan'd ;
Unrivalled land of science and of arts :
Land of fair faces and of faithful hearts ;
Land where religion paves her heavenward road ;
Land of the temple of the living God !
Yet dear to feeling, Scotland, as thou art,
Should thou that glorious temple e'er desert,
I would disclaim thee, seek the distant shore
Of Christian isle, and thence return no more.

LOVE.

Life were a wilderness of wrath,
A viper's den, a field of death,
Had Nature not devised the plan
By love to tame the savage man.

'Tis love inspires the lay in spring
That all the woodland warblers sing ;
And when the hour of love is o'er,
The forest song is heard no more.

Let tongue of inspiration speak
The blush that paints the maiden cheek.
The tear that trembles in the eye
When love exalts to ecstasy.

Oh ! could I paint thee in my verse,
Thou sun that gild'st the universe,
On high that light'st the angels' road,
And blazest round the throne of God !

YOUTH.

In boyhood's sweet and sunny vale
  No tear of anguish dims the eye,
The streams of pleasure never fail,
  Joy's silver fountains never dry.

The simplest bud that gems the hill,
  The daisies in the waste that rise,
By naked rock or scanty rill,
  Are fair as flowers of Paradise.

No sorrow shades the light of soul,
  Bright as the sun of summer day,
Nor like the ocean's billows roll,
  To sweep the shrine of bliss away.

Still, as new sport to sport succeeds,
  How lightly springs the elastic mind,
As after happiness it speeds,
  Nor disappointment fears to find.

WILLIAM CRAW.

1771-1816.

"DIED at Ayr, William Craw, mason, a native of Chirnside, in the Merse." So we read in the obituary column of an Ayrshire newspaper for the year 1816. William Craw (or, as the name is sometimes written, *Crow*) was the son of Ralph Craw, a weaver in Chirnside, and a noted Cameronian, while his grandfather, William Craw, was an eccentric character, who had been long a resident in Chirnside, and probably a descendant of an old Border family whose original seat was Auchincraw.[1] His wife, Madeline, had the reputation of being a witch, because, we suppose, she was ahead of her age in real intelligence. William Craw, the second, left Chirnside about the year 1792, and coming to the town of Ayr, found employment at his trade of mason in the building of the "New Brig" immortalised by Burns in his well-known poem. In 1796 he was "press-ganged"

---

[1] Auchincraw or Auchencrow, locally pronounced Edencraw, a hamlet in the parish of Coldingham, and a place of great antiquity, had a widespread reputation during last century for its frequent witch-burnings. Auchencrow seems to have been the centre of the witch community in the county, and has given rise to the sayings—

> "In the town o' Auchincraw,
> Where the witches bide a'."

and —

> "You're like the witch wives o' Auchincraw,
> You get mair for your ill than for your good."

That is, an individual is sometimes granted a favour for fear of his malevolence, or to get rid of his importunity.

and served for a time in a man-of-war. As a sailor he met with many adventures; he was present at the battle of Camperdown, and in the fleet that mutinied at the Nore. He never took the oath to remain a sailor, and when an opportunity presented itself, he deserted his ship and steered his course northwards. At that time, so great was the demand for seamen, that men were placed upon the public roads near Edinburgh to intercept sailors going to or leaving the capital. One of these parties encountered William Craw. When asked of what trade he was, he replied " a stone-cutter," but his querists made answer that " his hands smelt too strongly of tar for such a trade," and lugged him off on board ship again. About the year 1800 he managed to get rid of the miseries of a seafaring life, and returned to Ayr, where he married, wrought at his trade, died in 1816, and was buried in the old churchyard.

Now, there is nothing remarkable in all this, but our story is not yet fully told. This William Craw, as it will be seen, was far from being an ordinary man, and he has left behind him ample evidence of ingeniousness, perseverance, and carefulness that well entitles his name to a niche in the local Temple of Fame. He was a clever mathematician and draughtsman, a fair linguist, and a bit of a poet. One of his volumes now lies before us. It is entitled *The Parisians*, and comprises six books, "giving an accurate description of the French Revolution and the storming of the Bastile."[1] Other fragments in

---

[1] Kilmarnock, 8vo, 1815. Crawford.

the book are *The Jolly Sailors* and *The Dying Sailor.*
He is also the author of ten " Poetical Epistles"[1] and
of " The Naval Journal "—a record of naval engage-
ments concluding with Camperdown.[2]

When full consideration, therefore, has been given
to William Craw's worldly position as a common
sailor, and to the fact that nearly all his mathematical
treatises and a great many of his poetical addresses
were written on board ship, during the intervals of
hard toil, it will at once be conceded that here was a
man of no ordinary abilities, who might well have
taken, but for the untoward circumstances of his
early manhood and his all too premature death, a
high place amongst those whose life-work has been
a ceaseless contribution to the intellectual wellbeing
of the world.

[1] " Poetical Epistles," 8vo, Kilmarnock, 1809. Crawford. Four
of the epistles are addressed to Gavin Dalziel, the poet ; one to Joseph
Train, the antiquary, and the remainder to others.

[2] " The Banks of the Hudson "—a poetical description of life in North
Canada, appears also to have been the work of Craw.

ALEXANDER BROWN.

(*"Berwickshire Sandie."*)

1775-1834.

ALEXANDER BROWN was the son of William Brown and Marion Nesbit, and was born in 1775 at Thimblcha', a small farm near Spottiswood, in the parish of Westruther, which was tenanted by his father. He served an apprenticeship to the mason trade, after which he taught a side-school kept up by the farmers and others at Cambridge, a hamlet in the district. Then he removed to Glasgow, where he wrought for one of his brothers, who was a contractor for canals and bridges. After living for a short period in Edinburgh, he died in 1834. His father appears to have been a man of some intelligence, for he too taught a class of young lads during the winter. His brothers were also men of an intellectual vein, one of them, William, being a teacher of languages in Falkirk, Dunkeld, and latterly in Edinburgh. The mother, again, came of an intellectual family, and one of her near relatives, John Nesbit, a merchant in Leith, wrote several commendable poems. The following from his pen is copied from the *United Secession Magazine* for November, 1835. It is apparently a retrospect of his early days at Greenlaw.

MY NATIVE VALE.

Again I tread my native vale
  Where flowers are blooming wild,
And breathe once more the vernal gale
  That fanned me when a child.

And yonder is the aged tree,
  Still verdant in decay,
Round which, when from the school set free,
  I went at eve to play.

But, ah! my lonely native cot
  Has vanished from the scene;
A heap of ruins marks the spot
  To tell where it hath been.

Its rude remains are covered o'er
  With weeds and grassy sod;
And lambs are sporting on the floor
  My infant footsteps trod.

My early friends, in deep decay,
  Are slumbering in the grave,
And o'er the sod that wraps their clay
  The lovely wild-flowers wave.

And, oh! ere many years pass by
  They'll also bloom o'er me,
When I shall unremembered lie
  In Death's captivity.

Alexander Brown published, at Edinburgh, in 1801, 8vo, a selection of his poetical musings under the title, "Poems: Mostly in the Scottish Dialect; by *Berwickshire Sandie.*" This volume is now extremely rare. Perhaps Brown's most popular song is the one which follows—*The Eagle Troop*—written during the "false alarm" period, and sung with great gusto at various county gatherings.

THE EAGLE TROOP.

Besouth the hills o' Lammermoor,
The farmers, lairds, an' a' that,
Hae formed a band o' yeomen true,
The Eagle Troop they ca' that.
      A' that an' a' that,
      Our country's cause an' a' that.
      Shall Britons cower an' yield their rights?
      No! mortal never saw that.

In days o' yore, when lang-legged Ned
Strode ower the Tweed, an' a' that,
To rob our lairds, to burn our towers,
T' enslave our sires an' a' that.
      A' that an' a' that,
      Ding doun our kirks an' a' that :
      The Border lads their mettle shaw'd
      And prov'd it was no law that.

The trusty sons o' Berwickshire,
Aye loyal, brave, an' a' that,
Again resolve to say " stand yont "
To French and Dane an' a' that.
      A' that an' a' that,
      Wi' glittering sword an' a' that ;
      See Spottiswood[1] riding at their head,
      Wi' helmet, crest, an' a' that.

On S —— plain ye may rejoice,
Baith young an' auld, an' a' that ;
Your landlord will your right support,
The S * * * * bless an' a' that.
      A' that an' a' that,
      An' mony more than a' that :
      Let them wha thocht to coup the State
      Gae hide their heads frae a' that.

[1] The late John Spottiswood, Esq., of Spottiswood.

When Britain ca's her faithfu' sons
To run to arms an' a' that,
Whole legions to the standard flock
In Caledonia yet.
    A' that an' a' that,
    Their ancient fame an' a' that ;
    A braver than the Eagle Troop
    Auld Scotland never saw yet.

Our king may keep his mind at ease,
Laugh at his foes an' a' that,
His kingdom's safe—his throne secure,
While ilk ane mauna fa' that.
    A' that an' a' that,
    There's Louis too, an' a' that,
    Puir man ! oblig'd to beg his bread
    In foreign lands an' a' that.

Let Bonaparte through Britain peep,
He'll see her sons for a' that,
Like hearts of oak, unite and keep
Her frae his grasp an' a' that.
    A' that an' a' that,
    Our wooden walls an' a' that ;
    If he come here, we'll break his crown,
    An' send him hame to claw that.

ALEXANDER HEWIT.

1778-1850.

ALEXANDER HEWIT—"a Berwickshire
Ploughman"—was born at Lintlaw,[1] in the
parish of Bunkle, in the year 1778.   He and his
twin brother James were the youngest of the family
of Andrew Hewit and Mary Burk.   The two boys
were early sent to the school at Lintlaw, where they
received the greater part of their education.   Arriving
at manhood in the troublous times at the beginning
of the century, James enlisted in the navy, and was
shot while assisting to quell a mutiny on board his
warship.   Alexander followed agricultural pursuits
for a time, until he also enlisted in the Hopetoun
Fencibles, in which regiment he served for six years.
At the conclusion of the French war he returned to
his native county, and lived for several years in the
parish of Ayton, where he married.   Then he removed to the adjoining parish of Coldingham, where
we find him as ploughman on several of the surrounding farms.   In 1834 he became tenant of the farm
of North Fallyknowe, where he died in 1850.   His
poems were published at Berwick in 1807, while he
was ploughman at Cairncross.[2]   They consist of two

---

[1] At Lintlaw, it may be interesting to note, was born in 1735 the
celebrated medical theorist, Dr. John Browne, author of the system
called from him the Brunonian system.

[2] "Poems on various subjects, chiefly Scottish, by Alexander
Hewit—'a Berwickshire Ploughman,'" 8vo, Berwick, 1807.

parts—religious and secular—the latter, in native Doric, being particularly pleasing. Perhaps the best known of Hewit's local ballads is one entitled *William and Madeline* which may here tell its own tale·

WILLIAM AND MADELINE.

[See Dr. Henderson's "Popular Rhymes of Berwickshire," p. 109.]

Black night was clad in darkest gloom,
   And a' was fast asleep,
When Madeline lay by Willie's side
   In meditation deep.
A voice at last assail'd her ear,
   Wi' eldritch croon it cry'd ;
Three times she heard the awful roar,
   But not a thing she spy'd.
"O Madeline, hearken to my voice :
   The morn is a great day,
At Norham is a sacrament,
   An' you maun gang that way."
Though we into digression fa'.
   'Tis proper here to show
The voice that reached poor Madeline's ear
   Was only from below.
Some lads an' lasses, fu' o' glee,
   Crap close to Madeline's wa',
An' frae beneath the window board
   Gae her the kindly ca'.
She thought it was some angel guid
   That her sic warning gae,
She dunsh't on Willie, wakening him.
   And unto him did say :
"O Willie, lad, I got a ca'
   When you were fast asleep,
So I a vow hae made this nicht,
   An' I that vow maun keep.
The morn there's a sacrament
   At Norham—have a care
To do my bidden, an' be good,
   For we maun baith be there."

He promised fair, syne drowsy sleep
  Did weigh their eyelids down,
An' pleasant dreams that sousie nicht
  Did a' their wishes crown. . . .
Aurora now began to deck
  The morning clear and fair :
The cock frae hint the hallin wa'
  Did clap his wings and roar.
Up Willie rose, an' Madeline neist,
  And, when they supped their brose,
Lap on the mare aboon the sunks,
  Which off for Norham goes.
Wi' heartsome cracks upon the road
  They on their journey drew.
Till Ladykirk and Norham tower
  Stood fairly in their view.
But westlin winds had raised the flood,
  For Tweed ran wide and strong ;
Red was the water, black the clouds,
  An' boats were gaen ding-dong.
Nobody durst the water ride,
  But Willie without fear
Spurr'd down the brae, syne to the guts
  Plunged in the reckless mare.
Now fear and dread seized Willie's breast,
  His tongue on Madeline fell :
" Ye said ye got a ca' last nicht
  It's been a ca' frae hell."
The right hand rein in rage he drew,
  And, backward, gained the shore,
Syne hame in speed wi' full design
  To mind sic calls no more.

JOHN ROBERTSON.
1779-1831 (?).

THE author of "The Waddin' Day and other Poems"—a small volume published at Edinburgh in 1824, is described on the title page as "John Robertson, a native of Berwickshire." Born at Oldhamstocks on 4th March, 1779, of parents "without rank or possessions, but of respectability according to the place they held in society," he quitted his native village in his fourteenth year, made his way to Glasgow, where he learned the weaving trade, and married in 1801. In 1815 he removed to a weaving factory at Dunbar, where, in the space of seven years, he tells us, he lost his wife and four children. He died there several years later. "The Waddin' Day" is a characteristically Scotch production, full of homely incidents, and breathing a spirit of fervent piety in the recollection of past scenes and former days.

THE LASSIE BY THE WATER SIDE.

(TUNE—"O wat ye wha I met yestreen?")

O, ken ye where I was yon day?
  My dearest lassie was wi' me,
She was so comely, sweet, and gay,
  The blythesome blink was in her e'e.
We wandered east that day and wast,
  Wi' her I wandered far and wide,
But few sic days yet e'er I passed
  As that was on the water side.

Then first we gaed out ower the glen,
  The fields had a' a pleasing hue;
I sat down wi' my bonnie hen,
  Amang the heather bells so blue.

We were a while, syne ran our ways,
  As blythe as she had been my bride ;
Then we cam' doun to yonder braes
  That lie upon the water side.

An' there we were awhile on them,
  Where flocks they feed, and lambkins play ;
Then set our face towards our hame
  The e'ening o' that simmer's day.
An' as we cam' alang the plain,
  Near by the fields and meadow wide,
How pleasant this to be our lane
  That night upon the water side.

Then we sat doun awhile again,
  The birds sang sweetly as we gaed
Upon the grass baith soft and green,
  An' rowed us in her tartan plaid.
Then said to her, my only dear,
  What wad ye think to be my bride ;
While now our lane, come tell me here
  This night upon the water side.

An' lang I held her hand in mine,
  But still no answer did she gie :
Although a lassie sweet and fine,
  She blythesome was that day, and free.
But e'en was bashfu' here, and ta'en,
  She blushed, an' tried her face to hide ;
I took fareweel until again
  We meet upon the water side.

O' days like this I had but few,
  She was so comely, neat, and clean ;
Her goun was o' the silken blue
  Wi' ribbon o' the tartan green.
Whene'er I think on her I smile,
  An' though she ne'er should be my bride,
I'll no forget that night this while
  I wooed her on the water side.

THOMAS DICKSON.

1785-1857

THOMAS DICKSON was for many years schoolmaster of Chirnside, and a man of wide knowledge, great kind-heartedness, and deep piety. His poetry is mainly of a religious type, and generally in the form of hymn or paraphrase. He published in 1834, at Berwick, a small volume bearing the title, " Hymns and Paraphrases,"[1] from which the following is selected. He died 31st March, 1857.

"LOVEST THOU ME?"

Oh ! if I love not Thee,
  What can attract my love ?
For Thou art all on earth to me,
  All in the heaven above.
The rays that cheer this dark abode
All emanate from Thee, my God.

A mother's tender love,
  A father's ceaseless care,
All charities flow from above,
  And are unsullied there :
To creatures, Lord, I'd grateful be,
But look beyond them all to Thee.

Surpassing love, that brought
  The Saviour from on high !
Love far exceeding every thought,
  That He for man should die.
Oh ! may the love of Christ constrain,
To burn in love to Him again.

[1] Reprinted and enlarged, 1839. 8vo, pp. 108.

Lord, if I love not Thee,
   What can deserve my love?
For Thou art all on earth to me,
   All in the heaven above:
Each ray that cheers this dark abode,
Proceeds alone from Thee, my God.

JAMES SANDERSON.

1788-1861.

JAMES SANDERSON, only son of John Sanderson and Ann Haig, was born at Earlston in November, 1788. He received a very limited education, and at an early age began life at the loom. Earlston in those days was a weaving centre of much repute. Its ginghams, through the marvellous tact and industry of the Misses Christian and Marion Whale, were beginning to attract a considerable share of public patronage. The gingham was manufactured of cotton, and the weaving was done in private houses, in some of which there were as many as fifteen looms. The colours were woven into the cloth, not printed as is now generally done, and everything was of the best material.

Amid this community of weavers in the quiet old village James Sanderson passed his apparently commonplace life, varied only with occasional visits to the metropolis, borne thither by the carrier's cart or the lumbering stage-coach of those less advanced days. But, as we shall see, the life of this Scottish weaver was by no means a commonplace one. On the contrary, it was a life of active and unceasing service in the interests of others, and James Sanderson is thus well worthy of a prominent place in the local annals. He did not, it is true, acquire widespread celebrity, which was to a large extent

owing to his extreme modesty, but in the circle of
his nativity he shone a brilliant star. Amongst those
who really understood the man, there was no one
whose opinions was more respected. He was intelli-
gent in a very high degree, and won the praise and
friendship of the reading and thinking ones among
whom he lived and wrought. He has left behind
him a large collection of writings very varied in their
nature, comprising songs and poems, fragments of
dramas and Border romances, sermons, sketches,
theological essays, political speeches, etc., all of
which tell the one same tale of activity, earnest-
mindedness, and a desire to use his leisure for those
around him. In beautiful verse he sings of his native
village and its sweet surroundings. The tender
memories that cluster round the fairy-haunted Leader
have made his *Youthful Haunts on Leaderside*
deservedly popular with Earlstonians, young and
old, and no local re-union is complete without the
poem.

In his theology James Sanderson inclined to the
advanced school, and because he could not see eye
to eye with the more keenly orthodox, he suffered
frequently no little contempt and scorn from many
whose practice of religion differed very widely from
the thing itself. The practical side of Christianity
was that from which he viewed all its professors, and
he never failed to enforce the necessity of linking on
to the highest morality even the minutest details of
daily life. As a politician he was akin to the
modern Radical, living long before his time in this

respect. "Reform and progress" was the watch-word of all his projects, and the very measures he helped to advance more than half a century ago are the new-found experiences of these later Gladstonian years.

In fine, James Sanderson was a splendid type of an industrious, prudent, conscientious Scotchman, with the breadth of intelligence, deep-rooted sympathy, and ability to express heartily and sincerely his sentiments, that pertains only to a comparative few. He was an honour to the community among whom he dwelt and the humble craft which he so long and so ably pursued. The following extract gleaned from his papers will perhaps indicate the character of the man:

"My journey through life has by no means been easy. I have always had but a weakly and sickly constitution, and poverty's cold winds have blown continually in my face, but I thank my God that He has as yet given me fortitude to bear up. I have never yet made a sacrifice of my independence, and I can be as happy, when health permits me, as many who are much stronger, and much more happy than thousands who are rich. If my path has been through the desert, there has always been something to brighten my wandering and to lighten my burden. That 'man was made to mourn' is a truth forced upon all men by actual experience, but he was made to rejoice also, for even that which causes pain becomes often the source of pleasure. He who was never weary can never know the luxury of rest; and even poverty—that sterile god that ruled the star of my nativity—is a contributor to the general happiness of mankind, for what would be the condition of mankind if all were supplied with the means of dissipation? It is because we are poor that we work, and our work contributes to the happiness of the rich by increasing the means of their comfort and enjoyment, while their wealth confers the same blessings on us in return for our labour, as neither pleasure nor pain belong exclusively to either class. Since, then, this is so, and because it is clear that poverty and riches are only accidental circumstances, I can see but little cause to repine at my own lot or to envy those that are accounted above me. In truth, I have never acknowledged a natural superior, nor paid homage to the face of man, though I confess I am poor as a crow."—*April, 1837.*

He died at Earlston, 28th January, 1861.

MY YOUTHFUL HAUNTS ON LEADERSIDE.

On Tweed's pure stream and banks so green,
　Her mansions gay and grand ;
Her sunny bowers and silken flowers,
　The fairest in the land.
On these I've looked and felt the charm
　Such scenes alone impart—
Scenes that exalt, scenes that refine
　And purify the heart.

But still remembrance to my heart
　Its choicest blessings bring,
From Leader and its flowery banks,
　Dressed in the robes of Spring :
Where in the spring-time of my days
　I culled fresh rosebuds there,
With those whose silvery voices rang
　Like music in the air.

Thrice happy vale of Carolside,
　There lovely Flora dwells,
Nursing the early flowers of spring
　'Mong yellow daff-o'-dills,
Sweet vale of peace, where no rude storms
　Disturb thy soft repose !
Where green hills guard on every side
　From every storm that blows !

O'er pebbly beds, by wooded banks,
  The Leader rushes on,
By Rhymer's Tower and Blaikie's grave,
  That tell of times long gone :
When learning seemed a wizard spell,
  And kept the earth in awe,
And ghostly monks and purblind priests
  Gave the proud barons law.

O, Cowdenknowes, thy bonnie broom,
  So famous in old song,
Where shepherds tuned their Doric reed
  Its yellow blooms among :
And milkmaids sang sweet strains of love
  To their admiring swains,
Till echo rung from rocky glens
  The oft-repeated strains.

The broom is gone, the milkmaid's song
  No longer cheers the plain ;
But still the cuckoo's mellow voice
  Each morn is heard again.
High on the plane-tree's topmost bough
  The blackbird tunes his lay,
To cheer his mate that brooding sits
  The sultry hours away.

To me more dear these sylvan shades
  Than river more renowned,
Loved memories linger on thy banks
  As on enchanted ground.

THE BOWER BY LEADERSIDE.

There was no bower more beautiful
  Than that by Leaderside,
Green was the grass beneath our feet,
  The rose grew in its pride ;
And, waving on their leafy stems,
  Hung rosebuds red and fair,
While every balm that Nature breathes
  Came wafted on the air.

And sweetly sang the little birds
  Upon the budding trees ;
The cuckoo's soft and simple notes
  Came on the gentle breeze.
It was the poetry of life
  In that green bower to lie
And muse upon its varied joys—
  The Leader wimpling by.

No sorrow entered that green bower,
  Life's joys were all our own,
The world's cares, its toils and pains
  Were then to us unknown.
Oh, there were those in that green bower
  With whom I loved to meet,
Which made the oak trees' cooling shade
  More soothing and more sweet.

While memory still can hold her sway
  Within this breast of mine,
In that green bower my heart will rest
  With those I loved langsyne.

THE BANKS O' TWEED.

Ye banks and braes o' bonnie Tweed,
  Ye seem aye clad in summer's green,
Where spring's first early flowers are spread,
  And where the last o' summer's seen.
Oft have I wandered by thy side
  To hear thy gushing waters play,
And list the mavis woo his bride,
  And sing the e'ening sun away.

But ye have charms more dear to me
  Than gushing streams could e'er impart,
Or blooming flowers, so fair to see,
  Or song of birds devoid of art :
For there I first heard love's soft strains
  Come bursting on my ravished ear,
While thrilling joy suffused my veins,
  Locked in the arms of Jamie dear.

Now he and I have married been
  Twice twenty years and other twa,
But still our love burns pure and keen,
  And no a spark is lost ava.
We've seen our bairns' bairns grow up,
  And dandled them upon our knee,
But still we drink our ain love-cup,
  That will be brimful till we dee.

CAPTAIN JOHN MARJORIBANKS.

Fl. 1797.

INFORMATION concerning John Marjoribanks, "captain," as he styled himself, "of a late independent company," is scant. He appears to have been a native of Leitholm district, and to have served for a time in the army, chiefly in the West Indies. He died at Edinburgh about the close of last century, probably in the year 1797. The following compositions are from his pen:—

"Trifles in Verse, by a Young Soldier." Kelso, 1784.
"A Poetical Address to Rational and Genuine Liberty." Edin., 8vo, 1792. Creech.
"Slavery, an Essay in Verse." Edin., 1792. (Written in Jamaica in October, 1786.)
"Pieces in Rhyme." Edin., 1793.
"Posthumous Poems." Edin., 1798.

In Sir Walter Scott's copy of "Trifles in Verse" he has written the following marginal note:—"In 1783, or about that time, I remember John Marjoribanks, a smart recruiting officer in the village of Kelso, the *Weekly Chronicle* of which he filled with his love verses. His Delia was a Miss Dickson, daughter of a shopkeeper in the same village; his Gloriana a certain prudish old maiden lady, benampt Miss Goldie. I think I see her still with her thin arms sheathed in scarlet gloves, and crossed like two lobsters in a fishmonger's stand. Poor Delia was a very beautiful girl, and not more conceited than a

be-rhymed miss ought to be. Many years afterwards
I found the Kelso belle, thin and pale, her good looks
gone, and her smart dress neglected, governess to the
brats of a Paisley manufacturer. I ought to say that
there was not an atom of scandal in her flirtation
with the young military poet. The bard's fate was
not much better. After some service in India and
elsewhere, he led a half-pay life about Edinburgh,
and died there. There is a tenacity of thought in
what he has written, but his verses are usually easy;
and I like them because they recall my school-boy
days, when I thought him a Horace and his Delia
a goddess."— "Lockhart's Life of Scott," end of
Chapter III.

LIBERTY.

Come, blissful Liberty ! whose heavenly name
Still lights my bosom with the brightest flame !
Inspire with energy my feeble lay,
To bring thy beauties to the blaze of day.
Gay are the groves where thou delight'st to rove,
There all is peace and harmony and love.
There no oppressor binds the burdened slave,
But all enjoy what God and Nature gave.
There no one trembles at a Tyrant's wrath,
No lawless rabbles deal the shafts of death.
Smooth are the streams that lave thy blest domain,
Thy limpid waters flow without a stain :
Through fertile fields and flowery meads they stray,
For ever cherished by thy genial ray.
There Health and Happiness, thy offspring, shine,
And glorious Science is a child of thine.
There mild Philosophy still bends his way,
And Law and Reason rule with gentle sway.
There cheerful Industry, with willing toil,
Adds still new beauties to the grateful soil.

I

Thy peaceful citizen no poignard meets,
Nor havoc desolates thy crowded streets.
There busy Commerce, unrestrained and free,
Deals out the treasure of the land and sea.
Thy fostering hands fair Genius first produce,
And all the arts of elegance or use.
Soon may that epocha, Fair Queen, appear,
When thy glad presence all mankind shall cheer ;
When slaves no more shall till a stranger's ground,
And none but Freemen in the world be found.
But never may that fatal hour be known,
When savage Anarchy shall seize thy throne ;
And, paying tribute to thy spotless fame,
But spurn the Monster who usurps thy name.

JOHN WHITEHEAD.

1797-1879.

JOHN WHITEHEAD was born at Duns, in humble circumstances, in 1797. When little more than twelve years of age he was apprenticed to a shoemaker in the town, and continued this occupation until far on in life. Like many of the "craft," he was possessed of a vigorous intellect and fine literary taste. These he early turned to account in acquiring an extensive knowledge of general literature which, with an active and ready memory, enabled him in after years to converse fluently or use the pen readily on almost any subject. When a young man he evinced a strong passion for poetry, and verses from his pen, some of them of considerable merit, found their way into the local newspapers and at once drew attention to the writer. In this way he formed the acquaintance of the late Mr. John Mackay Wilson, of the world-renowned "Border Tales," and for a long period he was on intimate terms with the late Mr. Russell of the *Scotsman.* He died 3rd July, 1879, at the advanced age of eighty-two.

SONNET,

Written on a stormy night.

The tempest rages, and the sleety shower
In fitful volleys on the window pelts ;
The door-hinge creaks, and round the tottering tower
The threatening wind dreadful howls ; at this hour

Of midnight gloom and storm, what heart but melts
In sympathy for those who midst the lower
Of 'wildering elements have lost their way,
And find no shelter from the blast ? or those
Whom winds and waves in dreadful war dismay ?
Think on the half-starved poor, ye who repose
In snug and splendid halls—brook no delay
To send relief,   delay may make you lose
The power to make the widow's heart rejoice :
Then list, oh list, to pity's touching voice !

THE MISER'S HEART IS SET ON GOLD.

The miser's heart is set on gold,
  The soldier pants for glory,
The statesman loves a place to hold,
  The sage to live in story ;
But all I ask is a kindly glance
  From the eyes of my own Mary,
When at the gloamin' hour we chance
  Beside yon thorn to tarry.

Beside the thorn we aft have met
  When the weary world was sleeping,
When the moon's pale beam the landscape lit,
  And the stars their watch were keeping :
And there we felt what lovers feel
  When kindred hearts are blending.
No sordid thought would o'er us steal.
  The modest mind offending.

Beside the thorn we'll meet again,
  Where babbling streams meander,
And list the night-bird's plaintive strain,
  As through the grove we wander.
If there's a rapturous hour on earth
  To cheer life's path so dreary,
'Tis spent far, far from noisy mirth
  In solitude with Mary.

ROBERT MENNON.

1797-1885.

ROBERT MENNON, familiarly known as the "Ayton Bard," was born on the 29th April, 1797, at Ayton, where his father followed the occupation of village slater and glazier. After a meagre education at the parish school young Mennon proceeded in 1824 to London, where he made his home for twenty-six years. In 1828 he married Sarah Bridges, who had been a domestic servant with his employer. The union lasted for forty-eight years, her death taking place at Ayton in 1876. In 1850 Mennon returned to Scotland, and commenced business for himself at Dunbar. After nineteen successful years he retired and settled in his native village, where he died on the 30th January, 1885, in the same house in which he had been born eighty-seven years before.

Robert Mennon began in early life to cultivate the writing of verse, and in 1869 he issued a massive collection of his effusions with the title of "Poems, Moral and Religious," which had a wide circulation. He was a man of genuine piety, a keen observer of nature, of a lively and cheerful disposition, racy and good-humoured in conversation, a most agreeable companion, full of sage counsel and kindly, warm-hearted encouragement. His poetical productions are not of the highest merit, but they are generally pleasing, and show the writer to have been a man of refined feeling, and a good example of an honest, God-fearing, and patriotic Scot.

CHIRNSIDE.

On yon hillside where sunbeams play,
  Where health and happiness reside,
With dwellings meek and mansions gay,
  Stands cheerful, smiling Chirnside.

In bygone years, while yet a boy,
  Its landscape fair I viewed with pride ;
The fruitful Merse I hail'd with joy
  As seen from lofty Chirnside.

Fam'd Berwickshire, from east to west,
  Spreads out its treasures far and wide,
Till Cheviot Hills, with verdure dress'd,
  Seem in the clouds, from Chirnside !

The scene of Flodden Field I trace,
  By blood of noble heroes dyed ;
And mark the course of Chevy Chase,
  From vantage ground of Chirnside.

The famous Tweed rolls gaily on
  Past castles, erst the foe defied,
Whose ruins tell their glory's gone,
  As seen afar from Chirnside.

What anxious mothers here have stood —
  What new-made widows here have sighed,
While gazing on the Border feud
  Down in the vale, from Chirnside !

But better days we witness now,
  Which claim our thanks and rouse our pride ;
Our peasants whistle at the plough,
  A railway passes Chirnside.

When time admits and weather's fair,
  I'll on that railway take a ride,
Review afresh these beauties rare,
  And spend a day at Chirnside.

THE LILY O' THE VALLEY.

Doun in a vale begirt wi' trees,
  Where birds sing late an' early,
Where dewy flowers attract the bees,
  An' sunbeams sparkle rarely.
A cottage, frae the world exiled,
  Stands by a burn so gaily,
Where lives a lass the muse has styled
  The Lily o' the Valley.

Her cheek is like the lovely rose,
  Soft blended wi' the lily,
Her hair in wanton ringlets flows,
  She's slender as the willow.
She pure is as the snaw at morn,
  When frosts are keen an' chilly,
Gay as the birdie on yon thorn—
  Sweet Lily o' the Valley.

Her aged mither, a' her care,
  She helps wi' hand right tender,
An' vows wi' words an' heart sincere
  In troubles to defend her.
On a moss seat beside the door
  She plies her labour daily,
An' gaily sings, in Nature's lore—
  The Lily o' the Valley.

When Phœbus sinks beyont the hills,
  An' trees o'ershade the fountain,
When echo haunts the mossy rills,
  An' twilight gilds the mountain,
I aft a leisure hour beguile
  Where innocence dwells really,
An' count it bliss to share her smile—
  The Lily o' the Valley.

O may the rude, unfeeling heart
  Ne'er nip her tender blossom,
Nor cruel guilt's relentless dart
  E'er fester in her bosom !

Where'er I wander, far or near,
    Or dowie be or gaily,
To me she ever will be dear --
    The Lily o' the Valley !

JUKE AN' LET THE JAW GAE BY.

As musin' on the days o' youth,
    When impulse leads us aft astray,
Experience tells the precious truth—
    'Twas best when reason bore the sway.
I mind, when bathin' on the shore,
    When swellin' waves cam' boundin' high,
Their threat'ning wrath was quickly o'er
    We juked an' let the jaw gae by.

So I hae aften found since then,
    When cares cam' like a ragin' sea,
To calm my mind an' ease my pain,
    Was patiently to bend a wee.
For aft I've warsled lang an' sair
    To mak' contrary things comply :
But proved it best, beyond compare,
    To juke an' let the jaw gae by.

Oh ! if this maxim were oor guide,
    This warld wad be a heaven below
'Twad banish envy, strife, an' pride,
    An' kill oppression at a blow.
Nations an' tongues wad live in peace—
    War wi' its dreadfu' horrors fly ;
Friendships endure, an' law pleas cease
    Just juke an' let the jaw gae by.

An' sure 'twad bring its ain reward—
    What ills we'd shun, what cares we'd miss :
The stubborn will—the heart that's hard—
    Can ne'er enjoy the sweets of bliss.
An' when at peace wi' a' mankind,
    We calmly lay us doun to die ;
'Twill help to aid our fleeting mind
    To juke an' let the jaw gae by.

WILLIAM SUTHERLAND.

1797-18—.

WILLIAM SUTHERLAND, known as the "Langton Bard," was born at Choicelea, a farm place near Polwarth, about the close of last century. His father, of Highland extraction, had settled as cattleman at Choicelea, and there married Ann Tait, a native of Gavinton. The son's earlier years were spent in the joinery of old John Allan at Gavinton, but, not caring for this occupation, he and a companion started a grocery business in Coldstream. The venture, unfortunately, was not successful, and Sutherland emigrated about 1823 to America, and thence all trace of him is lost. In 1821 he issued from the press at Haddington a volume of his poems,[1] and these show him to have been a man of deep poetic feeling, in thorough sympathy with Nature in her many moods, drawing inspiration from the historic scenes of the Merse, and the daily round and common task of a simple, unassuming country life.

THE ENTHUSIAST LOVER.

Sweetly coos the gentle dove,
Joy sits smiling in the grove,
When a-wandering wi' my love,
My young, my charming Helen, O !

[1] "Poems and Songs," by William Sutherland, Langton, Berwickshire. Haddington, 8vo, 1821. J. Miller. [Now a scarce volume]

Sweetly blaws the hawthorn tree,
Flowers bloom bonnie on the lea,
Everything yields joy to me
When wi' my ain dear Helen, O !
Hills and dales look fresh and gay,
Harmless lambkins sport and play,
Hours like minutes flee away,
When present wi' my Helen, O !
But when alone, alack-a-day !
A' seems dowie, a' seems wae,
No flowerets smile, no lambkins play,
When absent frae my Helen, O !
Awake, my muse, awake, and sing,
Enraptur'd strike the vocal string,
Till hills and dales with echo ring
In praise o' my sweet Helen, O !
She's blooming sweet as rosy May,
Innocent and artless gay,
Curse on the wretch who would betray
My young, my guileless Helen, O !
For wit, for beauty, shape and air,
No maid on earth can e'er compare,
'Tis confess'd she has no peer,
My young, my charming Helen, O !
Could touch express as bosoms feel,
I might paint yon lassie leal ;
If hearts could speak, I then might tell
How dear I lo'e my Helen, O !
Queen of charms ! devoid of art,
Darling treasure of my heart,
O may we never, never part,
My soul's delight, my Helen, O !

DR. GEORGE HENDERSON.

1800-1864.

GEORGE HENDERSON, a most notable man of the Merse, was the eldest son of John Henderson and Frances Purves, and was born on 5th May, 1800, in the old farmhouse of Little Billy, in the parish of Bunkle, which had long been tenanted by the Henderson family. After an ordinary education in the village schools of the district, young Henderson repaired to Edinburgh to study medicine, qualifying himself for practice about the year 1827. In 1829 he took up his residence at Chirnside, married, and pursued with great popularity and success the somewhat arduous calling of a country doctor until his death on 4th July, 1864.

Of Dr. Henderson, more than of any other Merse man, it must be said that he excelled in love for his native county, and was justly proud of its record in the nation's history. He laboured with indefatigable diligence to draw, from every possible source, any item of interest regarding it. His busy professional career brought him in contact with every phase of life, and, never losing sight of his first duty, he yet gathered together an enormous accumulation of rare and curious facts relating to Berwickshire and its people. These, unfortunately, only exist in MS. Dr. Henderson undoubtedly meant to publish much of this collection, but the opportunity for his doing so never came. Besides many newspaper articles, his only work in book form is the well-known "Popular Rhymes, Proverbs, and Sayings of the County of Berwick," published at Newcastle in 1856. As a poet he takes a good rank. His powers in this direction are seen to greatest advantage in the descriptions of Merse scenery and life, that flow with such rare beauty and deftness of expression from his facile pen. He is equally at home in the harvest-field, the heathered moorland, or the grey hillside, and he loves to sing in pleasing idylls of the country and its charms.

CRUNKLY'S BRAES.

[Crunkly is a farm place on the estate of Nesbit, in the western extremity of the parish of Edrom, a few miles to the south of Duns.]

Now chill October strews the knowes
  Wi' yellow leaves and withered flowers,
And through the haugh the streamlet rowes
  Away to Nesbit's lofty bowers ;
The storm-blast comes, the welkin lowers,
  And drooping sad the bells decay,
That brightly blue, in harvest hours
  Bloomed by our path in sunlight gay.
    On Crunkly's bonnie braes.

The purple willow-herbs are gone
  That fringed the burn with gorgeous bloom ;
And withering where the Iris shone
  The sear flags sink in winter's gloom ;
The breezes pass without perfume,
  And moaning down the streamlet's side
The winds speak of decay and doom,
  While drumlie on the waters glide
    By Crunkly's bonnie braes.

Yon dark sloe-bower, now reft and torn,
  That shaded close the fountain clear,
Where violets met the April morn,
  And sweet primroses flourished near,
To me and mine will long be dear;
  Though slumbering cold in kirkyard green
Is she, who with young love sincere
  Shed o'er my heart a peace serene
    On Crunkly's bonnie braes.

We wandered aft down by the burn
  To mark the wild flowers springing sweet,
And slowly round the braes we'd turn
  Where hare-bells blossomed at our feet,
And hazels formed a cool retreat,
  And, 'twining round my Jessie's breast,
My arms were clasped in bliss complete,
  The mossy turf our pleasant rest
    On Crunkly's bonnie braes.

By Ladyflat came gently down
  Soft murmuring stream, where willows lean
Above the ford at Chatterton,
  Where aft our early sports have been ;
And wandering down thy margin green
  I've lonely mused the Craes below,
While gloamin' hushed the lovely scene
  Beside thy water's peaceful flow,
    On Crunkly's bonnie braes.

Now youthful years and loves are o'er,
  And sadly down life's path we go ;
In joy we'll trace those breaks no more,
  Nor see thy waters gliding slow ;
There aft the summer winds will blow,
  And laverocks sing above the corn,
While we, forgot, in grave lie low,
  And hail no more the autumn morn
    On Crunkly's bonnie braes.

Flow on, sweet stream, by lawn and lea,
  Still murmuring of departed days,
But ne'er again our feet will be
  Upon thy banks and flowery braes :
Life's troubled day in gloom decays,
  And, waning in the mist of years,
Our joys now shine in feeble rays,
  And no new hope for us appears.

A Fancy Flight to Leader Water.

Away to the west let my fancy fly,
  Away o'er the rustling corn,
And view the Leader flow shimmering by
  In the light of the harvest morn ;
O tarry not up in Lauderdale,
  The reapers are toiling there,
And stay not a minute by Tollishill
  To look on its daughters fair.

Up and away o'er the breezy hills
  Till you come to the Soutra steep ;
And then go down by the wimpling rills
  Where mists in the howes lie deep.
The flocks are raking the benty knowes
  On the side o' the Headshaw Law ;
Then away and away where the Leader rowes
  By many green brae and shaw.

Past Lauder town and the " darksome bield,"
  Where the Maitlands hae been lang ;
By Woodencleuch and St. Leonard's field
  We'll listen the lintwhite's sang :
On the Blainslie banks and Birkhillside
  We'll trace each nook and dell,
And in the groves o' the Chapel hide
  Till rung is the noontide bell.

There's mony a bonnie burn and rill
  That the Leader's stream doth meet
Before it has reach'd the Rhymer's mill
  And the " haughs " sae fair and sweet ;
Where stands in the vale "auld Ercildoun,"
  And the wa's o' the Rhymer's tower,
That held, in the ages long gone down,
  " True Thomas" of magic power.

And west, away on the Leader side,
  There's the pastoral Cowdenknowes,
Where lilted of old the shepherd's bride,
  By the green broom milking her ewes ;
O Leader Water and Cowdenknowes
  Live sweet in many a rhyme ;
And sweet down the vale the Leader rowes
  And murmurs of Rhymer's fame.

Long ages over the land have past
  Since these haughs the Rhymer trode ;
Or wended his way o'er the Leader fast,
  As he up to the Eildons rode ;
There's a charm in the haughs o' Leader side,
  For the Minstrel has been there ;
And the light o' his song doth yet abide,
  And makes a' its flowers more fair.

I love the land in ilk hill and glen,
  And its slopes o' the waving corn :
I love the land for its honest men,
  And its lassies bright as morn ;
But more I love its haughs and braes
  For the Seer once dwelling there,
And the songs that are sung in the Leader's praise
  Gar me love it mair and mair.

O what to me are the classic streams
  Of ancient Greece and Rome?
A fairer river is in my dreams—
  A fairer, and nearer home.

The wimpling rills o' my native land
  Fill my heart wi' a patriot's glow,
And I hear, at the touch o' Fancy's wand,
  The sound o' the Leader's flow.

And I see true Thomas, in baldric bright,
  Away with his hounds and horn,
To hunt the deer by the Eildon's height,
  Or roam by the Huntly burn ;
In the harvest morn he's off and away,
  The old harper, good and true ;
And, alone, on the Leader haughs I stray,
  And his ancient lays renew.

There sing we the song o' the Elfin Queen,
  Who loved true Thomas well,
And lured him away, 'mong her elves clad-green,
  In the Fairy's land to dwell.
Such legends old we have loved to croon,
  While the Leader we onward trace ;
And still we will love grey Ercildoun,
  Where lies the "auld Rhymer's race."

In the troublous times o' auld Scotland dear,
  On the Leader's green sunny side,
There trode true Thomas, the fairy seer,
  And harp'd by its shimmering tide :
And Thomas the Rhymer, and Elfin lore,
  In youth's fair morn were mine :
And, till my mortal course is o'er,
  May their light on my path still shine !

THE RETURN HOME.

To Lothian land I bade farewell,
  Up Danskein path I slowly trode,
And hailed with joy the heathy fell
  That lay around my homeward road.

Down Fasney Water's rugged side
  The fleecy mists yet lingering lay,
And far across the moorland wide
  Round shepherds wheel'd the lapwing grey.

The moss appeared in greener hue,
  And by the burn were fresher seen
Soft piles of grass with pearls o' dew,
  And budding briers were in the dean.

The gowan's rosy tips were gem'd
  With dew-drops of the April morn,
And while the mist the mountains seam'd,
  I lonesome pass'd Kilpalet burn.

The ploughman whistled o'er the lea,
  And gladsome, in the clear blue air,
The laverock sung his strains o' glee,
  And Nature's heart was joyful there.

The lambs were bleating yont the knowes,
  Where plaided herds roam'd pensively,
And wending south o'er heights and howes,
  I pass'd the waters of the Dye.

Then glad I hail'd grey Dirrington
  The shelter of my sires of yore—
And trod the heath, oft trode upon
  By men who Freedom's standard bore.

I left behind brown Lammermoor,
  And, passing east from Cattleshiel,
I saw the Merse wide spread before,
  And felt my heart with rapture reel.

K

Behind me lay the round bare hills,
    The Laws which ne'er had felt the ploughs,
The pastoral slopes and wimpling rills,
    The rushy bogs and ferny knowes.

The shepherd-shieling, wild and lone,
    The camps and cairns of ancient days,
I left them all, and hasten'd on
    To reach the Merse and Crunkly braes.

Dear native Merse ! a glorious plain,
    Streak'd wi' the sunbeams, mild and sweet ;
I gaze far o'er thy fair domain,
    Where true hearts in their gladness beat ;

I come to tread thy fields again
    Where long my fathers till'd thy soil,
And with thee and thy sons remain,
    Till there I end life's ceaseless toil.

To Cheviot's border hills I turn,
    O'er Teviotdale my view is cast ;
On Flodden field I sigh and mourn,
    And muse o'er days that long are past.

Far to the margin of the main
    See Halidon's grey skirts extend !
And wi' wild thoughts o' grief and pain,
    O'er Scotia's slaughtered sons I bend.

All that I love on earth is there,
    Land of my fathers ! happy land :
Be virtuous all thy daughters fair,
    And all thy sons in honour stand !

May tyrants and their minions flee
    Far from the Merse's bounds away !
May truth and genius dwell in thee !
    Thy toiling sons be glad for aye !

The land of Boston and M'Crie,
  Where Erskine preached and Baillie[1] sung,
Where, by the Leader's haughs and lea,
  The Rhymer's wizard harp was strung !

There, o'er thy waters, woods, and rills,
  My heart will pour its warmest lay ;
While morn and eve athwart thy hills,
  Shall all their varied charms display.

No land e'er blessed by sun or shower,
  Beneath the wide skies' azure dome,
Will e'er to me look half so fair
  As that which holds my native home !

Though bleak and bare thy hills may be,
  Though winter tempests scathe thy plain,
O Merse ! I could not part with thee,
  For all the gold beyond the main !

The shadows of the passing clouds
  On Bunkle-edge sweep slowly by,
And o'er those scenes my memory broods,
  That struck my young enthusiast eye.

My heart still clings to native scenes,
  And cling it shall for ever more ;
In thoughts by day, by night in dreams,
  I all their beauties wander o'er.

By woods and dells that skirt the Eye,
  'Midst heather bells, on moorlands bare,
In fancy, wandering lone, I hie,
  And sing their scenes and prospects fair.

Or down the hoary, rugged dean,
  'Mong sheltered rocks, with lichens grey,
I pluck the wild flowers, rarely seen,
  Or by Fast Castle's ruins stray.

---

[1] Lady Grisell Baillie, authoress of " Were na my heart licht I wad dee."

Or o'er the wild St. Abbs I roam,
  Or down the Ale I wander slow,
And mark sweet Nature's every form,
  And drink her spirit as I go.

By haunted streams let me repose,
  In Pease's deep sequestered glen ;
By fountains pure, in moss-grown howes,
  By limpid burn, or rushy fen.

O hide me in the wildwood glade,
  Or lift me to yon moorlands brown,
Where, watching slow the sunlight fade,
  I'll see the autumn day go down.

In fond delight I gaze each morn
  O'er scenes that pleased my infant heart,
And by the ripening, rustling corn
  I, lingering, muse and roam apart.

No other land I wish for mine
  Than my own fatherland—the best ;
I there content will spend life's line,
  And in its soil my bones shall rest.

When silent o'er my wasting frame
  The green Merse sod will dewy lie,
Few then will e'er repeat my name,
  Yet o'er me still the winds will sigh,
And evenings mild, in distant years,
Will steep my grave with Nature's tears,
  And soothe my " pale shade " lingering nigh !

WILLIAM AIR FOSTER.
1801-1862.

BORN at Coldstream, 16th June, 1801, was by trade a shoemaker, first in his native town, and afterwards in Glasgow, to which city he removed in 1842. He was a most enthusiastic Border sportsman, a distinguished champion in all games, excelling especially in archery, in which he had no rival at the time. His best songs are those animated by the thrilling excitements of this kind of life, and are characterised by splendid descriptive power and life-like touches. He was an attached friend of the Ettrick Shepherd, "for whom he had a great admiration, who warmly encouraged his poetic fancy, and in whom he met a congenial spirit," as the Shepherd was a keen angler, and used to spend a week or two at his father's house in Coldstream, from which they had many a fishing excursion. In Glasgow Foster enjoyed the acquaintanceship of a large circle of song-writers, in whose society he formed many of the strongest friendships of his life. Though a prolific versifier he published very little, his chief contributions being made to " Whistle Binkie " and the " Book of Scottish Song." His more sustained efforts he preferred to keep for the recreation of his friends and family. He died at Glasgow in 1862, much regretted by numerous friends for the kindliness of heart and generous sympathy which were so thoroughly exemplified in his life.

O! LIST THE MAVIS' MELLOW NOTE.

O ! list the mavis' mellow note
  Frae 'mang the aspen leaves,
While, big wi' sang, his swelling throat
  An' mottled breastie heaves.
O ! sweetly pours the bonnie bird
  His music wild and free,
But, Mary, song was never heard
  Could wile my heart frae thee.

The last bright tints o' sunset fair
  Gleam on the distant hill ;
Like threads o' polished silver, there
  Glow many a streaming rill.
The flowers smell sweet when gloaming grey
  Sends dews across the lea—
No odours sweet or colours gay
  Can wile my heart frae thee.

The blythsome lambs will sport at e'en
  On many a broomy knowe,
And through the gowan'd glen so green
  The mountain stream will rowe.
The trouts that sport aneath its wave
  Unguiled may live for me ;
No hackle bright, or harle grave
  Can wile my heart frae thee.

Beneath the gloaming's mellow light
  The landscape fair may lie ;
The laverock in his earthward flight
  May cleave the gowden sky ;
And Nature, baith wi' sicht and sound,
  May pleasure ear and e'e,
But, Mary, lass, the warld's bound
  Hauds nought so dear to me.

GUDE COLDSTREAM TOON.

My heartfelt thoughts to you are leal,
  Gude folks o' Coldstream toon !
My heart was sair to bid fareweel
  To a' the neebours roon'.
'Twas here my earliest breath was drawn,
  And mony a happy day
I spent wi' neebour callants then,
  Though I've been lang away.

But since I left gude Coldstream toon,
  O time has changed it sair,
The bairnie then upon the lap
  Has grown a woman fair ;
The young and comely lads I left
  Are now grown bald and grey,
And auld folks scarce, that ance I kenn'd
  Before I gaed away.

There's something in gude Coldstream toon
  That makes my bosom beat
Wi' an instinct like the hunted hare,
  To gain its native seat—
To see Tweed's bonnie stream again,
  Ilk plantain, haugh, and brae,
That bore the charm o' auld langsyne,
  When ane was far away.

I'll wear the gloamin' o' my days
  Where life's career began,
And breathe the latest breath o' life
  Just where the first was drawn.
In Coldstream toon, wi' Coldstream folk,
  A cosie bield I'll hae,
And fight the battles owre again
  I fought when far away.

THE TRYSTIN' TREE.

The birk grows green on Kennel banks,
   Brume flowers on Coldstream braes,
The plantains fair on Corn'el haughs
   Hae on their summer claes.
Tweed, rowin' in the gloamin' light
   That streams on haugh and lea,
Sheds beauty owre the landscape bright,
   Around the trystin' tree.

The merle likes the slae buss weel,
   Whar grows the berry blue,
The muirfowl likes the heather bell
   When draiket wi' the dew ;
And weel I lo'e the bonnie lad
   That comppit hearts wi' me,
When seated, on yon summer night,
   Beneath the trystin' tree.

A' Nature wears a summer hue,
   The sun sinks down serene,
The lamb sports round the bleatin' ewe
   On bonnie Kennel green ;
The mavis frae the auld kirk brae
   Pours out his notes wi' glee,
And the laverock twits a merry lay
   Aboon the trystin' tree.

Then wha wad hunt for warld's gear,
   Or sacrifice for gain ?
The hame spot hearts aye haud so dear
   When far across the main.
For lordly walth and a' its fyke
   I'm sure I wadna gie
The kiss I gat frae him I like
   Beneath the trystin' tree.

ON THE ETTRICK SHEPHERD BEARING OFF THE PRIZE AT THE COMPETITION OF THE BORDER BOWMEN IN 1832.

Our Minstrel Shepherd's won the prize
  Frae a' the gallant bowmen,
And mony a ane his fame envies
  Among the Forest yeomen.
For a' alang the Border now
  Where will ye find his marrow ?
He's won the sturdy Border bow,
  And borne it aff to Yarrow.

A glint o' langsyne was the scene
  To see the archers gather !
Our Shepherd drest in forest green,
  Wi' bonnet and wi' feather !
Out through the mark the arrows flew,
  They teeth'd it like a harrow—
But still the bonnie Border bow
  Has gane this year to Yarrow.

In manly sports the Shepherd's name
  Has rank'd amang the tightest.
And mair than a'—his minstrel fame
  Has ever been the brightest.
For wha wi' him can mak' a sang ?
  Wha draw a straighter arrow ?
Gae try—ye'll maybe find ye're wrang
  Ere ye come back frae Yarrow.

His sangs gie life when owre a glass
  They cheer us when we're eerie,
Wi' them the lad can woo his lass
  In strains that charm his dearie.
Ilk hill and dale, or broomy knowe,
  Frae him an int'rest borrow ;
Our shepherd—poet—archer now
  Whose genius hallows Yarrow !

Lang may our minstrel bowman feel
His arrow keen and true now,
Wi' energy frae hand to heel
Lang may he bend his yew bow ;
May plenty ever bless his hearth—
May't ne'er be scrimp'd or narrow,
For better man ne'er breathed on earth
Than Jamie Hogg o' Yarrow !

JOHN WILSON, D.D.[1]

1804-1875.

DR. JOHN WILSON, of Bombay, is one of the names that the Church delights to honour. And rightly so; for among Christian heroes there are none more worthy of being remembered than the men of earnest, self-denying, missionary spirit. John Wilson, by his labours in India, proved himself of this stamp, and has left behind him the rich record of a busy life that still bears much precious fruit.

The son of a small farmer, he was born at Lauder on 11th December, 1804; studied at the burgh school and University of Edinburgh; was ordained a missionary to India, 24th June, 1828; and arrived at Bombay in February, 1829. In 1836 he received the degree of D.D. from his *Alma Mater*, and revisited Scotland in 1842, returning to Bombay in 1848. In 1870 he was elected Moderator of the Free Church General Assembly. He died at Bombay in 1875. During his long and honoured career, Dr Wilson published several meritorious works, chiefly on missionary and Oriental themes. He wrote also a *Poetical Address to India*, which was printed at Bombay in 1872, and some other fragments, all of a religious character.

[1] An excellent biography is "The Life of John Wilson, D.D., F.R.S., for Fifty Years Philanthropist and Scholar in the East." By George Smith, LL.D., C.I.E., with portrait and illustrations. London: John Murray, 1879.

ALEXANDER HOME.

1807-1827.

THE following lines, amongst many others, were
written by Alexander Kinloch Home, of the
family of Home of Cowdenknowes, a student of great
promise, who died in 1827.   He rests in the ancestral
burying-ground at Earlston.

A WEEK IN THE COUNTRY.

[Written at Cowdenknowes, 20th May, 1823.]

Adieu, my books, adieu awhile,
  And welcome holiday and play,
For May invites, with gladsome smile,
  My steps to distant scenes away.

And now I trace each well-known spot,
  And roam o'er hill and valley fair ;
I pity much your harder lot,
  Whose hours are given to books and care.

O! who would give the simple joys
  Of country sports and healthful gales
For all the pomp of sick'ning noise
  A crowded city's pride unveils?

Now by the murmuring stream I stand
  And wish its sportive tenants mine,
Then seize the rod with eager hand,
  And launch with force the ample line.

The subtle hook, with tempting bait,
  Allures to death the finny prize ;
The victim, reckless of his fate,
  Springs at the bait, and wreathes, and dies.

Alas, even so our joys expire !
   For pleasure's paths are tracked with pain ;
The good our wishes most desire,
   When found, is transient, light, and vain.

Thus, too, my holiday is gone,
   Then farewell river, hill, and plain :
Adieu, adieu, ye hours pass on,
   And welcome to my books again !

ANDREW STEELE.

1811-1882.

ANDREW STEELE was born at Coldstream in 1811. After a moderate education at the parish academy he was apprenticed to the boot-making trade, and in a few years commenced business for himself. During his leisure time he strove arduously to add to his store of knowledge, and succeeded in acquiring a tolerably good under-standing of history and theology, subjects which seem to have had a special attraction for his mind. He was also a keen scientist. But perhaps he is best known as a cultivator of the Muse. He wrote a large number of poems, very varied in their nature and style, most of which appeared in the columns of local newspapers. About the year 1869, or earlier, he issued a volume of "Select Productions," and two years later a second edition,[1] both of which had a wide circulation in the Border country. He died at Wilton, Hawick, 20th February, 1882.

Steele's poetry embraces a wide range of subjects, and is in the main of a moral and religious character; but there are several bright lyrical touches of genuine beauty that show the author to have been influenced not only by the Divine life as revealed through the

[1] The Poetical Works of Andrew Steele. Edinburgh: John Forsyth, 1871.

Scriptures, but also by that same Divine life so richly manifested in the world of Nature and in the depths of human love.

MY NATIVE BORDER HOME.

O for yon heights where waves the pine,
  Again there let me roam ;
What charms on earth can rival thine,
  My native Border home ?

How sweet through blue-bells there to wade
  And see the primrose spring—
To hear beneath the vernal shade
  The mellow warblers sing !

And give me there alone to stray,
  In rapture to behold
The lovely landscape, fresh and gay,
  Its magic scenes unfold.

There wafts the Tweed her pearly tide,
  How soft her murmuring flow,
Bathing her osier emerald side,
  Where fragrant hawthorns blow.

And oh, yon hallowed craggy steep,
  Where silence reigns alone,
Where countless throngs oblivious sleep,
  Of years and ages gone.

And there the peaceful hamlet spreads,
  Where fields and orchards smile ;
And hail, embraced by deep'ning shades,
  Yon fairy portly pile.

And sweet the daisy-spangled mead,
  Where blithe the lambkin plays,
How bland its charms renew indeed
  The joys of other days.

Of life's ambrosial cloudless morn,
  Where now the seraph band
That gambolled gay beneath the thorn,
  Or gemmed yon pebbled strand?

I see them imaged in the clouds,
  On Cheviot's morning brow ;
While every grove and bower enshrouds
  For me but memories now.

Thus sacred thrice those scenes to me,
  How thrilling ! how benign !
Round which, as ivy round the tree,
  My sympathies entwine.

Then for yon heights where waves the pine.
  Again there let me roam ;
What charms on earth can rival thine,
  My native Border home?

THE HIRSEL[1] YET FOR ME.

Away ! ye orient groves, away !
  Where fragrant citrons bloom ;
The orange, lime, and myrtle gay,
  Exhale their sweet perfume :
Nor name those balmy, spicy dells,
  Though florulent they be,
Their fairy charms let others sing,
  The Hirsel yet for me !
Elysian spot ! while lasts a string,
  My lyre I'll tune to thee.

How sweet to roam thy sunny glades,
  Where wild the flow'rets blow !
Who for thy soft ambrosial shades,
  The world would not forego?

[1] The seat of the Earl of Home, near Coldstream.

Where native minstrels melting pour
  Their lays from every tree,
And every heart forgets its care :
  The Hirsel yet for me !
Elysian spot! while lasts a string,
  My lyre I'll tune to thee.

Unrivalled Flora's loved retreat,
  Thy smiling garden hail ;
An Eden here renewed to meet,
  What fancy now can fail.
As angels' breath thy zephyrs sweet ;
  And oh, the ecstasy,
When greets the eye thy blushing walls—
  The Hirsel yet for me !
Elysian spot! while lasts a string,
  My lyre I'll tune to thee.

Dear to my soul, thrice lovely bower,
  Those nameless sweets of thine ;
And oh, their heaven-inspiring power,
  How thrilling, how divine !
Here let me linger to enjoy,
  Alone, their luxury ;
I ask no higher earthly boon —
  The Hirsel yet for me !
Elysian spot! while lasts a string,
  My lyre I'll tune to thee.

And hail, yon venerable pile,
  Thy hospitable dome ;
May peace and plenty ever smile,
  To bless the house of Home !
And now adieu, thy magic scenes :
  My fondest memory
Shall ever homage with the lay—
  The Hirsel yet for me !
Elysian spot! while lasts a string,
  My lyre I'll tune to thee.
L

HEY FOR A WIFE WI' A HUNNER OR TWA.

Air—"The Laird o' Cockpen."

CHORUS.

Sing hey for a wife wi' a hunner or twa,
A canty bit wife wi' a hunner or twa ;
Contented and blithe, and hoo crouse wad I craw,
Gin I had a wife wi' a hunner or twa !

I've aft had a blink o' Dame Fortune's bricht e'e,
But passed her aye bye, as she cared na for me ;
What's wealth but a syren that sings to beguile ?
And honour a bauble that glitters a while ?
For them and for grandeur I little but care—
Eneugh be my lot, wi' a morsel to spare :
The sma'er the height, O the less is the fa',
So a' my ambition's a hunner or twa.

I care na for beauty, gin but she be guid,
I rate na her worth by connection or bluid ;
As the fairest o' flowers hae aft the least smell,
And the finest o' grapes by the tastin' we tell :
But if she is lovin' and modest and true,
Can wash a bit sark, can airn, and can sew,
And guide the bit penny wi' care aboon a',
She's naething the waur wi' a hunner or twa.

'Twad keep us fu' cosy—wi' that o' my ain—
When drifts the cauld snaw o'er the moor and the plain ;
Be to our wee blossoms a bield frae the blast,
That's withered the brightest and best as it passed.
O mony the pleasures that wait its command,
And hoo finely and freely it turns the hand !
" Your wit and your wisdom are naething ava,
Without," cries the world, "a hunner or twa."

WILLIAM BROCKIE.

1811-1890.

WILLIAM BROCKIE was born on 1st March, 1811, at Lauder East Mains,[1] of which farm his father was tenant. His parents—Alexander and Janet Brockie—had both sprung from well-doing Border yeoman families, and were fully qualified for the duties of parenthood. William was their first-born. His early days were spent in "sweet and pastoral Lauderdale," by the pleasant haughs of Leader. Romance reigns in this district; it is a tract of country of which it has been said that every field has its battle, and every rivulet its song. Nature, too, is here in all her glory. Wherever the eye may chance to wander it falls on a rich and varied landscape—hill and glen, field and moor, forest and river. And there is the added charm of legend and old-world story. This is the country of witch-lore and fairy tale. There is history also, dark and bloody, the revenge of Lauder Bridge, and, long years before, the defence of Thirlstane, by "Maitland with auld beard grey." The stream is the haunted Leader, bounding onward past many a broomy knowe to the Rhymer's Ercildoune and the silver Tweed. Surely, here indeed were attractions of highest value to a poetic soul! and it must be said that the home of William Brockie's childhood moulded

---

[1] *Not* at Smailholm, as Dr. Charles Rogers says in the "Modern Scottish Minstrel."

to a very large extent his future career. He received the rudiments of an English education, with a smattering of Latin, at the parish schools of Lauder, Smailholm, Mertoun, and Melrose. In February, 1825, he entered as a clerk the then well-known office of Messrs. Curle & Erskine, solicitors, Melrose. He was not given his choice of a profession, and had to submit to his father's determination to make his eldest son "a gentleman of the law." At Melrose his lot was by no means an easy one. The hours were long, the work irksome, the remuneration scant, and his masters hard and exacting. But the veriest drudgery is often accompanied with some charm, and our young law-clerk had his pleasure-able experience in the office at Melrose. He enlarged his knowledge of the world and of human nature, and came much in contact with many of the master minds of that day. He very frequently saw Scott, and many of the characters depicted in his novels ; the Earl of Buchan, of Dryburgh ; Sir David Brewster, who lived at Allerley, on the opposite bank of the Tweed ; Mr. G. P. R. James, who had taken a lease of Maxpoffle, near Bowden ; Mr. John Gibson Lockhart ; the Ettrick Shepherd ; and Colonel Ferguson, the author of "Cyril Thornton," who resided at Chiefswood.

At this time also, in spite of long hours and hard work, he found some leisure for self-culture, and, among other subjects, essayed the Muse. Soon, however, he left for Edinburgh, to assist in the office which, in consequence of extending practice,

Messrs. Curle & Erskine had established in that city. In the metropolis he took every opportunity of seeing and hearing the leading lawyers and divines —Lords Jeffrey, Cockburn, Skene, and Moncrieff, and Drs. Chalmers, Guthrie, Gordon, Henry Grey, and Andrew Thomson. But the destiny of William Brockie did not lie in the direction of the law or the Gospel. When he had completed his articles the country was passing through a severe commercial panic, and it was therefore a most inopportune period to get an engagement or to open chambers on his own account. Hence he returned home and farmed with his father for several years, during which time he applied himself vigorously to private study, chiefly linguistic and Biblical. In 1841 we find him at Galashiels as clerk and traveller for a wholesale establishment, and in 1843 he appears as a "dominie" in the small country school of Kailzie, in Peeblesshire. At the Disruption he cast in his lot with the Seceders, and was appointed to a Free Church school in Peebles. The editorship, with a share in the proprietorship, of the *Border Watch*, a Free Church journal published at Kelso, was offered to him about the same time, and this he accepted. In 1846 the headquarters of the paper were removed to Galashiels, when, mainly on account of the intemperate habits of his partner, Mr. Brockie determined to get rid of the concern, and it was sold to a gentleman who changed its name to the *Border Advertiser*, which is still published. This was the first paper printed in Selkirkshire.

In 1849 Mr. Brockie went to South Shields to edit
the *North and South Shields Gazette*, but loss of
health obliged him to forego this work in 1852.
Then he opened an academy, where for several years
he taught a thorough classical education. In 1860
he was returned to South Shields Town Council at
the top of the poll, and in the same year was united
in marriage to a very estimable lady, Miss Mary
Neil, daughter of the Rev. Robert Neil, of the
Presbyterian Church at Wallsend. In 1862 he went
to Sunderland to edit the *Sunderland Times*, but ten
years later had to resign this post also through
recurring ill-health. For a time, however, he continued to write the principal leaders, and contributed
frequently to contemporary journals. He was always
a busy man, an incessant toiler, and, up to the age
of seventy, wrought on an average between seventy
and eighty hours a week. He accumulated an
enormous quantity of material for literary under-
takings, and at the time of his death his library
contained upwards of two hundred bound volumes
of scraps and jottings on a great variety of subjects,
all duly collated and classified under distinct headings
and ready for reference. As a linguist few could
excel him. He acquired a competent knowledge of
all the modern continental languages—French, German, Italian, Spanish, Portuguese, Dutch, Danish,
Swedish, ancient and modern Greek ; and, with aids,
could make his way through Hebrew, Arabic, Syriac,
Polish, Russian, Welsh, and Gaelic. Some years ago
he entered into a correspondence with a poet in

Persia, which was entirely conducted in Arabic. He was a keen botanist, and was well versed in geology and natural history.

Besides his literary work for newspapers and periodicals, William Brockie wrote and compiled a large number of interesting Border books, chief among which may be mentioned his "History of Coldingham Priory," "The Gypsies of Yetholm," "A History of Shields," "The Folk of Shields," "Legends and Superstitions of the County of Durham," "A Day in the Land of Scott," "Leaderside Legends," "The Dark and the Dawn: A Poem," "The Confessional; and Other Poems," etc., etc. As a poet he does not attain any high eminence. His style is not the most attractive, and at times the thought tends to become mystical. But there are many pleasing rhapsodies, and one feels that beneath the surface there is, after all, a heart that understands the deep things of life—its joys and sorrows— that can sympathise very fully with a brother man in all the relations of his being. He is best in the Scotch pieces that comprise a part of his poetical musings, and delights to dwell on the scenes and incidents of early life in his beloved Berwickshire.

LAWTHER EAST MAINS.

I wadna gie the braes of Boondreich,
  That I used to speel langsyne,
For the olive groves of Lombardie,
  Or the vineyards o' the Rhine.

I wadna gie the auld toor perk,
    Wi' its ruin bald an' grim,
For the ducal palace o' Dalkeith,
    Wi' its lawns and gairdens trim.

I wadna gie the witches' thimmles,
    That grew near Howmeadows well,
For the fairest floors that florists prize,
    Or the royal rose itsel'.

I wadna gie the laich herd's hoose,
    Where I suppit nettle kail,
For the biggest and the bonniest ha'
    I' the Merse an' Tibbidale.

There's nae place like ane's native place,
    Nae hame like ane's first hame:
It mattersna hoo puir an' cauld,
    Oor love is a' the same.

We're drawn by some mysterious tie
    That nae man e'er defined,
To the sacred spot, hooe'er remote,
    Where licht first on us shined.

An' sae of a' the wide, wide warld,
    Scotland I loe the best,
An' dearest to me o' Scottish streams
    Leader dings a' the rest.

An' frae a' the ferms upon its banks
    I'd turn to Lawther East Mains,
Tho' nane that kens or cares for me
    For miles aroon' remains.

It's no that it's sae bonny a bit
    That nane wi't can compare;
I ken there's nae great beauty in't,
    But then it has what's mair:

A loving mother's gentle e'e
  There first waked luve i' mine ;
A gallant feyther's form first there
  To me appeared divine.

There first I heard the name o' Him
  That made the bonnie floors :
There first I saw the virgin snaw,
  An' the sparklin siller shoors.

Gae wa ! gae wa ! I pity ye a'
  That's been brocht up in toons :
Nae wonder that ye're timmer-tuned,
  Preekt, pauchty, padgel loons !

Yer bairntime amang styfe and reek
  In clarty closes spent,
Ye scarce e'er saw the green, green gerse,
  Or the clear blue firmament :

Ye never heard the humbee's drone,
  Nor the hurcheon's waesome cheep,
Ye never gumpt in a burn for troot,
  Or fand a young peasweep.

Ye never gat a drink o' milk,
  Sweet as it cam frae the coo :
Ye never built a rabbit hoose,
  Or fed a rookety doo.

Ye never watcht the fleeing ether
  Abune the mossy stank,
Or saw the huerunt catching eels
  Amang the reeds sae rank.

Ye never climbed a high hill tap,
  To see what ye could see ;
Ye never played hael simmer days
  On the bloomin' clover lea :

Ye never saw the Will o' the Wisp,
  Nor the flickerin Northern Lichts ;
Ye ne'er crap roon the kitchen fire,
  I' the lang wild winter nichts.

Ye never made a string o' beads
  O' the rountree berries ripe ;
Ye never blew a plane-tree whussel
  Or a green yit-stalk pipe.

A grown-up man may thrive in a toon,
  An' gather goud an' lair,
But ilka young thing sud enjoy
  The caller country air.

Better than schules and colleges
  Are hills and valleys green ;
For maist o' yer pedantic lore
  I wadna gie a preen.

Ye learn the Greek an' Roman names
  O' things ye never saw,
While aboot real existences
  Ye ken maist nocht ava.

For me, I had experience,
  Ere I was three year auld,
O' things that at the present, keep
  My hairt frae turnin' cauld.

An' hoo can I forget the place
  Where that experience grew ?
I wadna gie the memory o't
  For a' that Newton knew.

YE'LL NEVER GANG BACK TO YER MITHER NAE MAIR.

[New words to a favourite Scottish air.]

What ails ye, my lassie, my dawtie, my ain?
I've gien ye my word, an' I gie ye 't again—
　There's naething to fear ye,
　Be lichtsome and cheerie,
I'll never forsake ye, nor leave ye yer lane.

We're sune to be marriet—I needna say mair,
Our love will be leal, tho' our livin' be bare ;
　In a hoose o' our ain,
　We'll be cantie an' fain,
An' ye'll never gang back to yer mither nae mair.

We needna be troublet 'fore trouble be sprung,
The warld's afore us—we're puir, but we're young ;
　An' fate 'ill be kind
　If we're willint in mind,
Sae keep up yer heart, lass, and dinna be dung.

Folk a' hae their troubles, and we'll get our share,
But we'll warsle out throo them, and scorn to despair ;
　Sae cheer up yer heart,
　For we never shall part,
An' ye'll never gang back to yer mither nae mair.

While we live for each other, our lot will be blest,
An' tho' freens sud forget us, they'll never be missed ;
　We'll sit doon at e'en
　By the ingle sae bien,
An' the cares o' the warld 'ill a' be dismiss'd.

A couple that strive to be honest and fair
May be rich without siller, and guid without lair.
　Be gentle an' true,
　An' ye'se never need rue,
Nor sigh to win back to yer mither nae mair.

LADY HUME-CAMPBELL.

1812-1839.

THE following sweetly pathetic lines were written by the first wife of Sir Hugh Hume-Campbell of Marchmont, Bart. She was Margaret Penelope, younger daughter of John Spottiswood, Esq., of Spottiswood, and sister of Lady John Scott. She died 16th October, 1839. Dr. John Brown, in "Horæ Subsecivæ," after quoting the song, says: "Can the gifted author of these lines and of their music not be prevailed on to give them and others to the world as well as to her friends?"

WHEN THOU ART NEAR ME.

When thou art near me
Sorrow seems to fly,
And then I think, as well I may,
That on this earth there is not one
More blest than I.

But when thou leav'st me
Doubts and fears arise,
And darkness reigns
Where all before was light.
The sunshine of my soul
Is in those eyes,
And when they leave me
All the world is night.

But when thou art near me
Sorrow seems to fly,
And then I feel, as well I may,
That on this earth there dwells not one
So blest as I.

THOMAS KNOX.

1818-1879.

THOMAS KNOX was born at Greenlaw in June, 1818. He was educated at the parish school, and at the very immature age of thirteen was apprenticed to a firm of haberdashers in the High Street of Edinburgh. Upon completing his term in this establishment he entered a large warehouse in Dundee, where he remained for several years. During this period he exerted all his powers towards his self-improvement, and read and wrote extensively on subjects of passing interest. He took, for example, a prominent part in the agitation for shortened hours of labour in factories and shops, and was instrumental in securing a great reform in this direction. In 1843 he started, along with two partners, the well-known metropolitan firm of Knox, Samuel & Dickson, which soon grew to great extent, requiring large premises, and at one time nearly a hundred assistants. Notwithstanding the enormous labour thus entailed on his time and attention, he took a very active share in the work of various public movements. He was a vigorous temperance advocate, and did yeoman service to the cause in a multiplicity of ways. He espoused the sad lot of the poor, and drew public attention to the pitiful condition of the low and lapsed masses. His " Modern Chronicles of the Canongate " and " Social

Glimpses of Edinburgh" were not without their influence in urging on Dr. Guthrie's Ragged School system and Dr. William Chambers's well-known Improvement Scheme. He was one of the founders of the Association for Improving the Condition of the Poor, the Industrial Brigade, and Night Asylum for the Homeless. It might, in short, be said that Thomas Knox allied himself in a spirit of heartiest practical sympathy to every institution whose object was the temporal and moral elevation of the poor, the oppressed, and the sinful. He was, too, a devoted and energetic friend of education, and a strong upholder of its compulsory enforcement. He became a member of the Merchant Company of Edinburgh in 1856, passing through the offices of Assistant, Treasurer, and Master, and while thus connected inaugurated that special work which has made the Company's schools famous all over the land. He also took a prominent interest in the Watt Institution and School of Art—now the Heriot-Watt College—and his last work before retiring to rest on the night of his death was to draft the annual report. With other societies he was intimately associated, such as the Royal Society of Arts, the Geological Society, Edinburgh Border Counties Association, and Borderers' Union. He was a man of social disposition, warm-hearted and generous, true to the core—"one of Heaven's own aristocracy." His death occurred with startling suddenness on 4th December, 1879. He was buried in the beautiful Grange Cemetery.

Thomas Knox lived a life of sweet self-denial.
Not for the ambition of receiving plaudits from men
did he struggle bravely up life's steep ladder, but
from the grand desire, so strongly implanted in his
own manly heart, of benefiting humanity in his day
and generation. He wrote:

> Press on ! press on ! nor doubt nor fear,
> From age to age this voice shall cheer,
> Whate'er may die and be forgot,
> Work done for God *it* dieth not.

And these lines truly express the only motive of his
high-toned and public-spirited career.

A collection of Knox's poems, of which he wrote a
large number, mainly on religious and temperance
themes, was issued some years ago by William
Tweedie, of London, the well-known temperance
publisher, in a small volume of ninety-six pages
bearing the title, "Rhymed Convictions in Songs,
Hymns, and Recitations, for Social Meetings and
Firesides, by 'Walneerg ;'"[1] and in 1880 the Messrs.
Parlane, of Paisley, gave to the public a thin quarto
of "Scottish Temperance Songs to Scottish Airs," by
Thomas Knox. From the introductory note to the
latter publication we cull the following sonnet by
Professor Blackie, which appeared in *The Scotsman*
a few days after Thomas Knox's death:

----

[1] "Walneerg" is simply the name of his native village spelled backward.

ON SEEING A PHOTOGRAPH OF THE LATE THOMAS KNOX.

And art thou he—a shadow, a grey sign
  Of him who late, in fulness of a man,
Stood forth all fresh and strong in every line
  That with the Godhead links the human clan?
But yesterday, in proud view of this town,
  Loved by the good and honoured by the wise,
Now dimmed, disthroned, and cast obscurely down
  'Neath the cold earth, hid from all human eyes!
O, my dear brother, were the power with me
  To make thy name live with far-sounded men,
I'd pour thy praises forth as full and free
  As the well gushes from the cloud-capt Ben:
But I am weak; and with my tears alone
  Can tell how much I lack when thou art gone!

UNDYING WORK.

Though chilling years have o'er us rolled,
Warm at our hearts this faith we hold;
Whate'er may die and be forgot,
Work done for God it dieth not!

Though scoffers ask, Where is your gain?
And, mocking, say your toil is vain!
Such scoffers die and are forgot,
Work done for God it dieth not!

Press on, true men can never fail,
Whoe'er oppose, they must prevail;
Opponents die and are forgot,
Work done for God it dieth not!

Press on! press on! nor doubt nor fear,
From age to age this voice shall cheer,
Whate'er may die and be forgot,
Work done for God it dieth not!

EARTH AN EDEN-BOWER.

Air—"My love is like a red, red rose."

Oh, earth is yet an Eden-bower,
  Where man may happy be,
Creation's glories are His dower,
  By mountain, sky, and sea.
But chiefest joy to man e'er given
  Is hame wi' a' its bliss ;
A mother's love, there, emblems heaven,
  There childhood's angel-kiss.
There childhood's angel-kiss, my dear,
  There childhood's angel-kiss ;
A mother's love, there, emblems heaven,
  There childhood's angel-kiss.

Yes, earth is yet an Eden-bower,
  Where man may happy be,
Still sweetly blaws the auld wall-flower,
  And waves ilk forest tree.
Still Eden's milk-white thorn appears
  To deck the puir man's yaird ;
The thistle stands wi' bristlin' spears,
  His cottage door to guard.
His cottage door to guard, my dear,
  His cottage door to guard ;
The thistle stands wi' bristlin' spears,
  His cottage door to guard.

On earth we'll keep an Eden-bower,
  And happy will we be,
Our lives make fragrant as the flower,
  Majestic like the tree.
Round a' thing guid and a' thing kind
  Our hearts shall ever twine ;
We'll fling a' wicked things behind,
  And maist make life divine ;
And maist make life divine, my dear,
  And maist make life divine,
We'll fling a' wicked things behind,
  And maist make life divine !

M

THE TREE AND THE STORM.

[Hitherto unpublished.]

I've seen the storm with anger beat
  Against the lonely tree,
Until it swung and groaned as if
  In mortal agony!

Then sudden lift itself erect,
  Again defiant look,
As though the tempest's giant grasp
  In scorn away it shook!

Swift back the raging blast returned,
  And leapt upon the tree,
And, as two wrathful warriors,
  They wrestled furiously!

And deeper still the gallant tree
  Planted its mighty feet,
As rushed and roared the savage storm,
  And bough and stem did beat!

Till pithless branch and sapless leaf
  On high were hurled like dust,
Woe to the lonely wrestler,
  Had these been all thy trust!

But as they closed in sternest strife,
  And twig and leaf fell fast,
Still stronger seemed the smitten tree,
  And feebler seemed the blast!

At last the tree, with lighten'd arms,
  Could all the storm defy,
And mocked him back into his caves,
  A baffled enemy!

The calm returned, the tree remained,
  Majestic more by far,
The fading, worthless, only went
  In that tempestuous war!

Thus, thought I, fickle friends may leave
  On Truth's rough battle-day,
Yet nearer be the victory
  When such have passed away!

REV. ANDREW CUNNINGHAM.

1819-1879.

ANDREW CUNNINGHAM was the youngest son of William Cunningham, banker in Duns, and cousin of the eminent Principal Cunningham, of the Free Church College, Edinburgh. He was born at Duns in 1819, and received his education in the academy of that town, Edinburgh High School, and the University. Passing through the curriculum for the ministry in the Church of Scotland, he was licensed in 1842, but taking to the Free Church party, he was in the following year ordained to the pastoral charge of the first Free Church at Dundonald, in Ayrshire. There he remained for two years, when he accepted a call to the newly-formed congregation at Eccles, in his native county, over which he faithfully presided until his death.

He was known as an able preacher, a devoted pastor, and a warm-hearted friend. He was a valued leader in ecclesiastical affairs, and took a prominent part in every movement tending to the fuller development of his Church's work in the sphere of social reform. He was a skilful scientist, and he wrote poetry occasionally as a recreation. His musings are chiefly in the sonnet form, and indicate refined taste, good thought, and a capability of rising to higher achievements in the divine art of poesy.

KNOX.

A king of men behold : a man in truth—
Ay, every inch a man ; a spirit bold
But noble ; brave and warm of heart—not cold,
Not rough, unfeeling, rude—who, in his youth
To generous learning gave his soul away
With all a lover's deep devotion : who
Stood for his country and his kind ; and through
Evil and good report upheld the sway
Of what was true and just ; and founded all
On Christ's Evangel pure : having no fear
What man could do : and not prepared to fall
And worship despots even if death were near :
Not moved by blandishment in royal call,
Nor by fair face wet with deceitful tear.

LUTHER.

Strong monk of Wittenberg, thy homely face
And firm-set figure are the very type
Of what thou wroughtest for all time : the trace
Is still of thee, and of thy sturdy gripe
Even on the Book thy labour first revealed
To Europe and mankind : God's truth, concealed
By priestly guile, thou forth in language ripe
Did'st send to German homes : and darkness fled
From half a world : and Rome's blood stood congealed—
Her very heart ceasing to beat, stone dead
In blank dismay, while on the message sped
From town to castle ; they who in the field
Trained vines, or tilled the ground, the toil-bent head
Raised heavenward as they read in straw-roofed shed.

JOHN GIBSON.

1819-1882.

JOHN GIBSON, son of James Gibson and Barbara Muir, was born at Greenlaw, 24th December, 1819. After leaving school he wrought for a number of years with his father, who, for nearly half a century, carried on a tailoring business in the village. Latterly, he was employed as a colporteur under the Religious Tract Society of Scotland, during which period he resided at East Linton. In early life he showed indications of poetic taste, and contributed frequently to local newspapers. In 1875 he published a volume of his productions under the title of "Poems, Grave and Gay," which had a wide circulation.[1] He was a man of high character and sterling worth. His poetry echoes with honest sentiment and breathes a spirit of fervent piety, while here and there, in his lighter moods, he is exceedingly happy, and displays many excellent touches of bright, racy, good humour. Gibson died at Edinburgh, in January, 1882.

TAKE LIFE AS WE FIND IT.

We'll wait till doomsday ere we make
  Things marshal oor ain way ;
Ills oot life's lucky-bag we'll take,
  Nor cry, "Alack-a-day !"
Life at the best's a ravell'd pirn,
  With patience let's unwind it :
If fortune gowl we maunna girn,
  But take life as we find it.

---

[1] Small 8vo. Haddington.

If we had this, if we had that,
　　Hoo happy wad we be !
Oor outward fortune, without faut,
　　Each o' us langs to see.
Yet, though our hame were gilt wi' gold,
　　Heart-griefs might come behind it ;
Heaven may, to smite, our plans unfold,
　　Sae take life as we find it.

If friends forsake, we'll do oor best
　　To make their love return ;
If puir, oor hands will never rest
　　Till fortune cease to spurn.
But if our striving be in vain,
　　We'll whistle and ne'er mind it,
We've a' that's gude if Heaven remain,
　　And life just as we find it.

One grieves so little progress made,
　　So little ground we gain,
Condemned to roam the lengthening shade,
　　In hardship, woe, and pain.
Needful such frictions to the soul,
　　To polish and to grind it ;
We'll know, when we have reached the goal,
　　Why life is as we find it.

Young lads at school, strong men at work,
　　Maids singing all the day,
Wives full of married troubles, hark
　　And ponder what I say.
Your soul, though e'en to wealth ye climb,
　　Let not delusion blind it,
The present is your happiest time—
　　Then take life as ye find it.

There shines some light on every lot,
　　Thank Heaven, whate'er your store,
Though by proud fashion's ranks forgot,
　　God's mercies find the door—
The soul to its life-task God-given,
　　Through grief and toil to bind it,
And leave, by deeds for man and heaven,
　　Life better than we find it.

WILLIAM FORSYTH.

1823-1889.

WILLIAM FORSYTH was born at Earlston in 1823. His father, who came of an old Covenanting family, was a man much respected in the district, and strove to inculcate into his children his own deep religious convictions. While yet a child young Forsyth removed with his parents to Galashiels. After leaving school he wrought for a time as a spinner in Galabank Mill, and diligently applied his spare hours to self-improvement. He read much on questions of social and political importance, debated keenly on co-operative and temperance movements, and thus laid the foundation of his future useful and honoured career. At this time he very frequently contributed to the local newspapers articles and letters on a variety of subjects, sometimes venturing to address his readers in rhyme. After leaving Galashiels he spent a few years in Edinburgh, and thence proceeded to Aberdeen, where he established a prosperous temperance hotel. In 1863 he opened the Cobden Hotel in Glasgow, which soon became, under his management, of great proportions and world-wide fame. In 1885 he stood as a candidate in the Liberal interest for the Bridgeton division of Glasgow, but failed to find a majority. His death took place at Bridge of Allan, where he had gone for the benefit of his health, 28th May, 1889. He was thrice married,

and is survived by a family of four sons and four
daughters.

William Forsyth was all his life fond of literature,
and held correspondence with several well-known
journalists and authors. He was on intimate terms
with Russell, of *The Scotsman*, and the great Border
angler, Thomas Tod Stoddart. In 1887 he published
"A Lay of Loch Leven,"[1] dedicated to the Glasgow
Anglers' Association, which is profusely illustrated
with members' portraits. The following are the
introductory lines to the "Lay:"

> Loch Leven's old historic tide,
> Which erst had sheltered Scotland's pride !
> When strife and turmoil shook the throne,
> Retreat was found in island lone.
> The old grey keep, the castle hoar,
> Still seen from Leven's sedgy shore,
> Draws pilgrims from each foreign clime,
> To gaze on that, which, in its prime,
> Imprisoned Scotland's hapless queen,
> Unrobed and reft of royal sheen.
>
> What thoughts were hers ? Ah ! who can tell
> What tumults wild her bosom swell !
> What wild'ring fears and doubts arise,
> To wound her heart, to cloud her eyes !
> From palace driven to lonesome keep,
> To pine alone in anguish deep ;
> Imprisoned, captive, held in thrall,
> Nor longer courted, loved by all ;
> An outcast caged in lonely isle,
> Nought left to soothe or to beguile
> The tedium of her hapless fate,
> To shield her 'gainst a faction's hate.

[1] "A Lay of Loch Leven." By William o' ye West. 8vo. Glasgow:
Forrester

Dark were her thoughts, her prospects drear,
No ray of hope to gild or cheer ;
No longer peers and courtiers bow,
Or gallant yeomen take the vow ;
Torn from the pomp she prized ere while,
Reft of her crown—all regal style—
Denied the homage of a smile.

With blighted hope and broken crest,
Doomed with the mean to herd and rest,
Withdrawn the warrior's proffered aid—
His life, his honour, and his blade.
No minstrel's tale salutes her ear,
Silenced the harp she loved so dear ;
No courtiers fain her presence throng,
To fling the jest or raise the song.
Ah ! brilliant scenes, so joyous, gay,
To irksome solitude give way :
Pent and immured in hated keep,
Nought left but o'er the past to weep.
While base-born kerns keep watch and ward
O'er captive, held close under guard,
(How fitful fortune's changeful way,
By fickle freaks in one brief day,
Steals from our grasp the joys we prize,
Wounds the sad heart and blinds the eyes !)

At dark, ere day had closed its eye,
She sought retreat in turret high—
Retreat from menial's prying gaze—
To muse on bright or better days.
To Leven's placid western flow,
'Neath setting sun's soft amber glow,
Restful and calm, assuaged her woe.
Pensive and sad she seized the lyre,
This plaint of mingled grief and ire
Poured slowly forth through blinding tears,
And told, as caught by listening ears,
To men through long-descending years.

THE COTTAGE BY THE QUARRY.

What though no flowers our cot embowers,
  Our biggin' auld and hoary,
It has the charm o' leal hearts warm,
  O' mirth, o' sang, and story.

There aft we sing till rafters ring,
  And laud wi' rapturous feeling,
Our snug wee stead so near the Tweed,
  Our cosie fishing shieling.

There frien's we meet wha gladly greet
  Wi' eye o' welcome gleaming ;
We gather there, so free o' care,
  Our cot wi' kindness beaming.

Ilk fishing splore in days of yore,
  Ilk wondrous take and capture —
The lengthen'd run, the nichts o' fun,
  Rehearsed wi' kindling rapture.

The homely cheer, the mem'ries dear,
  O' days that wouldna tarry,
Endears the spot where Geordie's cot
  Snug nestles by the quarry.

PETER M'CRAKET.

1827-1882.

PETER M'CRAKET, son of Alexander M'Craket and Elizabeth Sanderson, was born at Lambden, near Greenlaw, in 1827. His great-grandfather was of Highland blood, and originally belonged to the Clan Cameron, while his father was a small farmer near Earlston, and latterly a wool-dealer and feuar in Greenlaw. Peter received a very limited education, but by dint of perseverance he assiduously applied himself during his occupation of " herd laddie " to his intellectual improvement, with such success that in a short time he had mastered the leading facts of Scottish history, and had acquired a considerable acquaintance with the great English and Scottish writers. He was for a time apprenticed to a draper, but not liking this employment, he went to Edinburgh, and, adding to his growing store of knowledge, commenced teaching at Abbeyhill. In 1847 he was appointed master of the Free Church School in the Canongate, and shortly afterwards he became headmaster of the Free New North Church District School, where he remained for four years. In 1853 he was elected headmaster of John Street School, Greenock, a position which he occupied with great credit and success until his death in 1882.

He wrote a large number of poems and songs, chiefly the former, which were printed only in

local newspapers and home journals.   They are
characterised by sweetness of diction, tenderness,
and sympathy, and impress the reader with the idea
that their author was a man full of love for Nature,
and of that higher love to the God of Nature which
is best seen in the spirit that seeks to elevate
humanity in the direction of goodness, truth, and
beauty.

THE LAMMERMOOR HILLS.

Though stately the hills in the North and the South,
No hills are to me like the hills o' my youth ;
There joys have an echo that time never stills
Frae the glens i' the bosom o' Lammermoor hills.

The steed o' the victor ance pranced on their plain,
An' his red banner waved ower the spoils o' the slain ;
For the camps ly yon corries and dark mossy rills
A' tell o' the Romans on Lammermoor hills.

Their wild heathy fells hae the cairns o' gloom,
Wi' the tales o' the perished or weird woman's doom,
An' the birds o' the muirland wi' lang crookit bills
Cryin' roun' them sae waefu' on Lammermoor hills.

The hills o' my hame where I lived an' I lo'ed—
Where I herded the sheep, an' the blaeberries pu'ed ;
As aft as I see them my heart and e'e fills
With the thochts o' langsyne on the Lammermoor hills.

The glad smile o' simmer wad light their black brows
As we played like the lambs 'mang the green hazel howes,
An' fished wi' a preen in the dam by the mills
Till the red sun gaed doon ower the Lammermoor hills.

Frae the blast that blew keen on the heathery dale
I can mind o' the shielin' weel thackit wi' feal,
An' the cosie red peat-fire that cauld an' care kills
To the lad wi' the plaid on the Lammermoor hills.

The lav'rocks and linties are dear aye to me,
As they sing frae the clouds on the bonnie ha' tree,
But their sang ower the heather like May-dew distils
On my heart never dowie on Lammermoor hills.

O, the sangs that they sung in our young days o' yore,
Ilk brood tak's the keynote and sings as before,
The true love and friendship that time never chills —
There's music for me 'mang the Lammermoor hills.

I lo'e the wild flowers by the brake an' the lea,
But nane smiles sae sweet an' sae charmin' to me,
Or sends to my bosom sic rapturous thrills,
As the heather that blooms on the Lammermoor hills.

O, gie me yon cot by the green burn side !
Wi' health and contentment 'twad be a' my pride :
My harp wad be tuned by the birds and the rills,
And my muse wad be nursed by the Lammermoor hills.

Dark changes hae left their deep trace on our brows,
Sin' we left the lane hoose 'mang the green gorsy knowes ;
But time kindly spares, wi' its furrows and drills,
The face aye the same o' the Lammermoor hills.

The sun of my youth is now rounded and set,
But the haunts of my childhood are dear to me yet,
Like friends fresh and fadeless through life and its ills,
To welcome me back to the Lammermoor hills.

THOMAS WATTS.

1845-1886.

THOMAS WATTS was a native of Ireland, but
from the age of eleven months until the day
of his death he resided almost entirely in Berwickshire.   His whole being was saturated with the
scenes and history of the Merse: he loved its people,
he sang its praises, and thus in a very true sense we
claim him as a Berwickshire bard.   He was born on
the 5th March, 1845, at Wexford Barracks, where his
father was a soldier and the trusted servant of Colonel
Logan Home, of Broomhouse, at that time an officer
in the Royal Marines.   On the colonel's retirement,
Watts obtained his discharge, and followed his
master to Berwickshire.   Young Thomas received his
education at Duns, and in his fourteenth year entered
upon an apprenticeship as a tailor in the same town.
When the four years were completed he resolved to
see life, and travelled through the chief cities of the
kingdom, working for a brief period in each.   During
his leisure hours he devoted himself to reading and
general intellectual improvement.   He became a
first-rate English scholar and formed a taste for
poetry.   Then he began to write verse himself.   In
summer time he would repair to the banks of the
Whitadder, and there, surrounded by the full beauty
of Nature, in some quiet and shady nook, his thoughts
shaped themselves into rhyme.   Many of these
effusions found their way into the columns of the

local newspapers, and in 1880 he published a selection, under the title of "Woodland Echoes,"[1] which was cordially received in the county. "It will now be more than ever prized as a memorial of one whose fine imagination, keen appreciation of Nature, dainty execution, high moral character, and early death will make his work and his memory ever tenderly cherished." In 1883 Watts paid a long-desired visit to London, and worked there for a little over two years. But his health, never robust, began to give way; a severe cold developed into consumption, and he returned to his home and friends by the banks of the Whitadder. Four months later he was laid to rest in the little churchyard of Edrom. The singer's voice is hushed, but the sweet cadence of his song yet lingers to gladden the memories of loved ones left behind, and there are few in the fair Merse land who knew him well that do not remember with keen delight and heart-felt gratitude the pleasant companionship, and the bracing, ennobling friendship of such a man as Thomas Watts, humble in station, but very high in worth.

THE FRIEND OF BYGONE DAYS.

Oh! rowan tree,
Ye bring to me
Sweet visions o' the past;
That tremble back
O'er memory's track,
Like sunbeams 'mid the blast;

---

[1] 8vo. Kelso: J. & J. H. Rutherfurd.

'Twas here, ere childhood's years were fled,
  In the autumn's gloamin' haze,
I cam' to pree thy berries red
  With the friend of bygone days.

    Oh ! rowan tree,
      I've stood by thee
  In the lang-gane summer hours,
      When whisp'ring gales,
      Like lovers' tales,
  Sigh'd 'mong thy virgin flowers :
In hopeful boyhood here I dream'd
  Aught but the warld's ways ;
Sae couthy, kind the warld seem'd
  With the friend of bygone days.

    Oh ! rowan tree,
      Again I see,
  Through the mist of memory's tear,
      A pairtin' scene,
      Where freends had been
  Sae happy and sae dear ;
The gloamin' had chas'd the last day-beam,
  And a cauld mist happ'd the braes,
When I bid farewell to the valley stream
  And the friend of bygone days.

    Oh ! rowan tree,
      There canna be,
  'Mang a' the scenes that vie,
      With charms combin'd,
      To soothe the mind,
  Or please the captive eye,
A scene like this, where now I roam
  In Fancy's fairy maze,
Through the dear old lane, by the valley home,
  With the friend of bygone days.

> Oh ! rowan tree,
> What wad I gi'e
> If my fondest wish could wile
> Frae yon far place
> The auld hame face,
> And the same auld kindly smile ?
> But, no ; though I ken that place be fair—
> Too fair for a mortal's gaze—
> In the "by-and-by" I may wander there
> With the friend of bygone days.

WINTER EVENINGS.

When all without, the wintry blast
  Comes sweeping 'long the lanes ;
When showers of drifted sleet are cast
  Against the lattice panes ;
When wildly from the upland heights
  The sounding tempest's hurl'd,
Drear as the screams of wand'ring sprites
  From some strange, ruined world :
    Oh ! the cosy winter evenings,
      How pleasantly they glide ;
    The love of Heaven was surely given
      To bless the ingle-side.

Not warmer glows the crimson flame
  That leaps in elfin mirth,
Throwing out its arms to clasp in love
  Those cluster'd round the hearth,
Than are the happy hearts, whose joys
  Home's social comforts prove ;
Nor brighter than the sparkling eyes
  Reflecting purest love.
    Oh ! the social winter evenings,
      What pleasures ye inspire ;
    Care's shadows pass, and vanish as
      We gather round the fire.

N

What memories throng the sacred place—
  Life's calendars that show
The outlines fair of many a face
  We cherished long ago—
'Twas here Hope waved her fairy wand
  To lure the buoyant heart,
When many a fort was traced and plann'd
  Upon life's glowing chart.
      Oh ! the hallow'd winter evenings
        Of our childhood far away,
      How fair ye seem, and brightly beam
        On Memory's dial to-day.

What though 'mid other scenes we roam,
  When Christmastide draws near,
Affection guides our footsteps home
  'Mid recollections dear ;
And as we meet those kindred eyes,
  With tender meaning fraught,
We feel that round the circle lies
  A realm of loving thought.
      Oh ! the homely winter evenings,
        May we, from wants secure,
      With Christ-like will remember still
        The hungry, homeless poor.

OOR WEE WEAN.

The canty Spring is past,
  The Simmer's worn dune,
While Autumn's soughin' blast
  Tells Winter's comin' sune ;
Ay ! sune the cauld, white snaw will hap
  Yon wee, wee mound again,
To rest, like mournfu' mem'ries, roond
  Oor ae wee wean.

An' life's glad day is by,
  Wi' a' its lo'esome smiles ;
Sad thochts, like shadows, lie
  Across the prospect whiles ;
Ay ! dreich an' dowie's been oor lot,
  An' fraught wi' muckle pain,
Sin' yon dool day we pairtit wi'
  Oor ain wee wean.

Ye mind the happy day
  We wander'd ower the lea
To Markle's whinny brae,
  Oor coortin' place to see?
A wee geni nestled on thy breist—
  A fairer there was nane—
The sinless pledge o' wedded love,
  That sweet wee wean.

We sat beside the breir,
  Near the auld trystin' tree,
While something like a tear
  Shone softly in your e'e ;
I watch'd its peerless beauty as
  Ye weav'd the daisy chain,
An' wreath'd it ower the curly broo
  O' oor wee wean.

I saw that simmer night—
  I think I see it noo—
A soft and holy light
  Illume thy thochtfu' broo ;
I couldna ken what 'twas that mov'd
  A mither's hairt sae fain—
Some lo'esome spell that circles roond
  The first wee wean.

Oh ! mind ye hoo we stood
  Ootside the shielin' door,
A-list'nin' unco prood
  Her pawky baby-lore ?

We kentna syne in a' the warl'
    A bonnier, sweeter strain,
Than infant lispings as they fell
    Frae oor wee wean.

An' mony a fear we've dree'd,
    When aff the cutty chair
She'd dunt her little heid
    Upon the yirthen flair ;
For mony a trial an' fa' she had
    Ere she could gang her lane ;
Ah ! methinks there's mony aulder anes
    Like that wee wean.

When Winter days cam' roon',
    An' nichts were wearin' lang,
To her ye'd sit and croon
    Some simple cradle-sang ;
Till, sleepin' soon', we'd breathe the prayer
    Faith never breath'd in vain,
And gied to Heaven the keepin' o'
    Oor wee, wee wean.

An' often wad we sit
    Lang at the ingle side,
While ower thy face wad flit
    A sunny smile o' pride,
As oft ye wad in fondness shape
    Some project o' yer ain,
Some plan anent the future weal
    O' oor wee wean.

But, oh ! that nicht sae drear,
    'Twill never be forgot,
While mony a joyless tear
    Revives the memory o't.
Toom is the wee, wee cottie noo
    Where, lauchin', she has lain,
While cauld's the snawy shroud that haps
    Oor ae wee wean.

Yet there's ae comfort still,
    It's calm'd me mony a day;
'Twill lighten a' life's ill,
    And soothe the hairt when wae;
Ay! tho' we've tint life's dearest joys
    In what we couldna hain,
A lammie in the Shepherd's fauld
    Is oor wee wean.

WALTER CHISHOLM.

1856-1877.

WALTER CHISHOLM was born on 21st December, 1856, at Easter Howlaw, near Chirnside, where his father was a shepherd. At the Whitsunday of 1865 the family "flitted" to Redheugh, a farm in Cockburnspath parish, and young Walter attended, until his twelfth year, the little school of Oldcambus, then under the kindly rule of Mr. William Cairns. At that age he became assistant to his father. In 1875 the family removed to Dowlaw, a neighbouring farm, and our poet took a term of shepherding near the gipsy village of Yetholm. In the winter he returned home, and attended for a time his old school. In the spring of 1876 he went to Glasgow, and found employment as light porter in a leather warehouse. At the end of this year, when on a visit to his parents, he was suddenly seized with a severe attack of pleurisy; and, though he rallied a little during the spring and summer, there was no hope of ultimate recovery, and he passed peacefully away on 1st October, 1877, a few months before completing his twenty-first year.

Had Walter Chisholm lived he would undoubtedly have taken a high place among Scottish poets. What he has left is amply sufficient to convince us of this. His life is another example of how much a man's environment will influence the inner being.

A herd laddie on the borders of Coldingham Moor,
and daily in the midst of Nature's many charms, it
is little wonder that a soul like his should have
expressed its feelings in song. He has given us
many bright touches of perfect poetry thrilling with
the music of country life, full of honest sentiment,
appealing to our noblest emotions and our loftiest
ideals, bidding us mould our lives in conformity with
the most lasting good. This Berwickshire shepherd
lad is an optimist in the highest sense of the term.
He sings his own experience. Much of sorrow and
suffering has been his lot ; but these are only means
to a great end. They are to act as the discipline of
life, and to accomplish its perfection. He is confident
that in all the affairs of this shifting scene there is that
" Divinity which shapes our ends, rough hew them
how we will," and by virtue of this faith he can sing
in exulting strains : " This, then, is the true solution
of human life. All things are controlled by an All-
Power Providence. God is good, and surely His
goodness shall ' fall at last, far off to all, and every
winter change to spring.' " All the events of man's
daily existence are wisely ordered, and not a single
item shall fail of the divinely-appointed plan.

> " All's well,
> God's in the heavens."

Walter Chisholm's " Poems " were published in
1879 in a neat little volume[1] edited by his old friend
and teacher, Mr. William Cairns, brother of the late
Principal Cairns.

[1] Small 8vo. Edinburgh : James Thin.

SCOTIA'S BORDER LAND.

Nae gentle muse will I invoke frae famed Parnassus' hill,
  To make my rhyme glide saft alang, and smooth each rugged line :
Nae high strung lay, for guerdon gay, shall task my rustic skill ;
  A hamely heart, a hamely harp, a hamely sang is mine.
I'll sing in the braid Doric tongue a lilt o' hill an' glen —
  O' muirlands wide and rocky dells, an' mountains green an' grand ;
I'll sing o' rivers winding fair, through mony a dowie den,
  O'er a' the storied length an' breadth o' " Scotia's Border Land ! "

From where, upon the eastern coast, the ocean floods before
  St. Abb's his rocky barrier rears deep-seamed wi' mony a scaur —
To where far Solway ebbs an' flows upon the sounding shore,
  Fame gilds the land wi' gowden light — a never-settin' star.
Oft has the yeoman's slogan cry re-echoed through her vales,
  When on her soil a Southron foe had dared to take his stand ;
And oft the stalwart Foresters have trooped from hills an' dales,
  And boldly dare l, or nobly died, for " Scotia's Border Land ! "

When from her highest mountain tops, around both far an' near,
  With fiery tongues the beacons sent the tidings of the fray,
The shepherd seized the barbèd crook, the hind the ready spear,
  And to the chieftain's banner thronged to swell his fair array.
From Liddel-side, in warrior pride, the doughty Elliot rode,
  And bold Buccleugh, 'mid kinsmen true, left Teviot's classic strand ;
From silvery Tweed Home's battle steed before his Merse-men strode,
  And many a laurel wreath was won for " Scotia's Border Land."

Then when the tempest brewed at Rome burst on the wondering world,
  When blood of martyr dyed the ground and priestly rage was high,
Within her verdant valleys was the Covenant flag unfurled ;
  A bright and sunny spot she shone in that dark cloudy sky.
Where was it that the Psalms were raised, as gloaming shades cam'
    doon,
  By buirdly men whose hands held baith the Bible an' the brand ?
Where was it kingly Cameron won the holy martyr's croon ?
  But 'mang the moors an' mosses wild o' " Scotia's Border Land ! "

There, guardian o'er fair Mercia's bounds, dun Lammerlaw is seen,
    Chief o' the hills that bear his name, a gallant train I trow ;
There Cheviot rules his craggy peaks, a giant broad and green —
    The traces of a thousand years deep furrowed on his brow—
There dark and heathy Ruberslaw towers silent and alone
    There Eildon shows his triple crest hewn by a master hand,
And many a hundred storied hills and many a lofty cone
    Proclaim the glory and renown of "Scotia's Border Land !"

Immortal bards have praised her worth in many a fadeless strain,
    Have sung the hallowed memories o' a' her winding streams—
Strains that can kindle aged hearts wi' youthful fire again,
    And memories bright that tinge wi' light the lanely exile's dreams.
O ! glorious land of love and truth, of song and battle fame !
    Where each grey cairn's a hero's grave thrice touched by glory's
        wand !
My heart aye bounds wi' quickened throb at mention o' thy name,
    The wale o' Freedom's pioneers, fair "Scotia's Border Land !"

OOR ONLY BAIRNIE.

Laddie ! wi' the lauchin' e'e !
    Bonnie, blythsome, little sonny,
Wha cou'd help frae likin' thee?—
    Aye sae pawkie, sweet, an' funny:
Thro' the hoose the lee-lang day,
    Hear his gleesome prattle ringin'—
Bent on naething but his play,
    An' his sang sae sweetly singin' !

Mammie there her bairnie sees,
    Playin' aye sae bricht and canny,
Whiles a kindly word she gies,
    Whiles she chides her little manny !
See him wi' his faither's hat
    Stickin' on his saucy croonie !
Off wi't noo !—I kenna what
    I'm to dae wi' sic a loonie.

In oor hame ye micht hae seen
  Twa-three weeks sin' sic a laddie,
But sin' syne has trouble been—
  Left us naething but his shaddie:
White as snaw his shilpit cheeks
  Reft o' a' their bonnie roses,
Laigh his voice whene'er he speaks,
  Een that lang e'er bed-time closes.

Puir wee chap! the stangs o' pain
  Thro' the nights sae lang and drearie,
Nocht hae left but skin an' bane
  O' that form sae blythe an' cheerie;
But that blight noo off we'll ca'—
  Mammie!   Fill the parritch coggie!
Chase that shilpit wean awa!
  Bring again oor lauchin' roguey!

"It Micht Be Muckle Waur."

O fain wad I that Fortune fair
  Wad deign to smile on me,
An' wi' my lip I fain wad try
  Her honeyed cup to pree:
But ne'er a blink o' Fortune's e'e
  E'er comes my airt ava',
An' at the bitter cup o' fate
  My mou' I still maun thraw.

I find, as thro' the warld sae wide
  I daunder up an' doon,
He wha has routh o' gudes an' gear,
  Aye hauds the causey's croon;
While mony men, wi' nobler minds,
  An' hearts mair tried an' true,
Maun toil aneath the froon that lurks
  On snell Misfortune's broo!

This life's a jumble at the best,
  Some sing while others moan,
Ane fa's, anither fills his place,
  An' sae the wheel rowes on;
Some toil wi' hard an' horny hands,
  An' some wi' weary brain,
Some dine on choicest venison,
  While ithers pick the bane!

But should we fa', an' ithers climb
  To where we ance hae stood,
Let's mind that ilka backward thraw
  Is gi'en us for oor good:
There's naething e'er sae ill, but that
  It micht be muckle waur;
An' Perseverance cleaves a way
  Thro' mony a rocky scaur.

Then fret na, freends, where'er we steer,
  Nor at oor lot repine,
The helm is held by higher hands
  Than either yours or mine;
But thro' the strife we'll strive to keep
  A conscience bricht an' clear,
An' bless the Hand that gi'es us health
  To fecht life's battle here.

An' shou'd the dull an' darklin' cluds
  O' Care come owre the sky,
We'll cower aneath some bieldy bush,
  · An' let the blast blaw by:
Then on, wi' Temperance for oor shield,
  An' Hope oor guidin' star,
An' sing—there's nocht sae ill, but that
  " It micht be muckle waur."

THE MISSED TRYST.

She trysted there to meet wi' him
  Between the licht an' mirk,
When e'enin's shadows grey an' grim
  Swathed auld St. Helen's Kirk ;
An' sune as e'er the sun had sunk
  Beyond the purple fell,
Altho' the nicht was wat an' cauld,
Wi' lowin' heart he left the fauld,
  An' socht the rocky dell.

Time dragged alang fu' wearily --
  The trystin' hour gaed by,
He heard the sad sough o' the sea—
  He heard the fox's cry !
"Oh ! has she feared to face the nicht?
  Or has she lost her way?
The Lan'sea links are lang an' steep,
The mermaid's floe baith braid an' deep—
  Gude send it be na sae !"

Wi' hurried steps he left the glen,
  An' socht the rocky shore,
Where wildly roon' the smuggler's den
  The seethin' waters roar ;
Is that a sea-bird's scream he hears !
  What form? what face is there?
He plunges in—he clasps her form ;
Though wilder blaws the blindin' storm—
  They'll miss their tryst nae mair !

Next morn when rose the sun, the lea
  In summer beauty smiled,
The winds were hushed, the changin' sea
  Had calmed her waters wild :
They found them on the rocky beach,
  An' bore them up the steep ;
By Helen's Kirk a mound is seen,
An' 'neath its canopy o' green
  A lang, lang tryst they keep !

MARGARET HAY HOME TOUGH.
MARY ANNE LORIMER.

THE following compositions are the work of two sisters, daughters of the Rev. George Tough, for many years minister of Ayton. On their mother's side they were connected with the ancient family of the Berwickshire Homes. In 1851 there appeared a small volume from the pen of the first, entitled "The Offering," and in 1864, the year following her death. a second was issued under the superintendence of her remaining sister, bearing the title of "Gathered Fragments." Miss M. A. Tough became the wife of the beloved Dr. Lorimer, of Haddington, and was herself an occasional writer of verse, mainly of a religious nature.

THE FAMILY GATHERING.

Deep thoughts are in those gatherings
  Of friends at festive times,
That 'mid the lighter play of life
  Wake low and solemn chimes,
As some cathedral bell is heard
  Amid the village glee,
Or some faint murmur borne along
  Of the far-sounding sea.

From wanderings in many lands,
  From scenes of many hues,
From the rose-bowers and the tangled brake,
  The frost blights and the dews;
From memories of other homes,
  That will not wear away,
From the ringing echoes of the past,
  'Mid the strains of a later day:

They gather round the festal board,
  With glowing hearts and glad,
And they smile and sing the hours away
  Too gaily to be sad.
But is there not a yearning,
  A sound like the night-wind's moan,
In the haunted chamber of the heart—
  A low, deep undertone—

For the fellowship of other days,
  For the links of broken chains,
For the old familiar faces, now
  In the halls where silence reigns?
Yes! though a goodly gathering,
  With greetings keen, are met—
All are not there of the olden time,
  And the heart doth not forget.

M. H. H. T.

MY LONGINGS.

I long for a breath of my native air,
With a perfume of flowers borne on the breeze,
And the sheltering shadows under the trees—
    I long to be there.

I long to roam by my native stream
As it ripples along 'neath the tall trees' shade,
And freshens all Nature down in the glade,
    Like my earliest dream.

I long for a glimpse of my once loved home ;
Peaceful its shelter, and lonely its bowers ;
I long for one of those moss-rose flowers
    In their fragrant bloom.

I long to rest in the quiet glade,
To wander at eve among mouldering graves,
Where the ivy creeps, and the tall grass waves
    By the ruin's shade.

But more I long for the living dead
To come to the fountain of life so free—
To hear the glad tidings for them and for me,
    What the Master said.

I long for more of Sharon's Rose,
To blossom there with His fragrant leaves ;
I long for the reaper to gather the sheaves
    That thy Father knows.

M. A. L.

LAMMERMOOR.

[The author of these lines was John Usher, son of Thomas Usher, shepherd, Byrecleuch, parish of Longformacus. Born in 1810, after a scant schooling, he was sent to herd sheep on the Lammermoors. About the year 1825 he entered the University of Edinburgh, bent on becoming a minister of the Secession Church. As a student he exhibited a marvellous amount of intelligence, and the professors took very kindly to the clever country lad, who, they said, knew almost as much as the most highly-trained town student. Before, however, young Usher reached the goal of his ambition, returning home on a snowy winter day, he caught cold, and died after a few hours' illness. He was buried in Melrose Churchyard. This was in 1829.]

> O Lammermoor, I love thee well,
> Each mountain brow, each hollow dell,
> Each craggy cliff, each rippling stream,
> Each fountain glimm'ring with the beam
> Of the fast-setting sun ; each scene
> Tells of what is, and what hath been.
> Oh, I could look on these for aye,
> Better than beautiful and gay ;
> Sublimely grand and roughly fair
> Stern Nature's majesty is there :
> The grey clouds swiftly passing by,
> The rainbow bursting on the eye
> In all the majesty of show,
> With every colour's richest glow :
> Or, when the mountain's giant form
> " Evanishes amid the storm,"
> And columned snow, by whirlwind driven,
> Hides the earth and veils the heaven ;
> And the loud fury of the wind
> Rouses the terror of the mind,
> And superstition's ghostly train
> Arise in all their strength again.
> These I love—on these to dwell,
> I know no thought I love so well :
> Whether in the summer's shine
> Or winter's mighty storm,
> Whatever's noble and sublime
> Is blended in thy form.

At evening fall, oh, let me still
Delight to linger on thy hill,
Or, enfolded in my plaid,
On thy heather lay my head,
And dream a thousand dreams of bliss
Of joy that knows no weariness,
Of warrior knight with iron glove,
Of rustic song and maiden love,
Forever with thee let me dwell—
O Lammermoor, I love thee well !

THE SABBATH.

[George Gilmour, the author of the following lines, was the youngest son of Peter Gilmour, mason at Edington—a small hamlet on the road between Chirnside and Berwick, in the former parish. He emigrated to America about the year 1833. The poem is copied from an old MS. volume in the possession of an aged inhabitant of Berwickshire.]

A Sabbath is a day of hallowed rest,
When all is peace within the unclouded breast ;
When the soul, panting for a loftier flight,
Views by faith's steadfast eye celestial light.
What though we tread not consecrated ground,
Nor hear a multitude's responsive sound ;
Nor priest with flowing vestment be our guide ;
Nor incense-breathing altar at our side ;
Nor burnished domes where thousand tapers gleam,
Nor turrets glitter in the moon-tide beam ;
Nor anthems swell the languid heart to warm,
Or soothe the senses with delusive charm —
Yet holiest worship owned by Him on high,
Such as alone can raise and sanctify,
May still from humble hearts accepted rise,
E'en from the dungeon where the captive sighs ;
From deserts where eternal silence reigns ;
From crowded cities, and from cultured plains ;
From boundless seas, or from the lonely isle,
Uncheered by love, and friendship's angel smile.

O

If in this little sphere of time and sense
Aught local could contain Omnipotence,
It were His own great works—these stately halls –
Of lakes, and hills, and rocks, and waterfalls ;
Whose deep, majestic shadows overspread
The waveless water slumbering on its bed.
In bright tranquillity all Nature glows,
She also has her Sabbaths of repose ;
The aspen leaf stirs not—the azure bell
Bends beauteously within the sunny dell ;
A solemn stillness—solitude profound
Breathes o'er the scene as it were holy ground.
Von little kirk so simple, poor, and low,
Where Sabbath melodies so sweetly flow,
May boast, begirt with Nature's grand attire,
An altar worthy of devotion's fire—
A temple more befitting prayer and praise
Than e'er the puny hand of man could raise.
And there, perchance, her worshippers are known
To Him, whose eye is on the heart alone ;
Who hail the joys of this Sabbatic day,
Joys which the world gives not, nor takes away—
So passionless, so peaceful, and so blest,
They seem the earnest of eternal rest !

LADY JOHN SCOTT.

B. 1810.

ALICIA-ANNE, eldest daughter of John Spottiswood, Esq., of Spottiswood, by his marriage with Helen, second daughter of Andrew Wauchope, Esq., of Niddrie, was born in the year 1810. On 11th March, 1836, she was married to Lord John Douglas-Montague-Scott, second son of Charles, fourth Duke of Buccleuch, who died 3rd January, 1860.

The family of Spottiswood have held for nearly four centuries a somewhat conspicuous place in Scottish history, and not a few of its members have achieved distinction in affairs of Church and State. The first of any importance is John Spottiswood, Parson of Calder and Superintendent of Lothian,[1] who in 1558 accompanied Lord James Douglas—afterwards the Regent Murray—to France to be present at the marriage of the young Queen of Scotland to the Dauphin. His son was the famous Archbishop

---

[1] " Which office," says an old historian, " he discharged with advantage to the Church, and with honour both to himself and to posterity."

Spottiswood, who in 1633 had the high honour of
crowning Charles I. at Holyrood, and who, two years
later, was advanced to the Lord Chancellorship of
the kingdom.   He is best known from his "History
of the Church of Scotland," a learned and judicious
work, full of sound judgment and diligent research.
The archbishop's son, again, was a celebrated
Senator of the College of Justice—Sir Robert
Spottiswood (Lord Newabbey)—a most scholarly
man, and the author of a well-known work, "The
Practice of the Law of Scotland," which has only
been superseded by the more elaborate treatises of
later times.   Other members of the Spottiswood
family have added to its reputation, and Lady John
Scott is still worthily maintaining the traditions of
her illustrious house.

As a writer of verse she takes a high rank.   Her
poetry is full of nature and the sweet scenery of her
Border home.   There is, too, a note of sadness run-
ning through it all, as if the writer were sighing "for
the touch of a vanished hand, and the sound
of a voice that is still."   Her style is in many
respects like that of another of Scotland's lady
song-writers — Lady Nairne — and there is much
justification for Sir George Douglas, in the dedication
of his "Minor Poets of Scotland," describing our
present poetess as the worthy successor of that noble
quartette—Lady Anne Barnard, Miss Jane Elliot,
Lady Grisell Baillie, and Lady Nairne.   Not only is
Lady John Scott the writer of the following beautiful
lyrics, but she is also the composer of their music,

and it is only proper to add that all her published songs have been sold in the interests of charitable organisations.

ANNIE LAURIE.

[Quite a controversy has been waged over the modern version of this well-known song. William Douglas of Fingland, in Kirkcudbrightshire, wrote the *old* version in honour of Miss Laurie of Maxwelton about the year 1700, of which the words are as follows :—

> " Maxwelton banks are bonnie,
>   Where early fa's the dew,
> Where me and Annie Laurie
>   Made up the promise true ;
> Made up the promise true,
>   And ne'er forget will I,
> And for bonnie Annie Laurie,
>   I'd lay down my head and die.

> " She's backit like a peacock,
>   She's breastit like a swan,
> She's jimp about the middle,
>   Her waist ye weel may span ;
> Her waist ye weel may span,
>   She has a rolling eye,
> And for bonnie Annie Laurie
>   I'd lay down my head and die."

But Fingland's lines are coarse, harsh, and unmusical. They have the ring of an old ballad, quaint and simple, but are too unrefined for modern delicacy. The new version, on the other hand, has a greater polish of diction, a freer, more natural grace, and a more tender pathos qualities essential to a lasting song. It was composed by Lady John Scott in 1835, while on a visit to her sister, Lady Hume Campbell, at Marchmont House. The tune had previously been written for an old ballad called *Kempye Kaye*, and was adapted to the improved and practically new song of *Annie Laurie*, now so universally known and admired.]

> Maxwelton braes are bonnie.
>   Where early fa's the dew,
> And it's there that Annie Laurie
>   Gi'ed me her promise true ;
> Gi'ed me her promise true,
>   Which ne'er forgot will be,
> And for bonnie Annie Laurie
>   I'd lay me doun and dee.

Her brow is like the snaw-drift,
  Her neck is like the swan,
Her face it is the fairest
  That e'er the sun shone on :
That e'er the sun shone on,
  And dark blue is her e'e,
And for bonnie Annie Laurie
  I'd lay me doun and dee.

Like dew on the gowan lying
  Is the fa' o' her fairy feet,
And like winds in summer sighing,
  Her voice is low and sweet ;
Her voice is low and sweet,
  And she's a' the warld to me ;
And for bonnie Annie Laurie
  I'd lay me doun and dee.

LAMMERMOOR.

Oh, wild and stormy Lammermoor !
  Would I could feel once more
The cold north wind, the wintry blast,
  That sweeps thy mountains o'er.
Would I could see thy drifted snow
  Deep, deep in cleuch and glen,
And hear the scream of the wild birds,
  And was free on thy hills again !

I hate this dreary southern land,
  I weary day by day
For the music of thy many streams
  In the birchwoods far away !
From all I love they banish me,
  But my thoughts they cannot chain ;
And they bear me back, wild Lammermoor,
  To thy distant hills again !

DURIS-DEER.

We'll meet nae mair at sunset, when the weary day is dune,
Nor wander hame thegether by the lee licht o' the mune ;
I'll hear your step nae langer amang the dewy corn,
For we'll meet nae mair, my bonniest, either at e'en or morn.

The yellow broom is waving abune the sunny brae,
And the rowan berries dancing where the sparkling waters play ;
Though a' is bright and bonnie, it's an eerie place to me,
For we'll meet nae mair, my dearest, either by burn or tree.

Far up into the wild hills there's a kirkyard auld and still,
Where the frosts lie ilka morning, and the mists hang low and chill ;
And there ye sleep in silence, while I wander here my lane,
Till we meet ance mair in heaven, never to part again !

KATHERINE LOGIE.

When the sun sets o'er the lily lea,
And the night is gathering silently ;
Oh, then my love I mourn for thee,
    My dearest Katherine Logie.

I wander awa' by the Heuch Wood Scaur,
And silently gaze at the evening star :
And I mind thy face that was bonnier far,
    My loveliest Katherine Logie.

The bird upon the forest tree,
Singing his wildest melody,
Had na a voice sae sweet as thee,
    My darling Katherine Logie.

The bright munebeam is no' sae fair
As the light that play'd on thy gowden hair ;
Waes me, I shall never see thee mair,
    My sweetest Katherine Logie.

Thou art far abune this warld o' pain,
Where I maun wander dull and lane ;
For the light o' my life wi' thee is gane,
    My dearest Katherine Logie.

To the depths of the sea!
Bright stream, from the founts of the west

It may be noted that Mr G. G. Napier for literary
material has traversed the haunts and countries of
Tennyson, Wordsworth, Cowper, and Byron, and, in
our own country, Scott, Carlyle, and Burns. Mr
Annan's (of Glasgow) chief coigns of vantage for
the taking of the panoramic view of Spottiswood demesne have been that part of the road
between "Steek the Yett" and Thorneydykes,
and the more high and distant promontory
of Hindsidehill (Mr Mill's) to the southward.
Lady John Scott, while in residence at Kirkbank,
used to make peregrinations into the wild fastnesses
of "Cheviot's mountains lone," for the purpose of
studying the wild scenery and collecting ballads and
traditions of that mountainous region. The result of
her investigations she embodied in her beautiful
song, "The Bounds o' Cheviot," which is as sweet to
the ear of a native of Cheviot as old Minstrel Burne's
(*circa* Charles II.) "Leader Haughs and Yarrow"
are to a Lauderdale man. The latter ballad was a
great favourite of Thomas Carlyle's, the great
historian and Scotch Borderer. According to
Emeritus Professor Masson, Carlyle was very fond of
quoting the concluding stanza—

"But minstrel Burne can not assuage
His grief, while life endureth,
To see the changes of this age,
Which fleeting time procureth;
For mony a place stands in hard case,
Where blyth folk kenn'd nae sorrow;
With Humes that dwelt on Leaderside,
And Scotts that dwelt in Yarrow."

In studying Carlyle's "French Revolution," I have
several times come across the quotation from "Leader
Haughs and Yarrow"—"Which fleeting time procureth." The flowery string of names, both in the
"The Bounds o' Cheviot" and "Leader Haughs and
Yarrow," as Mr Crockett comments on the latter in
his "Minstrelsy of the Merse," is very pleasing to
the men of the Border—to the "men of the south
countrie." We all know what impressive verse
Milton makes out of mere catalogues of localities.
We are charmed with the chanting verses which
embalm, as it were, the names of our country places,
and we love to hear them frequently awaken the
echoes.

"THE BOUNDS O' CHEVIOT."

Shall I never see the bonnie banks o' Kale again?
Nor the dark craigs o' Hownam Law?
Nor the green dens o' Chatto, nor Twaeford's mossy
    stane?
Nor the birks upon Philogar's shaw?
Nae mair! nae mair!
I shall never see the bounds o' Cheviot mair.

Shall I never watch the breaking o' the simmer day
Over the shouther o' the Deer Buss height,
When the Stainchel, and the Mote, and the flowery
    Bughtrig Brae,
Redden, slowly, wi' the mornin' light?
    Chorus—Nae mair! nae mair! &c.

Shall I never wander, lanely, when the gloamin' fa's,
And the wild birds flutter to their rest,
Or the lang, heathery muir to the bonnie Brunden Laws,
Standing dark against the glitter o' the west?
    Chorus—Nae mair! nae mair! &c.

Shall I never ride the mossy braes o' Heatherhope mair?
Shall I never see the Fairlone Burn?
Nor the wild heights o' Hindhope, wi' its corries green
    and fair,
And the waters twinkling down amang the fern?
    Chorus—Nae mair! nae mair! &c.

Shall I never win the marches at the Coquet head,
Through the mists and the drifting sna'?
Nor the dark Doors* o' Cottonshope, nor the quiet springs
    o' Rede
Glintin' bright across the Border far awa?
    Chorus—Nae mair! nae mair! &c.

* Lady John Scott-Spottiswood, the authoress,
explains that this is a curious rocky craig, a little
over the Fairlone Edge, well known to everyone in
that part of Cheviot—a great haunt of foxes.

WALTER LOCKIE.
Spottiswood, Lauder, 21st April, 1909.

THE FOUL FORDS.

The muirs and the waters remain !
  The road ower the brae
  We sae aft used to gae ;
But Jamie is gane !

And noo I gang wanderin' my lane !
  I keep frae them a',
  I've nae spirit ava,
Since Jamie is gane !

He'll ne'er come to Rathock again
  He's seen others ower fair,
  And he minds me nae mair,
And Jamie is gane !

Parting was never sae pain !
  For hope it was strang
  That it wasna for lang :
But Jamie is gane !

I ken that my grief is in vain,
  Yet my heart's like to break,
  wad die for his sake !
And Jamie is gane !

ETTRICK.

Oh, murmuring waters !
  Have ye no message for me ?
Ye come frae the hills of the west,
  Where his step wanders free.
Did he not whisper my name ?
  Did he not utter one word ?
And trust that its sound o'er the rush
  Of thy streams might be heard ?

Oh, murmuring waters !
  The sounds of the moorlands I hear,
The scream of the heron and eagle,
  The bell of the deer ;
The rustling of heather and fern,
  The shiver of grass on the lea,
The sigh of the wind from the hill,
  Hast thou no voice for me ?

Oh, murmuring waters !
  Flow on—ye have no voice for me ;
Bear the wild songs of the hills
  To the depths of the sea !
Bright stream, from the founts of the west
  Rush on with thy music and glee !
Oh ! to be borne to my rest
  In the cold waves with thee !

At a meeting of the Prim-
rose League, held in the Public Hall at Coldingham,
an address was given by Mr Fitzroy Bell, and the
following resolution was carried on the motion of Mr
Edington, Lumsdaine :—"That this meeting records
its renewed confidence in Her Majesty's Government,
and desires to express the hope that the war with
the South African Republic will be prosecuted with
continued energy, and that no settlement will be
arrived at which does not provide for the supremacy
of the Queen's authority."
Lady Sarah Wilson, who is abo...
writes the...

quoting the concluding ... of the ... Emeritus Profe... history ...

"But minstrel Burne can ...
His grief, while life endureth,
To see the changes of this age,
Which fleeting time procureth ;
For mony a place stands in hard case,
Where blyth folk kenn'd nae sorrow ;
With Humes that dwelt on Leaderside,
And Scotts that dwelt in Yarrow."
In studying Carlyle's "French Revolution," I have
several times come across the quotation from "Leader
Haughs and Yarrow"—"Which fleeting time pro-
cureth." The flowery string of names, both in the
"The Bounds o' Cheviot" and "Leader Haughs and
Yarrow," as Mr Crockett comments on the latter in
his "Minstrelsy of the Merse," is very pleasing to
the men of the Border—to the "men of the south

GEORGE PAULIN.

B. 1812.

GEORGE PAULIN was born at Horndean, in the parish of Ladykirk, 16th August, 1812. He was educated at the parish school and at Selkirk, till he entered the University of Edinburgh in 1832. Here he distinguished himself in more than one branch of study, winning, in particular, the friendship and admiration of Professor John Wilson ("Christopher North"). Having completed the required curriculum, young Paulin became successively parish schoolmaster of Newlands, in Peeblesshire, and Kirknewton, in Midlothian. In 1844 he was appointed to the important post of classical master and rector of Irvine Academy, Ayrshire, an office which he filled with the highest acceptance until his retirement in August, 1877. The work which he undertook to discharge at Irvine was a work which not one teacher in a thousand in those days would ever dream of attempting, even if he were competent to undertake it. For it required a careful understanding not only of the Greek and Latin tongues, but French, German, Italian, and Spanish also formed part of the curriculum. Besides, the rector at that time was expected to drill his pupils in the ordinary subjects of knowledge—arithmetic, grammar, and geography. When all this is considered, it will be apparent that Mr. Paulin is a man of no ordinary ability, but that he ranks exceptionally high as a scholar and

educationist. When he retired from the rectorship
his old pupils did not forget his services on their
behalf, and in proof of the esteem in which they held
him, presented him with a massive silver salver and
a cheque for £1000.

In 1876 Mr. Paulin published his only volume of
verse—" Hallowed Ground, and other Poems "[1]—
which was received with universal praise from the
press and public. The contents of this volume are
in two portions. The first consists of poems written
in early youth, long, long ago, when " North " and
the authoress of *Clanalbyn* swayed the magazine
literature of Scotland. The second portion is made
up of poems written in maturer years, and is chiefly
of a religious character. *Hallowed Ground*—the
principal contribution—gained the poetry prize in
Professor Wilson's class. It contains many elegant
passages, as it depicts in glowing language the power
of memory, hope, and imagination in hallowing spots
of earth. What is hallowed ground? is asked by the
mother, the lover, the patriot, the exile, the saint,
and each answers differently, yet truly. The poet
then enters the temple of Virtue and muses on the
deeds which have hallowed ancient Greece and
Rome, Helvetia and Britannia, dwelling fondly on
those of Scotia with all a patriot's enthusiasm, until
at length he is attracted to the land hallowed by the
footsteps of the incarnate Son of God—the most
hallowed ground on earth.

[1] 8vo. Edinburgh: James Taylor.

The poems that follow are not lacking in merit. Some of them are boldly conceived, are full of striking grandeur, and have the ring of true poetry. No analysis can convey their meaning—they must be read to be felt. In Mr. Paulin's minor musings he is intensely fascinating. He speaks in the simple but expressive language of common experience. There is something for all conditions of life—for prattling infancy, budding boyhood, mature manhood, the fresh, green prime, the whitening age.

His "Scotch poems" are probably his best. *The Covenant Sangs* inspires us with its deep feeling, and what heart has not bled at reading *Soun' Sleepin' Noo?* The whole realm of Scottish nursery literature, rich as it is, does not contain any sacred verses surpassing his tender, winsome *Baby Song.*

One characteristic of Mr. Paulin's verse is its wealth of religious feeling. He is a man of earnest piety, and this pervades his poetry as his life. He is a teacher of the highest righteousness. To be like Him who of old went about doing good is the grand motto of our singer, and he never fails to present this lofty ideal in thought and language of the purest tone.

As a Border man he reveals now and again a cherished love for the scenes of his boyhood. The ripple of the Tweed still rings in his ear, and as we read some of his fine descriptive scenery, our eyes unconsciously turn to the ivy-mantled wall of Lady-kirk Church, and the long row of tombstones in the churchyard beside it that bear the name of Paulin; we catch glimpses of Horndean village and the wooded braes and grassy haughs of Tweedside, all of which tell us that Mr. Paulin, notwithstanding his long residence in Ayrshire, is still a Borderer in spirit and affection.

To have written such as book as this of Mr. Paulin's—a book calculated to make men better and happier, to give them higher conceptions of the good, the true, the beautiful ; to teach them firmer trust in God and heartier love to man—is worth having laboured for—is not to have lived in vain.

THE TWEED REVISITED.

Oh, welcome, welcome, once again, my own, my native river !
The same calm, bright, blue wanderer, unchangeable as ever,
As when of yore on thy sweet banks, I thought the mighty sea
For wondrous width and soundless depth could hardly rival thee !

Thou singest still as when I heard, with hopes and feelings young,
First on thy bonnie primrose braes the water anthem sung,
And dreamed—a fond believing boy—it told of other years,
When maidens gazed from castle keep on glittering Border spears.

For with my infant lullaby was blent the mighty charm
Of song that told of Flodden Field and Randolph's potent arm ;
Of English blood, from Douglas' brand washed in thy azure tide ;
And all that Border minstrelsy has warbled on Tweedside.

The same wild song thou'rt singing now, the same wild witch-notes,
  burst
From memory's fount of melody, pure as they gushed at first,
When, innocent as thou, with brain unscorched by passion's fire,
To bound above thy sunlit waves was all my heart's desire.

I love thee, Tweed, with deepest love—though with no headlong shock
Thou fling'st thy flashing might of waves from foamy rock to rock—
Though thou hast not sweet Teviot's charm of haugh and heathery fell,
Nor Tay's far Highland solitudes, nor Clutha's water-bell.

I love thee, for thou wanderest through a land of song and beauty,
Where Loveliness is wooed by Truth, and Valour dwells with Duty—
A land of grey old castle walls and legendary lore—
A land of happy hearths and homes, where lances gleamed of yore.

I love thee, Tweed, for dear thou wert to Border minstrels' eyes
That often gazed with dreamy joy on thy sweet mirrored skies ;
Now dim the eye and cold the brow that wore the laurel meed,
And mighty Scott and Wilson sleep as erst they sung on Tweed.

I love thee, for thou art the same thou wert in days gone by—
The cloudlets of long years ago seem floating in thy sky !
And ne'er, my native stream, may change on thy loved borders be,
Till death shall darken from my eyes this beauteous world and thee !

BABY SONG.

Clap handies, bonnie wee thing, toddle up the brae,
Clap handies, toddle nearer, come, come away :
Daddy's wi' ye, mammy's wi' ye, nae ill can happen t'ye,
First ae fit, syne anither, toddle up the brae.

Clap handies, winsome wee thing, sune ye'll hae a hill
Ye maun set yer bonnie breast to wi' a right gude will.
Nae kindly hand to guide ye, muckle evil may betide ye,
But there's Ane will help my wee thing up the thorny hill.

Toddle up, my winsome wee thing, there's a hand aboon,
There's an e'e, a kindly e'e, watchin' late and sune,
There's a kindly ear to hear ye, and a kindly voice to cheer ye,
And a kind, warm heart is beatin' for my babe aboon.

Hear Him say, my bonnie wee thing, " Come to Me an' rest,
Rest within thy Saviour's arms, lean upon His breast ;
Up the brae I'll safely lead thee, wi' the bread o' life I'll feed thee,
First ae fit, an' syne anither, come to Me an' rest."

IT'S NO WORTH THE WARSLE FOR'T.

It's no worth the warsle for't
  A' ye'll get on earth,
Gin ye haena wealth aboon
  Mair than warl's worth.

It's no worth the lootin' for't
  Pickin' up a croon,
Gin ye haena in yer heart
  Arles o' ane aboon.

It's no worth the time it taks,
  Biggin' on the sand ;
Better be a bairnie yet
  Ridin' on a wand.

It's no worth a body's while
  Coortin' fame and glitter,
'T only maks the aftercome
  Unco black and bitter.

It's no worth the fisher's heuk
  Fishin' here for pleasure,
Gin we canna coont aboon
  Freends an' hame an' treasure.

SOUN' SLEEPIN' NOO.

He's soun' sleepin' noo, Willie,
  The warsle's ower wi' him,
The spraichle an' the hoast are ower,
  The bonnie e'en are dim.

We'll lay him i' the mools, Willie ;
  But, oh ! we'll think on Johnny,
No 'mang the worms and clammy clay,
  But 'mang the angels bonnie.

For haena we the blessed word,
  "Wha sleep wi' Me shall live?"
An' weel we ken his tender heart
  He to the Lord did give.

Then gang yer ways to bed, Willie,
  Oor weary watchin's past,
An' dinna look upon his face
  As ye would look yer last.

We'll ken the face aboon, Willie—
  Oor bonnie bairnie's face ;
He'll aye be oors and Jesus' too,
  Within God's holy place.

Kiss his cauld face aince mair, Willie,
  His thrabbin' broo's at rest ;
He never mair ken pain or wae
  Upon the Saviour's breast.

AUNTY'S SANGS.

I mind me fu' weel o' the blithe spinning wheel,
  An' the Covenant sangs o' the Auld Scottish Kirk ;
An' Aunty that sang to the birr o' her reel,
  I' the sweet gloamin' 'oor 'tween the daylicht an' mirk.
Though aftentimes eerie, we never were weary,
But liked when oor Aunty said, " Listen, my dearie."

She'd mony a rhyme o' the Covenant time,
  O' the mosses an' muirs where the brave martyrs fell
In dark days o' yore, when to pray was a crime,
  And the red blude o' saints was the dew o' the dell.
Tho' aftentimes eerie, we never were weary,
But liked when oor Aunty said, " Listen, my dearie."

But Aunty is gane, an' I croon a' alane
  O'er the lilt that was wed to the birr o' the reel ;
The bonnie birk waves o'er the cauld grave stane,
  But her spirit's awa' to the Land o' the Leal.
An' noo I am eerie an' dowie an' weary ;
I'll ne'er again hear her say, " Listen, my dearie."

RETROSPECT.

Where'er by isle or continent we roam,
In dreams we visit o't our childhood's home,
Though bleak its clime, and savage rocks arise
To cleave the cloudy terrors of its skies,
We know no place so dear, so sweet, so fair
As that which held our grandsire's old arm-chair.

At gloamin' hour we'd saunter by the stream
With Crusoe's tale or Bunyan's wondrous dream,
Or watch the westering sun refulgent steep
Its ball of fiery splendour in the deep.

Eve's sober grey our happiest daytime brought,
The ingle nook with eager feet we sought,
When tales of Eld were told or sung in turn
Of Border raids, of Bruce at Bannockburn,
Of haunted glens, of ghost-bestridden wight,
Of persecution's cold and stormy night
When Covenant men crept close to God in prayer,
Or hemmed by flashing spears stood calmly there.

God's blessing asked—the evening meal appeared—
A simple meal that satisfied and cheered ;
The psalm was sung, the Word with reverence read,
In heartfelt prayer all bent the lowly head.

O blithe springtime of youth ! how quickly flew
Your gales of fragrance and your skies of blue ;
Ye summer hours—days of romance and rhyme.
And russet autumn, life and labour's prime.
Till grey October, Nature's cloudy thief,
Stole the last lingering beauty of the leaf,
And wheeled in fitful gusts around my path
Winds heralding the howling winter's wrath.

Yet all in changing psalm sing Thy behest
Eternal Love.   Thy will is ever blest :
Who hears Thy voice and knows Thee as Thou art
In darkest hour has sunshine in his heart.

REV. JAMES BALLANTYNE.

B. 1820.

THE Rev. James Ballantyne succeeded the Rev. John Steuart Giffen as eighth minister of the West U.P. Church at Earlston. He entered the Divinity Hall in 1843, studying with distinction under Professors Lindsay and MacMichael, and was ordained at Earlston on 24th May, 1848, where he continued till 3rd September, 1850, when he was translated to Arthur Street Church, Edinburgh. This charge he demitted on 21st November, 1854, and proceeded to Australia, where he became colleague to the Rev. J. M. Ramsay, of Melbourne. He was known in Earlston as an eloquent and popular preacher, a faithful pastor, and a much-attached friend. He is the author of " Temperance Tales for Young Readers," "The Book of the Mother," and he edited for some time the *Juvenile Missionary Record* of the United Presbyterian Church. The following lines were written by him on reading the death-scene of a famous American free-thinker :—

THE DYING INFIDEL.

See'st thou that wretched man ?
  Cold sweats are on his brow ;
For but another hour to live
  He'd part with worlds now.

'Tis he whose puny arm
  Was late on high upreared,
The God of heaven to defy—
  That God by angels feared.

'Tis he who lately swore,
  With curses loud and deep,
The faith of saints from off the earth
  At one fell blow to sweep.

'Tis he whose impious boasts
  Defiled the very air,
Whose deeds were dark as hell itself,
  Who every crime could dare.

Behold him ! conscience now
  Asserts her awful sway,
And now he feels that he must die
  And meet the judgment day.

A thousand fearful thoughts
  His tortured bosom throng ;
O God, what living agonies
  To Christless souls belong !

Still hotter grows the strife,
  Still darker grows the hour,
Still fiercer burns the hell within :
  'Tis Satan's time of power.

Hark, how he groans—he cries—
  See how he gasps for breath ;
A curse is on his lips—he dies—
  It is the second death.

Young men, beware in time,
  Pride's fond delusions shun ;
Repent, believe, embrace the cross—
  Cling to the Saving One.

ANDREW WANLESS.

B. 1824.

FROM Longformacus, the "capital of Lammer-moor," have come two of our county's sweetest singers — Andrew Wanless and his gifted sister. They are now far from the old land and the familiar scenes of infancy, yet none the less cordially are they welcomed to these pages from their homes across the Atlantic.

Andrew Wanless was born 25th May, 1824, in the old school-house of Longformacus. His boyhood days were passed in this region of romance and story. Scott has made it the scene of his "Bride of Lammermoor," and the whole district is full of historical associations. He tells a good story of his pious-minded mother with reference to the death of Scott. "I have," he says, "a vivid recollection of my father's intense grief when the tidings of Sir Walter Scott's death reached him. He was an ardent admirer of the novelist. The mind of my mother, however, was strongly tinctured with Calvinistic doctrines, and she regarded the matter in a very different light. 'Houts, guidman,' said she, 'he's weel awa'. He was just fillin' the heads o' the folks fu' o' doonright havers!'"

At an early age young Wanless was sent to school, and received the usual education of the time which was supposed to fit a lad for almost any business. But Nature was perhaps his chief educator. "My keenest pleasure, in early life," he writes, "was found in wandering about my native land, visiting romantic haunts and burnsides. I was always of a studious and retiring disposition, enjoying the society of Nature more than that of man." After quitting school he served a seven years' apprenticeship as a bookbinder in Duns, and then removed to Edinburgh, where he obtained a situation as foreman in a large bookbinding establishment. In 1851 he emigrated to Canada, and after an unsuccessful venture at his trade of bookbinding in Toronto, he removed to Detroit, where he commenced business as a bookseller. In this he has been highly fortunate, and is now one of the best known and most respected citizens of the great Western Republic. He has published several volumes of poems, and in 1891 he issued a collection of "Sketches and Anecdotes" dealing mostly with the old home life, which has been very favourably received.[1]

Mr. Wanless is a true Scottish poet. He has been called the Burns of the United States. He writes in the "guid auld mither tongue" of his native land, and has a very wide circle of admirers in his adopted country. The memory of the past is his central theme. He is carried back to "auld Scotia," and returns laden with the wealth of her military and literary fame, with recollections of his youth and courtship, of the school and the "lonesome kirk"

---

[1] "Sketches and Anecdotes," by Andrew Wanless. 8vo. Detroit, 1891: Wanless. Pp. 300.

with the "auld kirkyard." It is no wonder he
breaks out into singing—

> "O ! let us ne'er forget our hame,
>   Auld Scotland's hills and cairns,
> And let us a', where'er we be,
>   Aye strive 'to be guid bairns.'
> And when we meet wi' want or age
>   A-hirpling owre a rung,
> We'll tak' their part and cheer their heart
>   Wi' our auld mither tongue."

This, then, is the power that has made him a genuine
poet of Scottish life and character, and for this
object he has written and sung so acceptably—"to
link the present with the past—to recall the
scenes of our early years—to bring up, in
imagination, the braw lads and the bonnie lasses
that we forgathered with in the days of the lang
syne, and attempt to describe, on this side of the
Atlantic, the wimpling burns, the gowany braes, the
bonnie glens, the broomy dells, and the heather-clad
mountains of our native land—the land where
Wallace and Bruce wielded the patriotic sword, and
where Ramsay, Burns, Scott, Tannahill, and many
more sang the songs of love and liberty."[1]

Our Mither Tongue.

[Read before the St. Andrew's Society, Detroit, 30th November, 1870.]

> It's monie a day since first we left
>   Auld Scotland's rugged hills—
> Her heath'ry braes and gow'ny glens,
>   Her bonnie winding rills.

[1] From Preface to "Poems and Songs." 8vo.   Detroit, 1878.

We lo'ed her in the by-gane time,
  When life and hope were young,
We lo'e her still wi' right guid will,
  And glory in her tongue !

Can we forget the summer days
  When we got leave frae schule,
How we gaed birrin' down the braes
  To daidle in the pool?
Or to the glen we'd slip awa
  Where hazel clusters hung,
And wake the echoes o' the hills—
  Wi' our auld mither tongue.

Can we forget the lonesome kirk
  Where gloomy ivies creep?
Can we forget the auld kirkyard
  Where our forefathers sleep?
We'll ne'er forget that glorious land
  Where Scott and Burns sung—
Their sangs are printed on our hearts
  In our auld mither tongue.

Auld Scotland ! Land o' mickle fame !
  The land where Wallace trod,
The land where heartfelt praise ascends
  Up to the throne of God !
Land where the Martyrs sleep in peace,
  Where infant freedom sprung,
Where Knox in tones of thunder spoke
  In our auld mither tongue !

Now Scotland, dinna ye be blate,
  'Mang nations crousely craw,
Your callants are nae donnert sumphs,
  Your lasses bang them a'.
The glisks o' heaven will never fade
  That hope around us flung—
When first we breath'd the tale o' love
  In our auld mither tongue !

O ! let us ne'er forget our hame,
  Auld Scotland's hills and cairns,
And let us a', where'er we be,
  Aye strive " to be guid bairns !"
And when we meet wi' want or age
  A-hirpling owre a rung,
We'll tak' their part and cheer their heart
  Wi' our auld mither tongue.

THE SCOTT CENTENARY.

[Read at the Banquet, Russell House, Detroit, 15th August, 1871.]

A hundred years have rolled away,
This morn brought in the natal day
Of one whose name shall live for aye.

Beside the clear and winding Forth
Was born the " Wizard of the North !"
The Muses circled round his bed,
And placed their mark upon his head ;
And Nature sang a grand refrain
As Genius claimed his wondrous brain,
For every bird in bush or brake,
Beside the silv'ry stream or lake,
Sang blythly on their leafy throne,
In honour of the " Great Unknown !"

The thistle raised its drooping head ;
The lark forsook his heather bed,
Shook from his wing the dew-drop moist,
And on the golden cloud rejoic'd ;
The classic Tweed took up the lay,
The Yarrow sang by bank and brae.
And Ettrick danc'd upon her way,
The daisies by the crystal wells
Smiled sweetly to the heather bells ;
And rugged craig and mountain dun
Exulted he was Scotia's son !

Time sped, and from that brilliant brain
There issued many a martial strain
He sang of knight and baron bold,
Of king and clown in days of old—
Though dead and gone, and passed away
Forgotten in the mould'ring clay—
We read, we trow, his magic brain
Brings back the dead to life again !
He sang of men who ne'er would yield
In Border fray or battle field.
Yes ! on the page of endless fame
He wrote of many a deed and name ;
How patriot heroes dared to die
For God, for right and liberty !

We see the beacon on the hill,
The slumb'ring earth no more is still,
For borne upon the midnight gale
The slogan's heard o'er hill and dale,
The din of battle and the cry
That echoed through the vaulted sky,
As warriors fell, and rose and reel'd,
And died on Flodden's fatal field !

The minstrel loved auld Scotland's hills,
Her gow'ny braes and wimpling rills,
He loved the land that gave him birth—
A land beloved o'er all the earth ;
There stood the brave in weal or woe,
Who never crouched to foreign foe—
Who stood in battle like a rock,
And snapped in twain the tyrant's yoke !

O ! Scotland, thou art dear to me !
Thou land of song and chivalry !
There Scott and Burns, and many more,
Did pencil Nature to the core—
There Wallace held the foe in scorn,
And Scotland lives in Bannockburn !

And every patriot, far or near,
In foreign land, or Scotia dear,
In castle proud, or lowly cot,
Reveres the name of WALTER SCOTT !

———

A SCOTCH SANGSTER'S COMIN'.

On Monday, in St. Andrew's Ha',
Rally ! men and brithers a',
Send the news baith far and near—
A Scottish Sangster's comin' here !
Deck'd fu' braw in Highland kilt,
He will sing us monie a lilt
'Bout auld Scotland's heath'ry hills,
Birken glens and wimplin' rills,
Where the lav'rocks sweetly sing,
Where the bonnie blue bells spring.
Hame ! we'll ne'er forget ava
'Till our latest breath we draw.

While the daisy decks the lea,
Scotia's sangs will never dee—
Floating down time's silent river,
Time and they will die together ;
Send the news baith far and near,
A Scottish Sangster's coming here !
Nane like him our sangs can han'le—
He's the lad to haud the can'le ;
Sangs o' Scotland he will sing,
Will make the very rafters ring ;
Sangs o' dule and dark despair,
Will mak' us rug and rive our hair,
Sangs wi' monie a weary mane,
Wad melt a very heart o' stane :
Sangs o' love, o' joy, and fear,
Heartfelt words forever dear.

Come, ye lasses blythe and braw,
Welcome to St. Andrew's Ha'!
His funny cracks will mak' for weeks
The tears rin down your bonnie cheeks.
Folk ! ye manna stay at hame,
That wad be a burnin' shame
Send the news baith far and near,
A Scottish Sangster's comin' here.

THE MEN O' THE MERSE.

Air—"Laird o' Cockpen."

Where the Watch and the Dye and the Whitadder rins
Doon to the Tweed where auld England begins ;
There lived the heroes, that whither or no,
Wad fight for their country and lounder the foe.
In the front o' the battle, sae gallant and true,
The Merse Men were there wi' their bonnets o' blue ;
The tyrants we read o' in prose and in verse
Ne'er wanted *twa strokes* frae the Men o' the Merse.

The Men o' the Border ! no tyrant could scare,
They ne'er run awa though the Percy was there,
When Liberty trembled, they never knew fear,
They aye did their best wi' the sword and the spear.
The Men o' the Border ! auld England kens weel,
Are made o' guid stuff frae the head to the heel,
At the war cry, " A Douglas !" the foe would disperse,
In terror they'd flee frae the Men o' the Merse.

How sweet are the haughs and the glens o' the Forth !
How grand and majestic the hills o' the North !
The Clansmen may brag o' their big Lochnagar,
But our bonnie Tweedside is sweeter by far.
Our lasses are sweet as the rose o' the bower,
Ye'll no find their match in the warld out-ower,
And men wha in English or Gaelic converse
Maun a' knuckle doon to the Men o' the Merse !

LAMMERMOOR.

Air—"Mary's Dream."

The heather blooms upon the knowes,
  Primroses spring in bielded dells,
The gowans smile on bank and brae,
  Amang the blue and bonnie bells.
Down o'er the rocks the burnies fa',
  They toddle on, they rin sae pure,
Through birken bowers and yellow brume
  That fringe the glades in Lammermoor.

The lark sings in the lift sae blue,
  The mavis sings upon the tree,
While lowly on the milk-white thorn,
  The robin chirps wi' gladsome glee.
I'll never see Auld Scotland mair,
  Misfortune's cloud does o'er me lour,
Nae mair I'll hear the linties' sang
  Amang the hills o' Lammermoor.

Yet there, in death's cold, cold embrace,
  Lies ane I'll ne'er forget to lo'e,
Through weal and woe her gentle heart
  To me was constant, kind, and true.
Our sindered hearts are in ae grave,
  Yet I maun still my griefs endure,
By day I mourn, by night my dreams,
  Are in her grave in Lammermoor.

JESSIE WANLESS BRACK.

B. 1826.

JESSIE WANLESS was born 30th September, 1826. Her early years were passed in the village of Longformacus. It was a happy period, and the memory of it pervades her song. But youth cannot always remain; the sterner business of life must be faced, and so we find our poetess at the age of nineteen in Edinburgh "keeping house" for her brothers, George and Andrew. Then death came to the old school-house, and she had to return home to take her mother's place in the family. "As the years sped along, one by one dropped from the family circle to make homes for themselves, the laughter of children passed from the auld hame, our dear father died, and the school-house was ours no longer." Several of her brothers and sisters had emigrated to Canada, and, together with her two youngest sisters, she also resolved to cross the Atlantic. "We landed," she writes, "in Quebec on 2nd October, 1866. I have now been in this country over twenty-six years, and I have never revisited the old land; but my thoughts fly often to bonnie Scotland —'to bonnie Scotland ayont the sea.'

> "'Yes, I long for a sight o' the heather bells,
> And a sound o' the wimpling rills,
> And a long, long breath o' the caller air
> That's blowin' on Scotland's hills.'"

Miss Wanless married in 1868 Mr. George Brack, a well-to-do farmer on the Huron River, Ontario.

Her poetry is full of the old home-life and the recollection of youthful days in " sweet and pastoral Lammermoor." She writes with bewitching grace, and the expression of all her songs is just what one might expect from a tender, sympathetic, womanly heart.

AMONG THE LEAVES SO GREEN.

Come to meet me, Nellie,
  When all Nature's clad in green,
Meet me in yon bonnie glen,
  Where often we have been.
I'm fain to sing a song to thee
  Wi' glints o' love between,
For lovers' songs are sweetest
  Down among the leaves so green.

Then come to meet me, Nellie,
  When the gentle breezes blaw,
Come down yon bonnie burn side,
  And through the birken shaw ;
And I'll be there before you, love,
  To watch your gracefu' mien,
When ye come to meet me, dearest,
  Down among the leaves so green.

Oh, come to meet me, Nellie,
  For the birds are singing sweet,
The mavis and the missle thrush
  Hae found out our retreat.
Oh, list the love-songs that they sing ;
  Yes, these at least are dear,
With all Nature for a chorus,
  In the spring-time of the year.

Then come to meet me, Nellie,
  For the flowers are blooming fair,
We'll wander through the woodlands wide,
  And gather clusters rare.
The sweetest flowers among them a'
  Shall deck my heart's ain queen,
For the blossoms are aye sweetest
  Twined among the leaves so green.

CHRISTOPHER DAWSON.

B. 1826.

CHRISTOPHER DAWSON is not exactly a Merse man in the stricter sense of the term, as having been born in the county, but from his long and intimate connection with Berwickshire he has a strong claim to be included among its poets. He came in 1830 with his parents to live at Coldstream, and in this ancient Border town, in the midst of its beautiful scenery, and within easy reach of many historic scenes, his boyhood and youth were passed. There can be no doubt that the nature of these early surroundings has done much to influence his character and work. It was here he acquired that keen appreciation and love of Nature which is so marked a feature in his writings, for even to this day he finds congenial employment in picturing through his verse the charms of fair Tweedside. Educated at Coldstream Parish School, he was there trained as a pupil teacher, and entered upon the work of his life in 1844 as assistant English master in Madras Academy, in his own native town of Cupar-Fife. His work here was no easy task, but success followed the enthusiasm and high purpose that nerved him on. Greatly to the regret of his pupils and the many friends he had made, he accepted in 1846 an offer to become master of Abercorn School, a picturesque village by the Firth of Forth. For forty-three years Mr. Dawson made this place his home. He quickly gained the goodwill of the people, and specially attached himself to the young men of the district, aiding and encouraging them in their work, and suggesting many plans for self-improvement. On his retirement in 1889 he received, at the hands of the Earl of Hopetoun, a handsome presentation from his friends and former pupils in the shape of a complete silver tea service and a purse of sovereigns.

Apart from his immediate professional duties, Mr. Dawson has found time to devote himself to other active work. He is a popular lecturer on historical, literary, and scientific subjects, and is a most acceptable platform speaker. He is fond of geological and antiquarian research, and has contributed several interesting papers on discoveries made by him to the Society of Antiquaries of Scotland. [See Transactions, Session 1876-7.] This love for research led him to gather together a very interesting collection of curios, relics, geological specimens, etc., which is being constantly added to; and occasionally there comes, even from distant lands, some much-prized contribution from an old pupil who has not forgot "the master's museum." Mr. Dawson is a Fellow of the Edinburgh Geological Society and the Educational Institute of Scotland.

In 1891 he published a volume of poems,[1] the

---

[1] "Avonmore and other Poems." London: Nisbet. 8vo.

fruit of leisure moments throughout many years. "Avonmore," which gives to the book its title, is the longest poem, and has a distinct claim to superior merit. The scene is laid in and near Coldstream, and the subject may fittingly be termed the history of a soul. It is a spiritual biography, finely conceived, touchingly expressed, full of lofty sentiment, and appealing to the highest emotions of man's nature. It tells of the gradual rising of a soul from the depths of the most horrible despair to a strong, exulting faith in the vital truths of the Christian religion. The life hid with Christ in God is shown to be no vain empty dream, but the most perfect form of life. True religion is the only real source of satisfaction for the troubled soul. God reigns, and the example of His Son is *the one* incentive to lead men upward to the completeness of true being. This is the grand lesson the author seeks to teach, and he has accomplished his task in a style at once meritorious and effective. Mr. Dawson's poems are all more or less on religious themes, and in each there is the ring of genuine poetry. And he, too, like George Paulin, has not forgot the Borderland. The Tweed at Coldstream and the old town are full of tender memories, and through the mists and gloom of more than fifty years he can look back on the sweet vision of his early life when he based his manhood on the determination to pursue the path of piety, to live for others, and thus to better the earth. As he very fittingly sings, so has he striven to realise the ideal that—

Life has a goal,
  A purpose and a prize—
Love welling out to guilt or woe,
  Love quickened from the skies,
Living for men, easing their load,
Leading their footsteps on to God !

TO THE TWEED AT COLDSTREAM.

I cannot turn, O Tweed, from thee,
  I lingering look behind ;
Yet all have sunk into the past
  That link thee to my mind ;
For what hath time now left to me
But memories of love and thee?

Thy waters roll as proudly now
  As when I was a boy,
And still unchanged thy sunlit scenes
  That gave my life its joy ;
I see along thy winding shore
The dear old spots just as of yore.

But where are they who played with me,
  Who made this holy ground,
Whose names are whispered by the breeze,
  And echoed all around?
I hear their voices rise to-day
Like angel music far away.

And they who taught my troubled soul,
  'Mid doubt's o'erwhelming strife,
To feel not time, nor yet the grave,
  The omega of life?
O from yon cloud-land let them rise,
And bless me 'mid my tear-dimmed eyes.

Thy silver willows swinging still,
   In cadence to thy song,
Press amorous kisses on thy waves,
   As swift they glide along;
While down beneath their shadows rest
A softer forest in thy breast.

How strange, O Tweed, thy magic power
   Fills all around with friends,
And ties long snapped by widening years
   Rejoin their broken ends;
The past returns, and on thy shore
My childhood days I live once more:

For, looking on thy sunny waves,
   All wrapped in flickering gold,
I throw away the rust of years,
   And feel not that I'm old;
And long-lost joys each spot invest,
And clothe all in a golden mist.

Hope smiled on sunny waters then,
   With rapture in her eye,
And all around, where'er I turned,
   A glorious earth and sky,
And life was wreathed in gorgeous beams,
Yet pure as holy angels' dreams.

The dews of life's young morning fell
   So soft on Hope's young root,
That none e'er dreamed such promise fair
   Would yield such bitter fruit,
Or prove our lives a chess-board game,
Victor or vanquished all the same!

O life! O vanished years and dreams!
   Where heaven, were you to last?
Your loves were blessed angel-guests,
   And these, O Tweed, are past;
And in dear memory's hallowed land
They move a silent shadow-band.

Away regret!   Life has a goal,
  A purpose and a prize,—
Love welling out to guilt or woe,
  Love quickened from the skies,
Living for men, easing their load,
Leading their footsteps on to God !

———

THE ROSE.

I gave a rose unto my love,
  Bright dreams my bosom swelled ;
I yearned it might an angel prove,—
  It was my all she held.

Leaf after leaf she tore away,
  The winds some sighing bore ;
While others scattered round her lay,—
  It was my hope she tore.

Her dainty feet toyed with them there,
  Then pressed them in the sod ;
I watched her in a wild despair,—
  It was my love she trod.

She bent the stem, it snapped in twain,
  A hell within me woke ;
I shuddered 'neath its burning pain,—
  It was my heart she broke.

WILLIAM TELFORD.

B. 1828.

WILLIAM TELFORD, for many years a respected resident of Smith, Peterborough, Ontario, is a native of the Merse, and was born at Leitholm, 6th January, 1828. He was sent to school in his seventh year; but on account of the long and serious illness of his father, which completely incapacitated him for work wherewith to provide for his family, he was compelled to relinquish his school life at the age of ten and join his brothers in their employment during winter of digging drains, and in summer of assisting them in a brick and tile yard. "But the severe labour he was forced to perform," writes one who knows him well, "did not crush out his aspirations for mental improvement. He rose superior to his prosaic environments, and triumphed over conditions that would have brought discouragement or plodding content with ignorance to a less aspiring soul. Day after day, in the rare intermissions of arduous toil, he strove, though but a child, with the energy and determination of a man to improve his mental condition. He had neither books nor means to procure them, and he had consequently to rely on the kindness of neighbours, who sympathised with his longings, and the scanty supply of books their cottage shelves contained; and in the long winter evenings he was to be seen sitting in the ingle-nook of his mother's cottage poring over some odd volume. In prose the books to which he had access were such works as Bunyan's ' Pilgrim's Progress,' Baxter's ' Saint's Rest,' Boston's ' Four-Fold State,' ' Josephus' History,' ' Hervey's Meditations,' ' Afflicted Man's Companion,' and such books—one would think, the least alluring in their ponderous sanctity to the lively temperament of youth. In poetry, Burns was his chief favourite, although Pope, Moore, Montgomery, Tannahill, and other poets were conned by him with diligent delight." At the age of twenty-two young Telford emigrated to Canada, where he has followed agricultural pursuits with marked success ever since.

During these many years, however, in spite of much hard, active employment, Mr. Telford has not been idle with his pen, and the fruit of his leisure moments was given a few years ago to the public in the shape of a large volume of his selected poems, which has been very cordially received by a wide circle of friends and readers who appreciate his talents and worth.

As a poet William Telford occupies no mean position. From humble circumstances he has risen to worldly comfort and prosperity. Yet he never forgets the old land and the hardships of life's young day. He looks back with a feeling even of pride to the dark and cheerless past, and knows right well that those times of trial have but proved the discipline of his life that present joys are but the result of the courage and indomitable perseverance then implanted in his soul.

SCOTIA'S HEATHER.

Yes, he brought it.   I have got it,
  Can you guess what it might be?
It's the heather John did gather
  On Auld Scotia's hills for me.

First he pu'ed it, then he viewed it,
  With its blossoms' varied hue,
Paper folded, therein rolled it,
  Saying, " Bill, this is for you."

When I took it, how I looket
  At the sprig I so well knew;
Silent blessed it, almost kissed it,
  For the sake of where it grew.

When I showed it, yes, they knew it,
  Every Scotchman that I met;
Fast they held it, and they smelled it,
  O! its scent they won't forget.

We adore it, true Scots wore it
  In their Highland caps of yore,
Their foes feared it as they neared it,
  Highland blood the heather bore.

Time has tried it, blood has dyed it,
  Yes, the best in Scotland shed;
They prayed on it, and laid on it
  Oft the martyr's dying bed.

You may prize it or despise it,
  As your inclination be ;
Don't annoy it or destroy it,
  'Tis a precious gem to me.

Yes, I have it, I will save it
  While its twigs will hang together ;
Time will move them, but I love them—
  Both Auld Scotia and her heather.

THOMAS MILLER.

B. 1831.

THOMAS MILLER, author of the well-known lyric, *My Heart aye Warms to the Tartan*, was born at Duns in April, 1831. His mother was maid to the wife of General Maitland, and his father also held employment in the Maitland family. When four years old he removed with his parents to Dumbartonshire, and then to Glasgow, where he got an ordinary school education. Entering a printer's establishment, he came much in contact with books and readers, and a perusal of Shakespeare awakened in him the poetic fire. He has now written many stirring songs, which have been set to music and sung in the principal theatres and music-halls of Scotland.

MY HEART AYE WARMS TO THE TARTAN.

O Scotland! country of my birth,
  My heart clings close to thee
As clings the tendril of the vine,
  And ivy to the tree.
The glorious East, the boundless West,
  The sunny South's rich charms
Are poor to him who Scotland loves —
  Whose heart the tartan warms!

    My heart aye warms to the tartan,
     And wheresoe'er I roam,
    The tartan kilt and plaid I'll love
     As dearly as my home.

Dear Scotland ! how thy memories crowd
  Within my fervent soul,
Thy fame shall make thy sons feel proud
  While years and ages roll ;
Unconquered in the grand old days
  By proud Imperial Rome,
And still we've tartan warriors left
  To guard our native home.

   My heart aye warms to the tartan, etc.

Our lion-hearted Wallace fought
  For home and freedom's sway,
And Scotch claymore and battle-axe
  Won many a glorious day.
And to the Bruce—great warrior king !—
  Our hearts shall ever turn,
For long as Scotland lives we'll sing
  The praise of Bannockburn !

   My heart aye warms to the tartan, etc.

On many a hard-fought battle-field
  Our tartan'd braves have bled
Like heroes, died before they'd yield,
  But never yet have fled.
On Alma's heights " the thin red line "
  Made e'en the bravest stare,
And Lucknow's March has taught the world
  What Highlanders will dare.

   My heart aye warms to the tartan, etc.

Long may the rose of England twine
  With Erin's shamrock green,
And long may Scotland's thistle wave,
  And lion flag be seen.
God grant our land the joys of peace,
  But should the war-blast roar,
The tartan kilt will to the front,
  And conquer as of yore.

   My heart aye warms to the tartan, etc.

THOMAS HAPPER.

B. 1835.

THOMAS HAPPER, like many of our Berwick-shire bards, is a member of the teaching profession, and diligently pursues his calling at the hamlet school of Millburn, near Duns. He was born at Earlston in 1835, and began life as a pupil-teacher in the old Free Church School of the village—now long defunct—then under the care of the Rev. Ebenezer Ritchie, who had been minister of an old Secession congregation in the Orkneys—"one of the saintliest of men," as Mr. Happer has styled him. Quitting Earlston, the young poet-teacher was appointed to a school in Ayrshire, but resigned this that he might further qualify himself for the work of his life by attending the classes in the University of Glasgow. This done, a round of teaching followed at various places—Smailholm, Coldingham, etc.—till finally he became settled in his present situation, a quiet nook at the foot of Cockburn Law, not far from the winding Whitadder.

Mr. Happer has written much good, sterling poetry, and has contributed largely to local journals on matters of general interest, but as yet no volume bears his name. Long may he wield the "kindly ferule" and the facile pen.

THE PARTING.

The pearly tear stood in her eye
  Like dewdrop on the violet blue,
The gentle girl breathed a sigh—
  She meant to say, " A fond adieu ! "

I kissed away the gath'ring tear,
  And pressed her beating heart to mine,
Then gently whispered, " Maiden, dear,
  Though absent I am ever thine.

" Thy parting tear I'll ever see,
  I'll ever hear thy farewell sigh,
Till, met again, my fate shall be—
  With thee to live, with thee to die.

" Can I forget how oft we've barred
  The world without, at evening hour ;
Adown the grove with sloping sward,
  And through the gate, and in the bower?

" The leafy branches o'er us hung,
  The moonbeam kissed the flashing stream,
The woodland breezes round us sung,
  And time passed like a fairy dream.

" The hours on moment's wing flew by,
  Till night too soon crept o'er the hill ;
We parted with the mutual sigh,
  And frequent kiss, that meant no ill.

" Oh, these are hours I'll ne'er forget,
  And scenes that must be ever dear ;
Too deep on mem'ry's page they're writ
  For ruthless time to cancel here.

" His hand may crop our leafy bower,
  And parch the stream meand'ring by,
And veil the moon : but vain his power
  To hide them from my fancy's eye.

" What though 'mid distant scenes I rove,
    Or haply cross the briny main,
We'll bind the knot of truthful love,
    The more to knit the more we strain.

" So does the mighty chain that binds
    The vessel to the wave-lashed shore—
The more the straining, tost large winds,
    The faithful noose slips fast the more.

" And when to other lands I'm gone—
    Though lashing seas between us fret
Oh, think, dear, on thy absent one,
    And know *he* never can forget.

" List not the wretch in friendship's garb
    Who hints my fond regard shall cease ;
He comes with doubly-pointed barb
    To steal thy heart and wound my peace.

" But we must part—the hour is come ;
    Stern fate now tolls our parting knell,
And calls me to an alien home,
    But still my heart with thee shall dwell.

" Part ! did I say ? how can it be ?
    True love's a being of the heart,
Our hearts are one ; then, dearest, we
    United thus can never part."

CHRISTIAN CHARITY.

(1 Corinthians XIII.)

Love bears long without repining,
    Ever gentle, ever kind ;
Love knows not the cold designing
    Envy frameth in the mind.

Love disowns all rash presuming,
  Arrogates no selfish praise;
Love is facile, unassuming,
  Prompt *another's* fame to raise.

Love, ingenuous and lowly,
  Ne'er is puffed with pride elate;
Love, disdaining ways unholy,
  Cultivates a seemly gait.

Love would fill a neighbour's coffer
  Rather than increase its own;
Love its only gem would proffer
  To adorn a brother's crown.

Love ne'er frets, nor ill devises,
  But delights in kindly ruth:
Love iniquity despises,
  But rejoices in the truth.

Love, all hardships meekly bearing,
  Trusts that good in all things lies:
Love is hopeful, ne'er despairing,
  Suffers all things, never dies.

ROBERT M'LEAN CALDER.

B. 1841.

ROBERT M'LEAN CALDER was born at
Duns in November, 1841. While yet a child
his parents removed to the village of Polwarth, and
it was here, amid the romantic scenes of the old
historic hamlet, that his love for the beautiful in
Nature was nurtured and his thoughts first shaped
themselves in verse. His education was begun at
the "bairns' school," kept up by the late Lady Hume-
Campbell, and afterwards continued at the parish
school. "The three R's," he writes, "were as far as
I got ; for at the age of nine I hired out at the farm
of Raecleughhead in the humble occupation of
'herding craws,' varying this with cutting thistles or
gathering rack." During this time, and later on
when herding sheep on the moors by Kyle's hill, he
supplemented the meagre education he had received
by taking his books with him to the fields and hillside. Whatever literature he could find was eagerly
devoured, and in this taste for knowledge he was
most generously encouraged by his parents, who
were both of more than average intelligence. Called
from the hillside to serve his apprenticeship to the
drapery trade with an uncle in Duns, he further
improved his education by attending evening classes
and studying music under the late Rev. D. Kerr, who

was one of the pioneers in the introduction of the Sol-fa system into Scotland. It was during this time that he first ventured to contribute to the local press, and the editor being kindly, he felt encouraged to further effort. Upon the conclusion of his apprenticeship he went to London, having obtained a situation in a leading drapery establishment, and in 1866 we find him emigrating to America and settled in Canada. Here he had great scope for his literary abilities, and during his residence in the country he was a constant contributor of verse to many weekly and daily newspapers. The *Scottish-American Journal,* a paper which has done much to foster the literary taste of Scottish-Americans, published a large number of his songs and other writings.

After remaining for some years in the town of Chatham, Ontario, he had, through ill-health, to relinquish his business and return to the old country. This was in 1882, and from that time he has resided in London, being now associated in business with his brother.

Several of Mr. Calder's songs have been published, and have had a wide circulation. For two poems he received gold medals from the St. Andrew's Society at Ottawa. In 1887 he published a small volume of verse under the title of " Hame Sangs,"[1] which has been very favourably reviewed by the press at home and abroad.

---

[1] London: 4to.

WHEN THE DAYS ARE CREEPIN' IN.

The simmer flowers are withered,
　The simmer winds are gane,
An' yellow leaves lie scattered
　On upland an' in glen ;
The burnie lilts sae dolefu'
　As its drumlie waters rin,
An' the sun curtails its glances
　When the days are creepin' in.

The stacks hae a' been thackit--
　We've laid aside the plough,
The tatties a' are howkit,
　An' the simmer dargs are thro',
An' noo beside the ingle,
　In the neuk sae snug an' clean,
Sae canty we foregather
　When the days are creepin' in.

Noo winter's comin' surely,
　Wi' cauldrife win's an' snaw,
We're thankfu' for oor biggin',
　Altho' oor cot's but sma',
We envy na the riches
　Sae mony try to win ;
We hae oor simple pleasures
　When the days are creepin' in.

An' for the helpless outcasts
　We never grudge a bite,
We're fain to gie them shelter
　Frae the nippin' winter's nicht ;
For we think o' oor ain laddie
　Far frae a' his kith an' kin,
Amang strangers may be fendin'
　When the days are creepin' in.

Auld age comes on us creepin',
  For oor simmer days are past,
An' sune we maun be sleepin'
  Amang the mools at last :
But yonder, where oor hame is,
  Free frae a' stains o' sin,
There will be nae cheerless winters
  When the days are creepin' in.

POLART BURN.

The frost has nipt the heather bloom,
  The brackens hing their dowdie leaves—
The hips are red upon the brier,
  An' paitricks whirr amang the sheaves :
Nae mair the bees roam o'er the muir,
  Or, laden wi' their sweets, return.
As I, to sniff the cauler air,
  Stray up the glen by Polart burn.

Here mony a happy day we spent,
  When we were laddies at the schule :
We sought the heather-linties' nest,
  Or gump'd for mennents in the pool :
We wist nae hoo the time sped on,
  Until we heard the cowboy's horn,
Yet, laith to lea', we linger'd on,
  'Till gloamin' fell o'er Polart burn.

We've wander'd 'mang the heather knowes,
  When frae oor feet the muir-cock whirr'd,
Or wander'd by the lower haugh,
  Where first the cuckoo's note was heard :
Syne hameward we would tread its banks,
  To watch the moss-grown mill-wheel turn.
Or note the foamin' mill-race rush
  To blend its flood wi' Polart burn.

R

There, wi' the love oor boyhood knew,
    We wander'd—prodigal o' time—
When eyes were brighter, lips mair sweet,
    Than ever met wi' in oor prime ;
Noo sad the memory that comes back—
    Its brightness never can return—
An' phantom hopes float 'mid the haze
    That e'ening brings o'er Polart burn.

The schuleboy friendships then begun
    Hae still grown closer year by year,
Tho' a' oor mates are scatter'd wide,
    In cauld nor'-land, or southern sphere :
But scarce a simmer time comes roun'
    But ane or ither maun return,
To see ance mair their native hame
    An' boyhood's haunts by Polart burn.

An' noo, amid the city's stir,
    The busy mart and crowded street,
Aft will my fancy wander free
    Ilk shady nook and calm retreat ;
Or as beside my fire I sit,
    Inclined o'er bygane joys to mourn,
The sunny glints come back again,
    Whene'er I think o' Polart burn.

———

THE AULD SCHULE HOOSE ON THE GREEN.

Oh ! weel I remember the schule hoose
    That stood fu' snug 'neath the trees,
Where the blaeberries grew in the plantin,
    An' the heather invited the bees ;
Where the bairnies' voices rang merry,
    As wi' faces an' daidlies sae clean
They scampered awa' thro' the bushes
    To the auld schule hoose on the green.

Oh! I mind when mysel' a bit laddie—
  When life wore its sunniest smile—
How blythely wi' licht heart I lilted,
  As I scampered through hedge-slap an' stile ;
Or climbed the scrogg tree in the meadow —
  Or waded the burn clear an' sheen—
Tho' aften I loitered ower late for
  The auld schule hoose on the green.

Still mem'ry delights to dwell upon
  The scenes o' those happiest days,
The burn where we gumpit for mennents :
  Or the blue bell and gowan-clad braes
Where we twined flower wreaths for the lasses ;
  For Mary, an' Lizzy, an' Jean,
Wha ilka morn toddled there wi' us
  To the auld schule hoose on the green.

Oh! I mind o' that wee theekit schule hoose
  Wi' the rose bushes grown at the door,
An' the apple trees in the wee gairden,
  Wi' bonnie white blossoms hung o'er.
The desks where we scribbled our copies,
  Or oftener, ate sweeties unseen,
While the lasses were clippin' and shoowin'
  In the auld schule hoose on the green.

An' still aft' I think o' the plantin
  Where the geens an' the blaeberries grew,
For aften we've sat there an' feasted
  Till our faces an' daidlies were blue ;
An' our legs wi' the whuns were a' scartet,
  But whilk we ne'er cared for a preen,
We were blythe as the lambkins that sportit
  Near the auld schule hoose on the green.

An' weel can I mind how we huntit
  The squirrel high up the fir tree,
Or the young cusha doo that had ventured
  Oot the nest afore it could flee.

Where we shunned the deep well where the hunter
  Had fa'n in, and ne'er was mair seen,
When the bell ca'd us back frae oor sportin'
  To the auld schule hoose on the green.

Oh, aften I think o' these playmates
  Noo scattered far, far frae their hames—
Where the laddies still search in the plantin
  For the trees where we cut oot oor names,
While they tell ane anither the story—
  That in many a strange foreign scene
Are the laddies wha were years before them
  At the auld schule hoose on the green.

I ken na if e'er I may wander
  Again by that auld cherished spot,
But those bright cludless hours o' my childhood
  An' those playmates shall ne'er be forgot.
While deeply engraved on my mem'ry
  Shall aye be each fair hallowed scene,
As in fancy I aften shall linger
  By the auld schule hoose on the green.

ROBERT PRINGLE.

B. 1841.

ROBERT PRINGLE was born at Duns in 1841, and, educated at the parish school, was for a time a pupil teacher therein. After passing with distinction through the training college at Edinburgh, he was appointed Latin master in Forfar Academy. He is now settled near Manchester as the head of a large educational institution. He has published several scholastic works of high merit, and is well known as a writer of verse full of thought and of graceful expression, such as befits a cultured wooer of the Muse.

THE VIRTUE WELL.

[A mineral spring in the neighbourhood of Duns.]

O'er-branched with waving shadows,
  Within a grassy dell,
Beside the virtue water
  Springs the virtue well.
In days of old we loved it,
  We love it now the same :
And on the dome above it
  The school-boy carves his name.

On early morn in summer,
  At dewy evening too,
Boys and girls we wandered
  Where the rushes grew,
We drank the healing waters
  Flowing from the well,
And laughing, homeward sauntered
  Our happiness to tell.

The old men from the village
  With tottering footsteps came
To sip the cooling fountain :
  The young men did the same.
And as the tinted sunset
  Yellowed all the dell,
Young maidens, too, came singing
  And tripping to the well.

And often when the moonbeams
  Softly fell from heaven,
And from the day's dull labour,
  Rest, sweet rest, was given.
Lovers met beside it
  To tell each others' love,
When nought could hear their story
  But the pale moon above.

Sunny, sunny memories !
  Ghost of joys gone by !
'Tis sweet to revel in dreamland,
  Yet still it brings a sigh ;
Mayhap the past was sunshine,
  The future sleeps in shade,
And pleasures, fondly tasted,
  Bloomed, but again to fade.

JEANNIE DODDS.

B. 1849.

JEANNIE DODDS was born in 1849 at Hills-house, in the parish of Channelkirk, where her father was the farm grieve. While yet a child the family removed to Fifeshire, settling in Kirk-caldy. At the age of twelve she entered a draper's establishment as a message girl, rising by her industry and perseverance to be head of the dress and mantle-making department. After fourteen years' service she commenced business on her own account, and has been highly successful. She is a frequent contributor to the local newspapers under the *nom-de-plume* of "Ruth." Her poetry is sweet and simple, displaying true depth of feeling, such as alone could proceed from the tender heart of a loving and sympathetic woman.

A MOTHER'S TEST.

There lay in the palm of a mother's hand
  A beautiful bunch of flowers,
And she said to herself, "I will try the strength
  Of this darling child of ours."

The little one bounded forth with a smile
  On her radiant, dimpled face,
And a chubby, soft, white hand held out
  With innocent, childish grace.

Just as she touched the stem of the flowers
  The mother closed her hand,
And the little one pulled, and pulled in vain—
  She could not understand.

The mother did not wish to withhold
　　The flowers from the child that day—
But to test the power of the little one's faith,
　　And the strength that in her lay.

Like children we reach out eager hands
　　For gifts kind Heaven denies :
But an unseen hand is holding them fast
　　Just to test what in us lies.

If we got all we longed for, and never were crossed,
　　Our hearts would grow selfish and vain ;
The finest of gold by the fire is refined,
　　And pleasure made purer by pain.

FRIENDSHIP.

In this bright world the storm succeeds the sunshine,
　　E'en midst our laughter, burning tears may blend ;
How sweet to think that on the earth's broad surface
　　There is some faithful soul whom we call friend.

What is a friendship? is it something subtle?
　　Like fragrance from a flower in shady nook?
Or just a sentiment to please the fancy—
　　Something existing only in a book?

A friend worth having must be noble, truthful,
　　Not one whose time is passed in dreams and myths ;
We want a friend high-souled and full of purpose,
　　Not one whose promise breaks like Samson's "withes."

True friendship is a gift direct from heaven,
　　Something that knits true souls in sympathy ;
Firmer than bands of gold the tie that binds them,
　　Each almost moulds the other's destiny.

In this bright world where death and separation
　　Make things too dark for us to comprehend,
Who has not felt just at life's darkest moments
　　The value of this heaven-sent gift　a friend?

GEORGE DEANS.

B. 1851.

A TRUE son of the Merse, George Deans was
born at Sisterpath Waukmill, in the parish of
Fogo, in 1851. The farm of Angelrow, a few miles
westward, was for many years tenanted by his
maternal ancestors—the Lyalls. From the banks of
the Blackadder his parents migrated to the village of
Wark, on Tweedside, in the northern corner of
Northumberland, where his boyhood was passed.
Here the usual varied experience of young Rusticity
fell to his lot: cow-herding, crow-herding, and the
wild, free delights of the fields in all seasons. The
murmur of the Tweed may be said to have made
music in his earliest dreams. From Wark the boy
was sent to Kelso, where he spent a few years in a
commercial sphere. But this kind of life being
unsuited to his inclinations, he made his way to
Glasgow when still a youth, and there, after a course
of arduous self-education, secured a position as
newspaper reporter. Mr. Deans is now a member of
the editorial staff of the *Glasgow Citizen*, the oldest
and most influential evening journal in the country.
In 1890 he produced a volume of poetry under the
title of "Harp Strums,"[1] which, savouring largely of
the famous Borderland, has been most cordially
received.

[1] 8vo. Kelso: J. & J. H. Rutherfurd.

HUME CASTLE.

Years and the blasts of war have wrecked thy form,
Old Time has hushed thee into dreamless sleep,
Silent and lonely on thy craggy steep:
Thou heedest not the fury of the storm,
Nor summer winds that o'er thy ramparts sweep.
No record tells of all the deeds thou'st done,
Yet any simple hind may guess thy story,
When, musing at the setting of the sun,
He sees thee looming through a cloud of glory,
And marks the scars upon thy visage hoary.

Of old thou wert the sentinel of the Merse:
When hordes on havoc's errand crossed the Tweed,
Quick was thine eye, thy valiant sword gleam'd fierce,
The trumpet called thy sons to doughty deed,
The lion rampant from thy turrets waved,
And peers and peasants, in their martial pride,
Rose up to guard thee round on every side—
Brave-hearted men who would not be enslaved.

Between the Cheviots and the Lammermoors
Thou kept thy watch defiant,
A grim unyielding giant,
Whose glance could range the far Northumbrian shores.

Strong foes have pressed and girdled thee about,
And leapt upon thy breast to lay thee low,
Then backward reeled from thy avenging blow,
Bleeding and broken, a disordered rout,
With valour songs all sunk to groans of woe !

Within the compass of thy sombre shadow
War, like a fiery storm, has roared,
And carnage has not sheathed his sword
Till heaps of slain lay red athwart the meadow !
And, wreathéd in a cloud of battle smoke,
Oft hast thou trembl'd on thy stubborn rock.

No more thou wakest at the clarion call,
Thou watchest for no foe by day or night :
The grip of ruin holds thee in its thrall,
Time with his shears has shorn thee of thy might.
Thy sleep is in an atmosphere of peace !
A drowsy village nestles at thy feet :
On thy green slopes the flocks, in snowy fleece,
Find grassy shelter from the noonday heat ;
The daisies cluster 'neath thy ample shade :
The shepherd there at gloaming woos his maid,
And whispers to her heart the old, old vow !

In thy decay thou still art beautiful !
No pennon floats from thy grim turrets now,
But summer flowers, with richest fragrancy,
Climb up thy rugged sides in fair array,
And hang in rosy garlands round thy brow !

In the wide Merse thou art a cherished feature—
No lifeless mass of crumbling stone and lime ;
To us thou hast become a part of Nature,
And old almost as anything of time !

A bearded host no longer owns thy rule,
But troops of children give thee high command,
When, homeward wandering on their way from school,
They linger 'mong the gowans round thy base,
And raise their laughing eyes up to thy face.
And call thee King of all the Borderland.
The peasant, far off, at his cottage door,
Tir'd with the heavy labours of the day,
Looks forth and sees thee—then he dreams of yore,
And warlike pageants that have pass'd away ;
He gazes at thee till his eyes grow dim—
A wizard from grey Eld thou art to him.

DARLINGFIELD.

Fair Darlingfield ! sweet Darlingfield !
Thy very name a joy can yield ;
At peace within thy cosy bield
   Among the woods o' Mellerstain.

How green the meadows round thee lie,
How blue above thee is the sky ;
The lark, upsoaring joyouslie,
Pours down his liquid song to thee.

I see the shepherd 'mong his sheep—
The flock is browsing, half asleep ;
A cushat murmurs in the trees ;
The clover grass is thronged with bees ;
A wimpling brooklet softly glides,
And charms the flowers that deck its sides :
Young winds that love the solitudes
Are wandering through thy shadowy woods.

'Tis June.   Thy cottages are bright
With woodbine, roses red and white :
And all about them, in the sun,
From morn to eve the children run—
Wee prattling things, with sunny hair,
That rob the hind of half his care.

Under a leafy beechen tree,
That throws a pleasant shade for me,
I lie and linger at mine ease,
And with quaint thoughts my fancy please.
Forgetting life's absorbing fray,
When summer gives me holiday.

Fair Darlingfield ! sweet Darlingfield !
Thy very name a joy can yield ;
At peace within thy cosy bield
    Among the woods o' Mellerstain.

BIRGHAM BOWERS.

Oh, bonnie are the Birgham bowers
Where the white haw blossom hings ;
Oh, bonnie are the bountrie trees
Where the thrush in simmer sings.

There Tweed rins clear, an' whispers
To the winsome nodding flowers,
As if she fain wad linger aye
By Birgham's bonnie bowers.

There first I met my dearie,
There, folded to my breast,
My gentle blue-eyed Jeannie
To me her love confest.

'Tis there we'll meet this evenin',
When shines the cludless moon,
Aneath the fragrant bountries
I' the balmy breath o' June!

O Birgham bowers, sae bonnie,
To me will aye bloom fair :
But fairest far, sweet lassie,
When thou art wi' me there.

AGNES MACK DENHOLM.

B. 1854.

AGNES MACK, of a worthy old Lammermoor family, was born at Abbey St. Bathans, 24th February, 1854. Her education was received at the parish school, and at the age of fourteen she entered domestic service. In 1888 she married Mr. William Denholm, overseer on the farm of Abbey St. Bathans, where she still resides.

Mrs. Denholm has written some really charming verse, which is deserving of a wider publicity than it meantime has. Her poetry is characterised by sweet simplicity of diction, and a certain tenderness of tone which can hardly fail to touch a responsive chord in the heart of the reader. In the *Legend of Lammermoor* the ancient ballad style has been faithfully imitated, and her other effusions prove their writer to possess, in no mean measure, the soul of a genuine poetess. We look forward to seeing, by and by, Mrs. Denholm's musings in a more tangible form.

A LEGEND OF LAMMERMOOR.

There lived a laird in Blackerstoune,
　And he had daughters fair to see ;
The youngest was plighted to Gibbie Craig,
　Wha lived in the west countrie.
Now Gibbie Craig has mountit his steed—
　Ane coal-black steed was he—
And he has ridden frae Lauderdale
　Fair Alison to see.

But when he had crossit the Edra's tide,
  And breistit the heather brae,
He saw a sight, in the fair munelight,
  That made his heart fu' wae.
There stood before him a goodly youth
  By the lanesome Butter Well.
And closely claspit in his arms
  Fair Alison hersel'.

He's loupit doun frae his charger then,
  An angry man and a grim;
Nae word spak' he to Alison,
  But turned to the youth sae slim.
He's pu'd out his dagger sae keen
  In the twinklin' o' an e'e,
And he's thrust the blade up to the hilt
  In that fair youth's bodie.

" My malison on ye, Gibbie Craig —
  An ill death may ye dee,
For ye hae slain my ae brither
  That was aye sae dear to me.
My faither had banishit him frae hame
  Away to the north countrie,
Because that he lovit a weel-faured maid
  Without either lands or fee :

" And he trystit me to meet him here
  By the lanesome Butter Well
Me, wha had been his only frien'—
  Ane secret to me to tell.
Alas ! alas ! my brither dear,
  Your secret I maun tyne,
But the hand that now has shed your blood
  Shall ne'er again touch mine."

He pu'ed his beard, he tore his hair,
  Doun on ane knee he fell.
And he prayed her sair to forgi'e him there,
  E'er they left the lanely well.

But she turnit away and left him there
  To dree the weird o' Cain ;
And nae mair by Edra's bonnie banks
  Was Alison seen again.

But for lang, lang years ane ghaistly form
  Hauntit that lanely well,
And waitit aye for Alison,
  His secret to her to tell.
And mony a ane run frightit hame
  When they the ghaist had seen ;
And men's knees did shake, and their hearts did quake,
  When they passit the well at e'en.

But after many lang, lang years
  The *Northern Mercurie*
Tauld of the death of Alison,
  And the weird that she did dree.
Now, whether it was the ghaist did read
  The *Northern Mercurie*—
I cannot tell ; but never again
  To the hauntit well came he.

But it well might be that where spirits meet,
  When they leave this warld o' care,
He had met wi' his sister Alison
  And tauld her his secret there.
Unawed the maids of Blackerstoune
  May roam the wooded dell ;
But never now is the water brought,
  Frae the lanesome Butter Well.

AFTER MANY YEARS.

Oh, do you mind the days, Jean,
  When you and I were young ?
When love's bewitching glamourie
  Was first around us flung ?

The joyous sun shone aye so fair,
  The birds so sweetly sung,
In that enchanted spring-time
  When you and I were young.

But clouds came o'er the sun, Jean,
  I thought ye false to me ;
And aye the rift was widened
  By artful trickery.
And tales were told to you, Jean,
  By that same spitefu' tongue ;
And so our hearts were sundered,
  When you and I were young.

Since then I've struggled sair, Jean,
  Some warld's gear to win ;
And seas have rowed between us,
  In shadow and in sun.
And ye are left your lane, Jean,
  To fight your bairns among ;
And we have met again, Jean,
  When we're nae langer young.

But though our hair is grey, Jean,
  Our hearts are warm and true ;
And happy days have dawned, Jean,
  At last for me and you.
And Jamie, Jock, and Janitie
  Shall rove the woods among,
And mind us o' the days, Jean,
  When you and I were young.

THE following pages comprise a number of writers of verse, who, although not natives of Berwickshire, have yet passed a considerable part of their life in the county, and may therefore be regarded as having some claim to recognition in the present work.

REV. CHARLES MILLER.

1811-1891.

THE Rev. Charles Miller spent half a century of his career in Berwickshire, thirty-eight years of which as minister of the United Presbyterian Church, Duns. He was born at Thornliebank, Renfrewshire, in 1811, and was educated at the parish school, Glasgow University, and the United Secession Divinity Hall. In 1841 he accepted a call to Duns as colleague to the Rev. John Robertson. After the long period of nearly forty years' active and faithful service, he demitted his charge in 1879 and retired to private life. He died, 12th June, 1891. As a preacher, Mr. Miller had great natural gifts. He possessed the true spirit of his calling, and by his polished, eloquent appeals attracted large congregations, while in private life he won for himself a large measure of popular esteem. He published in 1857 his only prose work, " Magdalene Nisbet, the Maiden of the Merse : A Tale of the Persecution of Charles the Second's time," which was cordially received. It is full of characters, incidents, and scenes of special interest to Berwickshire readers. Possessed also of true poetic genius, Mr. Miller from time to time contributed numerous poems to contemporary journals, and in 1882 he published a selection of these with the title, " The Three Scholars, and other Poems."[1]

[1] 12mo. Edinburgh : Elliot.

DUNS LAW.

We walk beneath the music of the lark,
Charming the ample ear of the lone sky.
Our lips are silent, oft we pause to hark
His clearer warblings flowing murmurous by.
And now the cloistering sylvan stripe is nigh,
Through which the panting path winds elevate ;
We climb, and frequent pause to feast the eye
At points of vantage ; now, with hearts elate,
We tread the springy hill beyond the wicket gate.

Welcome, once more, dear mount of solitude !
Loved tower of happy sights and musings.   Here
We mingle with a blessed brotherhood
Of trees, flowers, bees, and other objects near :
And with yon hills, and that cerulean sphere,
We move among the speechless, yet we talk —
Not by the tongue, but by the eye and ear —
With all that charm us, on this airy walk !
Down from the kingly sky to every blooming stalk.

This hill recalls the Past ; these slopes, that brow,
Were once alive with armed thousands, who,
Scorning beneath a tyrant king to bow,
Who strove their Rights of Conscience to undo.
Came hither, and unrolled their banners blue
In the Invader's face.   On yonder mound,
Whose camp-like lines still draw the curious view,
Stood Leslie's tent, and in great rings around
Ran tents and warriors over all the embattled ground.

Since then two hundred years have stamped their changes,
Few on this hill, but many o'er that plain ;
As the pleased eye discovers while it ranges
O'er ground once waste, now rich in grass and grain,
And decked with recent wood, and tower, and fane,
And that old Border town's new-fledged wings
Nestled among yon trees, through which the train.
Waving its smoky pennon, weird-like springs,
Like some huge dragon on its daily journeyings !

How sweet the air tastes on this goodly top!
How swift the eye flies o'er that pictured vale!
Like a young eagle, joying in the scope
For his strong wing. Hail, ye green pastures! hail,
Ye brighter corn-fields hued with emerald pale!
And hail, ye woods, from whose embowering shades
The stately mansion towers! Hail, clouds, that sail
With the soft summer shower, and come like maids
Who bring the fountain to the thirsty leaves and blades.

And hail! ye scenes of ancient Border war!
Ye Cheviot Hills, that gaze stern Flodden o'er!
And thou, Hume Castle, in the west afar
And Berwick town, dim on yon eastern shore—
Ah! once ye flowed with streams of human gore!
And war rang round you also, Eildons three;
But you, brave builders of the days of yore,
And Thomas True, beneath the fairy tree,
And Scott, have crowned with nobler immortality!

Lo! now the sun with western brilliance breaks,
And sullen Cheviot, smit as with a spell,
All down his side, with radiant laughter shakes;
And bloomed with splendour is his vaward dell,
'Gainst which the purple peak of Yeavering Bell,
And all her sister peaks, in clear outline,
Loom forth. O, light and shade! what muse can tell
With what a magic pencil ye define
The distant, formless mass, and make dull chaos shine!

The vale of Tweed a molten river washes,
Which, lake-like, o'er the distant east expands.
A thousand panes are bright with fiery flashes,
And every blade burns o'er the emerald lands.
How King-like in the glare huge Twisel stands!
And Berwick town, though thou art far away,
Standing obscurely on Northumbrian sands,
We see, amid the dazzling western ray,
White waves and sails flash brilliant o'er thy azure bay.

Good night ! brave, healthful hill ; and may the morn
Be not far distant when again our feet
Will walk amid the violets that adorn
Thy grassy brow.   Be oft-times our retreat,
Blessing our hearts, and pouring river sweet
Of bracing air through all our panting veins :
Raising our spirits to the mercy-seat
With thankfulness to Him, who loving reigns,
And round us pours the bliss of skies, and hills, and plains !

CHARLES PHILIP GIBSON.

1820-1888.

CHARLES PHILIP GIBSON was born in Leith in 1820, but, on the death of his father, he went to live in Northumberland, and received his early education at Wooler. Returning to Scotland he entered a lawyer's office in Edinburgh, and at the same time attended classes in the University with a view to becoming a barrister. His health, however, giving way, he turned his attention to agriculture. For over sixteen years he farmed Foulden West Mains, and in the district was, along with his first wife—a sister of Professor Marcus Dods—highly respected for his kind and genial disposition, and the keen interest he took in the welfare of the people around him. In 1862 he retired to Edinburgh, where he held several offices of trust in connection with benevolent institutions; then he removed to Dundee, and again to Leeds, where the remainder of his life was spent. He died suddenly on 3rd March, 1888.

In 1876 he published anonymously, through Messrs. Edmonston & Douglas, Edinburgh, a poem in four books, to which he gave the title of *Cheerfulness.* Pleasantly written, in the style of Goldsmith's *Deserted Village,* it is full of country life and the sweet scenes around Foulden, and is no mean contribution to the richness of Berwickshire minstrelsy.

From CHEERFULNESS.

Lo! Scotland's beauteous Merse enchants my eyes,
Where in calm loveliness fair Foulden lies:—
Dear scene of varied as of countless charms,
Fair woods embrace thee with their shelt'ring arms,
Nature round thee her gayest mantle flings,
While with her purest melody she sings;
With myriad flow'rs adorns the dewy ground,
And bids their blended fragrance breathe around:
Yes, earth thro' her wide realms few spots can show
Where more of Eden's charms still ling'ring glow.

Home of my happy youth!—Affection's seat,
My heart fond lingers near thy blest retreat,
And oft in musing mood I pensive mourn
O'er friends long lost who never can return;
While mem'ry's tones their forms so clear recall,
The heart is fain to let the curtain fall.

Methinks I see thee on thy em'rald mound
Which lofty trees with spreading boughs surround—
Far to the south our ravish'd eyes behold
A cultur'd plain immense its charms unfold—
(No fairer landscape boasts our lovely isle!)
Innum'rous fields as one great garden smile,
Tweed's classic stream meanders thro' the plain,
Gleams the bright grass, and waves the yellow grain:
The lordly hall 'mid wide-spread woods displayed,
The snug farm-house in homelier charms array'd,
The sacred spire, the churchyard, hallowed spot!
The ancient castle, and the poor man's cot,
All these, sweet blent in shadow and in light,
Refresh the heart while they regale the sight,
While, far remote, rise shadowy on the view,
The hoary Cheviots robed in misty blue.

Sweet Foulden! as on thee I lift mine eyes,
Bright'ning from out the past thy varied scenes arise:—
The modest church in ivy-robes array'd,
Round which in gambols whisp'ring breezes play'd,
High branching elms circling the still churchyard,
Where countless graves upheave the dark-green sward,

The sombre yews, like guardians of the dead,
Cast friendly shadows o'er their lowly bed,
While high in air the crows' tumultuous sound
In plaintive murm'ring music floats around.
    Hard by the churchyard wall, in sylvan shade,
The rural manse in mingled charms array'd
(Blest both by art and nature) gleams in view,
'Mid flow'rs of every scent and ev'ry hue.
    Sweet Foulden ! loveliest of the rural scene,
The trysting-place where all the charms convene,
Thee my fond heart with loving pride surveys,
Blest with the charms that bless'd my early days,
While em'lous art her utmost effort tries,
And to adorn thee e'en with Nature vies.
    The humblest cot has charms around its door,
Flow'rs on the air their blended fragrance pour :
I see thy features as of old displayed —
The joiner's shed where piles of wood were laid,
The dame-school (ivy-clad) whose cheerful din
Told of the youthful scholars rang'd within,
The village shop and post-office combin'd
Once dear to all—squire, farmer, cottar, hind ;
The parish school, whose tumults surging high
Startled the ear of strangers passing by,
While in the dreamy sunshine lay serene
(Soothed by the trees' deep shade) the village green :
The blacksmith's cot, with gorgeous ivy drest,
By woodbine, rose, and jessamine caress'd,
Smil'd like a bow'r, where e'en 'neath summer's ray
Noon's light shone, shaded, like to twilight grey.

REV. ROBERT NAISMITH.

1822-1891.

THE Rev. Robert Naismith, for over thirty years
an esteemed Berwickshire minister, was born
near Lesmahagow on 4th August, 1822.   He had the
advantage of a pious parentage, and received a
moderate education at various schools. The first years
of his active life were spent in clerking and teaching.
In 1841 he entered the Arts classes in Glasgow
University, and having passed through the Divinity
Hall of the Reformed Presbyterian Church, after
several broken and intermittent sessions, he was
licensed to preach.   In 1861 he accepted a hearty
and harmonious call to the pastorate of this denomin-
ation at Chirnside, where he continued, abundant
in labours of usefulness to his congregation and the
surrounding district, until his death on 31st January,
1891.   In 1847, whilst a teacher at Kirkintilloch, he
published a volume of verse entitled " Necropolis,
and other Poems," which met with a cordial welcome.
He wrote also a small collection of " Moral and
Social Songs for Children," and many fugitive verses
that are now only to be found in the "poets' corners" of
local newspapers, and in the religious and temperance
journals of the day.   He was also the author of a
" Historical Sketch of the Reformed Presbyterian
Church," and of a volume of " Sermons," published a
year or two before his death.

THE MARTYR'S GRAVE.

He sleeps beneath the sod,
  The patriotic brave ;
Who'd ne'er disown his God,
  Or live as Error's slave ;
Whose loyal spirit ne'er would own
As Zion's Head an earthly crown.

The grass waves o'er his head,
  The rude winds whistle by ;
They wake not now the dead
  Nor waft his prayerful sigh.
They only sweep now o'er his grave,
And make his grassy covering wave.

The wild storm on yon hill,
  The dirge-like sounding gale,
The murmuring of yon rill.
  Seem all for him to wail :
Seem all to whisper in my ear.
A martyred wanderer slumbers here.

But why does not some stone
  Mark where his ashes lie ?
Unpitied and unknown
  Must thus the martyr die ?
He who has fairer laurels won
Than heroes gained at Marathon.

His sufferings and his name
  May not mark history's page :
But these his sons will claim,
  In many a bitter age :
And many a fireside tale of woe
They'll tell of him who sleeps below.

Even those who scorned his cause.
  Who broke his solemn vow,
And bowed to perjured laws,
  Would fondly claim him now,
And say the truths for which he bled
Are those by which they now are led.

The rugged mountain steep,
  Or hollow caverned glen,
Where he might pray and weep
  Unknown to ruthless men,
Was all the home his life supplied,
And formed his death-couch when he died.

There he his song of praise,
  There he his solemn prayer,
With grateful heart would raise
  To God who cheered him there.
And thence his spirit took its flight
To realms of endless joy and light.

Let those who now would wave
  The banner he unfurled,
And now would deck his grave,
  Declare, before the world,
The whole cause of the honoured dead,
And show that Christ's their only Head.

E. V. O. E.
1833-1890.

[The writer of some charming lyrics under the above initials was Margaret Thomson, a daughter of the late Henry Beveridge, advocate, Edinburgh, of Inzievar, parish of Torryburn, Dumfriesshire. In 1862 she became the wife of the Rev. Stephen Bell, of Eyemouth, who died in 1881. Her death occurred on 9th August, 1890, at Kingswood Firs, Haslemere, Surrey, in consequence of a carriage accident.]

THE HERRING DRAVE.

O it's fine when the boats come in,
   When the boats come in so early;
When the lift it is blue, and the herring nets are fu',
   And the sun glints on a' thing rarely;
When the wives buskit braw, an' the bairns an a',
   Come linkin' doun to the quay, O,
The very fisher dogs pu' each other by the lugs,
   And join in the general glee, O.

      Then hey for the boats, for the bonny braw boats,
        That are bound for the Drave the year, O,
      Long live our auld toun, may she never gang doun,
        And God keep the men and the gear, O!

The auld, auld men come hirplin' then,
   And "ahoy" to the fisher lads so cheerily,
When there's so mony crans, there'll be plightin' o' han's,
   For the lasses lo'e a fine Drave dearly!
O there's mirth an' there's glee—on ilk face do you see
   The ghaist o' a gloom or a froun, O?
Na, na, though we may greet sair some other day,
   There's a laugh ower the hale o' the toun, O!
      Then hey for the boats, etc.

The sea is our ain, no lordly domain
   Can compare wi' our acres o' ocean,
As freemen we stand, and to bow to command—
   It ne'er entered our heads sic a notion!
Come woe or come weal, we'll stick by the creel,
   The yawl an' the net an' the line, O;
The storm may come soon, but there's Ane up abune
   Will carry us safe through the brine, O!
      Then hey for the boats, etc.

Low Summer Wind.

O low, low wind,
O sweet, sad wind,
What aileth thee this summer eve?
I cannot hear
Thy moaning drear,
But I, too, must in sorrow grieve!
I feel thy weird, unearthly touch,
Sweep o'er my heart -a harp for thee!
And oh, how mournful, sweet, and strange
Is that awakened melody!

Is't of the Past,
A lay thou hast,
Or of some coming grief or pain?
'Twixt thee and me
Some link must be,
Some chord that thrills between us twain!
In thy low, sobbing voice I hear
The voice I heard at eve and morn
Long since, when loud the branches swayed
Round the old home where I was born!

A Forest child,
Nursed in the wild,
Schooled early in sweet Nature's lore,
Though far away
From Nature's sway,
Her spell is o'er me evermore!
And chief of all her faëry wiles,
Hath thine, O Harper Wind, the power,
To stir old feelings into life,
E'en in the soul's most languid hour!

REV. PETER MEARNS.

B. 1816.

[The Rev. Peter Mearns is well known in Berwickshire, in which county he has now resided for close on half a century. Born at Glenconner, in the parish of Ochiltree, Ayrshire, in 1816, he was educated at Muirkirk and Lanark Schools, and at Glasgow University, being ordained in 1840 to the pastorate of the United Presbyterian Congregation at Coldstream. In 1887 he edited a very acceptable "Life of James Hyslop," author of the *Cameronian's Dream.* He has also published a book on "Muirkirk and its Vicinity," several sermons and tractates, and a large number of hymns.]

SCRIPTURE STUDY.

I saw her bend an eager look,
  As if intent to find
Some treasure in the Sacred Book
  Hid from the careless mind.

I saw the book of Truth reveal'd
  In which the treasure lay,
Which never fails its truth to yield
  To those who read and pray.

She read of threats and promises
  Inspiring hope and fear,
She read of loving-kindnesses,
  And righteousness brought near.

I saw again her placid mien,
  An angel's look was there ;
A Spartan virgin ne'er was seen
  Possessed of charms so fair.

JOHN REID.

B. 1836.

[The following poem is one of many written by Mr. John Reid, a native of
Ratho, Midlothian, but whose life has been largely passed in the fair fields of the
Merse. He is a frequent contributor to the local press, and worthily deserves a
place in this collection.]

THE LASS O' KIDSHIEL GLEN.

When summer's sun is sinking low
  Far in the distant West,
I feel the lover's genial glow
  With rapture fill my breast ;
For there is ane, a secret ane,
  I lo'e abune them a',
And I'll meet her down in Kidshiel Glen
  When the evening shadows fa'.

I'll rowe me in my shepherd's plaid
  And ower the Henly Hill ;
And the dreary dens o' Otterburn,
  I'll cross them wi' a will
For I ken my lassie's waitin'
  By the secret trystin' tree ;
There's virtue in that winning smile
  And true love in her e'e.

The gloamin' shadows saftly fa' ;
  A' Nature's gane to rest ;
The hills and vales and a' aroond
  In sombre hues are dress'd ;
But the flame that's in my bosom
  The power o't nane can ken,
It draws me, like the loadstone,
  To the lass o' Kidshiel Glen.

There's a grandeur in the solitudes
  O' the everlasting hills,
While nimbly doon their rugged sides
  Rin the merry ripplin' rills ;

Where the muircock, whaup, and plover
　By birthright have their home ;
'Mang these rugged scenes o' Nature
　'Tis my delight to roam.

There's serenity aroond me
　In the sweet, sequestered glen,
While musing by the purling stream
　Far frae the haunts o' men ;
But the burden o' my every thought
　Is centred, love, on thee,
And I ken that thou art waitin'
　Doon the gloamin' glen for me.

Wi' lengthy step I move alang
　Doon through the windin' vale,
'Mang the wild flow'rs nodding gaily
　In the evening's gentle gale ;
These modest gems o' beauty rare
　Seem whispering love to me
As they point me to yon hallowed spot,
　The secret trystin' tree.

As wi' manly pride I clasp her hand
　By Kidshiel's wimplin' stream,
There's a flutter in her bosom
　Where love's image rules supreme :
I feel my inward soul is moved
　By something that's divine,
When I rowe her in my shepherd's plaid
　And press her lips to mine.

The joy that oft has sealed my lips
　Nae langer will I hain,
But I'll speir my lovely Mary
　Gin she'll be a' my ain ;
And share wi' me yon shepherd's cot.
　Wi' its humble but and ben,
And by Heaven I vow I'll aye prove true
　To the lass o' Kidshiel Glen.
T

ANNIE BURTON EASTON.

B. 1844.

[The following verses were written by Mrs. Annie Burton Easton, a native of Yarrow Braes, but who spent many years of her life in Berwickshire. She is now a resident of Manitoba, having emigrated with her husband to Canada in 1884. Something of the old home-land still lingers in the name of their present abode—Huntly Brae. In 1883 Mrs. Easton published, through the Messrs. Rutherford, of Kelso, a small volume of her musings with the title, "The Tide of Life and other Poems" (pp. 48). These are full of tender memories, and breathe the gentle spirit of a true woman's loving heart.]

"DINNA FORGET ME."

"Dinna forget me!" When the glowing dawn
Bursts through the eastern haze upon the sight,
And, with still hand, night's curtain is withdrawn,
These words shall shine in rays of living light :
       "Dinna forget me."

"Dinna forget me !" When the noontide sun,
With bright effulgence, gleams o'er glen and glade,
Till in the west his glowing goal is won,
Their sound shall wrap me round like welcome shade :
       "Dinna forget me."

"Dinna forget me !" When the midnight chimes
Ring out with solemn peal upon the air,
Though far my feet may roam in distant climes,
I'll hear the echoes whispering even there :
       "Dinna forget me."

"Dinna forget me !" When misfortunes lower,
And hide the sunbeams 'neath a gloomy pall—
As on the earth, like soft reviving shower—
In gentlest accents, on my heart they'll fall :
       "Dinna forget me."

"Dinna forget me!" Sound they low and clear,
Deep in my heart to sweetest music set ;
In thrilling cadence, to each listening ear,
I'll softly sing them o'er : "Dinna forget ;"
        "Dinna forget me."

"Dinna forget me!" Though time's iron pen
Writes changes; though bright glittering stars may set;
Though silvery summer moons may wax and wane,
Till this heart cease to beat, I'll not forget :
        I'll ne'er forget thee !

MISCELLANEOUS.

SYMON GRAY, styled " of Dunse, Berwickshire," a curious character
about the end of last century, published a large number of pamphlets and
poetical fragments such as " The Rhymster " (1781); " The Rejoiciad "
(1786); " The Messiah ;" " Latin Poems and Verses in English, etc."
(1781). A historical catalogue of his writings, published and unpublished, was privately printed in 1840, containing a list of no fewer
than 158 articles and sketches from his pen. Burns came across Gray
during his Border tour, when the latter submitted several of his rhymes
for the approval of the former, which, not coming up to the poet's
standard, were returned with a stinging epigram of which only the
opening passage has been preserved : —

> " Dear Symon Gray, the other day
>   When you sent me some rhyme,
> I could not then just ascertain
>   It's worth, for want of time,
> But now to-day, good Mr. Gray,
>   I've read it o'er and o'er,
> Tried all my skill, but find I'm still,
>   Just where I was before.
> We auld wives' minions gie our opinions,
>   Solicited or no',
> Then of its faults my honest thought-
>   I'll give—and here they go."

The rest is lost, but we are told the piece concluded thus : -

> " Such damned bombast, no age that's past
>   Can show, nor time to come."

ALEXANDER PARK, author of " The Minstrel's Daughter," a tale of
the Scottish Border, in four cantos, printed at Edinburgh in 1824, and
dedicated to William Hay, Esq., of Duns Castle, may have been a
native of the county—possibly of Duns. No authentic information
concerning him has been procured. In the aforementioned work
there is an exceedingly able ballad in the old style on the murder of
the Chevalier de la Bastie.

"SERJEANT" DAVID BROWN, of Horndean, as he was commonly styled, was an old soldier, who, when his martial days were over, pedlared the Borderland with a variety of wares. He wrote a large number of rhyming epistles and other poems, nearly all of which, however, are of inferior merit.

JAMES ROBERTSON, presumably a native of the county, published at Berwick in 1835 a small volume of "Poems on Various Subjects, consisting of the beauty of Nature, Love, Morality, and Patriotism." He was the author of another work—"The Christian's Guide to Civil Liberty and Sacred Truth."

THOMAS WHITE, officer of Excise at Eyemouth, published in 1838, at Berwick, a small volume entitled, "Eyemouth Musings ; or, Poems on Humorous, Interesting, and Important Subjects." He was a man well known in the district, universally respected, and his poetry is clearly indicative of his high-toned character.

JOHN HEWIT, of Auchencrow, a labourer and farm-servant, wrote a number of songs and ballads on the "Witches of Edincraw," but none of these have been printed.

THOMAS LEGERWOOD HATELY (1815-1867), born at Greenlaw, hymnologist and composer of several very fine tunes in our Church Psalmodies—"Glencairn," "Leuchars," "Makerstoun," "Nenthorn," "Calwood," "Zwingle," etc. He occasionally wrote verse, but very little of it has been published.

THE BALLADS OF BERWICKSHIRE.

THE BROOM O' THE COWDENKNOWES.

> " O Cowdenknowes, thy bonny broom
> So famous in old song,
> Where shepherds tuned their Doric reed,
> Its yellow blooms among."—*Sanderson.*

[The well-known pastoral songs of *The Broom o' the Cowdenknowes* have undoubtedly sprung from some original ballad of the same name. Sir Walter Scott published in his " Border Minstrelsy " what professed to be a very ancient ballad bearing this title—(see below)—and there are several similar compositions both in English and Scottish collections. In the " Roxburghe Ballads," Vol. I., No. 190, we find the following broadside printed at London by Francis Cowles in the reign of Charles II., or earlier :

> " The lovely northern lass—
> Who in this ditty here complaining shews
> What harm she got milking her daddy's ewes,"

to a pleasant Scotch tune, called *The Broome o' Cowdenknowes*, with the refrain :

> "O the broome, the bonnie, bonnie broome,
> The broome o' Cowdenknowes;
> Fain would I be in the North Countrie,
> To milk my daddy's ewes."

Chambers tells that he saw a Jacobite song printed on a sheet at the time of the Rebellion of 1715, the burden of which was :

> "O the broom, the bonny, bonny broom,
> The broom of the Coldingknowes,
> O had I back my king again
> Then would my heart rejoice."

The tune a's appears to be of considerable antiquity. In the Pepys' collection of a very early date there is another song from the press of Cowles, entitled *The New Broome*, which is sung to a tune similar to the present *Broom o' the Cowdenknowes*. In Playford's " Dancing Master," as early as 1650, there is a tune called *Broom, the Bonny, Bonny Broom*, and it is likewise alluded to in the well-known book of that period—Burton's " Anatomy of Melancholy." It is also found, with a slight alteration in Mrs. Crocket's MS. book (1709), and Gay selected it for one of his songs in the *Beggar's Opera* (1728), beginning—"The miser thus a shilling sees."

Regarding the ballad, there are many versions of it. In Herd's collection (Vol. I., page 159), published in 1772, the ballad of *Bonnie May* is in its nature nearly identical with the *Broom o' the Cowdenknowes*. In Buchan's "Ancient Ballads and Songs of the North of Scotland" (Vol. I., page 172), there is a *Broom o' the Cowdenknowes* somewhat different, however, from Scott's copy, while Kinloch, in his collection, has printed other two—*The Laird of Ochiltree* and *The Laird of Lochnee*—both of which have a striking resemblance to the Border Minstrelsy version.

The song below which immediately follows the ballad is taken from Ramsay's *Tea-Table Miscellany* (1724), and is signed with the initials S. R. The author has never been discovered. Robert Crawford's version, which also was first printed in Ramsay's *Miscellany*, will be found at page 72 of this volume. Two modern versions of the song are appended.

Cowdenknowes, pleasantly situated on the banks of the Leader, a little over a mile from Earlston, is unquestionably one of the most beautiful spots in the Scottish Borderland. "The very word has a magical effect on our spirit; it has been embalmed by pastoral music, and carries us back to the simple usages of our ancestors—to the folds and bughts, and ewe-milkings of Scotland's olden time." The name is derived from the Cambro-British *Choille-dun*, which signifies "the wooded hill," thence transformed into Cohlen and Cowden. The etymology from the Scotch word *gowden*, for English golden, is plausible enough, but it is probably erroneous. The broom is not now so plentiful as when poets sang its praises in the by-gone days. Much of the land is under cultivation, and only here and there, in scattered patches on rough brae sides, are the sole remnants of its ancient glory.]

THE ORIGINAL BALLAD OF THE BROOM O' THE COWDENKNOWES.

[From Scott's "Minstrelsy of the Scottish Border."]

O the broom, and the bonny, bonny broom,
    And the broom of the Cowdenknowes!
And aye sae sweet as the lassie sang,
    I' the bucht, milking the ewes.

The hills were high on ilka side,
    An' the bucht i' the lirk[1] o' the hill,
And aye, as she sang, her voice it rang,
    Out o'er the head o' yon hill.

There was a troop o' gentlemen
    Came riding merrilie by,
And one of them has rode out o' the way,
    To the bucht to the bonny may.

[1] Hollow.

" Weel may ye save an' see, bonny lass,
  An' weel may ye save an' see."—
" An' sae wi' you, ye weel-bred knight,
  And what's your will wi' me ?"—

" The night is misty and mirk, fair may,
  And I have ridden astray,
  And will you be so kind, fair may,
  As come out and point my way ? "—

" Ride out, ride out, ye ramp rider !
  Your steed's baith stout and strang ;
  For out of the bucht I darena come,
  For fear 'at ye do me wrang."—

" O winna ye pity me, bonny lass,
  O winna ye pity me ?
  An' winna ye pity my poor steed,
  Stands trembling at yon tree ?"—

" I wadna pity your poor steed,
  Though it were tied to a thorn ;
  For if ye wad gain my love the nicht,
  Ye wad slight me ere the morn.

" For I ken you by your weel-busket hat,
  And your merrie twinkling ee,
  That ye're the laird o' the Oakland hills,
  An' ye may weel seem for to be."—

" But I am not the laird o' the Oakland hills,
  Ye're far mista'en o' me ;
  But I'm ane o' the men about his house,
  An' right aft in his companie."—

He's ta'en her by the middle jimp,
  And by the grass-green sleeve :
He's lifted her over the fauld-dyke,
  And speer'd at her sma' leave.

O he's ta'en out a purse o' gowd,
  And streek'd her yellow hair,
" Now, take ye that, my bonny may,
  Of me till you hear mair."—

O he's leapt on his berry-brown steed,
   An' soon he's o'erta'en his men ;
And ane and a' cried out to him,
   " O master, ye've tarry'd lang ! "

" O I hae been east, and I hae been west,
   An' I hae been far o'er the knowes,
But the bonniest lass that ever I saw
   Is i' the bucht, milking the ewes."

She set the cog[1] upon her head,
   An' she's gane singing hame—
" O where hae ye been, my ae daughter ?
   Ye hae na been your lane."—

" O naebody was wi' me, father,
   O naebody has been wi' me ;
The night is misty and mirk, father,
   Ye may gang to the door and see.

" But wae be to your ewe-herd, father,
   And an ill deed may he dee ;
He bug[2] the bucht at the beck o' the knowe,
   And a tod[3] has frighted me.

" There come a tod to the bucht door,
   The like I never saw ;
And ere he had ta'en the lamb he did,
   I had lourd[4] he had ta'en them a'."—

O whan fifteen weeks was come and gane,
   Fifteen weeks and three,
That lassie began to look thin and pale,
   An' to long for his merry twinkling ee.

It fell on a day, on a het simmer day,
   She was ca'ing out her father's kye,
Bye came a troop o' gentlemen,
   A' merrilie riding bye.

1 Milking-pail.   2 Built.   3 Fox.   4 Leifer. Rather.

" Weel may ye save and see, bonny may,
   Weel may ye save and see !
Weel I wat, ye be a very bonny may.
   But whae's aught that babe ye are wi'? "

Never a word could that lassie say,
   For never a ane could she blame,
An' never a word could the lassie say,
   But " I have a gudeman at hame."—

" Ye lied, ye lied, my very bonny may,
   Sae loud as I hear you lie ;
For dinna ye mind that misty night
   I was i' the bucht wi' thee ?

" I ken you by your middle sae jimp,
   An' your merry twinkling ee,
That ye're the bonny lass i' the Cowdenknowes,
   An' ye way weel seem for to be."—

Then he's leapt off his berry-brown steed,
   An' he's set that fair may on —
" Ca' out your kye, gude father, yoursell,
   For she's never ca' them out again.

" I am the laird of the Oakland hills,
   I hae thirty plows and three ;
An' I hae gotten the bonniest lass
   That's in a' the South Countrie."

THE BROOM O' THE COWDENKNOWES.
   [From Ramsay's *Tea-Table Miscellany*, 1724.]
How blithe, ilk morn, was I to see
   My swain come o'er the hill !
He skipt the burn and flew to me :
   I met him with good-will.
      Oh, the brume, the bonnie, bonnie brume !
         The brume o' the Cowdenknowes !
      I wish I were with my dear swain,
         With his pipe and my yowes.

I wanted neither yowe nor lamb,
  While his flock near me lay;
He gathered in my sheep at night,
  And cheered me a' the day.

He tuned his pipe, and played sae sweet,
  The birds sat listening bye;
E'en the dull cattle stood and gazed,
  Charmed with the melodye.

While thus we spent our time, by turns,
  Betwixt our flocks and play,
I envied not the fairest dame,
  Though e'er so rich or gay.

Hard fate, that I should banished be,
  Gang heavily, and mourn,
Because I loved the kindest swain
  That ever yet was born.

He did oblige me every hour;
  Could I but faithful be?
He stawe my heart; could I refuse
  Whate'er he ask'd of me?

My doggie, and my little kit
  That held my wee soup whey,
My plaidie, brooch, and crookit stick,
  May now lie useless by.

Adieu, ye Cowdenknowes, adieu!
  Fareweel, a' pleasures there!
Ye gods, restore me to my swain—
  Is a' I crave or care.
    Oh, the brume, the bonnie, bonnie brume!
      The brume o' the Cowdenknowes!
    I wish I were with my dear swain,
      With his pipe and my yowes!

S. R.

By ROBERT GILFILLAN [1798-1850].

[From Wood's "Songs of Scotland," Vol. I., p. 56.]

O thou broom, thou bonnie bush o' broom !
    I lo'e my land and thee,
Where thou and freedom flourished aye—
    Where Scotia's sons are free.
The Indian vales are rich and fair,
    And bright is their flow'ry bloom ;
But sad their flowers and myrtle bowers
    Without my native broom.
                    O thou bonnie, bonnie broom !

When wilt thou, thou bonnie bush o' broom,
    Grow on a foreign strand ?
That I may think when I look on thee
    I'm still in loved Scotland.
But ah ! that thought can never more be mine,
    Though thou beside me sprang ;
Nor though the lintie, Scotia's bird,
    Should follow wi' its sang.
                    O thou bonnie, bonnie broom !

Thy branches green might wave at e'en,
    At morn thy flowers might blaw,
But no to me on the Cowdenknowes,
    Nor yet by Ettrick Shaw.
O thou broom, thou bonnie bush o' broom !
    So sweet to memory ;
I maist could weep for days gane by
    When I think on days to be.

Scotland may ca' forth a sigh,
    And thou, sweet broom, a tear,
But I'll no tak' thee frae the braes
    To which thou'st lang been dear.
                    O thou bonnie, bonnie broom !

[From " Melodies of Scotland." By Archibald Bell, Esq. Edinburgh :
Privately Printed, 1849.]

When far awa' frae Cowden's bonny haugh,
　Frae Leader wimplin' clear ;
I sit my lane, and think o' days now gane,
　O' days baith sad and dear.
　　　O the broom, the bonny, bonny broom,
　　　　The broom o' the Cowdenknowes ;
　　　I wish I were amang the yellow broom
　　　　A-herdin' o' my yowes ;
　　　O the broom, the bonny, bonny broom.

And Jeannie fair, she aft wad meet me there,
　Sweet as the rose in June ;
We little fear'd the heavy, heavy weird
　Wad part us twa sae soon.
　　　O the broom, etc.

Amang the broom, sae bright wi' yellow bloom,
　We trystit aye the same ;
And ower the brae, when her wee lambs did stray,
　I wear'd them canny hame.
　　　O the broom, etc.

How sweet to share the soft and caller air,
　The grass so fresh and green ;
And, though her luve she wadna free declare,
　It meltit in her een.
　　　O the broom, etc.

But a' gaed wrang, and I was bowne e'er lang
　To cross the roarin' faem ;
Her puir auld daddy wasna fit to gang,
　She stay'd wi' him at hame.
　　　O the broom, etc.

So ower the sea she couldna follow me,
　Or cast her lot wi' mine ;
And, wae to part, my sad and dowie heart,
　It has no cheer'd sinsyne.
　　　O the broom, etc.

AULD MAITLAND.

"Wha does not know the Maitland bluid,
   The best in a' the land?
In whilk sometime the honour stood
   And worship of Scotland."
                    To the Castle of Lethington.

[This ballad was taken down from the recitation of the "Ettrick Shepherd's" mother, and first printed by Scott in the "Border Minstrelsy." In its present form there are distinct traces of modernisation, but the original version must have been of some antiquity, dating probably as far back as the end of the thirteenth or beginning of the fourteenth century. The incidents, if at all historical, seem to have occurred during the English and Scottish wars of that time, and the chief figure in the ballad is Sir Richard Maitland of Thirlstane, commonly called "Auld Maitland," one of the popular heroes in Gawain Douglas' allegorical *Palice of Honour* (1553), wherein he says:

"There saw I Maitland upon auld beird grey,"

that is, "with his auld beird grey." In the Maitland MSS. there is a copy of *Verses Addressed to the Castle of Lethington*, belonging to Sir Richard Maitland, the well-known poet and scholar of the sixteenth century—(see page 22)—and from these we gather that the renown of "Auld Sir Richard" was not merely local, but, on the contrary, was considerably widespread:

"Wha does not know the Maitland bluid,
   The best in a' the land?
In whilk sometime the honour stood
   And worship of Scotland.
Of auld Sir Richard of that name,
   We have heard sing and say;
Of his triumphant noble fame,
   And of his auld beard grey;
And of his noble sonnis three,
   Whilk that time had no maik,
Whilk made Scotland renouned be
   And all England to quake.
Whose loving praises, made truly
   After that simple time,
Are sung in mony a far countrie,
   Albeit in rural rhyme."

Is there not here, then, a probable allusion to the ballad of "Auld Maitland" in its primitive form, and upon which the present version has been based? The defence of Thirlstane and the courageous escapade of Maitland's three sons was surely a theme for the old minstrels. There is, therefore, nothing unreasonable in supposing that the earliest version of this ballad was as old as the events narrated, and that *it* was the "rural rhyme" referred to, through which the valour of Maitland and his sons was chanted "in mony a far countrie."

When Scott published " Auld Maitland," not a few suspected the ba'lad to be a clever forgery, and to rebut this idea the Ettrick Shepherd told how a number of the very old inhabitants of the district knew the greater part of it by heart long before it was either written or printed. " Indeed," he says, " many are not aware of the manners of this country ; till this present age the poor illiterate people in those glens knew of no other entertainment in the long winter nights than repeating and listening to the feats of their ancestors recorded in songs, which I believe to be handed down from father to son for many generations, although, no doubt, had a copy been taken at the end of every fifty years there must have been some difference, occasioned by the gradual change of language. I believe it is thus that very many ancient songs have been gradually modernised to the common ear, while to the connoisseur they present marks of their genuine antiquity." Professor Aytoun a shrewd critic had difficulty in accepting the ballad as one of ancient date. He states the matter very lucidly in his " Ballads of Scotland " (Vol. I., page 1), but admits that there are certain evidences which make him less confident in the opinion he expresses. Professor Child, of New York, and others, adopt Aytoun's view.

Thirlstane Castle, formerly called Lauder Fort, an edifice partly ancient and partly modern, beautifully surrounded by extensive woods, occupies a picturesque position on the right bank of the Leader, near the town of Lauder. According to tradition it was originally erected by Edward I. during his invasion of Scotland, being rebuilt by Chancellor Maitland, and subsequently improved by the Duke of Lauderdale.]

> There lived a king in southern land,
>   King Edward hight his name ;
> Unwordily he wore the crown,
>   Till fifty years were gane.
>
> He had a sister's son o's ain,
>   Was large of blood and bane :
> And afterward, when he came up,
>   Young Edward hight his name.
>
> One day he came before the king,
>   And kneel'd low on his knee
> " A boon, a boon, my good uncle,
>   I crave to ask of thee !
>
> " At our lang wars, in fair Scotland,
>   I fain hae wished to be ;
> If fifteen hundred waled wight men
>   You'll grant to ride wi' me,"

" Thou sall hae thae, thou sall hae mae ;
    I say it sickerlie ;
And I mysell, an auld gray man,
    Array'd your host sall see."—

King Edward rade, king Edward ran—
    I wish him dool and pyne !
Till he had fifteen hundred men
    Assembled on the Tyne.

And thrice as many as Berwicke
    Were all for battle bound,
[Who, marching forth with false Dunbar,
    A ready welcome found.]

They lighted on the banks of Tweed,
    And blew their coals sae het,
And fired the Merse and Teviotdale,
    All in an evening late.

As they fared up o'er Lammermoor,
    They burn'd baith up and down,
Until they came to a darksome house,
    Some call it Leader-Town.

" Wha hauds this house ?" young Edward cry'd,
    " Or wha gies't ower to me ?"—
A grey-hair'd knight set up his head,
    And crakit richt crousely :

" Of Scotland's king I haud my house ;
    He pays me meat and fee ;
And I will keep my guid auld house,
    While my house will keep me."—

They laid their sowies to the wall
    Wi' mony a heavy peal ;
But he threw ower to them agen
    Baith pitch and tar barrel.
U

With springalds, stanes, and gads of airn,
  Amang them fast he threw ;
Till mony of the Englishmen
  About the wall he slew.

Full fifteen days that braid host lay,
  Sieging Auld Maitland keen ;
Syne they hae left him, hail and feir,
  Within his strength of stane.

Then fifteen barks, all gaily good,
  Met them upon a day,
Which they did lade with as much spoil
  As they could bear away.

" England's our ain by heritage ;
  And what can us withstand,
Now we hae conquer'd fair Scotland,
  With buckler, bow, and brand ?"

Then they are on to the land o' France,
  Where auld king Edward lay,
Burning baith castle, tower, and town,
  That he met in his way.

Until he came unto that town,
  Which some call Billop-Grace ;
There were Auld Maitland's sons, a' three,
  Learning at school, alas !

The eldest to the youngest said,
  " O see ye what I see ?
Gin a' be trew yon standard says,
  We're fatherless a' three,

" For Scotland's conquer'd up and down ;
  Landmen we'll never be !
Now, will you go, my brethren two,
  And try some jeopardy ?"

Then they hae saddled twa black horse,
    Twa black horse and a gray;
And they are on to king Edward's host,
    Before the dawn of day.

When they arrived before the host,
    They hover'd on the lay—
" Wilt thou lend me our king's standard,
    To bear a little way?"

" Where wast thou bred? where wast thou born?
    Where, or in what countrie?"
" In North of England I was born:"
    (It needed him to lee).

" A knight me gat, a lady bore,
    I am a squire of high renowne;
I well may bear't to any king,
    That ever yet wore crowne."—

" He ne'er came of an Englishman,
    Had sic an ee or bree ;
But thou art the likest Auld Maitland
    That ever I did see.

" But sic a gloom on ae browhead
    Grant I ne'er see again !
For mony of our men he slew,
    And mony put to pain,"—

When Maitland heard his father's name,
    An angry man was he !
Then, lifting up a gilt dagger,
    Hung low down by his knee,

He stabb'd the knight the standard bore,
    He stabb'd him cruellie ;
Then caught the standard by the neuk,
    And fast away rode he.

" Now, is't na time, brothers," he cried,
   " Now, is't na time to flee ? "—
" Ay, by my sooth ! " they baith replied,
   " We'll bear you companye."—

The youngest turn'd him in a path,
   And drew a burnish'd brand,
And fifteen of the foremost slew,
   Till back the lave did stand.

He spurr'd the gray into the path—
   Till baith his sides they bled —
" Gray ! thou maun carry me away,
   Or my life lies in wad ! "—

The captain lookit ower the wa'
   About the break o' day ;
There he beheld the three Scots lads
   Pursued along the way.

" Pull up portcullize ! down draw-brigg !
   My nephews are at hand ;
And they sall lodge wi' me to-night,
   In spite of all England."—

Whene'er they came within the yate,
   They thrust their horse them frae,
And took three lang spears in their hands,
   Saying, " Here sall come nae mae ! "

And they shot out, and they shot in,
   Till it was fairly day ;
When mony of the Englishmen
   About the draw-brigg lay.

Then they hae yoked carts and wains,
   To ca' their dead away,
And shot auld dykes abune the lave,
   In gutters where they lay.

The king, at his pavilion door,
   Was heard aloud to say,
" Last night, three o' the lads o' France
   My standard stole away.

" Wi' a fause tale, disguised, they came,
   And wi' a fauser trayne;
And to regain my gaye standard,
   These men were a' down slayne."—

" It ill befits," the youngest said,
   " A crowned king to lee;
But, or that I taste meat and drink,
   Reproved sall he be."

He went before king Edward straight,
   And kneel'd low on his knee;
" I wad hae leave, my lord," he said,
   " To speak a word wi' thee."

The king he turn'd him round about,
   And wistna what to say—
Quo' he, " Man, thou's hae leave to speak,
   Though thou should speak a' day."

" Ye said that three young lads o' France
   Your standard stole away,
Wi' a fause tale, and fauser trayne,
   And mony men did slay;—

" But we are nane the lads o' France,
   Nor e'er pretend to be:
We are three lads o' fair Scotland,
   Auld Maitland's sons are we;

" Nor is there men, in a' your host,
   Daur fight us three to three."
" Now, by my sooth," young Edward said,
   " Weel fitted ye sall be !

" Piercy sall with the eldest fight,
    And Ethert Lunn wi' thee:
William of Lancaster the third,
    And bring your fourth to me !"

" Remember, Piercy, aft the Scot
    Has cower'd beneath thy hand ;
For every drap of Maitland blood,
    I'll gie a rig of land."—

He clanked Piercy ower the head,
    A deep wound and a sair,
Till the best blood o' his bodie
    Came rinning down his hair.

" Now, I've slayne ane ; slay ye the twa ;
    And that's gude companye ;
And if the twa suld slay ye baith,
    Ye'se get na help frae me."

But Ethert Lunn, a baited bear,
    Had many battles seen ;
He set the youngest wonder sair,
    Till the eldest he grew keen—

" I am nae king, nor nae sic thing ;
    My word it shanna stand !
For Ethert sall a buffet bide,
    Come he beneath my brand."

He clankit Ethert ower the head,
    A deep wound and a sair,
Till the best blood of his bodie
    Came rinning ower his hair.

" Now, I've slayne twa ; slay ye the ane ;
    Isna that gude companye ?
And tho' the ane suld slaye ye baith,
    Ye'se get nae help o' me."

The twa-some they hae slayne the ane ;
   They maul'd him cruellie ;
Then hung them over the draw-brigg,
   That all the host might see.

They rade their horse, they ran their horse,
   Then hover'd on the lee :
" We be three lads o' fair Scotland,
   That fain would fighting see."

This boasting, when young Edward heard,
   An angry man was he !
" I'll tak yon lad, I'll bind yon lad,
   And bring him bound to thee !"—

" Now, God forbid," king Edward said,
   " That ever thou suld try !
Three worthy leaders we hae lost,
   And thou the fourth wad lie.

" If thou shouldst hang on yon draw-brigg,
   Blythe wad I never be ? "
But, wi' the poll-axe in his hend,
   Upon the brigg sprang he.

The first stroke that young Edward gae,
   He struck wi' might and mayn :
He clove the Maitland's helmet stout ;
   And bit right nigh the brain.

When Maitland saw his ain blood fa',
   An angry man was he !
He let his weapon frae him fa',
   And at his throat did flee.

And thrice about he did him swing,
   Till on the ground he light,
Where he has halden young Edward,
   Tho' he was great in might.

" Now let him up," king Edward cried,
  " And let him come to me?
And for the deed that thou hast done,
  Thou shalt hae erldomes three !"—

" It's ne'er be said in France, nor e'er
  In Scotland, when I'm hame,
That Edward once lay under me,
  And e'er gat up again !"

He pierced him through and through the heart,
  He maul'd him cruellie ;
Then hung him ower the draw-brigg,
  Beside the other three.

" Now take frae me that feather-bed,
  Make me a bed o' strae !
I wish I hadna lived this day,
  To mak my heart sae wae.

" If I were ance at London Tower,
  Where I was wont to be,
I never mair suld gang frae hame,
  Till borne on a bier-tree."

LEADER HAUGHS AND YARROW.

"O Leader haughs are wide and braid,
And Yarrow braes are bonnie."—*Old Song.*

[There is something very sweet in the above song; there is a fine old rural and pastoral air about it, and it is redolent of Nature in her finer aspects. Dr. Robert Chambers says "it is little better than a string of names of places." On this point we differ from him entirely; we think it breathes the very essence of poetry, awakening sentiments and feelings that are truly poetical, carrying us back to a more simple and patriarchal age than the present, and calling up the scenes and pictures of Arcadia. Whatever of this kind that awakens feelings and aspirations for a more simple and innocent life is poetical. This flowery "string of names of places" is very pleasing to the men of the Border—to the "men of the South Countrie." We all know what impressive verse Milton makes out of mere catalogues of localities. We are charmed with the chanting verses which embalm, as it were, the names of our country places, and we love to hear them frequently awaken the echoes.

The author of *Leader Haughs and Yarrow* was Minstrel Burne,[1] presumed to have been a native of St. Leonard's, near Lauder, but nothing is known of him except the name. He is supposed to be one of the last of the old race of minstrels[2] who wandered about the country for the entertainment of the gentry. "In an old collection of songs," says Chambers, "in their original state of *ballants*, I have seen his name printed as 'Burne the Violer,' which seems to indicate the instrument upon which he was in the practice of accompanying his recitations. I was told by an aged person at Earlston that there used to be a portrait in Thirlstane Castle representing him as a douce old man leading a cow by a straw rope." Thirlstane Castle, the seat of the Earl of Lauderdale, is the castle of which the poet speaks in such terms of admiration. The Blainslie oats long held their repute in the county, and we have a proverb which is frequently used when speaking of those who inherit the attributes or propensities of their parents— "They have it by kind, like the Blainslie aits." The Leader Haughs possess much natural beauty, but are of course not so wild as in the days of Burne; they have been ornamented and cultivated in a high degree, and like most other places in Scotland, have been greatly changed by the hand of the modern improver. Still it is classic ground, and the lover of Border song will always delight to wander on the Haughs of Leader Water. We only once saw the Leader shimmering in the light of a harvest morning, and we thought there was something peculiarly enchanting in that stream, flowing past the ancient tower of Ercildoune where Thomas the Rhymer had his abode, when all the land was "full of fairy," and in our imagination it flows, and will still flow, till we lie down to rest "at life's brae-fit," one of the sweetest of earthly streams.—*Dr. Henderson's MS. Notes.*]

1 Minstrel Burne has been confounded with *Nicol* Burne, a Roman Catholic priest of the sixteenth century, author of "The Disputation Concerning the Controvertit Heads of Religion in the Realm of Scotland" (Paris, 1581), and of a scurrilous poem, entitled *Ane Admonition to the Anti-Christian Ministers in the Deformit Kirk of Scotland* (1581). Burne has been a common Berwickshire name. In the Tax-Roll of Dryburgh Abbey mention is made of "Burne in Ersiltoun," and of others of the same name.

2 Chambers ascribes to Burne another ballad after the style of *Leader Haughs and Yarrow,* entitled *Omnia Vincit Amor.* This he has printed in his "Songs of Scotland Prior to Burns," page 284.

When Phœbus bright the azure skies
  With golden rays enlight'neth,
He makes all Nature's beauties rise,
  Herbs, trees, and flowers he quick'neth:
Among all those he makes his choice,
  And with delight goes thorow,
With radiant beams, the silver streams
  Of Leader Haughs and Yarrow.

When Aries the day and night
  In equal length divideth,
And frosty Saturn takes his flight,
  Nae langer he abideth;
Then Flora queen, with mantle green,
  Casts aff her former sorrow,
And vows to dwell with Ceres' sel,
  In Leader Haughs and Yarrow.

Pan, playing on his aiten-reed,
  And shepherds him attending,
Do here resort, their flock to feed,
  The hills and haughs commending;
With cur and kent, upon the bent,
  Sing to the sun, Good-morrow,
And swear nae fields mair pleasure yields,
  Than Leader Haughs and Yarrow.

A house there stands on Leader-side,
  Surmounting my descriving,
With rooms sae rare, and windows fair,
  Like Daedalus' contriving:
Men passing by do aften cry,
  In sooth it hath no marrow;
It stands as fair on Leader-side
  As Newark does on Yarrow.

A mile below, who lists to ride,
  Will hear the mavis singing;
Into St Leonard's banks she bides,
  Sweet birks her head owerhinging.

The lint-white loud, and Progne proud,
  With tuneful throats and narrow,
Into St Leonard's banks they sing
  As sweetly as in Yarrow.

The lapwing lilteth ower the lea,
  With nimble wing she sporteth;
But vows she'll flee far from the tree
  Where Philomel resorteth:
By break of day the lark can say
  I'll bid you a good-morrow;
I'll stretch my wing, and, mounting, sing
  O'er Leader Haughs and Yarrow.

Park, Wanton-wa's, and Wooden-cleuch,
  The East and Wester Mainses,
The wood of Lauder's fair eneuch,
  The corns are good in the Blainslies;
There aits are fine, and sald by kind,
  That if ye search all thorough
Mearns, Buchan, Marr, nane better are
  Than Leader Haughs and Yarrow.

In Boon-mill-bog and Whitslaid Shaws,
  The fearful hare she haunteth;
Brig-haugh and Braidwoodshiel she knaws,
  And Chapel-wood frequenteth:
Yet, when she irks, to Kaidslie Birks,
  She rins, and sighs for sorrow,
That she should leave sweet Leader Haughs,
  And cannot win to Yarrow.

What sweeter music wad ye hear
  Than hounds and beagles crying?
The started hare rins hard with fear,
  Upon her speed relying:
But yet her strength it fails at length:
  Nae bielding can she borrow,
In Sorrowless-field, Clackmae, or Hags;
  And sighs to be in Yarrow.

For Rockwood, Ringwood, Spotty, Shag,
    With sight and scent pursue her;
Till, ah, her pith begins to flag;
    Nae cunning can rescue her:
Ower dub and dyke, ower sheuch and syke,
    She'll rin the fields all thorough,
Till, fail'd, she fa's in Leader Haughs,
    And bids fareweel to Yarrow.

Sing Erslington and Cowdenknowes,
    Where Humes had ance commanding:
And Drygrange, with the milk-white yowes,
    'Twixt Tweed and Leader standing:
The bird that flees through Redpath trees
    And Gladswood banks ilk morrow,
May chant and sing sweet Leader Haughs
    And bonnie howms of Yarrow.

But Minstrel Burne can not assuage
    His grief, while life endureth,
To see the changes of this age,
    Which fleeting time procureth:
For mony a place stands in hard case,
    Where blythe folk ken'd nae sorrow,
With Humes that dwelt on Leader-side,
    And Scotts that dwelt on Yarrow.

The following are the three additional verses as given in the Roxburghe Collection :

THE WORDS OF BURNE THE VIOLER.

What, shall my viol silent be,
    Or leave her wonted scriding?
But choose some sadder elegie,
    Not sports and mirds deriding.
It must be fain with lower strain,
    Than it was wont before, O.
To sound the praise of Leader Haughs
    And the bonnie banks of Yarrow.

But floods have overflown the banks,
  The greenish haughs disgracing,
And trees in woods grow thin in ranks,
  About the fields defacing.
For waters wax, and woods do wane ;
  More, if I could for sorrow,
In rural verse I could rehearse
  Of Leader Haughs and Yarrow.

But sighs and sobs o'erset my breath,
  Sore saltish tears forth sending,
All things sublunar here on earth
  Are subject to an ending
So must my song, though somewhat long,
  Yet late at even and morrow,
I'll sigh and sing sweet Leader Haughs,
  And the bonnie banks of Yarrow.

THE GREY PEEL GLEN.
(*A hitherto unpublished Border Ballad.*)

[This old ballad, now published for the first time, is supposed to be founded on
an incident of the year 1612.   In Pitcairn's "Criminal Trials" it is set forth
somewhat as follows :   The laird of Boon had a daughter who had two suitors
for her hand, namely, the tutor of Thorniedyke (in Westruther parish), Hay by
name, and Gilbert Cranstoun of Corsbie Tower.   One of these suitors was
returning from visiting her at her father's castle at Boon when he met his rival
crossing Boon hill on a like errand.   They had a quarrel about the fair damsel,
ending in a duel in which Hay, aided by his servant, soon overcame Cranstoun,
and killed him.   The murderers were tried at Edinburgh, were sentenced to
death, and their bodies hung for a time on chains on the Castle Hill.   The people
of the district in which the crime was committed, to mark their abhorence of the
deed, erected an old stone cross on the spot.   This relic stands below Old Boon,
in a plantation about a hundred yards above the public road leading to the farm
of Dods.   It is locally known as the Laird's Grave and the Dods Cross Stane.
Old inhabitants of the district also remember their fathers telling them that at
certain times the neighbouring farmers and others used to meet at this cross to
exchange their lint seed, etc., which gathering was called the Pirn Fair.   Not a
vestige of the Castle of Boon now remains, but it is supposed to have stood
somewhere to the west of " Dods Rauchan."   The Grey Peel of the ballad is an
old tower near Jedburgh.   The Merlindean is a dean or cleuch in the same

district.   The Cranstouns of Corsbie Tower (which still exists) were a branch of
the Cranstouns of Crailing.   Corsbie Tower, which was formerly surrounded by
a loch, has been supposed to be the scene of Scott's " Lady of Avenel."   It is only
proper to acknowledge an indebtedness to Mr. Walter Lockie, schoolmaster,
Gateside, Spottiswood, for rescuing this old ballad from the obscurity which
seems to have surrounded it for many years.]

Auld Wat o' the Grey Peel's dochter May,
    Perfection's maiden in form and mien;
Wi' face as bricht as a simmer day,
    I' the Grey Peel Glen nae mair is seen.

There's naething but grief within the wa's,
    Thereout there's dool 'mong women and men;
An ruefu's the strain o' the wind that blaws
    Through the shiverin' leaves i' the Grey Peel Glen.

Wi' frolicksome step i' the morning bright
    She brent her way to the Merlindean;
Where voices wail i' the darksome night,
    Or wildly laugh i' the moonlight sheen.

But the eerie glen i' the light o' day
    Revealed but charms to her laughin' een;
An' the sunbright morn that wiled her away
    Brought a dreary night, for nae mair she's seen.

Right ready o' help frae the Smaileleuch fit,
    Stern Ringan has flown to the sad Grey Peel;
Unpeered he stands i' the forest yet
    For a trusty hand and a bitin' steel.

An' gallopin' up comes Ruecastle Hew,
    On his Ruecastle naig o' the guid steel grey,
An' Fernihirst grim, but ever heart true,
    Whase ready Kerr hand redds mony a fray.

An' Rumpet Dowfort, the ae-lugget loon,
    An' lang-armed Tam o' the Waterside Toor;
An' muckle Wull Elliot o' Jethart toon,
    Wi' staff aye ready for ony stoor.

Baith east and wast they muster and rin,
  Wi' eager speed the fair May to trace;
But the sad days close as they begin,
  And auld Wat manes for her bonnie face.

Six heart-fearin', heart-wearin' weeks are away,
  In forest and open a' search is vain,
And hope seems dead for the lang-lost May,
  Its mystery a' ower hill and plain,

But, hark, what news is this by the way,
  Whilk auld and young gaurs loup i' their shoon;
That May was seen i' the gloamin' grey,
  On the toor o' the treacherous laird o' Boon.

And Gilbert o' Corsbie, ready and sure,
  Up faced wild Boon wi' an angry ee,
An' vowed he wad clear his lady's bour,
  Or he or himself wad surely dee.

Now Boon for man had never a fear,
  Had sinew an' heart o' granite stane:
But his flashin' swurde an' his fiendish leer
  On dauntless Gibbie effect had nane.

On Boon hill back they take their stand,
  An' draw their brands o' the Spanish steel;
Then fit to fit an' hand to hand,
  They thrust an' parry syne slash and reel.

But Gibbie has pricket the laird o' Boon,
  An' rage-blind now that sic should be,
He springs on Gibbie, but that nimble loon,
  Strikes life wi' death frae his fause body.

They bury him speedily where he fa's,
  An' rush frae the fatal spot away,
To search the holes o' the auld toor wa's,
  Wi' beatin' hearts for the lang-lost May.

She's found i' the hour proteckit right weel
    By Boon's auld tittie—Black Marjorie;
But soon they light doon at the blythe Grey Peel,
    Where auld Wat laughs and greets wi' glee.

Frae east to wast to the Grey Peel gay,
    Gude sprinklings o' blythe company ride,
To pleasure auld Wat an' his winsome May,
    Now gallant young Gilbert o' Corsbie's bride.

There's naething but mirth within the wa's,
    Thereout there's joy 'mong women and men,
An' sweet is the strain o' the wind that blaws
    Through the whisperin' leaves i' the Grey Peel Glen.

THE BALLAD OF THE TWINLAW CAIRNS.

[The Twinlaw Cairns are situated on Twinlaw Hill, on the farm of Flass, belonging to the extensive domain of Spottiswood. Twinlaw Hill is 1100 feet above sea level, and commands one of the most magnificent views in the Border country. In the north-west you see far into the fertile Lothians, while to the south and south-wast the whole panorama of the Merse lies at one's feet with its wealth of wood and cultivated land, stretching away out to the long wavy line of "Cheviot's mountains lone." The Cairns are two in number, some ten feet high, and stand about seventy yards apart. Circles of loose stones lie round the base of each Cairn. There are winding steps leading to the top from the outside, and a recess with a seat fronting southwards. It is to Lady John Scott—perhaps the most zealous lady antiquary in Scotland—that we owe the careful preservation of these ancient monuments. Some years ago, when the stones were showing signs of crumbling, she had the Cairns thoroughly repaired, and every opportunity is now afforded to strangers for visiting this interesting locality so full of history and tradition, and so richly dowered with Nature's own wealth. The ballad tells its own tale. There is but to add the further tradition of the two armies standing in line from the Watch water at the foot of the hill to the top of Twinlaw handing on stones to one another as they gathered them from the streamlet, and by this means forming the rude and simple memorial. The legend of the Twinlaw Cairns is common to many parts of the county · indeed to many parts of Scotland. Near the hamlet of Gateside, which is close by, is a field bearing the name Brotherfield, in which formerly stood a large cairn known as Brotherfield Cairn. The same tradition was told of it as of the Twinlaws, and in the parish of Mertoun, to the south of the county, on the top of Brotherstone Hill are two tall whinstone slabs concerning which also there is a story similar in most respects to the present ballad.

The whole of this region around Twinlaw and Spottiswood is one of deep romance. The supernatural has a firm hold of the native imagination. It is a fairy-haunted land, and old inhabitants will tell you how, on pleasant summer evenings, just when gloaming begins to shade the scene, the little green-clad elves are all astir, and chorusing their favourite " Fairy rhyme :"

> In the parks o' Thystie we mowed our corn,
> We thrashed it up in Bruntyburn ;
> We grund our meal at Clacharie Mill ;
> We carried our meal up to Boon Hill ;
> We bakit our bread in the Fairy Glen,
> An' we eatit it up in the jolly Dod Rauchan."]

In days of yore, when deeds were rife,
  And wars on banks and braes,
And nought but strife on every side,
  Which brought on dule and waes.

The Anglo-Saxon's restless band,
  Had crossed the river Tweed ;
Up for the hills of Lammermoor
  Their hosts march'd on with speed.

Our Scottish warriors on the heath
  In close battalion stood ;
Resolved to set their country free,
  Or shed their dearest blood.

A chieftain from the Saxon band,
  Exulting in his might,
Defied the bravest of the Scots
  To come to single fight.

Old Edgar had a youthful son
  Who led the Scottish band,
Who bravely met the Saxon's challenge
  To fight it hand to hand.

The armies stood in deep suspense
  The combat for to view ;
While aged Edgar stepped forth
  To bid his son adieu.

X

" Adieu ! adieu ! my darling son,
   I fear that ye be lost,
  For yesternight my troubled mind
   With fearful dreams was tossed.

" I dreamed your mother's parted shade
   Between two armies stood ;
  A lovely youth on every hand,
   With bosom streaming blood.

" My heart will break if you should fall,
   My only prop and stay ;
  Your brother when in infant years
   The Saxons bore away."

" Delay it not," young Edgar said,
   " But let the trumpets blow ;
  You soon shall see me prove your son,
   And lay yon boaster low."

The trumpets raised with deafening clang,
   The fearful onset blew ;
  And then the chieftains stepped forth ;
   Their shining swords they drew.

Like lions in a furious fight,
   Their steeled faulchions gleam ;
  Till from our Scottish warrior's side
   Fast flowed a crimson stream.

With deafening din on the coats of mail
   The deadly blows resound ;
  At last the Saxon warrior
   Did breathless press the ground.

An aged Saxon came to view
   The body of his chief ;
  His streaming eyes, and downcast looks,
   Bespoke a heart of grief.

" He's dead," he cried, " the bravest youth,
    Ere sprang from Edgar's line;
I bore him from the Scottish coasts,
    And made him pass for mine.

" And in the days of youthful prime,
    He was my pride and boast;
For oft to bravery he has
    Led on the Saxon host."

Old Edgar heard the Saxon's moan,
    His cheeks grew deadly pale;
A great convulsion shook his frame,
    His strength began to fail.

Frantic he tore his aged locks,
    With time and trouble grey;
And faintly crying, " My son! my son!"
    His spirit fled away.

The Scottish chief, as his father fell,
    He raised his fading eye;
And tore the bandage off his wounds,
    To let life's stream run dry.

He kissed his sire, and his brother's wounds,
    Which ghastly were and deep;
And closed him in his folding arms,
    And fell on his long, long sleep.

POLWARTH ON THE GREEN.

ALLAN RAMSAY [1686-1758].

[The first four and the last four lines of this song are old, the rest are by
Ramsay. Chambers is wrong in ascribing the song to Captain MacGregor of
Balhadies, and Burns also was misinformed on this point. There was a very old
song of " Polwarth on the Green," which is now lost. Polwarth was made a
baronial burgh in 1587. Two old thorn trees formerly stood in the centre of the
village green and the bridal party at every marriage in the village for upwards of
three centuries, till about the beginning of the present century, danced round
them. The " Polwart thorne" is referred to in the *Flyting* of Montgomery and
Polwarth. The air of *Polwarth on the Green* is inscribed in Mrs. Crocket's book,
written in 1709, and in Craig's " Old Scottish Airs" in 1730. Gay selected this
tune for one of his songs in the opera of *Polly*, beginning " Love now is nought
but art," 1729.]

At Polwarth on the Green
　If you'll meet me the morn,
Where lads and lassies do convene
　To dance around the thorn ;
A kindly welcome you shall meet
　Frae her, wha likes to view
A lover and a lad complete -
　The lad and lover you.

Let dorty [1] dames say *Na*,
　As lang as e'er they please,
Seem caulder than the snaw,
　While inwardly they bleeze ;
But I will frankly show my mind,
　And yield my heart to thee
Be ever to the captive kind,
　That langs na to be free.

At Polwarth on the Green
　Among the new-mown hay,
With sang and dancing keen
　We'll pass the live-lang day.
At nicht, if beds be ower thrang laid,
　And thou be twined of thine,
Thou shalt be welcome, my dear lad,
　To take a part of mine.

_____

[1] Saucy.

POLWARTH ON THE GREEN.

JOHN GRIEVE.[1]

'Twas summer tide: the cushat sang
  His am'rous roundelay:
And dew, like cluster'd diamonds, hang
  On flower and leafy spray.
The coverlet of gloaming grey
  On every thing was seen,
When lads and lassies took their way
  To Polwarth on the Green.

The spirit-moving dance went on,
  And harmless revelry
Of young hearts all in unison
  Wi' love's soft witcherie;
Their ball the open-daised lea,
  While frae the welkin sheen,
The moon shone brightly on the glee
  At Polwarth on the Green.

Dark een and raven curls were there,
  And cheeks of rosy hue,
And finer form, without compare,
  Than pencil ever drew;
But ane, wi' een o' bonnie blue,
  A' hearts confess'd the queen,
And pride of grace and beauty too,
  At Polwarth on the Green.

The miser hoards his golden store,
  And kings dominion gain :
While others in the battle's roar
  For honour's trifles strain.
Away, such pleasures ! false and vain;
  For dearer mine have been,
Among the lowly rural train,
  At Polwarth on the Green.

---

[1] John Grieve, born in 1781, was a hat manufacturer in Edinburgh, of literary tastes, and one of the Ettrick Shepherd's earliest friends and patrons. Hogg dedicated *Mador of the Moor* to him and introduced him as one of the Minstrels in the *Queen's Wake*. He died in 1836, long after retiring from business. He was the author of a large number of poetical compositions.

TIBBY FOWLER.

[We claim "Tibby Fowler" as a Berwickshire song. By constant tradition its locality has been fixed in a glen near Edrington Castle on the Whitadder. Allan Ramsay, being a west country man, wished no doubt to make it appear as a production of his native soil, and accordingly, in the *Tea-Table Miscellany*, he localised it by the introduction of "Tintock Tap," which we here alter to its probably original "Cheviot." The song is old, and was well known in the early part of last century. There is a tradition in Leith that Tibby Fowler was a real personage, and married sometime during the seventeenth century to the representative of the attainted family of Logan of Restalrig. A marriage contract between Logan and Isobel Fowler is still extant.--Campbell's "History of Leith," note, p. 314.]

Tibby Fowler o' the Glen,
  There's ower mony wooing at her;
Tibby Fowler o' the Glen,
  There's ower mony wooing at her.
    Wooin' at her, pu'in' at her,
      Courtin' her, and canna get her;
    Filthy elf, it's for her pelf
      That a' the lads are wooin' at her.

Ten cam east, and ten cam west;
  Ten cam rowin' ower the water;
Twa cam down the lang dyke-side:
  There's twa-and-thirty wooing at her.

There's seven but, and seven ben,
  Seven in the pantry wi' her;
Twenty head about the door:
  There's ane and-forty wooin' at her!

She's got pendles in her lugs;
  Cockle shells wad set her better!
High-heel'd shoon, and siller tags;
  And a' the lads are wooin' at her.

Be a lassie e'er sae black,
  Gin she hae the name o' siller,
Set her up on Cheviot tap,
  The wind will blaw a man till her.

Be a lassie e'er sae fair,
  An' she want the penny siller,
A flee may fell her in the air,
  Before a man be even'd till her.

THOMAS THE RHYMER.

" Oh ! long shall Scotland sound with Rhymer's name,"—*Finlay's Wallace.*

[The opening pages of this volume treat of Thomas the Rhymer, the prophet-bard of Ercildoune. In Scott's " Border Minstrelsy" there are three ballads concerning this mysterious personage, one of which purports to be of great antiquity, while the others are merely modern imitations. The first is given from a copy obtained from a lady residing not far from Earlston, corrected and enlarged by one in Mrs. Brown's MSS. The second is made up by Scott himself from the printed prophecies vulgarly ascribed to the Rhymer, and the third—entirely modern—is founded on the popular tradition of his returning with the hart and hind to dree his weird in the realm of Faëry. For our present purpose the last of these is selected—the portion descriptive of Thomas's disappearance]

The feast was spread in Ercildoune,
   In Learmont's high and ancient hall:
And there were knights of great renown,
   And ladies, laced in pall.

No lacked they, while they sat at dine,
   The music nor the tale,
Nor goblets of the blood-red wine,
   Nor mantling quaighs [1] of ale.

True Thomas rose, with harp in hand,
   When as the feast was done:
(In minstrel strife, in Fairy Land,
   The elfin harp he won).

Hush'd were the throng, both limb and tongue,
   And harpers for envy pale;
And armed lords lean'd on their swords,
   And hearken'd to the tale.

In numbers high, the witching tale
   The prophet pour'd along;
No after bard might e'er avail
   Those numbers to prolong.

Yet fragments of the lofty strain
   Float down the tide of years,
As, buoyant on the stormy main,
   A parted wreck appears.

[1] Wooden cups, composed of staves hooped together.

He sung king Arthur's Table Round:
  The Warrior of the Lake;
How courteous Gawaine met the wound,
  And bled for ladies' sake.

But chief, in gentle Tristrem's praise,
  The notes melodious swell:
Was none excell'd in Arthur's days,
  The knight of Lionelle.

  . . . .

There paus'd the harp: its lingering sound
  Died slowly on the ear:
The silent guests still bent around,
  For still they seem'd to hear.

Then woe broke forth in murmurs weak;
  Nor ladies heaved alone the sigh;
But, half ashamed, the rugged cheek
  Did many a gauntlet dry.

On Leader's stream, and Learmont's tower,
  The mists of evening close:
In camp, in castle, or in bower,
  Each warrior sought repose.

Lord Douglas, in his lofty tent,
  Dream'd o'er the woeful tale:
When footsteps light, across the bent,
  The warrior's ear assail.

He starts, he wakes—"What, Richard, ho!
  Arise, my page, arise!
What venturous wight, at dead of night,
  Dare step where Douglas lies!"—

Then forth they rush'd; by Leader's tide,
  A seleouth[1] sight they see—
A hart and hind pace side by side,
  As white as snow on Fairnalie.[2]

---

[1] Wondrous.   [2] An ancient seat upon the Tweed, in Selkirkshire.

Beneath the moon, with gesture proud,
  They stately move and slow :
Nor scare they at the gathering crowd,
  Who marvel as they go.

To Learmont's tower a message sped,
  As fast as page might run ;
And Thomas started from his bed,
  And soon his clothes did on.

First he woxe pale, and then woxe red :
  Never a word he spake but three ;—
" My sand is run ; my thread is spun :
  This sign regardeth me."

The elfin harp his neck around,
  In minstrel guise, he hung ;
And on the wind, in doleful sound,
  Its dying accents rung.

Then forth he went : yet turn'd him oft
  To view his ancient hall :
On the grey tower, in lustre soft,
  The autumn moonbeams fall :

And Leader's waves, like silver sheen,
  Danced shimmering in the ray :
In deepening mass, at distance seen,
  Broad Soltra's mountains lay.

" Farewell, my father's ancient tower !
  A long farewell," said he :
" The scene of pleasure, pomp, or power,
  Thou never more shalt be.

" To Learmont's name no foot on earth
  Shall here again belong,
And, on thy hospitable hearth,
  The hare shall leave her young.

" Adieu ! adieu !" again he cried,
　All as he turned him roun'—
" Farewell to Leader's silver tide !
　Farewell to Ercildoune !"

The hart and hind approach'd the place,
　As lingering yet he stood ;
And there, before lord Douglas' face,
　With them he cross'd the flood.

Lord Douglas leap'd on his berry-brown steed
　And spurr'd him the Leader o'er ;
But, though he rode with lightning speed,
　He never saw them more.

Some said to hill, and some to glen,
　Their wondrous course had been ;
But ne'er in haunts of living men
　Again was Thomas seen.

REFERENCES TO THOMAS OF ERCILDOUNE BY OLDER SCOTTISH AND ENGLISH WRITERS.

Additional note to Thomas of Ercildoune—see note, p. 17.

Robert Mannying of Brunne (1303) commemorates him as the author of an incomparable metrical romance entitled *Sir Tristrem*. His words are—"It is the best geste ever was or ever would be made, if minstrels could recite as Thomas composed it." His description of the style in which it is written—"quaint Inglis"—and the complicated nature of each stanza, corresponds with the modern copy.—"English Chronicle," Vol. I., p. 90.

Sir Thomas Gray, Constable of Norham (1355), in "Scalcronica"—a French chronicle of English history—apparently written in the reign of Edward III. says "William Banestre and Thomas Ercildonn, whose words were spoken in figure, as were the prophecies of Merlin."— LELAND.

In Barbour's *Bruce*, composed about 1375, there is a reference to a prophecy of Thomas concerning the exploits and succession of Robert the First.—*The Bruce*, Book II., Chap. 86.

Andro of Wyntoun (1424) refers to the poetic fame of the Rhymer. His words are—

> " Of this fycht quhilum spak Thomas
> Of Ersyldowne, that sayd in derne, etc."

—"Original Chronicle of Scotland," Vol. II., p. 292 ; Book VIII., Chap. 31.

Bower, who flourished about the year 1430, has given a circumstantial account of the celebrated prediction of the Rhymer relative to the untimely and disastrous fate of Alexander III.—"Scotichronicon." Book X., Chap. 43; Spottiswood's "History," p. 47.

Henry the Minstrel, who is supposed to have written his metrical history of Wallace in the early part of the fifteenth century, represents Thomas as alive in 1296, the year in which Wallace took up arms, and as predicting that before the death of the Scottish hero,

> " Many thousand in field shall make their end,
> Off this region he shall the Southron send ;
> And Scotland thrice he shall bring to the peace,
> So good of hand again shall never be kend."

— *Wallace*, Book II., Chap. 3.

Hector Boece or Boyce, Principal of King's College, Aberdeen (1465-1536), in "Scotorum Historia"—a work in which history is largely mixed with fable—narrates the story of Thomas's prophecy concerning Alexander III., and concludes thus—"This Thomas was ane man of great admiration to the people, and shewed sundry things as they fell, howbeit they were aye hid under obscure words."—Bellenden's translation of Boece, Fol. 208, Book XIII., p. 291. Boece appears to be the first who puts on record the tradition that the Rhymer's name was Learmont.

John Mair or Major (1430), in his " History of the Nation of the Scots," also inserts this prophecy, but he adds the following caution—"To this Thomas our countrymen have ascribed many predictions, and the common people of Britain yield no slight degree of merit to stories of this kind which I for the most part am accustomed to treat with ridicule."—" De Gestes Scotorum," p. 157.

John Leslie, Bishop of Ross, in his " History of Scotland " from 1436-1561, has commemorated Thomas as a personage of extraordinary character.—" De Rebus Gestis Scotorum," p. 220.

John Spottiswood, Archbishop of St. Andrews, in his " History of the Church of Scotland," refers to Thomas as a prophet, and pins his faith to the alleged prediction concerning the Union through one in the ninth degree of Bruce's blood.— " History," p. 47.

Nisbet the Heraldist, in his great work, styles Thomas as " Sir Thomas Learmont of Ersildoun, in the Merss," and attempts to prove his knightly lineage.

THE TOWER OF ERCILDOUNE.[1]

There is a stillness on the night ;
Glimmers the ghastly moonshine white
On Learmont's woods, and Leader's streams,
Till Earth looks like a land of dreams :
Up in the arch of heaven afar
Receded looks each little star,
And meteor flashes faintly play
By fits along the milky way.
Upon me in this eerie hush,
A thousand wild emotions rush
As, gazing spell-bound o'er the scene,
Beside thy haunted walls I lean,
Grey Ercildoune, and feel the past
His charmed mantle o'er me cast ;
Visions and thoughts unknown to Day,
Bear o'er the fancy wizard sway,
And call up the traditions told
Of him who sojourned here of old.

Backward my spirit to the sway
Of shadowy Eld is led away,
When, underneath thine ample dome,
Thomas the Rhymer made his home,
The wondrous poet-seer whose name,
Still floating on the breath of fame,
Hath overpast five hundred years.
Yet fresh as yesterday appears.
With spells to arm the winter's tale,
And make the listener's cheek grow pale.

[1] David Macbeth Moir, a distinguished writer under the pseudonym of " Delta,"
was born at Musselburgh, 5th January, 1798. In 1817 he graduated in medicine
at Edinburgh University, and practised with much success as a physician in his
native town until his death on 6th July, 1851.   He wrote, amongst other stories,
the famous Scotch novel " Mansie Waugh," besides much charming poetry which
has for long held a high place with readers. His poem on *Ercildoune* was the
result of a journey to that place during an interesting Border tour.

Secluded here in chamber lone,
Often the light of genius shone
Upon his pictured page, which told
Of Tristrem brave, and fair Isolde,
And how their faith was sorely tried,
And how they would not change, but died
Together, and the fatal stroke
Which stilled one heart, the other broke :
And here, on midnight couch reclined,
Hearkened his gifted ear the wind
Of dark Futurity, as on
Through shadowy ages swept the tone,
A mystic voice, whose murmurs told
The acts of eras yet unrolled ;
While Leader sang a low wild tune,
And redly set the waning moon.
Amid the West's pavilion grim
Old Soltra's mountains vast and dim.

NOTE.

Among Berwickshire ballads may also be mentioned the following:—*The Shepherd's Antiquity*—a curious rhapsody consisting of eighty-one stanzas, by " Andrew Hardie, shepherd, Leader Water, Berwickshire." This elaborate effusion was printed at Haddington by James Miller in 1823, and sold for one penny. The late Mr. Thomas Gray, gingham manufacturer, Earlston—a gentleman well known throughout the Merse for his antiquarian tastes and extraordinary book-collecting zeal—had it republished many years after (1856) by Mr. D. Jerdan, of Dalkeith. The Haddington copy, now extremely rare, bore the following title—" A Poem to the praise of the Shepherds; or, The Shepherd's Antiquity, being a true account of the rise and progress of the shepherds, and of their heroic actions ; as also giving an account of the dreadful storms of snow, thunder, and wind which happened in 1729 and 1731. By a Gentleman." Haddington : Printed and sold by James Miller, 1823. The tradition of Andrew Hardie, to whom the ballad is ascribed, is that he came into the Leader district sometime well back in last century from the North—Forfarshire or Aberdeenshire,—and though he gave himself out for, and worked as a common shepherd, it was quite evident that this was not the rank he had been born into, nor was Hardie more than an assumed name. He was a man of education, as may be seen from the classical knowledge displayed in the ballad. A silent, moody man, he kept very much by himself, and the mystery of his life is not now likely to be known.

The Gudewife o' Tulloshill, in James Miller's " St. Baldred of the Bass," pages 299-310. Edinburgh, 1824.

The Murder of De la Bastie, in Alexander Park's " The Minstrel's Daughter," 1824.

The Auld Wife o' Lauderdale, in Lyle's " Ancient Ballads and Songs," London, 1827.

The Castle of Bonkyll—an unpublished ballad of which only a few verses have been preserved.

The Laird of Boon—a ballad evidently referring to the same incident as that of *The Grey Peel Glen*.

The Brethren Stanes, by the late William Brockie, published in his " Leaderside Legends." Sunderland, 1876.

Edom o' Gordon. This ballad is wrongly inserted in some collections as a local or Border ballad. The scene of it is laid in Aberdeenshire.

ADDENDA.

PETER COLDWELL.

1811-1892.

PETER COLDWELL was a native of the royal burgh of Lauder, where he was born in 1811. Educated at the parish school, he had for a time as his teacher a youth known as "The Little Maister," from his assisting the smaller children with their lessons, who was destined to become the famous Indian missionary and Orientalist—Dr. John Wilson. After a long separation, it is recorded how these two "Lawther bairns" had the unexpected pleasure of renewing their friendship by mutual recognition at Galashiels railway station, when both were well tinged with "the seer and yellow leaf." While still a young man Coldwell started a grocery business in Galashiels, which he successfully carried on for a large number of years, retiring with a competency to spend the evening of life in restfulness and peace. He died at Kelso on 17th July, 1892. Peter Coldwell was endowed with literary gifts of no mean order, and produced some humorous ballads which procured him fame, not limited to this country, but extending to America and all the English-speaking colonies. and to Germany, for, greatly to his surprise, he learned some years ago that his well-known production, *Cuddy Peggy*, which is a favourite recitation at home, had been translated into German and published in the Fatherland. The heroine of the ballad—for it is simply a humorous narrative of a real incident—was a well-known Galalean, who earned a livelihood by itinerating the district with her donkey, vending smallwares and groceries. She was a "character" all through, and would reproach or remonstrate with " Dauvit," as her donkey was named, as if he understood the English, or rather the Scottish tongue, as well as herself. The hero was the late Rev. Dr. Henderson, an able and amiable minister of the United Presbyterian Church in Galashiels, who fully appreciated the humour of the ballad, and greatly respected its author. Perhaps nothing in the Scottish language has been so frequently recited as this ballad, which never grows stale, and is a never-failing source of enjoyment and laughter. It is not a little strange that the only publication this piece ever had was in the columns of various local journals, though a few copies privately printed obtained some circulation. For the first time it is now printed in a collection of local verses. This piece was not our author's only essay in humorous composition, and those who have heard him recite *The Deil in Darnick Toor, The Painters*, or *The Droonin' o' the Deil*, will hardly admit that his best production is best known. Though often urged by his friends to publish his various poetical pieces—for he sometimes wrote in other and graver moods—in a volume, he never could bring himself to adopt the advice, and thus his name and powers will likely never be known as they deserved. The fame he acquired while in life brought many whose faces he had never before seen to seek his acquaintanceship and advice ; and he also knew some celebrities in the literary world, among whom may be mentioned Mr. Gerald Massey and the late Mr. Russell of the *Scotsman.* He may be said at one time to have known all Galashiels, and especially those who had a taste for literature, or things above the mere food and work of daily life, with whom he would meet and discuss the politics of the day, and the world of mind and morals.

[For much of the above sketch the editor is indebted to Mr. J. H. Rutherford, Kelso.]

CUDDY PEGGY.

In the high town of Gala lived auld Peggy Tinlin,
Wha was blessed wi' content, though at times took to grumblin' :
Her calling in life was provisions to hawk,
And David, her cud, bore them a' on his back !
Each morning they marched to their daily employ,
Nae task did they think it, but rather a joy ;
And David jogged on wi' his weel-laden creels,
While Peggy half-bent, hirpled after his heels.
Frae morning to nicht thus wandered alane,
But aye at the dusk o' the gloamin' cam' hame :
And when Peggy had selt aff the guids o' her pack,
Then she mounted astride and rode hame on his back.
For mony a long year thus they toiled on thegither,
And the longer they toiled they grew fonder o' ither :
For David she seldom had reason to flog,
Though gently she touched him at times wi' the brogue.
But it happened ae day that poor David took ill,
Which the heart o' auld Peggy wi' sadness did fill,
And a sorrowfu' tear filled the auld body's e'e
As she thought to herself puir David wad dee :
And seeing him placed in this helpless condition
She thocht it her duty to get a physician,

Y

So away for that purpose she hurriedly set,
When just on her way she the minister met.
" Well, Margaret !" he said, " I hope you are well."
" I thank you," said Peggy, " I'm gaily mysel':
But I'm sorry to say oor David's no weel,
An' I'm just gaun awa' to get medical skill."
" Indeed, to hear that I'm exceedingly sorry,
But, if spared, I'll come down and see him to-morrow.
So wi' that Peggy bowed and speedily withdrew,
Syne awa' like the wind on her errand she flew.
The doctor came prompt at auld Peggy's request,
Thinkin' a' the road up what he might suggest :
So his patient wi' skill he minutely surveyed,
And then shook his head and reluctantly said—
" His case it is bad—nay, hopeless, I doubt--
But I'll try what I can to bring him about."
So he blistered and bled him, and gave him a dose
O' the best o' strong physic, as one might suppose ;
And these means they were blest to bring David relief,
And to ease at the same time the auld body's grief,
For as David grew weel her spirits grew licht,
And her e'e, lichtly dimmed, shone wonderfu' bricht.
The minister, who, to his word ever true,
Came down the next day as he promised to do,
On purpose, nae doubt, as a matter of course,
To see whether David was better or worse.
" Well, Margaret," he said, " how is David to-day ? "
" Deed, sir, he's some better, I'm happy to say ;
The doctor's been here and used every means,
And to outward appearance some better he seems."
" I'm glad to hear that ; I hope he'll recover,
And that both may be spared for a while to each other."
" Deed, sir, I'm glad and thankfu' atweel,
For little I thocht to have seen him as weel :
But come in, sir, and rest you a bit."
" Oh ! thank you," said he, " I scarcely must sit,
But, if it's convenient, with David I'll pray."
" Lord bless me, sir, what on the earth do you say ? "
" I'll pray with your husband that's now in distress."

" The deil's in the man—would you pray for an *ass* ? "
" Oh, fie ! Margaret, fie ! why don't you think shame
To call your poor husband by such a vile name ? "
" My husband !—I daursay the minister's mad—
It's mony a long year sin' my husband was dead."
" Oh, Margaret, you don't mean to say it is true ? "
" It's as true as this minute I'm speaking to you."
" Then is David your son, or relation in blood ? "
" Guid gracious ! the man ! isn't David the cud ! "
" A cud ! " cried the parson ; " Aye, a cuddy ! " cried she :
" Sic a farce to compare a dumb creatur' to me."
" Oh, Margaret ; I find I've been quite mistaken,
I David your cud for your husband have taken,
So pardon what I've in my ignorance said,
And the awkward mistake into which I've been led."
So the priest he no longer protracted his stay,
But wi' reverence bowed, and syne went away,
And laughed a' the road hame till nearly distracted,
To think sic a part in the drama he acted.

MARY INGLIS.

[The following compositions are from the pen of a lady once well known in the
Merse—Miss Mary Inglis, daughter of the late Rev. D. M. Inglis, minister of the
United Presbyterian Church, Stockbridge, Cockburnspath. On her father's death
in 1858, Miss Inglis removed near Glasgow, where she has led a truly devoted life.
" Her poetry, which evinces a gentle, sympathetic nature, is expressed with a
quiet and melodious grace, and with fine poetic sensibilities." It is just the kind
of verse that one expects from a writer in full touch with everything that is good
and true and beautiful in humanity and in the world. The poems are selected
from a small volume which Miss Inglis has entitled " Croonings."]

THE AULD MANSE.

The auld manse ! the auld manse !
  Was neither grand nor braw ;
The passages were narrow,
  The rooms low-roofed and sma' ;
But dear to me was every stane
  In each time-worn wa'.

Hoo sweet the sunny garden looked
 Wi' a' its flowrets fair,
That wi' their mingled fragrance
 Perfumed the summer air,
And fed the hungry honey-bees
 That flocked and feasted there.

The auld manse! the auld manse!
 Was filled wi' memories sweet
O' days when each spot echoed wi'
 The din o' dancin' feet,
And nichts when blithe young faces
 Smiled round the hearth sae neat.

The dancin' feet hae lang been still,
 The faces hid away
Beneath the grass and gowans
 For many a weary day;
Hoo aften the bonniest blossoms
 Are the first to droop and decay!

The auld manse! the auld manse!
 Is altered noo and fine,
Rude hands hae torn down the porch
 Where the roses used to twine
Sae lovingly about the stems
 O' the starry jessamine.

I miss the shady summer seat,
 The apple trees are gone,
Whose rich ripe clusters keeked langsyne
 Through each bricht window pane;
It does na please *my* e'e sae weel
 That cauld bare front o' stane.

The auld manse! the auld manse!
 The hame o' infancy,
When each sma' grief was soothed away
 On a loving mother's knee;
A fairer, sweeter, sunnier spot
 I ne'er expect to see

Till life's lang journey ower, I reach
  The heavenly hame sae fair,
Where they drap nae tear, and breathe nae sigh,
  And ken nae grief or care—
The hame where earth's lost loved ones
  Re-unite for ever mair.

YON BURNSIDE.

Ah, me ! what gleefu' days I've seen
      By yon burnside ;
What ploys among the brackens green
      By yon burnside !
But noo nae bricht-e'ed bairnies meet
To climb the cliffs wi' tireless feet,
And pu' fair flowers and berries sweet
      By yon burnside.

There's nae din' or daffin' noo
      By yon burnside ;
There's nae licht-hearted laughin' noo
      By yon burnside.
Still high on the thyme-scented brae
The wild wee lambies blithely play,
But a' the bairnies are away
      Frae yon burnside.

It's lanesome noo to dander doon
      By yon burnside ;
And waefu' noo the waters croon
      By yon burnside.
The laverock's lilt that used to be
Sae fu' o' mirthfu' melody,
Noo sounds like some sad dirge to me
      By yon burnside.

But aye I like to wander yet
      By yon burnside ;
The flowery knowes I'll ne'er forget
      By yon burnside ;

For oh ! sic visions haunt me there,
O' gracefu' forms and faces fair,
A' gane, a' gane, for evermair
    Frae yon burnside.·

— ·

LAST LONGINGS.

" Oh ! bring me a deep cauld draught," he said,
  " O' the water I used to drink,
Frae the well at the foot o' Ewieside,
  Wi' the buttercups round its brink ;
And there grew the sweet-spotted orchis
  Amang the rushes green,
And the bonnie blue-e'ed speedwell,
  And the scented meadow-queen."

They held a cup to his pale parched lips,
  But he turned his head away,
And yearned on still for a " deep cauld draught "
  Frae the well in the howe o' the brae.
On Memory's wings his thochts had flown
  Away from the close dark room,
To the sunny hillside where he used to play,
  'Mang the feathery ferns and broom.

Upon his ear there fell ance mair
  The sang o' the Heriot burn,
As it rippled alang 'neath the alder boughs,
  Wi' mony a curve and turn ;
And he heard again the bees' blithe hum
  Amang the heather bells ;
And the waefu' wail o' the new-spained lambs
  High up on the grassy fells.

And ane by ane before his e'e
  Rose pictures sweet and fair,
O' the dear auld hame sae far away,
  That he wad ne'er see mair.
But fairer than a' were the sichts he saw,
  Lang ere the end o' the day,
In the blessed land where they thirst nae mair,
  And a' tears are wiped away.

LET THE BAIRNIES PLAY.

Oh! let the bairnies play themsels.
　I like to hear their din,
I like to hear each restless foot
　Come trippin' oot and in;
I like to see each face sae bricht
　And each wee heart sae gay;
They mind me o' my ain young days—
　Oh! let the bairnies play.

Oh! dinna check their sinless mirth,
　Or make them dull and wae
Wi' gloomy looks or cankered words.
　But let the bairnies play.
Auld douce wise folks should ne'er forget
　They ance were young as they.
As fu' o' fun and mischief, too—
　Then let the bairnies play.

And never try to set a heid,
　Wi' auld age grim and grey,
Upon a wee saft snawy neck --
　Na! let the bairnies play,
For, oh! there's mony a weary nicht,
　And mony a waefu' day
Before them, if God spares their lives—
　Sae let the bairnies play.

INDEX OF NAMES.

Baillie, Lady Grisell, 53.
Ballantyne, Rev. James, 226.
Barrie, James, 97.
Binning, Lord, 66.
Brack, Jessie Wanless, 237.
Brockie, William, 163.
Brown, Alexander, 110.
Brown, David, 293.
Buchan, Earl of, 91.

Calder, R. M., 254.
Chisholm, Walter, 198.
Coldwell, Peter, 335.
Craw, William, 107.
Crawford, Robert, 70.
Cunningham, Rev. Andrew, 179.

Dawson, Christopher, 239.
Deans, George, 265.
Denholm, Agnes Mack, 270.
Dickson, Thomas, 119.
Dodds, Jeannie, 263.
Dudgeon, William, 99.

Easton, Annie Burton, 290.
Ercildoune, Thomas of, 9.
Erskine, Sir David, 95.
Erskine, Ralph, 82.
E. V. O. E., 285.

Forsyth, William, 183.
Foster, William Air, 149.

Gibson, Charles Philip, 279.
Gibson, John, 181.
Gilmour, George, 209.
Grainger, M.D., James, 74.
Gray, Rev. James, 102.
Gray, Simon, 292.

Haddington, Earl of, 64.
Happer, Thomas, 250.
Hately, T. L., 293.
Henderson, Dr. George, 139.
Hewit, Alexander, 114.
Hewit, John, 293.
Home, Alexander, 156.
Hume, Alexander, 38.
Hume, Anna, 51.

Hume, David, 48.
Hume, M.D., James, 50.
Hume-Campbell, Lady, 172.
Hume, Patrick, 63.
Hume, Sir Patrick, 37.
Hunter, Mrs. John, 85.

Inglis, Mary, 339.

Knox, Thomas, 173.

Lauderdale, Earl of, 36.
Lorimer, Mary Anne, 205.

Maitland, Baron, 29.
Maitland, Mary, 35.
Maitland, Sir Richard, 22.
Maitland, Thomas, 34.
Marjoribanks, Captain John, 128.
Mearns, Rev. Peter, 287
Mennon, Robert, 133.
Miller, Rev. Charles, 275.
Miller, Thomas, 248.
M'Craket, Peter, 187.

Naismith, Rev. Robert, 282.

Park, Alexander, 292.
Paulin, George, 218.
Pringle, Robert, 261.

Reid, John, 288.
Robertson, James, 293.
Robertson, John, 117.

Sanderson, James, 121.
Scott, Lady John, 211.
Steele, Andrew, 158.
Sutherland, William, 137.
Swinton, Sir John, 83.
Swinton, Lord, 84.

Telford, William, 245.
Tough, Margaret H. H., 205.

Usher, John, 208.

Wanless, Andrew, 228.
Watts, Thomas, 190.
White, Thomas, 293.
Whitehead, John, 131.
Wilson, Dr. John, 155.